ANIMA RISING

Also by Christopher Moore

Razzmatazz

Shakespeare for Squirrels

Noir

Secondhand Souls

The Serpent of Venice

Sacré Bleu

Bite Me

Fool

You Suck

A Dirty Job

The Stupidest Angel

Fluke: Or, I Know Why the Winged Whale Sings

Lamb: The Gospel According to Biff, Christ's Childhood Pal

The Lust Lizard of Melancholy Cove

Island of the Sequined Love Nun

Bloodsucking Fiends

Coyote Blue

Practical Demonkeeping

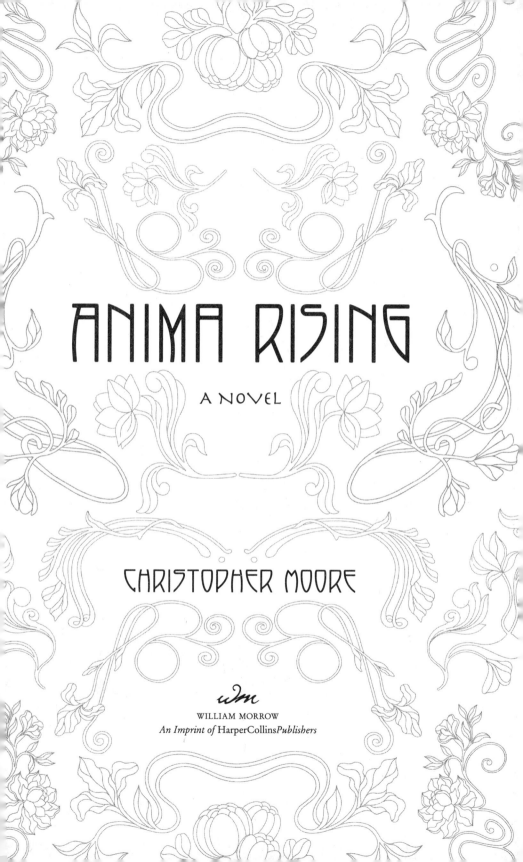

ANIMA RISING

A NOVEL

CHRISTOPHER MOORE

WM
WILLIAM MORROW
An Imprint of HarperCollins*Publishers*

Note on the Illustrations: All the art in *Anima Rising* is in the public domain. Photographs are provided through Wikimedia Commons license or by the author.

This is a work of fiction. Names, characters, places, and incidents are products of the author's imagination or are used fictitiously and are not to be construed as real. Any resemblance to actual events, locales, organizations, or persons, living or dead, is entirely coincidental.

ANIMA RISING. Copyright © 2025 by Christopher Moore. All rights reserved. Printed in the United States of America. No part of this book may be used or reproduced in any manner whatsoever without written permission except in the case of brief quotations embodied in critical articles and reviews. For information, address HarperCollins Publishers, 195 Broadway, New York, NY 10007.

HarperCollins books may be purchased for educational, business, or sales promotional use. For information, please email the Special Markets Department at SPsales@harpercollins.com.

FIRST EDITION

Designed by Elina Cohen
Art Nouveau florals courtesy of Shutterstock / Anna Mariukhno
Letter art courtesy of Shutterstock / Helga_creates

Library of Congress Cataloging-in-Publication Data has been applied for.

ISBN 978-0-06-243415-9

25 26 27 28 29 LBC 5 4 3 2 1

AUTHOR'S NOTE AND TRIGGER WARNING

This is a work of imagination. While some of the characters are based on historical figures, the events and dialogue are entirely fictitious.

This is a horror story. Herein are described incidents of sexual assault, violence, and profanity, as well as references to sex and sex work. Those with a sensitivity to such elements would do well to avoid this text.

Finally, and I can't stress this enough, if you are listening to this book in audio format in the car, with a kid or your grandma, turn on something else. Now.

ANIMA RISING

OPHELIA RISING

*S*he was born of electric fire into ice and torment and there had never been anything like her. At dawn, a century later, in Vienna, the painter Gustav Klimt, making his way home after a night of opera and dalliance with a wealthy widow, found her dead in the Danube Canal.

Still in his top hat and tails, Klimt paused on the Rossauer Bridge when he spotted a pale lavender figure lying against the concrete stairs on the platform at the water's edge. She lay face up, nude, her torso on the stairs, arms akimbo, her hips and legs like ghosts just under the surface of the muddy water. Tendrils of yellow hair flowed over the edge of the platform and waved in the slow current.

Klimt looked around for someone to call out to, but at this hour, while he could hear the clop-clop of horses' hooves in the distance, and the electric whir of the streetcars on the Ringstrasse, there was no one to be seen. He snatched off his top hat, tucked it under his arm, and hurried off the bridge to the stairs at the bank of the canal that led down to the loading platform.

He was forty-eight, powerfully built, strong from fencing and long hours standing at an easel, but with a slight swaybacked shape to his body from his weakness for large portions of breakfast cake smothered in whipped cream at the Café Tivoli. Balding, he sported a stalwart island of blond hair at his forelock, and a short, pointy beard that often framed a Puckish smile that crinkled the corners of his eyes.

He hurried down the stairs to the loading platform, not sure what he was going to do when he reached her. She might have slid slippery out of one of his paintings: his *Water Serpents*, or *Fishblood*, fantasy motifs of pale, lithe women gliding indifferently through pools of desire. Paintings built from thousands of drawings and hundreds of hours in the studio with young models, yet only at this moment, standing above the corpse, did it occur to him that all the women in the paintings, like this poor drowned girl, were oblivious to his presence.

She might have slid slippery out of one of his paintings:
his *Water Serpents*, or *Fishblood*, fantasy motifs of pale, lithe
women gliding indifferently through pools of desire.

He knew he should call for a policeman, or perhaps a doctor, but he just stood, looking at her. There were white lines, finer than a hair, hatching the mottled lavender of her skin, as if some artist had drawn her figure, traced out the contours of her limbs, then erased them. Or, perhaps better, had laid down watercolor on paper threaded with wax. It was curious. Fascinating. *In life you would never have seen the lines,* he thought, *because she would never have been this color in life.* With that thought, he pulled a leather-covered notebook from the inside pocket of his overcoat and, with the nub of a pencil, began sketching her. Her figure he could record, preserve as a note in his memory, and perhaps, with that, he could remember and reproduce the colors.

"Hey," came a voice from above. "Is she dead?"

Startled, Klimt looked up to see a young boy, perhaps ten years old, in a newsboy cap, looking down over the wall of the canal. He folded the pencil quickly into his notebook and held it inside his coat as if hiding evidence.

"Yes," he said, now transported from the ethereal fairyland of his imagination to the stark reality of this situation. "I think so."

"Did you kill her?" asked the boy.

"No. I just found her. I think she drowned in the canal."

"Were you drawing her picture?"

"Yes. I am an artist." He wanted to tell the boy that drawing was his natural response to things.

"Were you drawing her because you can see her boobies?"

Klimt wanted to tell the boy that he was Gustav *fucking* Klimt! founder and leader of the Vienna Secessionists, the most famous painter in the entire Austrian Empire, the darling of Viennese high society, sought after by every major museum in Europe to exhibit his paintings, and he could draw boobies any time he wanted to, but he thought the proclamation might constitute a bit of overkill, delivered to a smudge-faced urchin while standing on a dock in a top hat, sketching a corpse. Instead he pulled the notebook from his coat, measured his sketch against the dead girl, then flipped the page and, humbled by the blank sheet, began to draw again. "No, I've never seen skin this color before," he mumbled.

"Me either," said the boy. "Do you want me to fetch a policeman?"

Klimt felt panic rise in his chest. No, he wasn't finished.

Then the dead girl coughed. The boy screamed and jumped back from the edge of the canal. Klimt retreated a step. The drowned girl spewed a stream of canal water, then gasped, and, without opening her eyes or moving otherwise, said, "*No.*" It was English, but everyone knew the basics of all the major languages: "yes," "no," count to ten, and "Where's the fucking library?" Even the boy knew what "no" meant.

"So *now* should I fetch a policeman?" said the boy.

"No," said Klimt. "No, help me get her out of the water. Please."

Klimt gathered the girl's arms above her head, then, as gently as possible, tried to pull her up onto the concrete dock. The boy had scampered down the stairs and stood behind Klimt, not sure what to do.

Klimt laid the girl down again, cleared her hair from over her face, then took off his top hat and handed it to the boy. "Hold this."

"Do you want me to fetch a doctor?"

"No," said the girl, as if she'd been startled awake; then she slipped back into her limp, dead aspect.

"I guess not," said Klimt. He shrugged off his overcoat and laid it on the damp concrete beside the girl. Starting with her shoulders, then one leg at a time, he moved her onto the dark wool and pulled it tight around her. Being careful of his balance on the narrow platform, he squatted, gathered her up, and lifted her in his arms.

"I have a cart," said the boy.

Klimt didn't know what he was going to do with the girl, beyond getting her out of the canal. He followed the boy up the stairs, turning sideways to keep from scraping the girl's head or toes against the canal's wall. At street level, he saw the boy's cart, stacked high with newspapers. He and his brother Ernst, when they were poor boys from the suburbs, had run a newspaper cart just like this, delivering stacks of papers to the newsstands, cafés, and newsboys on the street, except he and Ernst had had a swaybacked horse to pull it. This boy had no horse.

Klimt rolled the girl onto the stacks of newspapers, then gathered his coat around her. Finally, after checking to see that she was still breathing, he concealed her face in the fur collar. He stepped back and bent over, resting his hands on his thighs as he caught his breath.

The boy held out Klimt's top hat. "To the hospital, then?"

A muffled "No!" sounded out of Klimt's overcoat.

"I guess not," said Klimt. Where to take her, then? He couldn't very well take her to the apartment he shared with his mother and youngest sister, even though it was only a few blocks away. *Good morning, Mother, I've brought a naked, drowned girl home for breakfast.* Perhaps not. His studio, however, was in a small house on Josefstädter Strasse, perhaps a half hour's walk away.

"We can take her to my studio," he said to the boy. "Number two Josefstädter Strasse."

"That's too far," said the boy. "I have to deliver my papers."

"I'll pay you for your time."

"How much?"

"Fifty heller," Klimt offered, thinking that would be about what the boy would make each day for hauling his papers.

"Two crowns," said the boy.

"One crown," countered Klimt, wondering if the poor girl might expire atop the newspapers while he bargained with this child.

"One crown and the drawing you made," said the boy.

Klimt heard men's voices nearby and looked up to see two policemen, with their spiked helmets and swords, making their way across the Rossauer Bridge.

"Fine. One crown and the drawing," said Klimt.

"And you have to help me pull the cart," said the boy.

"Why don't you have a horse?"

"I had a donkey, but it died."

"Fine," said Klimt.

"Fine," said the boy.

The painter snatched his hat away from the boy and lifted the carriage shaft on one side, waited for the boy to take the other shaft. The cart creaked and shimmied as they made their way along the bricks.

After they'd gone a block, the boy asked, "How do you think she got in the canal?"

"Jumped, perhaps," said Klimt. "Young women her age are often overcome with despair. Freud calls it hysteria."

"Jumped? Naked?"

"Fell, maybe."

"Did you see the bruises on her neck?" asked the boy.

"Of course," said Klimt. He hadn't. He'd been concentrating on the lines of her figure and the color of her skin and hadn't even noticed any bruises.

"Handprints," said the boy. "I thought you had murdered her."

"I didn't."

"I will believe you for two crowns," said the boy.

Klimt's studio was a modest stucco house just across from the Rathausplatz, one of the multitude of white, neo-Gothic public buildings that made Vienna appear a city designed to top an elaborate wedding cake. When they arrived at the studio they found a red-haired teenage girl in a tattered red coat, sitting on the steps on a suitcase, petting one of the many cats who lived there.

Klimt dropped the cart brace, pulled his watch from his vest pocket, and checked the time: five thirty.

"Wally, what are you doing here?" asked Klimt. Wally Neuzil, seventeen, had modeled for him off and on for months. She was a petite redhead with wide blue eyes, a little shorter of limb than what he needed for the project he was working on, so he hadn't had her come to the studio for a couple of weeks.

"I'm short on my rent this month," said Wally, "so I thought I'd get some extra hours in."

"Good morning, Fräulein," said the boy.

"Good morning," Wally said. Then to Klimt, "Is this your son, maestro?"

"No, no, not my son," said Klimt. He had four sons that he knew of, all named Gustav, by four different mothers who had modeled for him. He kept his children and their mothers in apartments around Vienna in the hope they would grow up under better circumstances than this poor newsboy.

"I'm Maximilian, Max for short," said the boy. "Pleased to make your acquaintance, Fräulein." The boy set down his cart brace, removed his cap, and bowed over it.

"And I am Wally, young gentleman, short for Walburga," she said, with a giggle and a smile at the boy's formality.

Klimt said, "Wally, I will help you with your rent, but I can't pay you for hours that I'm not here." No one was to come to the studio before nine a.m., and then only at the maestro's invitation. There was a secret knock.

"We brought a dead girl," said Max, whipping back the collar of Klimt's overcoat to reveal the unconscious girl beneath.

Wally gasped and leapt up from her seat to examine the girl on the cart. She looked to Klimt. "Why have you brought a dead girl? Because you won't have to pay her?"

"No," said the maestro. "I'm rescuing her. And she's not dead."

Wally pushed a tendril of hair out of the drowned girl's face. "She is very pretty, but pale."

"I found her in the canal."

"He was drawing her boobies," said Max.

"Maybe you should call a doctor to help rescue her," Wally said.

"I think a doctor would want to take her away, and I still need to draw her."

"Do you want me to pose her pleasuring herself?" Wally asked.

"No!" said Klimt. "Help me get her into the studio. The key is in my coat." He looked around to make sure no one could see them moving the girl. *My next studio must have a walled garden with a locking gate*, he thought.

"He likes to draw us pleasuring ourselves," Wally explained to Max. "I am an expert at that pose."

"He likes to draw us pleasuring ourselves," Wally explained to Max.

"Does he find all of his models dead in the canal?" Max asked Wally. He took the girl's feet, while Klimt took her by the shoulders, carrying most of her weight. Wally pulled Klimt's overcoat from the cart, took the keys from the coat pocket, unlocked the front door, and held it open while they carried the drowned girl in.

The studio consisted of six rooms and a foyer. The foyer opened onto a parlor that had once been a dining room, and a formal living room to the right that now served as his portrait studio, the walls covered with Klimt's collection of Japanese prints. The living room and parlor both opened onto a third, large room that ran the length of the house, which Klimt used for a drawing studio. Across the back of the house were a kitchen; two bedrooms, one of which served as a supply closet; and a bathroom.

"We'll put her on the divan in the parlor," Klimt said. "Wally, can you fetch some sheets and a blanket from the other room?"

Wally scampered off to the next room, the drawing studio, and began gathering sheets off of chairs and various wooden platforms. Max craned his neck to watch Wally as he helped lay the drowned girl on the divan in the parlor. Although only ten, Max was relatively sure that he was in love with Wally and would marry her as soon as possible and they would eat cake in the park together while watching swans and carriages and fancy people go by.

Wally came back into the parlor with an armload of linen, continuing her narrative as if she'd never stopped, and as if Klimt weren't in the room. "Sometimes he likes to pleasure ourselves himself," she said. "But he doesn't draw that part because I don't think he can hold his pencil steady. Maybe that's why he has four or five of us here all the time. You'd rub yourself raw trying to pleasure yourself the whole day while he draws." She tossed the linen on top of the supine drowned girl. "Although sometimes he just has us drape ourselves over those platforms." She shot a thumb toward the room where she'd gotten the linens and Max looked over and nodded. "Draping is easier."

"Wally!" Klimt barked. "He's just a boy!"

"He's fine. I'm just talking about my work. You're fine, yes?" She looked at the boy. He nodded. "See, he's fine."

"You," Klimt said to the boy. "You go on." The painter dug into his pocket and retrieved two crown coins and handed them to the boy.

The boy squirreled the coins away in his pocket, then held his hand out. "And the drawing."

Klimt acted as if it had slipped his mind. Wally pointed to his overcoat, which she'd hung on the hall tree when she'd brought it in. Klimt retrieved his notebook from the inside pocket and carefully tore out a leaf, the first sketch he had tried. He held it out to the boy.

"Have him sign it," said Wally.

Klimt snarled at the petite model. "Wally, you need to go away. I don't need you today, and I have to lock up while I go home to change."

"You can't leave her here alone," Wally said. "The cats will eat her." A coven of cats had been milling around in the parlor, looking to be fed.

"Sign it," said Max.

Klimt fished the pencil from his vest pocket and quickly signed the drawing, then handed it to the boy.

"You can sell that for far more than two crowns," Wally said. "Tell them it's a Klimt."

"Don't tell anyone that," Klimt said. "Our business is done. Now on your way, boy."

"I want to stay with Wally while you go home to dress."

"Wally isn't staying."

"Then who will keep the cats from eating the drowned girl?"

This situation was spinning out of control. He didn't want to let the boy go out running around telling the tale of how he acquired an original Klimt, at least not without some warning, yet he really did need to get home and change before the streets filled up with people and he was seen wandering around in his opera clothes. The only clothes he had at the studio were the caftans he wore while painting, and he couldn't very well be out and about in one of them.

"Wally, a word please." He signaled for her to follow him into the drawing studio, where the models normally posed. She followed him, wearing a silly smile as if she'd just prevailed in a game of checkers.

"Wally, I need you to fix the bedding for the girl, and impress upon the boy that he mustn't tell anyone how she came to be here, then send him on his way. You stay with the girl, keep an eye on her. I'll be back in an hour."

"And you'll pay me?"

"Of course. I'll bring your rent current, too."

"I'm afraid it may be too late. I was evicted last night."

"Where did you sleep last night?"

"On your front stairs."

"I'm sorry, Wally," Klimt said.

"Perhaps I can stay here?" Wally added. "Watch over the drowned girl until she's better."

"We shall see. I know a young artist who may be able to help you. He needs to find new accommodations himself and he also needs models. You might work something out."

"Oh, would you ask him?"

"I will send him a message today. Now, get rid of the boy. I should be able to catch a cab at Rathausplatz."

"I will." She scampered out to the parlor and began tucking the linen in under the drowned girl, who hadn't moved or made a sound since they'd brought her in.

On his way out, Klimt checked on the drowned—well, *damp*—girl. She was breathing steadily and had lost her lavender color as well as the fine white lines that had hatched her skin. He pushed aside her hair to get a good look at her neck. There were no bruises there at all—the boy was daft.

"What should I tell her if she wakes up?" asked Wally.

"That we saved her. Then ask her how she came to be in the canal." He turned to the boy. "Max, Wally wants to talk to you, but then you must go."

The boy nearly swooned at the instruction and Klimt felt as if he might have just pimped Wally out to a ten-year-old.

"I have to deliver my papers," the boy said.

"Thank you for your help this morning. You were a gallant knight in service," Klimt said. Then he snatched up his hat and coat and strode out of the house wondering how he was going to explain his night at the opera to his mother and sister.

2

A FRIEND FOUND

Dearest Sister:

Who would have thought that after weeks at sea, hundreds
of miles from land, our ship blocked in by great ice sheets, I
would, at last, find a friend? (And ne'er did I have to develop
a personality, as you always teased, as my new friend finds it
sufficient that I saved him from freezing and being eaten by a
great white bear, and he said not a word about my deficit of charm
or conversational acumen. So there.) We had been mired in the
ice for four days when one of the mates stationed in the rigging
to look for the edge of the ice spied a lone figure in the distance
pulling a sledge upon which rode a long wooden box, perhaps
three feet on each side and eight feet long, and upon that stood
a single sled dog. It was a clear, windless day, and we could see
the figure dark against the endless white of the ice even with the
naked eye once directed where to look. Some of the men stood at
the rail watching, passing the lieutenant's spyglass back and forth
as they watched the figure's slow progress, making comments in

Russian or Swedish, which the lieutenant translated as "How did he get out here?" and "Why does the dog get to ride?"

We passed several hours watching the traveler, who struggled and fell every few minutes, and the men had begun to lay bets on when he would fail to get up again, when the lieutenant spotted one of the white bears several hundred yards behind, stalking the trudging figure. I ordered rifles fetched and loaded, but the lieutenant assured me that the bear was beyond the range of our munitions, and the shot well beyond the ability of any of the men, who were whale fishers and merchantmen, not marksmen.

I ordered the nets dropped and I, four sailors with rifles, and the bosun, who was the only one besides the lieutenant who spoke any English, joined me on the ice to make our rescue. I tell you, dear Margaret, that I did not feel fearful being on the ice with the white bear, but instead a rush of the blood I had only experienced when shooting with Father on fall mornings—an excitement a man only feels when pitting himself directly against nature itself. Granted, the great bear was somewhat larger than the grouse Father and I blasted upon the moors, but grouse are wily, and I have been told they will charge when wounded, although I have never witnessed this myself. Besides, the bosun is a portly fellow, slow of foot, and I felt sure if the bear should charge, and not be stopped by the rifles, I could make it to the safety of the ship before the bear finished eating him.

Our progress on the ice was slow. After a quarter of an hour we seemed no closer to the man pulling the sledge, although he did have the courtesy to fall facedown on the ice and lie still, so it became less a matter of catching him and more of a race with the bear. When we were within a hundred yards of the traveler, as was the bear, I had the men fire a volley at the bear. All the shots missed, but the bear did pause at the noise and regarded us with interest, as if he might have been deciding to abandon the downed traveler and have a go at the lot of us. (A whale fisher in a tavern in Archangel once told me that the white bears are the rulers of their realm and consider anything that moves on the ice to be food, so I suppose our group appeared to be a more abundant repast for the creature than the fallen sledge man.) The lone sled dog, perched atop the crate, began to cry, an almost howling whine rather than a quick bark, as if he were mourning that he and his master were about to be eaten.

I ordered the men to reload, but only one of them had remembered to bring powder and shot.

"I thought you lot were hunters," I scolded them. "How is it you can't shoot and don't remember to bring the basic kit of hunting?"

"They hunt whales," the bosun reminded me. "You hunt whales with a harpoon, not a gun."

"Well it's shoddy work," I told him. I snatched the only loaded rifle from the bewildered whaler, checked that the pan was primed, and took aim at the bear. Dear sister, while I know that many of the aspects of the adventurer's life may seem fanciful to you, a lady, who has spent her sheltered days plying her needlepoint and powdering her pretty bosoms, trust me when I say, these white bears are quick and cunning rascals, and no sooner did hammer strike flint than the bear leapt five feet to starboard, saving him from my deadly accurate shot.

"Reload," I ordered the bosun, rather sternly, to show him I was displeased at him for bumping my shoulder just as I fired, perhaps. I handed him my rifle, and when I turned back, the bear had reconsidered his stalking of the sledge fellow and had set a loping course toward our little hunting party.

"You know," said the bosun, "I can load all of the rifles from this one powder flask and shot pouch, it will just take longer."

I *did* know that, of course, but as a commander, one must let one's men learn for themselves, although one would hope that one's men are not so thick that the lesson would occur to them only upon the attack of a ravenous bear.

The bear wasn't charging us, exactly, as if we were prey that might elude him, but rather approached in a more leisurely manner, like a man might stalk a can of beans, confident it would not make an escape before he pounced. Before the bear had crossed fifty yards, the bosun had loaded three of the rifles and had handed them back to the men. I bade them stand in a line in front of me and, upon my signal, fire at once. When I felt the bear was close enough for a successful shot, I called "fire." The volley went off with a magnificent display of noise and smoke, doing no harm whatsoever to the bear, but the great ghost of smoke that drifted in the bear's direction caught his attention, and he stopped, stood on his hind feet, and sniffed at the air.

The creature stood some ten feet tall, and I thought at that moment I might dash back to the ship while the beast feasted on my less fortunate compatriots, but as we watched, a stripe of red bloomed on the bear's arm and we realized at the same time as the bear, I think, that a rifle ball had grazed him. The beast dropped to all fours and licked the wound, then, as if he had had enough, turned and loped away several steps before he simply disappeared.

"Where did he go?" I inquired.

"Hole in ice," said the bosun. "White bears swim."

I nodded as if I had known that the white bears could swim under the ice, and as we resumed our progress toward the sledge fellow, I could see the hole into which the bear had slipped. I moved away from it with a newfound alacrity, lest the beast resurface and attack.

When we reached the downed sledge fellow he appeared to be dead. We rolled him onto his back and he muttered, "Save the crate.

My work," in German first, then in English after I assured him he was safe. Then he fell unconscious, his breathing so shallow that steam barely rose in the cold air. His sled dog must have sensed that we were there to help, as it whimpered and lowered its ears in submission.

The men loaded the traveler atop the crate, and four of the men pulled the sledge back toward the ship, while the bosun and I pushed at the back, with loaded rifles slung at our shoulders should the bear appear again. When we reached the ship the traveler sat up and grabbed me by the front of my coat.

"Friend," he implored. "You must bring the crate. My work. Save the crate and the dog, too. Please, friend."

Yes, he used the term "friend," so I do not exaggerate that I have, indeed, found a friend, and before I even found the Northwest Passage, so you were wrong about that, too, dear Margaret. A friend!

"We will," I told him.

The sledge and the crate were so large that the men had to use the tackle for raising and lowering longboats. They hoisted the whole rig aboard, with the traveler atop it. As they pulled him up, he leaned over the edge of the box and said, "And do not look in the crate, friend. Promise."

"I promise," I told him as they hoisted him away.

I watched from the ice as they pulled the crate and sledge on board. One of the men carried the dog up in a cargo net slung over his shoulder and handed him to another—the hound was passive, as if resigned to whatever fate we had in store for him. Once the dog was on board, the rest of the party scrambled up the cargo net, then pulled it up behind them, leaving me standing on the ice. I thought perhaps they would lower one of the longboats and heave their captain aboard in honor of his having saved them from the white bear, but such was not the case. In fact, I could hear a lot of scrambling as they moved about on deck, followed by the battening of the hatches, and then only the cold wind through the rigging.

"Gentlemen, I believe you've forgotten something," I called, but there was no answer.

I tell you, sister, despite having just made a friend, the only time I have felt more lonely was that time when we were children, and Father sent us to town to fetch some sugar, and you sold me to the bachelor vicar. The fortnight Father spent bargaining a fair price to buy me back was my most lonesome time until now. I sat on the ice plotting my revenge on the bosun and the others, until my bottom froze, and was ready to resign myself to a frosty death, when a half-dozen of the men burst out of the hatches laughing and threw down the net, allowing me to climb to safety and share in the jest. And while the feeling is yet to return to my nethers, even as I write this, I feel as if the men and I have bonded in fellowship. I may have made more than one friend, dear sister. Now my new friend, the frozen traveler, after having been stripped and rubbed down head to toe with warm brandy and salt to promote circulation, lies sleeping under a pile of furs on a cot in my cabin. My watch finished, I too must rest. I will write more when I can. But perhaps first I will have a look inside the mysterious crate, which is still up on deck.

With deepest affection,

R. A. Walton

Dearest Margaret:

I know not when I might be able to post these letters, but writing them makes me feel less lost and closer to home, so I will continue to write, even if it is their fate to be found with my frozen corpse by future travelers. Forgive my untidy penmanship, as I have just had a severe shock and have quaffed quite a bit of the Russians' vodka to steady my nerves, but I must get this down. We are yet icebound, but the one good fortune is that the wind has not blown the ice into great mountains that might crush the ship's hull, so there is still some hope that we will be free before winter.

Meanwhile, my new friend seems to have thawed, warmed by my good company and copious amounts of tea and brandy. While he is yet unwell, sometimes racked by chills and fever, he has regained enough of his mind to tell the tale of how he came to be traveling upon the ice in the middle of the sea, and his story seems a marvel that I would ascribe to myth if he were not such a sincere and humble fellow.

His name is Victor Frankenstein, and he is the eldest son of a Swiss family of the landed gentry, so already we share the commonality of the burden of inheritance. How liberating it must be for you, a woman who can neither inherit nor own property, who need only find a husband and squirt out sons to assure the legacy of some other family to fulfill her destiny, while I, having received my estate, must make a Herculean effort to bring honor and acclaim to our family name. If I am the one to find the Northwest Passage, the name Walton will be long remembered. In this, Victor and I are alike: my quest, to find the Northwest Passage, and his, to transcend the very limits of human mortality. I shall explain.

Victor, it seems, studied the practices of the ancient alchemists at university, as in Switzerland it was one of the few nonclerical fields of study available to him, the others being chocolate and cheese. He decided to specialize in the ELIXIR OF LIFE, as all the philosopher's-stone and turning-lead-into-gold classes were full. Thus, he tells me, after much study of arcane and forbidden texts, and no little bit of dissecting dead animals, he graduated with honors and moved to Heidelberg, where he continued his studies at the medical school, focused on discovering the very ELIXIR and, as he calls it, the spark of immortality. In telling his story, Victor seemed to find his strength, and I thought he might be on to a speedy recovery, even as he recited hours' worth of procedures and chemical formulae, most of which slipped my mind as I dozed off several times. But I will take better notes when he repeats his story, as all men do under the influence of spirits, in which we indulged mightily to fend off the cold and the monotony of hours' worth of procedures and chemical formulae.

At last, my friend felt he had concocted this ELIXIR, and after several experiments on small animals, he thought he might be able to strike the spark of life into the body of a deceased human, if only he could repair that condition which caused their death. His animal experiments had taught him that the mere shock of reanimation caused damage so severe that his subjects survived only minutes. Thus he resolved to construct a larger, more durable human, one who might survive to live a full life. To this end, he began to haunt the graveyards and charnel houses of Heidelberg, even going so far as to attend executions, then purchase the corpses of the condemned, saying they would be used for study at the medical school, which, in a way, they were. He picked the largest, most robust of subjects, stitching together the best bits, until he had constructed the patchwork body of a man nearly eight feet tall. He bathed each intersection of joint or organ in his precious elixir, and even though the subject remained dead, the junctions healed together, leaving only thin, white scars. Such a massive subject, he postulated, would be able to withstand the reanimating process.

With his animal subjects, Victor had applied electricity from Leyden jars* to the animals to revive them, but this method, he found, did not produce enough electricity to jolt his man creature to life. He resolved to capture the power of lightning from a storm, by attaching a copper cable to the steeple of the university chapel. But while trying to scale the church, he was discovered by other students, who reported him to their professor. If Victor had made his creature from a single corpse, his experiment might have been dismissed as youthful misadventure, but because he had constructed his man from the best parts of no fewer than eight different corpses, and, after taking the best parts, chucked the remaining parts into the Rhine, where they washed up on the banks, terrifying local fishermen and farmers, the authorities were quite cross with him. He was expelled from the university, and the local constabulary promised to bring charges against him but did not take him into custody. Under dark of night, Victor fled Heidelberg with his patchwork man and his instruments, and made his way home to Switzerland.

Once at his family's estate, he set up a laboratory in a folly they built on a hilltop, a small-scale replica of the Parthenon. (Dear Margaret, we simply must build a folly on the grounds when I return. Perhaps on the hill where Father built that wretched monument for Mother. Perhaps a miniature St. Paul's? I know you haven't seen it, but take my word for it, it is smashing.) Once installed in his new laboratory, Victor hired an assistant, a twisted

---

* Early batteries.

dwarf from the local village, who helped him with any last-minute grave robbing and climbed onto the dome to attach the lightning rod. Upon the first electrical storm, Victor was able to capture a thunderbolt and send its spark through a copper cable into his patchwork man, who rose from the table screaming like a newborn, as he had just been soundly toasted with lightning.

The massive creature, whom he referred to as Adam (a wholly unoriginal name. I think if I should decide to create life after building our folly, I should name my first man Malcomb, or perhaps Reginald, to give him a better chance to make a good impression in polite society), was still smoldering from the lightning as he scowled at Victor, then ran off into the hills, not to be seen again for several years, when they happened upon one another on an Alpine glacier, as one does, I suppose, in Switzerland.

Victor's story becomes clouded now, and I wonder if it is because we were both drinking heavily while he told it, or if, as you already suspect, it is because he is a raving lunatic, but evidently Adam told a long and eloquent tale of stealing food and learning to speak by watching a blind fellow and his family through a crack in the wall of a pigsty attached to their cabin. Evidently, as well as being quite tall, Adam's mismatched parts made him horrible to look upon, and he terrorized any persons he approached on his odyssey, so he took to staying away from towns during the day, only going among civilization to steal food and murder the odd child, one of whom was Victor's younger brother William. Adam, or "the creature" as Victor calls him, then explained that he should not be condemned to a life of loneliness, and if he weren't so alienated, he wouldn't need to go about killing children and framing the housekeeper for the murders. Oh, I forgot, the creature not only strangled Victor's brother but planted a locket belonging to Victor's housekeeper by the child's body, and she was summarily convicted and hanged for William's murder, which charred Victor's crumpets no little bit, housekeepers being terribly hard to come by in Switzerland. Anyway, the creature demanded that Victor must make him a mate as hideous as himself, and he and his ugly wife would live away from others in the far north, with no need to perpetrate violence on anyone. And, should his creator refuse his request, the creature promised to destroy everyone Victor loved.

Which put me in mind of the time when we, as children, found that rather surly stray dog in the corner of the stables, and you said he would be less growly if someone simply petted him. Oh, the joke was on me, you little scamp, and I still have one small finger that refuses to work in concert with the others due to my injuries. My fault, I suppose, for not knowing a badger when I saw one. I'll not make that mistake again any time soon.

Anyway, to draw the creature away from his family, Victor went to Scotland, having heard they had the best grave robbers in Edinburgh, because of the medical school, and proceeded to set up a laboratory in which to build the creature a wife. But the grave robbers were not forthcoming, and when Frankenstein tried to do his own grave robbing, he found the best bits had all been picked over, leaving little but bones and hair. Victor had suspected all along that the creature would follow him across Europe, so he was not entirely surprised when one evening, as he was perfecting the chemistry of his life elixir in the lab, the fiend kicked in the door.

"That wasn't locked," Victor told him.

"I have endured untold suffering and alienation from mankind, if I wish to kick in a door I shall kick in a door and all who say otherwise may be damned to perdition," the creature replied.

"Well, see if you can prop it in place," Victor said. "It's cold out and I need a steady hand for this work. I can't be shivering."

The creature said, "Don't talk to me of cold, Creator. I have suffered the cold of a thousand—"

"Tea?" Victor said.

"Yes please," said the fiend.

So, amid the arcane volumes and bubbling laboratory glass, Frankenstein served the creature tea, with milk and sugar, it turns out, but no lemon, as there was no lemon to be had.

And yes, dear sister, as I listened to this tale, fraught with detail such as how the monster took his tea, I too was thinking *Quoi is in the fucking box?* If you'll pardon my French, dear sister, as I am approaching the answer to the mystery, my hand shaking from the revelation, even as I write.

"Why have you made no progress on my mate?" Adam demanded.

"I have not been able to obtain the necessary parts," Frankenstein told him, and he proceeded to tell his tale of grave-robbing woe, summing up with "I checked at every charnel house and they didn't even have anything in the sale bins except for that big hand over there, which I paid dearly for." (Victor did mention that he had acquired a large hand, I'd forgotten that bit.)

"Would you suggest that a hand be my companion in life?" the creature asked.

Here Victor assured me that an incorrect answer to the question might have seen him murdered on the spot, but, before he could answer, mercifully, the fiend finished his tea and proclaimed that he would find the "necessary parts" and with that was off into the night, pausing only to roughly refit the door into the jamb and suggest that Victor have someone in to fix it.

Several hours later Adam returned carrying the body of a young woman, which he laid out on the table Frankenstein had set up for the assembly of the creature's bride. She was young, perhaps twenty, and dressed in the simple attire of a shopgirl, with an apron, and she appeared to be completely intact. Victor was horrified, and as he suspected, when he examined the corpse, while there was no heartbeat, it was still warm.

"You've murdered this poor woman," Victor told the creature, but the fiend knew.

"Less digging, really," said the monster. "Now you will bring her back to be mine. We will go away together, away from other people, just wretches content in our wretchedness."

The girl was quite attractive, Victor said, and had no deformities at all that he could detect.

"But she's not wretched at all. She's perfect. How will you be wretched together?"

"You can sew the big hand on her."

"I cannot. It would not fit. You are enormous because I began your construction with an enormous head, and everything was built to scale from there."

"Perhaps a large nostril. You're a surgeon. Give her a dozen nostrils."

"I don't know how to do that. And I don't have any donor nostrils. You can't just make her wretched."

"You don't know, my creator, what it is to go into the world with a mind fully developed but empty. Everything is a terror. Everything is pain. You know how to walk, to run, to feed yourself, even to talk, but you do not know what words mean, or that you are an abomination to others. Life is a horror. And it will be that for her. I will teach her, my mate, that she is wretched. She will know the world is cruel because I will make it so. She shall be a blank canvas and I shall paint her with the stuff of nightmares."

Victor was horrified at the very idea of subjecting a person to the torment of his creation. This girl of sweet countenance, yanked from life only to be restored into a life of torture. "I will not do it," Victor told the fiend. "I will not bring an innocent creature into a life of suffering."

"But you have already. Was I not an innocent creature? Did you not bring me into a world of torment and suffering?"

"You are a fiend, a thief, a murderer."

"All because of my alienation, my misery."

"So you will inflict that on another creature? No. I tell you no," Victor cried. And with that he snatched up a surgical knife and plunged it into the corpse's chest. "There, now she is beyond your reach, for I cannot repair a damaged heart."

"I will fetch you a new heart," the fiend said. "You can restore her."

"I will not do that. I will not!"

"You would deprive me of companionship, then I shall deprive you of the same. I will take from you everyone you care about. I shall be with you on your wedding night," the creature roared. Then he was gone, into the night, pausing momentarily to again try to fit the broken door into the jamb. Then he was gone.

Here Victor stopped and lay back on the cot, breathless from telling his tale.

"What happened then?" I implored.

But Victor was exhausted and waved me off. "I cannot go on, good Captain. Allow me to rest and I will continue my tale on the morrow."

And so I turned out the lamp and made a bed for myself in a hammock on the far side of my cabin and before long I could hear my guest softly snoring. You'll note, dear sister, that Frankenstein referred to me as Captain, even though that is a title reserved for military ships, and I am merely the master of this ship. Still, my affection grew for him even more for the error.

I lay there in the dark, for perhaps an hour, listening to the wind whipping through the masts, the occasional footfall of one of the men on watch, as I considered the fantastical tale. I had so many questions: How did all of this lead to an educated and refined man of means pulling a heavy sledge across the Arctic ice, hundreds of miles from land? And why was the dog so precious? Frankenstein would not settle until he knew the dog was inside, and well-fed and watered. And what of the mysterious box, so precious that he would not even board the vessel of his salvation until it was secured?

Finally, I could stand it no longer. I rose and wrapped myself in furs, grabbed a storm lantern, and made my way to the deck, making an excuse to the mate as I passed his quarters that I wanted to see if the wind was driving masses of ice that might crush the hull. The mate, knowing the wind was not so ferocious as to do any such thing, but convinced of my incompetence, allowed that this was good thinking. (My ineptitude is a convenient ruse I often play to my advantage among the crew.)

Upon the deck I found Frankenstein's crate and examined it as best I could under the dim lantern. The crate was secured with latches and straps, like a cabin trunk, and I used a rigging mallet to break the ice from the buckles and latches, and a hatchet to pry them open. I only had my hands out of my mittens for a few seconds, yet I lost feeling in my fingertips, which is just as well, as I also lost skin trying to work the metal buckles. At last the lid opened and I shone my storm lantern over the contents. I expected food, medicine, and tools one might use to survive on the ice, but instead I found scientific equipment, some packed haphazardly, some in sturdy hardwood boxes. I opened some of these to find optical instruments in one, surgical tools in another, and I shuddered at the thought of what Frankenstein had assembled with these. Various iron rods, brass balls at their ends, fitted so they might be fastened together, and great coils of braided copper cable, no bigger in diameter than the shaft of a quill pen, but hundreds of feet long. I stirred through the contents, placing the sturdier elements like the iron rods on the deck, so I could see what might lie below. At one end of the box I cleared the way until I was nearly an arm-length down, then I reached a woolen cloth that padded something at the bottom of the crate. I pulled this aside and opened a small hatch. To my shock, I saw a young woman's face. I nearly cried out but fought to regain my composure and leaned in for a closer look. While she was undoubtedly frozen, she appeared only to be sleeping peacefully, her golden hair arranged around her face on a pillow. This must surely be the corpse from Victor's story, the one he had stabbed in the chest. But why? I noted then that he had built a structure into the box so the corpse was not crushed by the weight of the instruments, not that it would be a danger in these temperatures.

I held the lamp close again, examined her, forgetting for a moment the elements swirling around me. She was the very picture of peace, a frozen Venus, as fair as any painting I have seen. Then her eyes opened. I screamed, casting my lamp aside, and it went sailing out over the ice. I made to run, then, thinking perhaps the drink and cold had gone to my head, I peeked back into the crate.

"What are you looking at, butt puddle?" she said.

Forgive me, dear sister, Frankenstein is stirring on his cot and I have urgent questions for him. More later.

Yours,

Robert

3
EGON RISING

"Mama, Egon is painting Gertie's naughty bits again," called Melanie, at twenty-two, the second-oldest sister.

"We're making art," said Gertie, seventeen, who sat on the bed in nothing but her stockings, her knees pulled up to her chin, trying to project a coquettish smile while her brother, Egon, a painfully thin young man of twenty-one, with wide, haunted eyes and a great explosion of disheveled dark hair, scratched away at a sketch pad. "I'm drawing, not painting," said Egon.

They could hear steps approaching, Mother's stout shoes on the wooden floor. Gertie looked around in a panic.

"Stay still," Egon said. "I'm almost finished."

Frau Schiele stormed into the room, brushed Egon's sketchbook aside as she passed, then grabbed a folded blanket from the foot of Melanie's bed and threw it at Gertie. "Cover yourself, child."

"See," said Melanie, "they're at it again."

"It is only practice," said Egon. "I have to draw every day. I am an artist. If I played piano, I would have to practice every day."

"And you would not be allowed to play piano on your little sister's naughty bits, either," said Melanie.

"I wouldn't mind," said Gertie.

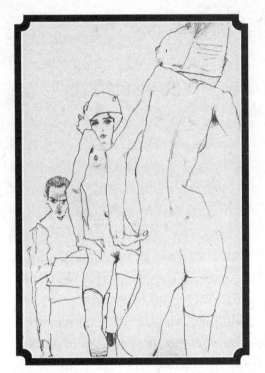

"Much of Egon's critical success is due to my
snatch, Mother," said Gertie.

"No more," said Frau Schiele to her son, alternately waving a
scolding finger under his nose, then tapping it on his sketch pad,
then waving again. "No more of this, you two. I told you."

"But, Mama, we are making art," said Gertie. "Egon's genius
shines best when it shines out of my—"

"You are not too old to be beaten, Gertie. Put on some clothes."
Frau Schiele turned to her son again. "Out! I forbid you to even see
your sister, and you are not staying here. Go back to your flat and
your whores."

"Models," said Egon. He'd been evicted from his apartment only
a week ago because of his models, a dozen of them, who had been
lounging around his studio as a place to get out of the cold, as they

were all very young and needed a place to smoke, sip the sweet wine Egon bought for them, and get away from parents who didn't understand art. The landlord hadn't understood either, when an angry father dragged his thirteen-year-old daughter out by the hair and threatened to kill Egon and burn the building down if he found his daughter there again. Pity, too. Not only had Egon produced hundreds of drawings of the girls, he was able to sell a few of them to pornography dealers to help pay for supplies. Unlike his mentor, Gustav Klimt, Egon was not able to pay his models and was less careful about checking that they were over fourteen, the age of consent, before allowing them in the flat.

"Mother, I have no funds to pay models and Gertie has some experience."

"Much of Egon's critical success is due to my snatch, Mother," said Gertie.

"Oh my God!" said Melanie. "These two!"

"Well, it is!" Gertie insisted. "Tell her, Egon."

"No more in this house," said Mother. "Out, Egon."

"But I had to give up my flat. For artistic reasons. I thought you knew that."

"Then rent another one."

"But I have no money. You are quenching the light of genius, here, Mother. You, who should be honored to have given birth to such a talent."

"Melanie," said Frau Schiele, "bring me the coal shovel from the parlor. I am going to thrash your brother, one last time."

"Philistine," Egon said. He gathered up the loose drawings that were spread around Melanie's bed and tucked them into his sketchbook. His older sister stood in the doorway, holding his coat, waiting.

Egon took the coat from her as he passed her. "Harridan," he whispered.

"Lecher," she retorted.

His mother followed him out into the hallway. "You can send for your clothes."

"What of my art supplies? My paints?"

"We will keep them safe until you send for them."

"But I have no place to go."

"You will find a place."

"But I have no money."

"Go see your uncle Leopold. He believes in your enormous genius."

They had all been living off the largesse of her brother, Leopold, a successful railroad man, who took the family under his wing when Egon's father went mad with syphilis he'd caught from streetwalkers and burned the family's savings (in railroad bonds) in the stove, then unceremoniously died in an asylum.

"Uncle Leopold never respected Father," Egon said as he reached the front door, as if that made any difference.

"For much of his life, your father was a libertine and a raving lunatic," said his mother.

"How can you say that in front of the girls? You sully his memory."

"Your lunatic father would beat you within an inch of your life if he were alive, and it would be the first sane thing he had done in years."

That was probably true. Father had been very angry indeed when, at sixteen, Egon had taken Gertie, who was twelve at the time, to Italy for a romantic reenactment of their parents' honeymoon in Trieste. Father had beaten him unconscious and Gertie was spared only when Mother and their two older sisters threw themselves in front of her and kept her safe until Father drank himself into a stupor.

"Here," said Mother, picking up an envelope from the hall tree and handing it to him. "This came for you while you were molesting your sister."

"I was making art."

"And when you find a flat," said Mother, "Gertie is forbidden from visiting you there." She pushed him out onto the landing and closed the door behind him.

"Goodbye, Egon," he heard Gertie sing from the other room.

"Goodbye, Gertie," he mumbled as he opened the envelope. Inside was a card that said, simply, *Come to my studio today at noon. Opportunity. —Klimt.*

Ah, Klimt would understand. He, too, was a genius. Yesterday's genius, to be sure, but a true artist, not one of these Philistines who understood nothing.

*S*he woke up and vomited some canal water," said Wally. "But she didn't talk, even when I asked her questions."

The drowned girl was wrapped in blankets, only her face peeking out, sleeping on the divan. It had taken more than the hour he'd promised to return, mainly because his mother had wanted to be told the entirety of the story of the opera he'd seen, and after he started, he found he was reciting the plot to Wagner's entire Ring cycle, and finally, realizing both of them might expire from exhaustion before he finished, he said, simply, "Then everybody died." (He'd been reading a lot of Shakespeare lately in translation, and the Bard seemed to think that was a completely acceptable way to end a story.) Mercifully, it had worked.

"She said nothing?" Klimt asked.

Wally shook her head. "I think she might be mute."

"She's not mute. The newsboy and I heard her speak. Did you feed her?"

"I gave her some tea. You don't have any food. Well, cat food. I fed the cats."

"Did she seem hurt? Could she sit up?"

"She just seemed tired," said Wally. "And damp. I helped her wash off the mud on her feet and legs with a flannel. Some gravel was stuck to her, but I didn't see any cuts or bruises. She let me give her a sponge bath, like she trusted me."

"Thank you for that, Wally," said Klimt. He dug into the pocket of the tweed trousers he'd changed into at home and came out with a handful of notes. "Can you go to the market? Get some food. Bread, cheese, sausages, maybe some pastries. Enough for yourself, too."

She took the bills. "Do you want me to stay, take care of her?"

"Yes, maybe, for a while. I sent a message to the young artist I mentioned, telling him to come at noon. And I have a portrait sitting in the afternoon, so we'll need to move her to one of the rooms in the back."

Wally was quite pleased with herself when she returned to the studio with a shopping bag full of food, including some hearty strudel that she thought she might like to eat if she were drowned, and she had kept enough change to get a room for the night if the drowned girl died and she was out on her own. When he was working, the maestro could be intense to a point where he was frightening, but he was generous to a fault, or perhaps just completely shit at keeping track of money, or both. Either way, she knew he would not remember he'd given her too much money for what he'd sent her to buy.

She performed the secret knock, then pushed through the front door before there was a response. The maestro and a younger man stood over the drowned girl, who lay on the divan sleeping or possibly dead. The blanket that had covered her was pulled back and the two men were studying her naked body.

"I brought food," Wally said.

"Put it away, please, Wally." Klimt waved toward the kitchen. "Wally, Schiele. Schiele, this is Wally."

Schiele was very thin—swimming in his linen shirt
and wool trousers as if he'd borrowed them from a larger
man and cinched up the difference with a belt.

Schiele was very thin—swimming in his linen shirt and wool trousers as if he'd borrowed them from a larger man and cinched up the difference with a belt. He didn't look up.

"*Enchanté*, Herr Schiele," Wally said with a curtsy. She extended her hand for him to kiss it, because artists loved all things fucking French and she expected him to be charmed, but he simply muttered, "Good morning," without looking away from the drowned girl.

"I can see the fascination," Schiele said. "But why did you bring her here—"

"Her color. I have never seen skin the color she had turned," said Klimt. "An opalescent lavender, like the inside of an abalone shell, with very fine white lines all over her, which disappeared after she warmed up."

"You could drown her again, see if the lines come back," said Wally, apparently to no one at all, because neither artist responded nor even looked up. She slunk off to the kitchen and began to unload the groceries. *Just wait until they notice how tall the drowned girl is,* Wally thought. *She won't even fit on a canvas unless she puts her heels behind her head.* Klimt's change from the groceries felt righteous and plump in her pocket. It had become *her* change by the *transitive property of men behaving like shits.*

She opened one of the cans of broth she'd bought, poured the brown liquid into a pan, then lit the cooker with a match. She put the pan on the flame and scampered back to the parlor, where she found the two artists looming over the drowned girl like drooling vultures. Schiele was arranging the drowned girl's hair so it flowed off the divan "to extend the line of her figure," he said.

The drowned girl opened her eyes. Wally moved to the divan and pushed Schiele out of the way. "You are safe," Wally said, covering the girl with the blankets and helping her sit up. Wally sat and held the girl like a mother might cradle a sick child. "There is some broth on the cooker," Wally said to Schiele. "It should be warm, if you two are finished talking about her like she's a piece of wood."

Schiele looked to his mentor for permission to be outraged at Wally's insolence. The maestro was already on his way to the kitchen, slinking away, really, after being scolded. Schiele pretended to look at the Japanese prints decorating the parlor.

"Can you speak?" Wally said to the girl.

The drowned girl went wide-eyed, but she didn't respond. Didn't seem to understand. Klimt returned with a cup of broth and handed it to Wally, who tried to feed it to the girl with a spoon.

"Try it. It's not too hot," said Wally. She slurped a bit of the broth herself and smiled. The girl returned Wally's smile and took a spoonful of the broth, then another, then another. Wally was trying to get her to hold the cup herself when there came a knock at the front door.

Schiele and Wally looked with panic in their eyes at Klimt, who looked back at them with equal panic. Wally gestured to the drowned girl to be quiet, then shouted, "That's not the secret knock, you'll have to come back later, the maestro is working."

"Police," came the reply from the other side of the door.

Now the drowned girl looked alarmed and began shaking her head furiously and glancing toward the back room.

"One moment," Wally called. She got the girl on her feet, wrapped the bedding around her, and steadied her as she led her out of the room. At the doorway she gestured over her shoulder for Klimt to answer the door.

There was another room beyond the drawing studio that had once been a bedroom but was now stacked with canvases and cans of solvent. Wally got the girl seated on the floor in the corner, tucked the blankets around her, then caressed her cheek and said, "Quiet now. We'll send them away."

Klimt opened the door just a crack. A stout man of about forty with a mustache stood outside, wearing an overcoat and bowler hat. Klimt was surprised. He had expected to see the military-style coat and shiny spiked helmet of Federal Gendarmerie.

The man flashed an identification card quickly and put it away before Klimt could get a look at it.

"I am looking for a woman. It was reported she was brought here this morning."

"I am a painter," said Klimt. "I work with many women. Models."

"May I come in?" asked the policeman.

"No," said Klimt. "I am in a portrait sitting now. My clients are assured the utmost respect for their privacy."

Schiele stepped into the policeman's view. "Don't you know who this is? This is the studio of Gustav Klimt. *The* Gustav Klimt. The master. Leader of the Secessionists."

"I know who he is," said the policeman. "But who are you?"

"This is Herr Josef Hoffmann, of the Wiener Werkstätte," Klimt said. "Surely you've heard of him."

"Of course," said the policeman. "Herr Hoffmann, were you here this morning when a woman was brought here?"

"I've only just arrived," said Schiele, "but as the maestro told you, there are always women at his studio."

"This woman was pulled from the canal and brought here on a newspaper cart this morning at dawn," said the policeman, who seemed to be getting angrier with every second that passed.

"I have no idea what you are talking about," said Klimt.

The policeman stepped on the threshold and began to push his way in. "You were seen—"

Then Wally, completely naked, stepped under Klimt's arm and into the narrow open gap. "Were you talking to Max?" said Wally. "That little scamp."

The policeman now backed off a step, confronted by a naked Wally standing in the doorway, making no effort at all to cover herself. "I spoke to a boy . . ."

"Yes, that's Max," said Wally. "Gallant young gent helped Herr Klimt rescue me this morning."

"You?" said the policeman. "But—"

"I had a bit too much to drink last evening," said Wally.

"And you fell in the canal?" The policeman seemed uncomfortable with how comfortable Wally was being naked in front of him, which was exactly what she had hoped.

"Near the canal. A friend and I were deep in our cups—I passed out and she just left me there, the bitch."

"Nude? The boy said you were nude."

"As a professional model, I am often nude," said Wally. She put her hands on her hips, shoulders back, and turned from side to side as if her breasts were searchlights and she was scanning the garden for escaped prisoners.

"This is true," said Klimt. "But I was shocked at the time."

"Shocked," said Schiele.

"I'm fine now, thank you," Wally said, twirling in the doorway. "You may please fuck off now."

"Yes," said Klimt. "And I am fencing with the commandant of this district after lunch. I will give him details of the situation, Officer . . . ?" Klimt raised an eyebrow in question. Waited.

The policeman seemed to have forgotten his name, then said quickly, "Kraus. Inspector Kraus."

"Kraus," Klimt repeated. He closed the door in the policeman's face, then turned to Schiele and winked.

"You are not fencing with the commandant after lunch," said Schiele.

"No. And he is not a policeman. At least not Viennese. Anyone from here would have recognized Hoffmann's name and known he is more than twice your age."

"Yes, that accent," said Schiele. "What is that, the outer districts?"

"No, I have the accent of the outer districts. He was Dutch, I think. Do you think you could draw his face from memory?"

"Yes."

"Please do then." Klimt took a small sketch pad and pencil from the hall tree by the door and handed them to Schiele. "I think we may be looking for him soon."

Wally breezed into the room, now wearing a short silk robe. "That man was not a proper police," she said.

"That was really something. *You* were really something," said Schiele, as if he were seeing Wally for the first time.

"*Merci*," she said, with a curtsy. *The fucking French thing, they love it*, she thought.

"Wally is the reason I sent for you," said Klimt. "Well, indirectly. I know you are looking for a place to live and you need models."

"I am, more desperately than when I last saw you. My mother

has evicted me. But I do not think I have funds. I have several paintings up at Hauptmann's for sale. And as soon as I can make some more drawings—"

"I will help you," said Klimt. "I know someone who has a flat with studio space to let. Wally can stay with you in exchange for modeling, and when you sell some paintings or drawings you can pay me back. Would that be acceptable to you, Wally?"

I slept on your front steps in the cold last night, she thought. "Perfect. See if it will have access to a tub. I love a bath."

"I would love to draw you in the bath," said Schiele. "Yes," he said to Klimt. "That would be most acceptable to me, thank you."

"I have a bottle of schnapps," said Wally. "We can celebrate in our new flat." *Well, I guess I'm fucking this skinny wretch tonight*, she thought.

"Good," said Klimt. He took a slip of paper from his billfold and handed it to Schiele. "This is the address, tell him I sent you. And now, that drawing of the false policeman, if you please." (Schiele was a marvel at speed drawing.) "While you do that, Wally and I must talk to our little mermaid."

"She's better. Sitting on the floor in the storeroom eating like a savage when I came out. She ate a whole strudel."

"Perhaps she will have the strength to tell us who she is and why a Dutchman pretending to be a policeman is looking for her."

4

INVENTING SURREALISM

*H*e had painted her before, eight years ago, and had produced one of his most celebrated portraits, despite its residing in her husband's personal collection. Adele Bloch-Bauer was a tall, thin, delicate Jewish socialite, the wife of wealthy industrialist Ferdinand Bloch. She could be morose at times, but Klimt could find a light in her eyes if he could capture her interest, perhaps with a story or a compliment. She'd been only twenty-two when he first painted her, and although unhappy in her arranged marriage, and racked with the despair of having lost two babies (she'd revealed her grief to him in one of their sessions), she had been resilient, defiant even, and he found it easy to get her to shine, perhaps from such close attention from the master painter—a novelty at the time for the young bride. Now, at thirty, she was more world-weary and wary, and after two hours he was exhausted. She wore a big sun hat and flowing silk wraps in the colors of spring, and he had posed her in front of some of his brightest Japanese prints, but he could not make her shine as she had before. Was it *he* who was missing something?

"Frau Bloch—Adele, I fear we are losing the light. Would you mind if we resumed later in the week, perhaps Thursday afternoon?"

She wore a big sun hat and flowing silk wraps
in the colors of spring, and he had posed her in front
of some of his brightest Japanese prints.

"Oh, you're tired, poor lamb. You haven't had a break today, Gustav," she said. "Maybe you should take some time to restore your powers."

She was right, of course. Normally, during a sitting, for a half hour at a time, he would leave his portrait studio, which had once been the house's living room, and escape to the drawing studio, where several of his young models waited in various stages of undress, and there he would draw and talk and laugh with them, a master of his domain, comfortable in his skin, a creative animal, not under the scrutiny of a grand lady upon whom his income depended, and return refreshed. He was the toast of high society, and so in demand he could have painted the wives of bankers and industrialists until he was perched atop a small mountain of gold. The coveted maestro. But this work didn't hold the fascination for him that it once had—perhaps a life of comfort had inured him to inspiration.

"Thursday, then?" Klimt said.

"Thursday," she said. She shed the sun hat and her spring wrap and he helped her with her coat at the door. "Can I fetch you a taxi, Adele?"

Again the smile, almost wistful. "My driver is waiting," she said. "Herr Bloch is in London on business for two weeks. I would love if you could come by for coffee some afternoon," she said. Ah, there it was—that shine.

"I would quite enjoy that," he said. "I will check my diary." He bowed over her hand. She pulled it away coquettishly and sashayed out the door and across the garden. He closed the door, took a deep breath, then headed to the drawing studio to check on his guests.

Wally was reclining on one of the posing platforms, flipping through a magazine and nibbling on a croissant. The drowned girl was nowhere to be seen. "Where is she?"

"In the storeroom. She's fine. Quite mad, but fine."

Klimt headed toward the door to the storeroom, then paused, turned. "Mad? Is she talking?"

"Gibberish," Wally said. She flipped her magazine shut and sat up. "Why did you offer to help Schiele find a flat and not me?"

"I didn't know you needed a place until this morning. Schiele has needed to leave his mother's home for some time. He has an unsavory relationship with his little sister."

"Unsavory? Like he's boinking her?"

"She models for him. In the nude. His mother doesn't approve."

"And he's boinking her?"

"I thought this arrangement could work for you both. He needs a model, you need a place to live."

"You live with your mother and your younger sister, don't you?"

"I am *not* boinking my sister," Klimt said. "Look, Wally, I have one acquaintance who has one flat available. Just stay with Schiele until you can find another place."

Wally waved it off, subject dismissed. "She built a nest."

"My sister?"

"The drowned girl. She built a nest in the storeroom." Wally hopped off the platform and padded over to the door—stood aside as she opened it. *"Voilà!"*

The girl was sitting cross-legged in a nest made of blankets, sheets, and Klimt's overcoat, wearing one of Klimt's blue painting smocks hitched up over her hips. Snuggled around her were five—no, six—of the studio cats, looking quite content. When the door had opened the girl had snatched up a bread crust and held it to her breast as if to keep it safe.

Klimt took a step toward her and crouched down. One of the cats, a little calico female he quite liked, arched her back and hissed at him. *His cat. Hissed at him.*

"She talks to them," Wally said. "She's mad as a bedbug."

"That's not mad," said Klimt. "I talk to them."

"They talk back to her. They do what she asks. She speaks cat, I think."

Klimt scoffed. "Don't be silly. She's just frightened." To the girl, Klimt said, "My name is Gustav. What is your name?"

"She tried to eat one of them," Wally said. "You only have one knife in the kitchen and I hid that from her—well, I don't think she knows how drawers work—so she just tried to eat it whole. The little orange one. It didn't go well for her. It scratched the hell out of her."

Klimt noted the small orange cat that was snuggled by the girl's left thigh. Its fur did appear to be damp in places. And checking, he could see the girl had some orange cat hair stuck to her cheeks.

"I don't see any scratches on her," Klimt said. Although he did note she seemed to have some blood smeared on her wrists and the back of one hand.

"Do you like my kitties?" Klimt asked the girl. "They seem to like you."

"I gave her a loaf of bread and she stopped trying to eat the cats. But there's only half a loaf left. We're going to need more groceries."

Klimt looked up to Wally. "Has she said anything else? Anything about how she came to be in the canal?"

"No, nothing. Just some gibberish, in English, I think."

"You said you could speak English."

"I said I could speak *a little* English. I asked her where the fucking library was. What do you want from me?"

"I died four times!" the girl blurted out in English.

"That's it," said Wally. "That's what she's been saying."

"She's saying she's died four times," Klimt said.

"I told you. Mad as a bedbug. Shall we send her to the hospital?"

"No, no, we can't send her away until we know why that man who was pretending to be a policeman wanted to find her. Perhaps she has family looking for her. For now, she can stay here."

"A complete stranger? Who you just pulled out of a canal? And she can stay here as long as she needs to? Yet I, a loyal employee, a hard worker who has buffed herself to the bone for your work, and who has amicably boinked you upon several occasions, I—I am cast out into the street like so much—"

"I will need you to stay with her overnight. Watch over her. I'll pay you half your modeling rate."

"Half?"

"Most of the time you'll be sleeping."

"Right. Good. I've already taught her how to use the toilet. She was a little afraid of the water at first, but I suppose that's understandable for someone who recently drowned. She might not be mad, she might just be feeble-minded."

"We'll tell Schiele you'll be staying here for a while when he returns."

"Do you want me to get her to pose for you? There's still some sausages I could lure her out of the storeroom with."

"No, not today. I think I will go over to Café Landtmann for coffee to gather my thoughts. I'm feeling quite drained."

"Will you bring me back a pastry?"

"Yes, of course. What would you like?"

"Something delicious. Surprise me. And bring one for the drowned girl so she doesn't attack me for mine."

"She won't do that."

"She tried to eat one of the cats."

"I'll bring one for the drowned girl." He made his way to the front studio to change out of his painting smock.

"We have to think of something to call her besides 'the drowned girl,'" Wally called from the other room.

"*I died four times!*" said the drowned girl in English.

"Ask her name," Klimt called back.

*A*h, Vienna in the spring, a city of infinite possibilities, of inspiration and hope that even forty-eight-year-old Gustav Klimt could feel rising in him as he strolled across the park to the café, passing the market stalls opposite the great Burgtheater, where he and his late brother Ernst had painted the murals above the stairs and stage. Flowers were blooming in the gardens, and blossoms from the fruit trees were falling like fragrant snow. Vienna, monumental city of wide boulevards, concert halls, and palaces. The seat of a thousand-year-old empire, the home of many of the world's greatest painters, composers, scientists, and philosophers. Vienna, a shining jewel on the Danube; birthplace of the waltz, X-rays, psychoanalysis, mathe-

"No, not today. I think I will go over to Café Landtmann for coffee to gather my thoughts. I'm feeling quite drained."

matical genetics, tiny spiced sausages in a can, and before long, Surrealism, just as soon as the trout hit the cream cake.

The waiter at Café Landtmann showed him to a table under the great glass awning. Gentlemen in suits sat at the tables around him, alone and in pairs, reading papers, drinking coffee, conversing, and smoking cigars. Among these, Klimt spotted the renowned doctor Sigmund Freud, who was reading from a brief and diligently not talking to his companion at the table, a younger man who looked to be a doctor as well. At the other end of the café, tablefuls of ladies in fine hats sipped tea served from silver pots and nibbled pastries as delicate as a butterfly's dream. Klimt ordered coffee and a plate of cookies, instead of the Gugelhupf cake that was his usual morning preference. The waiter delivered two evening papers from the rack, where they were threaded through long sticks, for Klimt to peruse while waiting for his order.

As he stirred sugar into his coffee he turned and picked up *Die Stunde*, the evening paper he preferred because they wrote about him and his artist friends, as well as the rest of Vienna's cultural scene, but instead of another glowing review or denouncement of the decadence of current art, a news headline nearly caused him to choke: *HEADLESS BODY FOUND IN DANUBE CANAL*.

He sat up straighter and scanned the article with his finger to make sure he missed no detail. Where? Near the Rossauer Bridge. When? Approximately 8 a.m. Passersby saw the man's headless body floating in the river. Who? The police said the credentials of a Dutch citizen were found on the corpse. Witnesses? A street sweeper had spotted a man in a top hat on the dock near the bridge several hours before. He may have had a sword.

Nothing else? No newsboy? No girl in the water? No newspaper cart? But a sword?

Klimt set the paper down. He took deep, measured breaths to try to bring his heart rate down, as his lady friend Emilie always reminded him to do when he became incensed over a review or an uncooperative painting. Well, the witness was obviously pathetic. A sword? Klimt hadn't even been carrying a walking stick. Obviously it was a detail added after the street sweeper had heard the body was headless. But still, what were the chances that the headless body of a Dutchman, the drowned girl, and a false Dutch policeman showing up at his studio were unconnected? None at all. Perhaps he should go to the police, confess that he had found the girl and thought that she had simply fallen into the canal and hit her head. He was merely helping her until she could remember. He needed to talk to the girl and find out how she had come to be in the canal so near the headless Dutchman.

He signaled to the waiter to bring the bill, and, in doing so, caught the eye of Dr. Freud, who nodded with recognition. They had met, and promised to discuss the influence of primitive African art on modern art at some point, never actually meaning it, of course, and right now the last thing Klimt wanted was to be recognized. As he stood, a quick and shallow bow toward the scientist said everything he needed to say, and he thought he might escape the café without being noticed further, when the trout hit the cream cake.

The drowned girl ran into the café patio near where Freud was sitting, wearing one of Klimt's blue painting caftans, but with the front part of it cinched up before her into a pouch, so she appeared nude from the waist down, her bottom and bits open to the air as she ran, holding up the front of the caftan with one hand, while reaching into the great bundle with the other to retrieve trout and toss them on the tables and to the patrons as she passed.

"Fish!" she said as a trout landed in Freud's companion's cream cake. "Fish!" she shouted, chucking another peschedellian to a table of lunching ladies. She had reached the middle of the patio, and was distributing her fourth fish, when Wally came running around the corner, barefoot in a short kimono that had come unbelted, and so she appeared even more naked than her predecessor.

"No! No! No!" Wally called. "Please keep the trout," she said as she passed one gentleman whose cigar had been extinguished by a flying fish.

"Meat!" said the drowned girl as she pulled a cat from her pouch and cast it into a silver tea set.

"I'm sorry," Wally said, scooping up the cat as she ran by. "She's quite mad. You may keep the fish."

Another fish. Another cat. And the drowned girl reached the restaurant door but was blocked by a brave waiter who barricaded the entrance with a service cart.

"No fish for you," said the drowned girl, her German quite clear and with little accent, Klimt thought.

She turned from the door, spotted Klimt standing by his table, and headed his way, tossing a cat to another waiter as she ran, calling, "Meat! Eat! Good!"

Wally handed another cat to the waiter, stopped to tie her kimono, then took both cats back, thanked him, and headed after the drowned girl, shouting, "No! No! No!" as she went.

"Those are my fish!" shouted a man in a waxed canvas apron who had just run onto the patio.

The drowned girl ran up to Klimt and let go of the caftan, spilling another dozen or so trout and a distressed calico cat onto Klimt's table. "Fish! Meat! Eat!" she said, then paused with a big grin as if waiting for praise.

Klimt scooped up the kitten and held it to his chest.

"Those are my fish!" shouted the fishmonger. He was charging Klimt's way.

"This is my cat," Klimt said.

The fishmonger drew a fillet knife from a sheath at his belt and brandished it as he ran.

"Oh balls," said the drowned girl, and she sprinted past the ladies who lunched and out into the park.

"You need to pay him," Wally said over her shoulder as she ran after the girl. "Those are his fish."

"My cats," Klimt replied.

"Not all of them," said Wally. She trotted after the drowned girl, swinging a cat in each hand as she went. Klimt lost his grip on the trout-slimed cat he was holding and the kitten darted after Wally.

"Those are my fish," said the fishmonger. "That girl took them from my cart and ran off, giving them to people as she went. The red-haired one was helping her. Someone must pay."

Klimt reached into his jacket for his billfold. "How much?"

The fishmonger quoted an amount that seemed absurdly high to Klimt, but he needed to go after the girls, so he shrugged and handed the fishmonger a wad of bills. "Apologies," he said. "She's new." He put another note on the table amid the trout and dishes to cover the bill, then turned to leave as a gentleman nearby spoke.

"Herr Klimt," Freud said. "Am I to understand that those two young women are in your employ?"

"Dr. Freud," said Klimt, offering his hand, then pulling it back when he realized it was covered with slime and cat hair. "Yes, models. Not to be left unsupervised, I have just learned. My studio is only around the corner."

"I see," said Freud. "I confess, the artistic soul is a mystery to me. My young associate is doing a study of hysteria among young women of the lower classes. Perhaps you could send your models around for an interview."

Klimt bristled at the "lower classes" pronouncement, then willed himself to relax. It wasn't untrue, his models did hail from the lower classes, most from the poor suburbs where he himself had grown up, but he didn't care for the implied judgment. "I will ask them, Doctor. Thank you. But I must be off. Good to see you."

"And you. We must have that discussion you've been threatening."

"Primitive African motifs in modern art? Yes, I remember," said Klimt. "Yes, I will send a message to your offices. Now, Herr Doctor, if you'll excuse me, I have girls, cats, and fishes to collect."

Which was exactly the sort of thing he'd rather not have said to the world's leading psychiatrist.

5

RAVEN RISING

"Did you bring me a pastry?" Wally asked. She knew the master hadn't brought her a pastry as both of his hands were full, one with a kitten and the other with a trout, but it was always a good idea to keep him thinking he owed her.

"Where is she?" Klimt asked.

"In her nest. In the storeroom. With all the cats. She's sharing a trout with them."

"What happened? How did that happen? You were supposed to watch her."

"I did, I watched her run out and the cats run after her. They really like her, even the one she tried to eat. Then she scooped up the trout as she ran away from the fishmonger's cart and the cats jumped into the"—Wally gestured as if she were forming a pouch in front of her stomach—"into the smock she was wearing."

"Why didn't you stop her?"

"She's very strong for a skinny girl. Also very tall. Did you notice how tall she is?"

"So you *did* try to stop her?"

"I said '*stop*,' if that's what you mean. She didn't stop."

"It doesn't sound like you tried very hard."

"I'll try to do better the next time you bring a drowned lunatic to my workplace."

"She's not a lunatic," Klimt said. "She needed help."

Wally held up a hand to stop him from talking, then crooked a finger signaling for him to follow her through the parlor and into the drawing studio, where she bowed deeply and held her arms out toward the open storeroom, as if presenting one of the dancing white stallions from the Spanish riding school. The drowned girl sat in her nest, tearing pieces of a trout with her teeth and feeding them to the cats, who were circling her and purring as they waited for their snack.

"She's going to need a bath," Wally said. "I don't know how to light the water heater." She had never taken a bath at Klimt's studio, but she knew the tub was there. "I need a bath, too." Wally was still naked but for the short, open kimono. She gestured to a trail of fish slime running down between her breasts. "She tried to feed me a trout before she stole the rest of them off the cart. I think to thank me for looking after her."

Klimt looked at the slime on Wally, then at the feral drowned girl, then back at Wally. "She frightened everyone in the café."

"Don't change the subject just because you don't know how to light the water heater."

"I *do* know how to light the water heater. And you *weren't* looking after her."

"I *was*, until she ran off. I was cleaning the blood out from under her fingernails when she started chanting and ran out."

"Blood? Chanting? Blood?" Klimt seemed to be losing the thread of the story.

Wally sighed, she hoped like a tolerant and understanding sister would sigh, because she didn't want Klimt's confusion to turn to frustration, then anger at her. She still wasn't sure where she was sleeping tonight, nor, for that matter, from where her next meal was coming.

"There was blood under her nails, even after I cleaned her up."

"From the fish?" Klimt asked.

"No, not from the fish. This was before the fish." Wally suppressed the urge to scold him for not keeping up. "So I got one of those bendy little knives from your studio and started to clean her nails for her. As soon as she saw a glob of the blood on the knife her eyes got big like she was frightened and she started chanting."

"Chanting what?"

"I don't know. Some nonsense. *Tulu*-something."

"*Tulugaak makittuk!*"* said the drowned girl, looking up from her fish. "*Tulugaak makittuk! Tulugaak makittuk!*"

"Yes, that's it," said Wally. "Nonsense. English maybe?"

"It's not English," said Klimt, moving closer to the drowned girl. She gave the last of her trout to a black kitten and the other cats pounced after it and scuffled in the nest for a share. "Not English I've ever heard."

Klimt crouched down so he was eye level with her. She brandished her hands at him as if they were talons. "Tulugaak *makittuk*," she said. She looked at the gore under her nails, then at him, and she said it again.

"That's what she did before," Wally said. "When she saw the blood under her nails."

Klimt scooted closer to her on the floor. "My name is Gustav," he said. He pointed to Wally. "That is Wally."

"Short for Walburga," Wally said.

"And you are?" Klimt said, pointing to her chest, the front of her smock, dark and well slimed with fish offal. "Your name, is it Tulugaak?" Klimt tried.

"Tulugaak?" the drowned girl said, and she laughed manically, her mouth open, like a toddler who was just learning to laugh and wanted to make sure it was good and loud. "Tulugaak?" Again the laugh.

---

* "Raven rises!"

"Mad as a fucking hatter," said Wally. "Probably from syphilis. We should take her to the nuthouse."

"She's not mad, she's just distressed. Freud calls it *trauma*."

"You can't even light the water heater and you are quoting the great doctor Freud?" Wally had left a box of matches in the soap tray for him.

"I will light the fucking water heater," Klimt said, standing and heading toward the bath. "Get her ready."

"You could use a bath too, maestro. You are ripe."

"I am not ripe," he called from the bath. There was a knock at the front door. "Answer that, please," he said.

"It's not the secret knock."

"It might be Schiele. He doesn't know the secret knock."

"Then why did we let him in? He's very thin. I think he might be ill."

"Answer the door, please, Wally."

Klimt struck a match on the underside of the tub and turned on the gas under the water tank.

"It's a policeman," Wally called.

"No! No policeman," shouted the drowned girl, in German, from her nest.

"A real one," Wally said. "He has a boy and a trout with him."

The gas made a *whomp* sound, like a muted explosion, as it ignited.

Klimt was determined that if this was another scoundrel posing as a policeman he would box his ears. Yes, he was a gentleman, and moved among the highest levels of Viennese society, but he had not grown up thus, and he and his brothers had fought like cats as boys, with each other and with the other boys from the suburbs. He knew how to fight. He would box this policeman's Dutch or possibly Flemish ears. As a precaution, though, he snatched an unopened bottle of wine from the credenza as he passed through the portrait studio, just in case he had lost a step or two in his ear-boxing game and the charlatan required a braining blow from a nice gray Riesling he kept around for the ladies.

Wally scampered out of the foyer as Klimt swung the door back, fully ready to bring the Riesling around in a crowning slam. Which he did not. Because the policeman standing there wore a spiked helmet and a brass-buttoned military uniform with silver braid, epaulets, and a sword. *This* was a Viennese policeman, a stout fellow in his late forties with a flamboyant handlebar mustache. In one hand he held the boy, Max, by the scruff of the neck; in the other, as Wally had promised, a trout.

"Herr Klimt, I found this boy in the square trying to sell a dirty picture. He says you gave it to him." The policeman handed the boy the trout, then pulled the drawing of the drowned girl from inside the front of his jacket.

"I've never seen this boy before in my life," said Klimt.

"Papa?" said Max.

"Herr Klimt," said the policeman, "I have heard that you have many children wandering the outer districts. I understand, a man must be a man, but if this boy—"

Klimt hung his head in surrender. "I gave the drawing to the boy. But it is not a dirty picture." He braced himself to defend dragging the drowned girl out of the canal, but Max simply snatched the drawing from the policeman's hand and said, "I told you."

"To be sure," said the policeman. "It's just that it is signed, and I thought the boy might have stolen it. He was trying to sell it for ten crowns. I recognized your signature from your work at the Secessionist Gallery. The wife and I, we are fans."

This was not at all what Klimt was expecting, but he supposed he shouldn't have been too surprised. Vienna's people, even the working-class people, were proud of her artists, her composers, her writers, her actors. Citizens who could never afford to attend the theater followed the reviews and gossip about actors in the papers and magazines.

"Thank you," Klimt said. To Max, he said, "Perhaps you would like to find something to eat in the kitchen."

"Is Wally back there?" asked Max.

"Of course. Go ask her to help you find something."

"I had to leave my cart in the square," said Max.

"We will fetch it directly," said Klimt. To the policeman he said, "Thank you for your vigilance."

The boy breezed by him, trout in hand.

The policeman, looking very self-satisfied, leaned into the doorway. "If you don't mind my saying so, Herr Klimt, you should have your prostitute register with the Gendarmerie. That way if she's picked up on the street she won't be put in jail or forced into medical treatment."

"She's not a prostitute. She's a model. I employ many models and they often model nude."

"As you wish, sir. Well, I'll look out for her if I see her on the street. Any of your *models*, if they say they work for you."

"Very kind of you, Officer . . . ?"

"Bauer. Sergeant Richter, Central District, *mein Herr.*" He came to attention and clicked his heels, then immediately looked uncomfortable. "Sorry."

Klimt recognized that the poor policeman was starstruck, which amused him, since the artist had been terrified when Wally announced a policeman at the door, although he was relatively sure he hadn't done anything illegal. Profoundly stupid, perhaps, but not illegal. "Sergeant, again, I thank you. Tell me, do you know anything about that body they found in the canal this morning? The papers said it was near the Rossauer Bridge. I often take that bridge on the way to the studio. Not this morning, thank the graces, but still . . ." Klimt trailed off, hoping the policeman would volunteer some information.

And he did, leaning in conspiratorially: "Nasty business, that. It was a policeman from Amsterdam, too. Still had his wallet, so it wasn't a robbery. Detective Sergeant Thiessen. We're waiting to hear what he was doing in Vienna."

"And the paper said his head was cut off. A sword?"

The policeman shook his head and shuddered as if recalling something particularly unpleasant. "No, no, the papers got it wrong. His head was *torn* from his body, not cut. Perhaps caught in a cable trailing a ship, or even a propeller, we don't know. The doctors haven't reported yet. Of course they won't tell me, but I know the investigator."

"*Torn* from his body?"

"One hopes it was an accident," said Sergeant Richter. "If we find his head we'll ask him what happened." The big policeman laughed at his joke.

"Well, I thank you for your concern, Sergeant Richter, but I must go back to work."

"Oh yes, the muse does not wait, I am told. Tell me, Herr Klimt, why did you give the boy such a valuable drawing?"

"Oh, that. I passed him this morning on the way here and I wanted to buy a paper but I didn't have any coin. I simply tore a sheet from my sketchbook in exchange. It was nothing."

"Well, next time, perhaps don't trade a nude to a child. You know there are those in Vienna who are not so sophisticated as we are and could make a stink."

"I'll remember that, Sergeant. Thank you."

The policeman touched the silver brim of his helmet in salute and said good day as Klimt closed the door. "Wally!" he called as he made his way through the studio.

"In here," came the answer from the bathroom.

The two of them, Wally and the drowned girl, were both in the long clawfoot tub, which was filled with steaming water, milk white from soap. The boy, Max, stood by the sink holding a paint-stained towel in front of him.

"I'm helping," said Max.

The drowned girl, far from frightened or feral now, lay back in the water with her eyes closed, smiling.

"I used some of that brown soap you had in the kitchen," Wally said.

"I use that to clean sizing brushes," Klimt said. He wanted to grab a sketch pad from the other room and draw these two in the bath. Record the line the water made on the contours of their bodies where they emerged from the water. Of the drowned girl he could see only her face, her hair, and the swell of her breasts above the waterline like islands, the feminine archipelago. Wally was sitting up—head and shoulders above the surface, her red hair, in still-dry curls, a splash of color amid all the pale skin and bathwater.

"Perhaps you can find something in the kitchen for Max to eat," Wally said.

Was a seventeen-year-old girl telling him what to do? In his own studio?

"For being such a good boy and not telling the policeman about her." Wally splashed a small wave at the drowned girl.

"What?" said Klimt. "Oh, of course. Max, come with me please."

The boy followed him, holding the folded towel fast in front of him.

"Do you want to leave that with Wally?" Klimt asked.

"No," said Max.

When they had passed down the hall to the kitchen, Max said, "Something funny is happening to me."

Klimt made a great show of searching the kitchen for something to eat, despite there being a half loaf of bread and butter on the counter right in front of him. "You'll be fine in a minute. How old are you?"

"I am ten."

"Surely this isn't the first time you have experienced that."

"When I wake up sometimes, but not like this, in the middle of the day."

The boy seemed more distressed by his spontaneous erection than he had been by finding someone fishing a body out of the canal. If Klimt had wanted to have this kind of conversation with a child he would have been raising his own children, and even then he would have told them to ask their mothers. He sighed. "Max, that is something that happens to all men sometimes when they are around pretty ladies. Especially if the pretty ladies have no clothes on."

"Why isn't it happening to you, then?"

"It does sometimes, but not now, because I am old—older— and I have learned to control it. I work with pretty naked ladies all the time, so I must control myself to do my work." This was a lie, of course. He didn't control his urges at all; he channeled them. Pretty ladies, particularly pretty *naked* ladies, were his raison d'être, and if he actually had developed the control he professed, he wouldn't have been supporting four different families spread across Vienna. He secretly believed that lust, channeled through craft learned in eight years of study at the University of Applied Arts, was the key to his success.

"I think I should like to be a painter," Max said.

"It is a noble calling, but you will have to work hard to learn."

"Mostly it's naked ladies, though," said Wally, who was coming down the hall wearing her white cotton knickers and a matching chemise, rubbing her hair dry with a towel.

Klimt noted that Wally was leaving thin stripes of black paint in her vivid red hair from oil paint that was still tacky on the towel, but he thought it might be better if she discovered that herself. "Did you just leave her—?"

"If you become a painter, Max, be sure to bathe often
so your models are not disgusted by you."

"The drowned girl is still in the tub. The water is still hot if
you'd like to join her."

"No, I wouldn't do that," said Klimt.

"She's very pretty with the filth washed off of her."

"But she's simpleminded. I would not—"

"You will do anything to avoid a bath, won't you?" Wally looked
at the boy. "If you become a painter, Max, be sure to bathe often so
your models are not disgusted by you."

"I am not disgusting," protested Klimt.

"You're the maestro. She's going to need clothes. All your smocks
are dirty."

"Can you lend her some of your clothes?"

"I only have two dresses, and besides, she's too tall for my clothes."

"I will lend her some of mine," said Max.

"That is very sweet of you," said Wally. "But she is also too tall for *you*, and you'll need your clothes to wear home."

Max suddenly looked distressed. "I need to fetch my cart from the square before someone steals it."

"Wally," said Klimt, "would you take Max to fetch his cart?"

"Yes."

"And perhaps buy some clothes for the drowned girl? Something simple."

"Of course."

"And more groceries, if you don't mind?"

Klimt pulled his billfold from his jacket and stared into its inky depths. The last of the bills had gone with the fishmonger. "I'm going to need to go to the bank to get more money."

"An artist should never have to think about money," said Egon Schiele, stepping through the swinging door. "The state should see to our needs as we perform a service to society."

"Schiele," Klimt said.

"You didn't use the secret knock," said Wally.

Schiele ignored her. "Maestro, may I borrow a sketch pad and an oil crayon? That drowned girl is nude in your drawing studio being licked dry by cats. I've never seen such a thing. I must get a sketch."

"We forgot to leave her a towel," said Wally.

Max clutched the folded towel fast to his crotch.

"Cats!" said Klimt. He pushed through the kitchen door. "We need to count the cats. See that they made it home safely. They are house cats, not used to being outside of the garden."

"Did you get the flat?" Wally asked Schiele as they both followed Klimt into the drawing studio, where the drowned girl was now sitting on one of the posing platforms, petting the little calico.

"Oh, this is even better," said Schiele, ignoring Wally's question. He snatched up a sketch pad and pencil from one of the cushions and flipped over one of Klimt's drawings already in progress to a fresh page.

"My kitties," said Klimt. "Where are all my kitties?"

"All here," said the drowned girl, calmly, in unaccented German. "All good."

Klimt stepped back from her. The cats were patrolling the room now. Two played in the corner. He counted nine, including the one she held. They were all there. "They are all here," Klimt announced.

"Can you move your knee?" Schiele gestured for the drowned girl to sit with one knee up. "I like to confront the viewer with everything."

"Oh joy," said Wally.

Klimt, who could often be dismissive and obsessive when he was drawing, felt the hairs on his neck prickle watching the young painter work. *What a ravenous creature is talent!* Schiele would endure much suffering feeding his talent, but how much would he inflict? Klimt wondered for an instant, just the blink of an eye, if *he* had caused suffering while feeding his talent. Then he tried to shake the thought out of his head like a dog clearing water from its ears. Better to worry about money.

"Did you remember who you are?" Schiele asked the girl.

"Do you remember who you are?" she asked Schiele.

"I am Egon Schiele," Schiele said. He offered his hand to shake. She looked at it.

"I am simpleminded," she said.

"No you're not," said Wally. "Klimt was just saying that because he didn't want to take a bath."

"I will need to go to the bank and get some money," Klimt announced to the room.

"Do you remember who you are?" the drowned girl asked Klimt.

"I am Gustav Klimt," Klimt said.

"I am also Gustav Klimt," the girl said to Schiele.

"She's like a parrot," said Schiele.

"I am like a parrot," said the girl.

"No you're not," said Wally.

"I'll get you money to buy clothes and groceries," Klimt said to Wally.

"And to pay me for the day," Wally said.

"Of course," Klimt said. "And to buy that drawing from you," he said to Max, who was mesmerized by the movement of Schiele's crayon on the paper.

"What?" said Max.

"Twenty crowns, for your drawing."

Max looked away from Schiele's drawing and grinned widely. "Twenty crowns? Twenty?"

"Gather your things, we will fetch your cart on the way to the bank and then I will pay you for your drawing."

The boy scampered off to the front rooms.

Klimt said to Wally, "Could you bundle the laundry so the boy can carry it? And would you stay here? Make sure the drowned girl stays here as well, and if that Dutchman pretending to be a policeman returns—"

"Kill him," said the drowned girl.

And everything stopped. Even Schiele stopped drawing, dropped his crayon.

"What?" said the drowned girl.

"You're speaking better," said Wally, to clear the murder from the room. "Very good."

"Perhaps she's Dutch," Schiele said. "Do you know where you are from?"

The girl glared into the air as if searching for an errant mosquito. Finding none, she shook her head.

"Ask her something in Dutch," Wally said.

Klimt said something in Dutch.

The drowned girl slid off the posing platform and stepped up to Klimt with a growl. Although slight, she was half a head taller than his six feet, and somewhat mad, so he stepped back in spite of himself.

"Why would I know where the fucking library is? I don't even know who I am!" she said in German. She pivoted on a bare heel, tossed her hair behind her, and strode out of the drawing studio into the storeroom, then snatched up the little calico who had followed her and shut the door behind her.

"Well, the drowned girl speaks Dutch," said Wally with a smile, as if the day had not been a complete circus.

"I don't think we should keep calling her 'the drowned girl,'" said Schiele. "Although I would like that to be the title of my drawing."

"'The Dutch Girl'?" Wally suggested.

"Judith," pronounced Klimt.

Schiele's prodigious eyebrows lifted like levitating badgers. "Really?"

"Yes," said the maestro.

Wally looked to each of the men to see if there was consensus, then walked over to the storeroom door and tapped gently. "Pardon me, Fräulein, but would you have any objection to being called Judith?"

"Bring back sausages," said the drowned girl. "This kitty wants sausages."

Wally turned to the artists. "Judith it is, then."

6

PROMETHEUS BOUND

Dear Sister:

Please forgive the abrupt ending of my last missive, but I felt it urgent I ask my new friend why he had locked a woman in a box and left her there to freeze, but I have since discovered it was nothing so horrible, merely a simple case of reanimation of the dead gone wrong. Upon awakening, Victor scolded me for what I felt was an unreasonable amount of time for opening his crate, before explaining that the young woman inside was not an unwilling hostage, but instead the girl-corpse the creature Adam had brought to him to make into his bride. When Victor plunged the knife into her chest to show his unwillingness to give her life again, only to be the companion of a monster, he had quite purposely missed her heart, and, in fact, having gained a thorough knowledge of anatomy in constructing his prior abomination, guided the knife so it missed all her vital organs. After Adam made his escape into the night, Frankenstein injected the girl with all that was left of his ELIXIR OF LIFE, which he'd been steadily trying to improve since first raising Adam.

"She never came to consciousness," Victor told me, "but there was a heartbeat there, so faint and irregular that had I not touched her neck, examining the bruise left where I presume the creature had strangled her, I might have never felt the pulse. Her breath was shallow and sometimes a minute would pass between breaths, when I thought she had expired again, only to be surprised a full moment later. But she is not alive. I suppose because I was not able to apply sufficient electricity to shock her to life. She is in a state of catatonia, not alive, not dead. Undead, I suppose."

"She spoke," I said.

"She does not speak. She does not move. She is simply a still body with a heartbeat."

"She called me a butt puddle."

"I don't know what that is," said Frankenstein.

"Shall we ask her?"

"We must bring her inside." Suddenly a fellow I had thought at death's door a moment before had found new energy. He was off the cot and dressing in an instant. "My dear Walton, this is a revelation!"

I had the men lower the crate through one of the hold hatches, then six of them carried it to a spot outside of my cabin. The crate was far too large to fit through the door. The entire time the sled dog, who had been fed and rested and was living in my cabin with myself and Victor, followed and guarded the crate as if this had been his duty all along. When the men were called to the galley for breakfast, Victor and I opened the crate and moved all the scientific equipment into my cabin. We laid the young woman, who was wrapped in Native-sewn furs like Frankenstein's, on the chart table.

She was very pale; her skin had taken on an almost bluish hue, which faded to a pale pink as she warmed in my quarters. The whole time the sled dog, whom Frankenstein had named Geoffrey, or Geoff, stood by whining, as if he was anxious for her safety. Upon Victor's instruction, I placed my finger upon her neck and felt her pulse.

"How long has she been like this?" I asked.

Several months, he told me. He had given her the elixir and discovered her slow state in Scotland, then had packed her into the crate with his instruments and returned to Switzerland, thinking he would reach there in time to protect his family. If the girl survived the trip, perhaps he could replicate the electrical process used on Adam to bring her fully to life. He fed her only small quantities of rich beef broth, most of which she absorbed, for he had fitted her with a nappy, which seldom became more than a little damp.

"When I reached our estate outside of Basel, mercifully, I found my father and my fiancée, the lovely Elizabeth, alive and safe. I installed the girl in the folly where I had animated Adam and bade my assistant, Waggis, to live there and care for her in secret, which involved little more than keeping her clean and pouring small quantities of broth and water into her lips, while we waited for an electrical storm so I might jolt her to life."

Weeks passed; while Victor again enjoyed the company of his family, the little dwarf cared for the undead girl, whose heartbeat increased, although this was only discovered by Waggis meticulously timing her heartbeat and respiration and recording them in a ledger. Meanwhile, Victor found two young men from the village who had finished their military service, and employed them as guards. They patrolled the estate every night, with loaded rifles, and neither Elizabeth or Victor's father was permitted to leave the estate unless accompanied by a guard, or by Victor himself, who had taken to carrying a brace of loaded pistols under his coat. It was not until the night of the very storm for which they were waiting that the fiend appeared.

Waggis had already climbed to the top of the folly and installed the copper cable and lightning rods. On the night of the first storm after Victor's return, however, the little man was distraught and refused to assist Victor as he had on the night that they had raised Adam. He did not want to connect the cables to the copper table where the girl lay, afraid that she might be burned, or that she might wake up to become a monster.

"I confess," Victor told me, "that ensconced in the bosom of my family, and pretending to have returned to normal life, I left too much of the girl's care to Waggis. Sometimes when I would tread up the hill after supper, I would find him sitting next to her, talking quietly to her. I couldn't hear what he was saying, but it was gentle, and had the tones one might take when comforting a sick child. He brushed her hair and found a new dress for her somewhere; I suppose he stole it from the wash lines of one of the villagers, as it was the simple dress of a milkmaid or shopgirl, not as fine as anything he could have found among Elizabeth's things.

"When I would spy him through the windows, talking to her, I would retrace my path and cough loudly as I approached, or call out that I was on my way. So intimate did the little man's moments seem with her that I did not wish to disturb or embarrass him.

"I thought perhaps Waggis had gotten over his fixation on the undead girl when I heard laughter one evening as I approached the folly to find him playing gleefully with a gray mouse. Talking up a storm to the little creature and giggling as if he were being tickled.

"'What is this?' I called to him, relieved a bit, that he had found another source of entertainment. 'Have we found a small friend?'

"'We have created a friend,' Waggis replied. He insisted that he had suffocated the little rodent in one of the vacuum jars in the laboratory, then had reanimated it by applying a light current from one of the smaller Leyden jars."

Surely the mouse had only been stunned, I told him, and he had simply awakened it, for the application of electric current in any amount would not reanimate dead flesh—the experiments had been tried all over the world and resulted in little more than convulsing frog legs and scores of small, broiled animals. One needed the elixir, and there was no more.

"'I used some of her blood,' Waggis said, pointing to our undead guest. The mouse, he told me, had been quite dead—he'd let it sit for two hours, had even tried applying current without the girl's blood, which did nothing at all. I was stunned, both by his ambition and by his success. I hadn't even attempted to create more of the elixir since my return—the ingredients were expensive and difficult to obtain, especially in useful quantities, and my work had brought so much misery so far, my only concern had been to undo some of the suffering I had caused, to see if I could return the poor girl who had been murdered by my creature to life, as a way to atone for my sins. It was the success of the little man and his mouse that reignited my enthusiasm for science. What power there was in this new elixir, that even the trace amount that remained in the undead girl's blood might return a dead creature to life. And with that, I resolved to manufacture an even more refined batch. Little did I know that once again, the desire to overcome death would be the very thing that invited it into my world.

"There were certain ingredients, rare, arcane mineral compounds, that I had only been able to obtain through a dealer in Prague, a Jewish fellow whose family had been supplying these compounds since the Dark Ages. I could get to Prague by stagecoach, do my business, and return in under four days if I slept on the coaches, perhaps three if I could book a ride on a mail coach, although there would be no sleep in such an arrangement. I had become somewhat complacent since my return from Scotland, between the guards and my own habit of carrying a pistol about my person at all times, for which my lovely Elizabeth called me mad. I had come to think of the estate as secure, a safe harbor, so to speak. Even so, before I left, I hired extra guards to patrol the main house day and night, and even gave Waggis my small pocket pistol and instructed him on how to use it.

"I was lucky to secure a rear seat atop a mail coach, so was able to reach Prague in only eighteen hours, but exhausted and very sore of flank. I did my business and acquired a sturdy valise full of chemicals and slept on the coaches home to arrive only forty hours after I left, and apparently only hours after complete calamity had struck.'"

At this point, dear sister, Victor nearly succumbed to tears, and I pretended to fuss with charts and other nautical things until he regained his composure. In short, he found the guards and his family slain, his fiancée strangled in her bed, the guards with their necks snapped, their rifles unfired, his father still in his dressing gown, in the parlor, his brains bashed in with a candlestick.

"I became breathless with grief as I wept over my lifeless Elizabeth," Victor told me, "but when, after what was perhaps a half an hour, the sable-colored melancholy receded, I found my feet and rushed up the hill to the folly to find the undead girl and the crate in which I had transported her gone, along with all the cable and lightning rods, and much of the laboratory equipment you have seen in the crate. I found poor Waggis unconscious under a stack of books that had fallen over him from an oak shelf, shattered, no doubt, from the impact of his small body. Blood was pooling on the floor about his head and I thought him dead like the others until he moaned as I removed the books. I sat him up and was able to staunch the blood flowing from a gash in his scalp.

"'He took her,' Waggis said. As I stitched his wound he told me his narrative. He had drawn the pistol I had given him when Adam crashed through the glass doors, but before he was able to cock the hammer the monster had snatched him up by the front of his coat and tossed him across the room, knocking him unconscious. He awoke long enough to see the creature gathering up the undead girl and putting her into the crate, then packing the instruments and even the lightning rods and cable on top of her. Waggis looked for the pistol as Adam was retrieving the lightning rods but fell back into a ruse of being dead when the monster returned to the room. 'I could not find it,' Waggis said. 'And without a weapon, the giant would render me as dead as I looked, so I had to listen as he packed the instruments into the crate. As he carried it out, he said, "I know you are not dead, little man. Tell Victor Frankenstein I will await him, with my bride, in the land of the dead."

"'You have to get her, bring her back,' Waggis pleaded. He did not know that everyone in and around the house had been murdered, and while my grief was turning to anger and desire for vengeance, I knew I would have to bury Elizabeth and my father, and somehow explain the massacre to the local authorities. When I explained this to Waggis, he said, 'I will bury them. You go, bring her back.'

"As I contemplated the coming days, burying my family and trying to return to some sense of normalcy, I could not see beyond my sorrow and anger. There would never be a new dawn, only darkness. I cursed all the gods I could name at the top of my lungs. I ran into the fields until I was breathless, then fell to the ground and sobbed, wishing for death to take away my pain—pain I had created. Then, after some time passed, I heard Waggis speak from alarmingly close to me. I looked up to see the little man holding a rolled-up map. As I blinked away my tears, he unrolled it—a map of Europe, with a bold black line drawn from Basel, tracing waterways to Norway and into the frozen north. Written next to the line were the words 'The Land of the Dead.'

"'He left it for you,' Waggis told me. 'In the big house. You need to follow. Kill him. Bring her home.'

"I protested, poured out my troubles and tasks, and the little man looked from me to the map. 'You brought this evil into the world and you must remove it. Go now, before he is too far ahead of you.'

"Waggis had an answer to my every objection. If I waited, I might lose the trail, even with a map to follow. The little man promised to bury my family and inform the authorities, even tell them that I pursued the perpetrators. I had thought Waggis a simpleton, his mind as broken as his little body, but such was not the case—which I suppose I should have realized when he reanimated the mouse. If I gave him the authority, I was sure he would be able to handle the affairs of the estate, so I relented. In the library I drafted a document giving my power of attorney to the little man, then, with his help, I packed for the journey, light, but with all the currency the monster had not taken and several pistols with shot and powder. The creature had taken the only wagon, so I saddled a horse and the two of us rode into Basel. I outlined my wishes as we rode and Waggis suggested a strategy for pursuing Adam. He had been wearing a cloak with a hood, Waggis said, so he might hide his face, but he would not be able to conceal his great height. He would book passage in cargo, where he could hide, so I would find witnesses to his passage among the stevedores and cargo clerks.

"'I know,' said Waggis, 'because I too have a form that I would hide away, and that is what I would do.' Adam would have to change ships when changing rivers heading out onto the sea.

"In Basel I woke up the family attorney, who, after much protest and scolding, notarized the document and assured me he would help Waggis see to my wishes. He even suggested I hire more guards for the estate or even some men-at-arms who might accompany me in my pursuit, but I would not have it. Waggis rode with me to the docks on the Rhine and waved from horseback as I boarded the first ship headed north."

Victor paused here and I could see his newly found energy had waned. He sat back on the cot. I was eager to know how the undead girl in the box got to the frozen north and onto Victor's sledge, but he could go on no more, despite my stating rather sternly, "For fuck's sake, man, how did the frozen undead girl in the box end up on your sledge in the frozen north?" But he had no more to give. He fell back on the cot and I covered him with the blanket. "Later," he said. "I fear my fever has returned." Then he fell asleep or unconscious, but he would talk no more.

Perhaps I had been too quick to ply him with tankards of brandy while he told his story. I will write again when he awakens. For now I am being regarded skeptically by the sled dog, Geoff, whom Victor insisted I allow to stay in my cabin with us, and who is now guarding the body of the undead girl as she thaws.

Until the morrow, I remain,

Your adventurous brother,

Robert

P.S. Since Victor passed out I have asked the undead girl several times what was the meaning of calling me a butt puddle but she has remained stubbornly silent.

7

THE PRODIGAL SON
RETURNS

Letter #4: August 11, 1799, Aboard the Ship Prometheus,
Icebound in the Far North

My Dear Margaret:

Forgive my unsteady hand, but the events of the last day
have shaken me so, I can barely hold the pen. Victor regained
consciousness some eight hours after my last letter, but if
anything, he was weaker than he had been before his excitement at
hearing that the frozen girl had spoken. After the steward poured
some porridge into him, I asked, "If Adam left with the girl and
the box full of instruments, how is it we found you sledging across
the ice with both in your possession?"

Indignant, he replied, "Are you accusing me of stealing the
property of a monster? I have created human life here, I will not have
my ethics questioned."

He was feeling stronger, then, I think, so I said, "My sister rattles
on about the very same thing, but she can't be trusted with the
silverware." I knew you would be touched that I thought of you in
these harrowing moments.

Then, after I saw to it that he was fortified with porridge and brandy, Frankenstein related the story of how he had come to recover the girl in the box. I shall attempt to relate the story in the manner in which he told it, while it is fresh in my mind.

"I followed Adam's path to the very northernmost regions of Europe, doing as Waggis recommended, bribing stevedores and cargo clerks for clues to the fiend's progress along the way. When at last I arrived in Hammerfest, the northernmost port in Norway, I found a clerk who was still shaken from his transaction with the grim giant. I was less than a day behind. With my father's pilfered gold, Adam had purchased provisions, a sledge and a team of dogs, two sets of furs, as well as passage on a fishing boat large enough to transport him and the kit to the northern ice. Everyone he encountered cautioned the giant about taking the large crate as cargo onto the ice, but relented when they surmised that the more quickly the foolhardy creature perished, the better for everyone.

"I bought kit of similar description, a sledge, dogs, provisions, furs and boots made by the Natives who thrived in the frozen north. Upon the dawn, which comes quickly in summer in the far north, I departed on the fishing sloop that had taken Adam to the ice. It was an open boat, except for a very small cabin in which the fishermen could retreat during rain—much like the Viking ships one sees in book illustrations—and I marveled at how these hearty fishermen endured the elements in such a craft.

"The captain explained that it was less than half a day's sail to the edge of the ice and he would try to land me at the same spot where he had taken Adam. The fishermen had been frightened during their transport of the giant, and the captain confessed that he had stood at the rudder with a primed and loaded pistol prominent in his belt the entire time, but the monster had paid them a year's wages for the passage, so despite their misgivings, they had accepted the commission and they had offloaded him without incident.

"The fishermen dropped me on the ice at a spot where, from the disturbance of the hardened snow, I could discern there had been considerable activity recently, and they assured me this was from Adam and his sled dogs. Then, after a quick lesson in driving a dogsled, the captain bade me good luck and said that if I should change my mind, he would make an effort to return four days hence, and if I was able, I should return as well and he would rescue me from my folly. The entire journey he had lectured me, in his broken German, on dangers I might encounter, from the white bears to the sea ice breaking up and stranding me.

"It had not snowed overnight, nor had the wind been strong, so the creature's path through the snow was as clear as if drawn in ink. I set the dogs on what I thought an easy pace as I became accustomed to driving the sledge. From the depth of the tracks, I could tell that the creature's sledge, with his bulk and the crate, was much heavier than my own, and therefore I should be able to travel at a more rapid rate. If I did not rest, and if the weather cooperated in not covering his tracks, I should overtake him in less than a day.

"I drove the sledge through the night, which was only a few hours long, and even then never fully dark under the full moon. By dawn of the second day, when I was wearing the goggles the captain had given me (small eye cups carved from ivory with a thin slit through which to look, which he admonished me to wear at all times during daylight, lest I succumb to snow blindness and haplessly plunge into the inky sea), I spotted a dark figure on the horizon, merely a comma on the snow at a distance, but I could perceive movement. After checking with my spyglass I saw I had, indeed, caught up to the fiend.

"The cargo clerk had assured me that Adam had not purchased a rifle, even when warned about the white bears. He had told them he feared nothing on this earth, and instead took a whaler's harpoon and a knife as his only weapons. Still, even with my brace of pistols, I did not want to rush headlong at the monster. I resolved to stay at a distance until darkness or weather could cover my approach, and if luck was with me, I might see surprise in the monster's yellow eyes as he awoke to the touch of the barrel of my pistol to his ear just as I blasted his malignant brain out of his enormous skull.

As I pursued Adam farther onto the ice, the surface became uneven, the ice jutting up in great mounds, slowing my progress as I tried to steer the dogs around the obstacles to more even ground, but also to cover my approach. I lost sight of the fiend at times, and feared that I might top the crest of a hill to find him waiting for me, harpoon in hand, and after a full day and night of keeping my distance, it nearly happened. At the base of a mound of ice perhaps twenty feet in height, I heard a racket like nothing I had encountered on the ice. I left my sledge and dogs and climbed to the top of the rise with my spyglass to see Adam not a hundred yards away, holding what appeared to be the bloodied carcass of a small bear, the creature no bigger than one of the dogs. His sled dogs were yowling and struggling to run away with Adam's sledge, and indeed, while I watched, they dashed away, the sledge in tow, while Adam shouted at them. He dropped his harpoon and the carcass of the bear cub and ran after his sledge, but made only three strides before the mother bear burst out of her snow den. She must have been in there while her baby was out playing on the ice. I suppose Adam thought the cub would be easy game, without consideration for the enormous fury of maternal vengeance that might follow.

"The bear reared up on its hind legs and loomed even over Adam's great height. He tried to snatch his harpoon from the snow but missed it as the great bear swiped at him, knocking him several yards. Before the giant could draw his knife the bear was on him.

I folded my spyglass and slid down the ice mound to my own sled and dog team, the latter whimpering and stirring as if wanting to bolt. And bolt they did when I climbed aboard and cracked the whip, calling "mush" at them as the outfitter had taught me.

"I had come to the ice to kill my creation, but it seemed the white bear was fulfilling that task, so I took off after the runaway sledge, driving the dogs at such a pace that the steam of their breath rose over us as if from a locomotive. I had scarcely glanced back toward Adam and the bear before they were but a distant tumble of darkness and blood against the snow, when all my concentration was jolted back to staying on the sledge and driving the team. The dogs seemed to sense the urgency of their task, while, with the bear hundreds of yards distant, Adam's team began to slow.

"As we closed on the team, slowed I think by the great weight of the crate, they entered a field of rough, jagged ice, and the dogs followed their instinct to tread the valleys between the jutting ice crags. But the sledge was not designed for such rough going. I trusted my team to follow, the way one trusts a good horse to navigate a forest, but there was no familiarity to this ever-changing landscape and the dogs became confused as I drove them after Adam's team, which was hopelessly lost and bounding away out of fear. Soon the lead team broke out of the crags and pulled up a gradual slope of hardened snow, giving me hope that we might catch them before they reached the top. Indeed, when they were so close that I was steering my team alongside Adam's sledge, I thought if I timed it right, I might grab one of the ropes binding the crate to the sledge and perhaps tie the two teams together, but as Adam's team crested the hill, the dogs began to yelp in terror as the hill ended in a sudden drop-off. My team followed and I was thrown from my sledge. The drop was not sheer but very steep, and covered with knifelike spikes of ice. Adam's sledge rolled, and dragged the dogs behind it as it slid down the precipice. Their harness caught on a great ice spike and snapped, sending the sledge and one dog down one side, while the rest of the team scuffled and bolted away into a valley. My own team stayed barely ahead of our sledge until it reached the bottom, then took off after the loosed team. I lay in shards of ice and snow, trying to assess if any of my limbs were broken. I could hear the dogs' calls in the distance, fading.

"I confess, I had pain in my ribs such as I had never felt before, but I could move. With great effort and concentration I found my feet. I was surrounded by more ice mounds, so there was no distance to survey. Fortunately, my snow goggles had stayed attached around my neck, so I donned them and climbed to the highest point I could see. I realize now, in the telling, I should have opened the crate and checked on the girl, but to my mind she was still dead, and I had designed the crate so she would be isolated from the instruments, so I thought only of my own escape at first. At the top of a hill I could see the trail the dog teams had made that disappeared into the distance. I don't know how far we had traveled from Adam and the bear, but I could see no trace of them, even with my spyglass. In the other direction I could see no sign of the two dog teams or my sledge, but I did see a path out of the rough ice onto a smoother plane, so I returned to the sledge to measure my resources.

"I had an overturned sledge, a badly injured sled dog, and a crate with a dead girl inside. I unbuckled the straps on the crate to find that Adam had stored his supplies inside, on top of the girl in her isolated compartment. There were food, dried fish and meat, some tins of broth, tools, a small oil stove and fuel, a lantern, and a pot for cooking and melting snow for drinking water, as well as my scientific instruments. For shelter there were a tent and several more large white bear furs. I still had those things I carried inside my furs, my spyglass, my compass, and two loaded pistols, although

I'd lost the powder horn and shot pouch along the way. Strangely enough, Adam had also packed compact volumes of Shakespeare and Chaucer, both in English.

"I used the stove to melt some water, which I shared with the dog, along with some salt fish. My strength somewhat renewed, I spent the next hour trying to right the sledge, which I was able to do by completely unloading the crate, then pushing the sledge upright, replacing the crate, and reloading it, checking to see the girl still had her slow heartbeat. It was there, and wrapped in the bear fur, she even seemed to have produced some body heat. My heart broke again, for my Elizabeth, my father, my friends, all the people the monster had murdered, and I vowed again that I would not cause the death of another innocent.

"I managed to make a windbreak with the lid of the crate and kept the little stove lit long enough to warm some broth, which I poured into the girl's mouth. She was more responsive than I remembered, but then, it had been little Waggis who had done the patient caring for her. He must have told Adam how to care for her, perhaps even how he might reanimate her, otherwise why would the fiend have dragged heavy lightning rods and cable to the top of the world?

"By the time I had the girl fed and secured in the crate, in her own furs, with one of the polar bear furs on top of her compartment, the wind had whipped into a fury, and the sun had fallen below the horizon for the long cold twilight that would be night. There was no hope of raising a tent in the storm, so rather than pack my scientific instruments, I lifted the injured dog into the crate, crawled in myself, with the other bear rug, and managed to fasten the lid over us. In that way, the three of us weathered the storm, and when, at last, the wind subsided, I crawled out to find we had been buried in snow overnight, but we were alive—well, two out of three of us—and with some digging I was able to free the sledge and pull it out of the valley and onto smoother ice.

"Geoff was completely useless, of course, as his injuries were so severe that he whined even at being lifted into the crate."

And here, dear sister, I had to interrupt the narrative, because even amid such a fantastic tale, my curiosity overwhelmed me, as it would have any educated man. Again, I am thankful you were not made to suffer the burden of education, and therefore intellectual curiosity. So I inquired, "Geoff?"

He explained: "When we were in the crate, hiding from the storm, I lit the lamp, mostly for warmth, which it provided in that confined space. And I read aloud from the book of Chaucer's tales, which I endeavored to translate into German as I read, although I don't know why, as the dog probably spoke Norwegian or Eskimo, if at all, but still, every time I stopped the dog would whimper. I realize now it was because I was going to put out the lamp before we were asphyxiated by the fumes, but delirious from exhaustion and injury, I took it that he had a passion for Chaucer, thus I named him Geoffrey, with a G, after his new favorite poet."

So, Margaret, there you have it: a dog called Geoff. Chaucer, by the way, is a tedious and incomprehensible medieval teller of pornographic tales who is inflicted upon educated men so they will appreciate the clarity and economy of Shakespeare, whom you know from that play Father took us to see with the fairies and the fellow with the head of a donkey. So yes. Geoff. But Frankenstein's tale continued until the most horrifying of interruptions ensued.

Victor resumed: "I know that bringing the injured dog along seems foolhardy, but I didn't know if I would ever be rescued, or make it to land, so I thought if supplies ran low, the dog might serve as fresh meat."

"You were going to eat Geoff?" I exclaimed, with enough ardor to startle poor Victor. In my defense, Victor was looking increasingly weak and unwell, and should he expire, I would again be left friendless except for Geoff and the recently thawed girl, neither of whom was a scintillating conversationalist.

"He wasn't called Geoff when the plan was set," Victor said. "I reconsidered once I realized I was much more likely to freeze or be slaughtered by one of the white bears than to starve to death."

"Of course," I allowed. "Pray continue."

"There is not much beyond that. I found my way out of the rough ice onto a smoother ice plane, then followed the compass south in hope of encountering either a landmass or a passing ship, sleeping and sheltering inside the crate as I went. I never again saw sign of the dog teams or my original sledge. Then I happened upon your lot, or you upon me, I don't know."

"We saved you from a white bear," I said.

"I am grateful. But I fear my rescue has only delayed my fate," he said. He winced then, and his breath started to come in gasps. "Something is wrong." He clawed at the blanket, then at his shirt, pulling it up to reveal his entire abdomen had turned the deep purple color of a bruise.

"Some soup?" I offered. But he shook his head violently to deny my kindness.

He was fighting for breath as he spoke. "No, I think I have been bleeding internally, perhaps since I came on board. But you may save me yet, my friend. You will find among my instruments a leather box, and in it, glass vials and a machine for spinning them, as well as hollow needles and tubes for drawing blood into them. I will instruct you how to draw blood from the girl, spin it in the machine until it separates, then through the same needles introduce it into my veins. This may be my only hope."

"That won't work," I said, my pitch rising to panic as I feared I was losing my only friend. "She is barely alive herself."

"It will work," Victor insisted, his breath becoming shorter with each second. "I gave her blood to Geoff, when he was at death's door, perhaps even across the threshold."

The intrepid sled dog perked up at the mention of his name, and, indeed, he appeared perfectly healthy.

"You need only fill five of the vials, seal them, then spin them in the machine—less than a quarter hour, I think. The machine is very finely geared and easy to turn. A clockmaker in Geneva made it to my specification, so if it hasn't been damaged it should do the job. Then draw off the clear bit to administer to me. You should be able to complete the whole process in less than a half an hour, so please . . ."

And so I did as he asked, step by step, locating the instruments and bleeding the girl from a vein in her arm until all five vials, each the size of my small finger, were full, then bandaging her arm.

"You must finish the process even if I lose consciousness, Robert," Victor gasped. "My life depends upon it. If you must, plunge one of the longer needles into my heart and drive the blood in with one of the small bellows."

And I followed his instructions, continuing to spin the little machine even after Victor passed out, and I could not leave the machine to check his pulse or breathing. I shouted for one of the young midshipmen to come in and spin the machine while I tended to Victor. Soon his breathing eased, and even after the lad finished his task spinning the vials, and the blood was separated into its two colors, I decided to wait before introducing it into Victor's veins. I am no man of science, but he seemed to be sleeping now, and I was exhausted. I had the midshipman watch Victor, called the bosun in to translate instructions into his native language, to have the boy wake me should Victor's breathing or pulse change, and with that, exhausted, I took to my cot and slept.

And here, dear sister, is where I can scarcely steady my hand, although a day has passed since the events that next transpired, for the next thing I knew, I was startled from sleep by the sound of my cabin door shattering to splinters, and when I sat up there stood a creature so horrible in aspect and scale that I shudder at the memory.

His height was such that he could not stand fully in my cabin, but slouched with his shoulders against the ceiling. His bulk, enhanced by the full set of furs, made me cease to wonder how he had survived mauling by one of the great white bears. Indeed, one side of the furs by his shoulder was shredded and encrusted with frozen blood, and his scalp, covered mostly with black, stringy hair, had been raked by the bear's teeth, the wound already scarring white, and part of one ear was missing altogether. His countenance was pulled into a horrendous grimace, as if the skin was too tight, and appeared to be constructed completely of scar tissue, an unnatural shade of bluish-white, and his eyes were unevenly set, wide and rheumy, but fierce.

He stood for a moment after bursting in, as if taking inventory, and in that moment the young midshipman tending Frankenstein bolted at him, I know not if to attack or to try to escape through the splintered doorway behind the fiend, but Adam snatched him up by his hair and threw him across the cabin as if he were no more than a bundle of yarn. The boy's body shattered the doors of a cabinet and he fell motionless. The fiend then looked to the girl, still lying on my map table.

"My love," he said, his voice deep but with a rasp, like someone tearing canvas at the mouth of a cave. Then I realized it was not a grimace but a horrible smile he wore. He stroked the girl's hair with his massive hand and I could see his fingernails, thick, ragged, and caked with filth.

I looked for how I might escape, for there was no defending against such a monster, and my only weapon was a short-bladed rigging knife that would do no more damage than to draw his attention to my destruction. There were windows behind heavy draperies at the rear of the cabin, but no chance I would get through the draperies and the ice on the exterior before I would be crushed like my midshipman.

Adam looked from the girl to Victor. "Ah, Father, the prodigal son has returned. Won't you rise to greet him?"

"He's dead," I said.

Adam crossed the cabin and loomed over Victor's supine form. He poked Victor sharply in the solar plexus and my friend let out a cry of pain. "No, but he shall be," said Adam. "He who birthed me into this pain and misery, this torment, this suffering, shall return to the land from whence he yanked me"—the fiend reared up until his shoulders were flat against the ceiling—"in pieces!"

Had I known what would transpire next I would have averted my eyes, for then the monster plunged his hands, stiffly held, into my friend's throat, the great, horny nails tearing the flesh like blades, and ripped Victor's head from his body. The cot beneath Victor's body shattered with the impact and from beneath it poor Geoff yelped, then bolted through the broken cabin door and away onto the deck of the ship.

Adam held Victor's head, dripping with gore, and, in his hellish voice, recited, "Alas, poor Yorick. I knew him, Horatio, a fellow of infinite jest." Then he tossed back his head and laughed, the sound more horrible than any I had ever heard, and I thought at that moment I might lose control of my bladder, but no, it was then I could see light on the snow outside my cabin door and made my dash. And I escaped.

Once out of my cabin I sounded the alarm by screaming in the accepted manner of a lunatic, until four of the men found my side.

I ordered them to fetch guns, but before I could convey my order in pantomime, as the bosun was not one of the four and there was no one to translate, Adam emerged from my cabin with the girl thrown over his shoulder.

My men bolted from my side and I was turning to follow them when Adam shouted, "Stop!" and as if I had reached the end of a leash, I did. I peeked over my shoulder, cringing at what might come my way.

"Call your men if you will," Adam said, "and I will gladly kill you all and live out my days on this ship, feasting on your frozen bones. Or you can direct me to the crate in which my lady was bound, and I will lower it to the ice, where my sledge awaits with most of what was two dog teams, and I will be gone, never to be seen by living man again. What say you, Captain, would you live, or shall I make a puppet of your head to join Frankenstein?"

"The crate is on the deck near the bow," I told him. "Take it and go. We will neither hinder nor molest you."

"Wise choice, Captain," he said. Then he made for the bow.

I headed belowdecks and to the stern, where I found the bosun and most of the crew. I instructed them to first find rifles, and load them, but to put up a defensive position belowdecks at the bow, and barricade themselves in. I told them to bring their harpoons, their killing lances, their pistols and knives, not to come up on deck or try to impede the monster. He had defeated one of the white bears and appeared to be thriving. I was not sure our few rifles and spears could stop him before he slayed us all.

I instructed two men to go fetch the midshipman in my cabin and, if he had survived his ordeal, bring him to their barricade and tend his wounds. Then I borrowed furs from one of the men and, with a loaded rifle, went above to monitor Adam's progress. I told the men that if they heard a rifle shot they should assume I had perished and prepare for an attack, but I had no intention of provoking the monster's wrath.

I stood on the poop deck and watched as he dragged the crate to one of the gunnels by the winches we used for the lifeboats. He pulled the lightning rods and cable, and the other remaining instruments, from the crate, then carefully lowered the girl into the compartment Frankenstein had built for her. I thought he might leave the heavy instruments on the deck, but he packed them carefully as he went. For a moment I feared he might look for the blood-drawing instruments that were still in my cabin, but he took no notice that they were missing. He hoisted the crate over the rail and lowered it to the ice, then looked back to me as I watched from above on the poop deck.

As he made to climb over the rail, the dog, Geoff, attacked, going for the monster's throat, but Adam pressed his forearm in Geoff's jaws and, wrapping his other arm behind the dog's head, swiftly snapped its neck with a sickening crackle. He grabbed Geoff's corpse by the scruff of the neck and tossed it against the cabin bulkhead, then looked up at me and grinned.

"What are you looking at, butt puddle?" he called. Then he laughed again and leapt over the side of the ship. I heard his heavy boots crunch in the snow below and soon the ropes that had been attached to the crate went slack and were blowing in the wind.

He was gone. I stood there, my breath shallow in my chest, waiting for his horrific countenance to rise again above the rail, but it did not come. In time I heard him crack the whip upon his dogs and he came into sight as he took off over the ice behind a very long team of dogs.

I hurried down the ladder to the deck and knelt over the fresh corpse of the intrepid sled dog that had been saved by my one and only friend, Victor Frankenstein.

"What does it mean, Geoff?" I asked the dog, but he was still. I lifted his corpse in my arms and carried him into my cabin.

I do not know if these letters will ever reach you, dear sister, and if they do, I hope that I have not terrified you beyond sleep, but for now I am shaken, exhausted with grief, and deeply frightened that I will never escape this icy prison with my life. Whether I see you again or if these letters are the last you see of me,

I remain, your dedicated brother,

Robert Allen Walton

8

THE WOLF AT THE DOOR

*T*here's a wolf at the door," Wally said.

She'd been on her way out to buy pastries and tobacco when she opened the door to find a wolf there.

"That is just a saying we artists have," Klimt called from the drawing studio, where he had been obsessively sketching the nude Judith as she reclined on the posing platform. This had gone on for most of the week. "It means we are always running from the need to make a living, to feed ourselves."

"This one is black, gray, and white," Wally said.

"What?" said Klimt.

"I want to see," said Ella, who had been sitting in the drawing studio, watching and sulking. She jumped up and padded to the door. Ella (short for Camilla) was fifteen, a willowy blonde, barefoot, and wearing one of the kimonos the master kept for his models. She was five months pregnant and, because she was thin, was just starting to show, which was one of the reasons she had been sulking. "It's very large," Ella called.

"It's just a saying," said Klimt, now sounding annoyed. "You know, an adage, an aphorism."

"Although this is my first wolf," Ella said. "So it might be normal size."

"I think it is large," said Wally.

"It's just a fucking saying," Klimt shouted. "*We do what we must to keep the wolf from the door.*'"

"Is it called Geoff?" Judith said. "Geoff with a G?"

"Are you Geoff?" Wally asked.

"With a G," Judith specified.

"With a G?" Wally repeated. Then, back to Judith, "I'm not sure. When I asked about Geoff he wagged his tail, but he didn't change when I asked if it was with a G."

"Probably Jeff with a J," Ella volunteered. "Short for Jürgen?"

"I don't think he's German," said Judith, still posing like a water nymph, which is what Wally had told her to pretend she was, even though she didn't know what that was, exactly.

"It's just a saying!" Klimt slammed his sketch pad and crayon down on the portable drawing board, stood, and stormed through the parlor to the front door, where he saw his two models standing on either side of the door facing a rather large, fluffy gray dog with crystal-blue eyes. He pulled up quickly and brushed down the front of his caftan to compose himself. "That's not a wolf," he said.

"Well, it's not a fucking *saying*," said Wally.

"Come, Geoff!" Judith called from the other room. The wolf dog shot by them.

Unable to completely assess what had just happened, Klimt said, "What are you two doing?"

"I came out to see the wolf," said Ella.

"I was going to the store to get us pastries and cigarettes," Wally said.

"Ella shouldn't be smoking," Klimt said.

Ella pouted. "I was just here looking at the wolf."

"Put on some clothes," Wally said. "You can come along." To Klimt she said, "Can we buy a Victrola?"

"No," Klimt said.

"Then how can we hear the genius that is Beethoven that you're always talking about?"

"I would like to go to the symphony," said Ella. "I will need a dress."

"I will get you a Victrola," Klimt said.

"Oh, you are wonderful, maestro," Wally said. She leaned up and kissed his cheek. "Thank you!" To Ella she said, "Put on some clothes and come with me to the store."

"I can't," said Ella, looking sullen again. "I need the money. I have to stay and work."

"You can come. The maestro will pay you. We'll be back in half an hour anyway."

"Really?" Ella asked Klimt.

He nodded. "Don't be long," he said, which sounded very much like a surrender.

Ella padded off to the storeroom to retrieve her clothes. Klimt shuffled back to the drawing studio, where Judith was ruffling the ears of the wolf dog.

"It's Geoff," she said with a big smile, the first smile he'd seen on her face other than when food was involved.

"How do you know?" Klimt asked.

She looked up from the dog, bewildered. "I—I don't know."

"Where do you know this dog from? You must have known him very well to know how his name is spelled."

Judith shook her head, stopped, then stared into the air as if she were trying to conjure a memory, but instead tears welled up in her eyes. "I don't know. I don't know. I can't remember. I don't know."

Wally entered the drawing studio and sat on the platform next to Judith, put her arm around her, and said softly, "It will be all right.

You've been working hard and you need a break." She looked at Klimt. "She needs a break."

"I don't know who I am," Judith said.

"But you know this fuzzy fellow," Wally said, reaching out and petting Geoff on the head with her free hand. She looked at Klimt. "You said you were going to get help for her from your fancy doctor friend."

"Dr. Freud is not a friend. He is an acquaintance."

Wally glared at him with what she hoped looked like disgust.

"I will," Klimt said.

Ella skipped out of the storeroom fully dressed in a blue frock with a white lace collar and a straw sun hat. "I'm ready."

A black and white cat had followed Ella out of the storeroom into the studio and caught sight of Geoff, just as he caught sight of the cat. And they were off, the cat scrambling away, claws skittering over hardwood, the large furry dog taking the corner behind without skidding at all, ice dog that he was.

"My kitties!" Klimt called, and took off after the dog.

"Geoff!" Judith called, and took off after Klimt.

"We should go," Wally said to Ella. She held her hand out and led Ella out of the house and into the garden as if they were heading into a magical summer adventure.

As they walked, still hand in hand, down the boulevard, Ella said, "She is his favorite now. He hasn't asked me to pose since she arrived."

"He is fascinated with her because he pulled her from the canal. Also, she has nowhere to go, so she's always around."

"I think he is in love with her. Do you think he's in love with her?"

"I think he is in love with every girl he sees naked. Although some before he sees them naked, I think."

"Do you think he still loves me?"

Wally sighed. She wondered if she had been such a naïve child when she was Ella's age, two years ago. She couldn't remember, but she didn't think so. "Of course, silly. He has you come to work and doesn't even make you pose. He's making sure that you have money to live on. That's why I knew you could come to the store with me and he would still pay you."

"Oh. Yes, I suppose. But she's so tall. It's rude."

"You are also tall." Wally bumped her head against Ella's shoulder playfully, to illustrate how much taller the younger girl was.

"Do you think he's making love to her?"

"No," Wally said definitively. "That I know for sure. I have been at the studio almost all the time since she arrived, looking out for her. He hasn't touched her." She was going to say that Klimt said he wouldn't touch Judith because she was simpleminded, but the more she talked to Ella the less that seemed like a credible explanation for his abstinence. "I think he might be afraid of her."

"But she's his favorite," said Ella.

Wally sighed again. "Ella, we are like his kitties to him."

"Are you saying he's boinking his cats? I will not believe it. He can be crude and sometimes smells bad, but he is a genius, and he is kind, and he is not a cat boinker."

"I am not saying that. I am saying that he loves them and he likes having them around and he takes care of them but he doesn't know their names."

"Well, he knows my name," Ella said. "He says it quite a lot when he makes love to me, especially toward the end."

"Yes, that is because you are his favorite kitty."

"I knew it," Ella said.

Wally pulled her into a magazine shop. "Come, I'll teach you how to roll a cigarette and blow smoke rings." Wally looked back as they entered the store and saw a man in a bowler hat duck behind a vegetable cart to avoid her gaze. Wally sneered at him and pulled the door shut behind her.

Yan Beek was hiding among the peaches and he felt ridiculous. They were young girls, of no threat at all. Of course, that's what the cop, Thiessen, had thought, and he'd ended up in the canal minus his head. Van Beek wasn't even sure if one of them was the girl he had been sent to find. The taller, blond girl might be her. He'd only seen her from a distance, and then it had been dark and she'd been nude. The shorter redhead was the girl who had met him at the door of Klimt's studio and pretended to be the one he was looking for. Smart mouth, full of herself. He wanted to hurt her, badly, slap the taunting grin off her face, but that would not help to get him paid.

Still, if she got in the way, it would become part of the job. You had to enjoy your work or why do it? He'd still be a cop in Rotterdam if he hadn't tried to make knocking little tramps around part of the job. Ah, water under the bridge, so to speak, he was self-employed now, a *security specialist*, it said on his business card. Of course, that's *all* it said on his business card. He hadn't even had his name printed on the card. If someone needed it, he could write it in. He was a fixer: find an errant wife, make a mistress go away, ruin a rival, frame a competitor, threaten a debtor, hide a body. A fixer—working now for another fixer who would not tell him who he was actually working for. But he had a clip full of banknotes as retainer and all he had to do to collect the rest of his fee was get one blond chippy halfway across Europe, alive and against her will. And without the dog.

The fucking dog. He had wondered about the dog when he first saw Thiessen had it on a leash on the train. If you're looking for someone, and you don't know where they are, follow someone who does. He was following Thiessen, and Thiessen had been following the dog. He'd never heard of a dog that could track a subject by train, but evidently the fluffy wolf dog could, because after a few days in Vienna, into the wee hours of a Tuesday morning, he followed the cop and the dog to an apartment building in the Second District, near the canal. Once he determined there was only one entrance to the building, he had just found a good spot across the street to watch, hidden by a news kiosk, and was taking a sip from his brown bottle of Mother Hagen's Cough Killer (Moeder Hagen's Hoestmoordenaar) when the girl came through the window three stories up and landed on her feet, naked, in the street in front of him amid a shower of glass shards. Before he could pocket the cough killer the girl was off down the street, her hair flying out behind her. He'd taken just two steps after her when Thiessen came out of the building, dragging the reluctant dog behind him. The Dutch cop looked his way. Van Beek tried to duck behind the kiosk, but Thiessen had seen him and paused his chase long enough to point to him to let him know he'd been spotted. *Balls,* how were you supposed to maintain a surreptitious tail with bitches jumping out of third-story windows?

He waited for Thiessen and the dog to round the corner before heading down an alley in the same direction, hoping he might intercept them on the next block. He heard a commotion as he approached the corner, a truncated man-scream followed by a splash, but when he rounded the corner, he saw nothing but an empty bridge. He hurried out to the bridge, where he found nothing but a dog leash with a broken collar attached. He looked down to the dark water and watched the ripples of a disturbance and a red stain swirling in the slow, moonlit current.

When Wally and Ella returned from the store they found the master sitting on the floor in the corner of the parlor, cradling two of the cats in his arms. The doors to the drawing studio were closed. Judith was nowhere in sight.

"Why are you in here?" Wally asked.

"*Bonjour*," Ella said. She blew smoke in the air in a way she thought quite sophisticated.

"I'm teaching her French," Wally said.

"Why are you smoking?" Klimt asked.

"I'm also teaching her to smoke," Wally said. "Where is Judith?"

"She's in the drawing studio with her giant dog."

"The wolf," said Ella. To Wally she whispered, "How do you say 'wolf' in French?"

"It's a Malamute," Klimt said. "Not a wolf."

"How do you know?" Wally asked. "It looks like a wolf."

"Judith said it's a Malamute."

"How does she know?" Wally said. "She doesn't know anything."

"Because she's simpleminded," Ella added with a little cough.

The door to the drawing studio opened and Judith stuck her head out. "I am not simpleminded."

Wally crossed the room, kissed Judith on the forehead, and pushed her face back out of the doorway. "Yes you are, but it's not your fault. Now please fuck off until we have spoken to the master."

"Did you bring pastries?" Judith called through the door.

"We bought croissants," said Ella. "They're French."

"No they're not," said Klimt. "Croissants were invented right here in Vienna and taken to France by Marie Antoinette."

"I would like one of those, please," Judith said through the door.

"In a minute," Wally said. "Go play with your Malamute."

"*You're* a Malamute!" Judith shot back.

"Would you all pretend like I am drawing you and not move your mouths?" Klimt asked.

"That Dutchman, the one who was pretending to be a policeman, he's back," Wally said.

"He followed us to the boulevard," Ella said. "He must have been waiting outside when we left."

Klimt let his kitties go. They ambled away casually, as if they didn't know him. "You're sure?"

"I am a pretty girl who grew up in the city," Ella said. "I think I know when a creepy old man is following me."

"He was younger than me," Klimt said.

"It was him," Wally said. "I think he might have followed the dog here. If Judith knows the dog, he might be her dog, and the Dutchman might know him too."

"Geoff," Ella added, to clarify which enormous and mysterious dog they were talking about.

"You need to help her," Wally said. "Given how you found her, and that dead policeman they found near her in the canal. If the Dutchman wasn't up to no good he would just ask after her by name. At least ask your policeman friend to find out who he is."

"Or we can just go kill him," Judith said through the door.

"Shut up, whore!" Ella said. She looked from Klimt to Wally and back to Klimt, who both seemed astonished at her ferocity. "What? We're trying to have a discussion."

Klimt stood now, took the paper bag from Wally and dug out a croissant, then plopped down on the divan and began crunching away while he watched a constellation of crumbs form between his feet. "I don't know how to go about it, Wally. I can't very well go to the police. I am fencing colleagues with the commandant of this district, but how do I express my suspicions without revealing how I found Judith and why I've waited this long to report it?"

"You can tell him the truth," Wally said. "That she asked you not to talk to the police and you took pity on her."

"Because she's a simpleminded whore," Ella offered. "And you are kind."

"What do I tell Dr. Freud? He is a world-renowned scientist. He will think me common for plucking a girl out of the canal and bringing her home. And on the same night a man is found decapitated in that same canal."

As Klimt spoke, Wally took the bakery bag from him and sidled over to the drawing studio door—opened it slightly and chucked a croissant through the gap.

"Thank you," said Judith from the other side.

"Tell him the same thing," Wally said. "You were helping her. You don't have to talk about the creepy Dutchman. Wait, decapitated? You didn't tell me he was decapitated. Is that why you gave her the name Judith?" She'd seen what was perhaps his most famous painting, of Judith, the Hebrew heroine from the Bible.

"It just came to mind," Klimt said, "for some reason."

"They stole his cap?" Ella asked.

"She didn't know how to use a toilet when she came here, and you believe she cut a man's head off?"

"*Tore* a man's head off," Klimt said, correcting her.

"So not his cap?" Ella asked.

From the other side of the drawing room door Judith said, "May I have another? Geoff got that one."

Geoff made a singsongy howling-talking noise.

Wally chucked another croissant into the drawing studio and shut the door.

"Thank you," Judith called.

"Fine," Klimt said. "I'll send a message to Dr. Freud, asking if he will help. I fear my writing isn't sophisticated enough, though."

"If we had a telephone here you could just call him," said Wally.

"Oh, we should get a telephone," said Ella.

"And a gramophone," added Wally.

"I don't want a telephone in the studio. If I had a telephone people would call me and I'd have to talk to them. I just want to paint and draw. I don't want to talk to people."

"You talk to us," said Ella. "Sometimes all day."

"You're not people," Klimt said. "You're models."

Wally snatched the half-eaten croissant from Klimt's hand and returned it to the bag. Ella dropped her cigarette on the floor and ground the stub into the boards, never taking her eyes off of the painter. She continued to grind her foot for what seemed like a long time.

The drawing studio door opened a crack and Judith stuck her face in the gap. "So, when do we murder the creepy Dutchman?"

Grateful for the break in the tension, Klimt said, "I'll send a message to Freud. Maybe he'll be able to help you remember where you came from."

"And the police?" Wally said.

"I'll go to my fencing club this afternoon to look for my friend the commandant."

"And buy a gramophone." Wally raised an eyebrow and leaned in toward the painter to project her petite ginger scrutiny.

Klimt nodded in defeat. Wally held out the bakery bag to him so he could retrieve his croissant.

9

THE INIMITABLE
DR. FREUD

As they rode in the taxi to Dr. Freud's office, Klimt lectured Judith on what he expected to happen. They'd hired a taxi even though Klimt's studio was only a short walk from Freud's office because Klimt never allowed himself to be seen in public with his models. Judith had never ridden in a taxi before that she could remember. It was a horse-drawn cab, because Klimt wanted the privacy and a longer ride, but automobile cabs putt-putted by them on both sides as they rode. She wore Ella's blue dress with the white collar. Wally had lent her a pair of shoes, pinned up her hair, and painted her face. "There," Wally had said, with a kiss on the forehead. "Pretty as a painting. You would never even know that you were drowned. Dr. Freud will put you to sleep and have his way with you." Wally had a jaded and often accurate view of the self-control of older gentlemen.

In the taxi, wearing a brown tweed suit and bowler hat, Klimt said, "No, Dr. Freud will not touch you, except, perhaps, to take your pulse. He will put you in a trance and help you remember who you are—where you came from."

"That would be wonderful," Judith said.

"You must answer his questions, but you mustn't tell him that I found you in the canal."

"I won't. Where shall I tell him you found me?"

"I don't know. Say I found you wandering in the garden outside my studio. I'll tell him I think you had been hit by a car or a carriage."

"I was hit by a car or a carriage? Not a streetcar?"

"There is no streetcar near my studio."

"You can hear the bells from the Ringstrasse streetcars. What if I was hit by a streetcar on the Ringstrasse?"

"We don't know what you were hit by. You were in an accident and I found you."

"What about a horse? I think I'd like to be run down by a horse."

"Fine, a horse."

"You could feed a lot of people with the meat from a horse. We should find the horse that ran me down and feed it to the people."

"Fine, after you see Dr. Freud. And don't tell him about the Dutchman."

"Which one, the one in the canal or the one we are going to murder?"

"We are not going to murder anyone. But don't mention either one of them."

"No Dutchmen," she said, making a mental note. She imagined a written checklist in her mind. She'd recently remembered that she knew how to read, and while Klimt worked on portraits of fine ladies in the painting studio, Judith had regaled the other models with readings from a smutty novel that Wally had found called *Josephine Mutzenbacher: The Story of a Viennese Whore*, by Felix Salten, the fellow who wrote *Bambi*.

"What is *Bambi* about?" Judith had asked.

"A baby deer," Wally had answered. "That talks."

"Not if Bambi has as many dicks in its mouth as Josephine Mutzenbacher," said Ella, who was cranky and jealous that Judith could read so well and she could not.

In the cab, Klimt said, "And don't speak English, or Dutch, or any other language. Just German."

"Just German."

Their coach stopped at 19 Berggasse, a five-story building in the historicism style, which means it would be suitable as a model for a dome cake or a Greek temple, all white with a central arched entrance and some neoclassical flourishes here and there, although the only really ornate elements were a set of curly cornices holding up a faux balcony that looked like albino rams being wound onto an enormous fork.

"Is this his house?" asked Judith as Klimt, ever the gentleman in public, helped her out of the cab.

"He lives here but I think only one floor is his house. Much of it is his clinic."

"So he lives among the lunatics?"

"No, why would you say that?"

"Because Wally said she heard that he lives among the lunatics."

"You know Wally is young and sometimes misinformed?"

"So he doesn't live among the lunatics?"

"I don't know, but I can't very well ask him, can I? He's the most famous scientist in Vienna."

Klimt led her across the sidewalk and through the double doors into a lobby, where a young man in a white lab coat stood at a tall desk.

"Gustav Klimt, to see Dr. Freud," Klimt said. "And Judith." Judith grinned at the mention of her name.

"Oh yes," the young man said, the picture of enthusiasm. "Herr Klimt, I am honored to meet you. Please, the doctor is expecting you. Just up the stairs to the second floor and through the door on the right. I am happy to show you."

"We will find it," said Klimt with a smile. "And what is your name, young man?"

"I am Bauman. Hans Bauman. Dr. Bauman."

"A doctor, working at the desk?" said Klimt. "It is we who are honored."

The young doctor blushed and looked at the floor. "Well, I am a resident here, studying under Dr. Freud."

"Thank you, Dr. Bauman," Klimt said. He bowed and made way for Judith to lead him up the stairs. "After you, mademoiselle. Let's go find out who you are."

"And while we're there, do you mind if I ask him who *you* are?" Judith had never seen Klimt functioning outside of the studio, where he could often be petulant and morose but completely preoccupied with his work. She found his charm suspicious.

"You threw a trout in that young man's cream cake," Klimt said out of the corner of his mouth.

"Oh, right. I remember."

"See, you're doing better already."

The second-floor landing led to a hallway with a bench upholstered in wool carpet woven with a colorful tribal pattern. Freud came through double glass doors to greet them in the hallway. He was older than Klimt by a few years, bald, with a white fringe and short white beard. He was shorter than either of them by a head, wearing a black suit with vest and watch chain, and thick-rimmed black spectacles. He switched his cigar to his left hand and shook Klimt's hand warmly. Klimt, in turn, introduced Judith.

"One of my models," Klimt said. "Unfortunately I can't tell you much more about her than that, which is why we're here."

"A pleasure," Freud said to Judith, but from his expression, it did not look like a pleasure for him.

"Charmed," she said, as Wally had instructed her. "*You say 'how do you do' if you don't think you'll see them again, 'charmed' if you might*

need something from them, and 'enchanté' if you want to make them
think you might let them shag you. It's the fucking French that gives it
away."

"If you wouldn't mind waiting here," Freud said, "I'd like to have
a word with Herr Klimt in my study before we begin."

Judith sat on the bench while Freud led Klimt through glass
French doors into a room with a swooning couch covered in more
exotic carpets, and tables on which sat dozens of carved figures from
different cultures and religions. Some looked very old, worn, carved
from stone; others were finely detailed standing figures. Judith
thought she recognized one, a man with a dog's head and a golden
walking staff, but she couldn't remember where she might have seen
it. Perhaps the doctor would use these figures to remind her who she
was, and she very much wanted to know who she was, and where the
voices in her head that guided her came from. Two were very distinct:
One encouraged her to feed people, help the unfortunate; it was this
voice she had heard when she stole the fishmonger's trout and distrib-
uted them to the café-goers. And the other voice spurred her toward
mischief and trickery, and it was this voice that always told her to talk
of murder, or sex, or to say the most inappropriate thing for a situation, even when she didn't know what was appropriate, and it was this
voice that had told her to ask if the wolf at the door was Geoff, and
helped her recognize and speak different languages—all languages,
she thought. There was a third part of her that was not so much a
voice but a presence of feelings, raw and unarticulated—fear, hunger,
anger, joy, gratitude—and this amorphous mass within her felt like
it must be who she was, *what* she was, and it desperately wanted context, shape, history. *Well, Dr. Freud has his work cut out for him.*

After perhaps ten minutes the two men returned to the hallway
and Klimt offered his hand to help her stand. "Judith, the doctor is
going to spend some time talking to you, but I will be in the next
room if you need me."

She nodded. Freud led her to the room with the couch and asked her to sit on its edge while he examined her. He asked her if she had been having headaches, and she said no; then he had her look at the window and covered each of her eyes with his hand in turn to watch her pupils react. He asked her to squeeze two of his fingers with each of her hands, and asked her to squeeze as hard as she could, which she didn't do, and instead gave him a firm squeeze that wouldn't break his fingers.

"Will you put me in a trance now?" she asked. *And have your way with me?* the mischievous voice in her head wanted her to ask, but she resisted.

"No, I don't think so. I haven't used hypnosis in my practice for nearly fifteen years. We will try something I call free association. I will say a word and I want you to say the first thing that comes into your head. In this way, we may be able to access the memories in your subconscious and perhaps find out who you are. You may sit, or lie back on the couch. I will sit behind you so you aren't distracted by my taking notes."

"What is subconscious?"

"That is the part of your mind that functions below the surface. Your mind is like an iceberg. Do you know what an iceberg is?"

"Yes."

"There is the part of your mind that is above the water, which is your day-to-day thoughts, reactions, new things you learn—that is your conscious mind; then there is the part that is below the water but can be seen, which is called your preconscious mind. This is where you have information that you can access anytime but is not in your conscious until needed, like when I asked you if you knew what an iceberg was. You hadn't been thinking of it, but you knew immediately when you needed to. This is where most of what we would normally think of as your biography is stored—where you would know what your name is, who your family members are, where you were born. For some reason, perhaps from physical injury or emotional trauma, this part of your mind isn't storing the normal information a person would have, yet you know how to speak, to read, the conventions of day-to-day life. Finally, below what is visible in the water is your subconscious, and here are stored memories that we do not have access to. Here, I believe, everything is remembered, but is sometimes suppressed, by fear or trauma, and we can only access it indirectly—through dreams, through hypnosis or association—and the suppressed memories in our subconscious can often cause problems in our day-to-day life, make us anxious, or melancholy, or make us act irrationally. By bringing these suppressed memories to the surface, we can address the source of the patient's problem. In your case, we need to find out who you are, where you came from, and, if your loss of memory is not from physical damage, what is causing it. Do you understand?" He sat back and puffed his cigar.

"Yes. Most of my mind is underwater and we don't know what is down there."

"Then let us begin. Why don't you lie back, relax, close your eyes if you wish, and I will ask you a few questions. Herr Klimt has told me some of your recent history, so I may ask something to confirm that. First, do you remember anything about your life before Herr Klimt found you?"

"I remember that I knew Geoff."

"The dog?"

"Yes."

"And yet you didn't remember him until he appeared at Herr Klimt's studio."

"Yes."

"Can you think of the context when you knew the dog? Where you knew him? Perhaps feeding him?"

"No, I just knew it was him."

"Herr Klimt has told me your dog is a Malamute—a northern dog, often used for pulling loads on the ice and snow. Do you have memories of any of those landscapes?"

"No—well—no."

"And you have no memory of growing up? Of your parents or siblings?"

"No." She had tried to remember, but there just didn't seem to be anything there. It was like staring into a steaming cauldron, and she could never see below the vapors to the surface.

"What about dreams? Since Herr Klimt found you, have you had any dreams you remember?"

"Yes, I dream of drowning."

"Anything else? Any details?"

"No, just drowning. That's all I remember. The water is clear and cold, but I don't remember anything else."

"Perhaps there are other events around the drowning—"

"Have you ever drowned, Dr. Freud?"

"No."

"It occupies your full attention."

"But you have not drowned either, Judith. Or you would be dead."

That's right, she wasn't supposed to tell him about drowning. She laughed. "Oh, I am being silly. I'm not dead, Doctor. Never been dead. Wouldn't know what to wear. Ha ha."

"I see," said Freud as he wrote in his notebook.

"Are you writing that I'm dead, there? Because that is a mistake. It was only a dream."

"I am not writing that you are dead, Judith. But let's try the free association. If you would lie back on the couch." He stood and moved to a chair behind the raised end of the couch.

"Are you sitting there so I can't see when you're writing in your notebook?"

"Partially, but mainly so my presence doesn't distract you."

"But you're still going to be talking, right?"

"Yes. I'll say a word, then you say the thing that first comes into your mind. There are no wrong answers. Ready?"

"Burning hair."

"What?"

"You said 'ready' and I said 'burning hair.'"

"Oh, right."

"Because your cigar smells like burning hair."

"It does not."

"That's what came into my mind. You said there are no wrong answers."

"Let's move on," Freud said. He read from the list. "'Head.'"

"Kill!"

"'Cold.'"

"Strangle."

"'Voyage.'"

"Bludgeon."

"'Home.'"

"Sandwich."

"'Pride.'"

"Sandwich."

"'Finger.'"

"Slaughter."

"'Money.'"

"Sandwich."

"'Cow.'"

"Assassinate. Also sandwich."

It went on like that for nearly ten minutes, Freud reading *pride, luck, family, flower, box, pamphlet, new, salt, ship, ink, angry, bread, pity, yellow, mountain, house, carrot, frog, old, cup, pencil, book, unjust, child*, and on and on. And Judith answering *murder, sandwich, stab, sandwich, crush, sandwich, hang, sandwich, behead, sandwich, sandwich, sandwich, strudel, slay, sandwich, murder, kill, kill, kill*, and so on, until she said, "I have to pee"—at which point Freud put down his pen, stood, and went to a humidor on the desk, where he retrieved a fresh cigar and clipped the end.

"Why did you say 'kill' so many times?"

"Because that's what I was thinking."

"I don't think it was."

"Because I thought you would find it the most disturbing."

"And you wanted to disturb me?"

"Yes."

"Why?"

"Because you look down on me."

"I'm trying to help you."

"Oh, I don't doubt that, but you think I'm a loon."

"I don't think that's true. You are my patient. I am concerned with your well-being."

"I should have said 'penis' instead of 'kill,' shouldn't I?" The mischievous voice in her head had told her to say "penis."

"That would be more in line with what I expected."

"Because you think I'm some penis fiend with no memory?"

"No, because I think it would explain your resentment. Toward me. Toward men. I think you have resentment toward men, probably due to something that happened in your past that you are suppressing."

"I don't resent men. Herr Klimt is lovely."

"He tells me that he is the one who decided to call you Judith."

"That's true."

"Do you know who Judith was?"

"No."

"She was a Jewish heroine from the Bible. When her city
was under siege by the Assyrians, she went to the tent of the
Assyrian general, Holofernes, seduced him, then, when he
fell asleep, sawed his head off, thus saving her people."

"She was a Jewish heroine from the Bible. When her city was
under siege by the Assyrians, she went to the tent of the Assyrian
general, Holofernes, seduced him, then, when he fell asleep, sawed
his head off, thus saving her people. It is a very famous story."

"Klimt probably meant some other Judith."

"One of his most famous paintings is of Judith holding the sev-
ered head of Holofernes."

"I don't want to talk about cutting people's heads off anymore. So penises, those are my problem?"

"Penis envy."

"Penis envy? If I wanted your penis I'd cut it off and take it with me."

"That *is* disturbing."

"Ha! Penises in my pockets. A chain of bloody penises on a string around my neck—"

"Perhaps we *will* try hypnosis," the doctor said.

"Do you have anything to eat in here?"

"Thus your repeated response of 'sandwich'?"

"And 'strudel.'"

"I will have something brought for you from my kitchen."

"Aren't you going to hypnotize me?"

"I think we should save that for our next session. We'll just talk while you eat."

"So I won't get to find out who I am today?"

"You are a very attractive, confident, well-spoken young woman. For now, that will have to be enough. If you remember any of your dreams, however, be sure to write them down. You do know how to read and write?"

"Of course."

"Do you remember learning to read and write?"

"You're just being tricky now, aren't you?"

"Yes," said the doctor. "Do you still need to pee?"

*I*n the taxi back to the studio, Judith said, "You named me after a woman who saws people's heads off?"

Klimt cringed. "Yes. But no. I named you after her because of the sensuality of the character. I still have some of the studies I did for that painting back at the studio. I'll show you. I think you'll be pleased."

"Dr. Freud thinks I have penis envy."

"I don't know what that is."

"I think it means that I resent men because they have penises and I don't have one and my mother got all the penis from my father when I was little."

"Then you remembered your mother and father? That's fantastic."

"No, he just explained penis envy to me. Evidently all girls go through it when they are little and the rest of their lives they are all about getting penis revenge, which is power."

"That doesn't sound right," Klimt said.

"It's total *bollocks*, if you ask me, but what do I know?"

"What is *bollocks*?" Klimt asked. She'd used the English word, which he didn't recognize.

"It means 'hogwash, rubbish.'"

"I see," said Klimt. "Judith, I want to do a painting of you. It will take more time and more patience on your part to pose than for a drawing."

"I will check my schedule. I may have some heads to take."

Klimt laughed. "I have some ideas, I will work on sketches today, but I will also need to get you a gown."

"I would like that. I think Ella and Wally are getting tired of me borrowing their clothes. Especially Ella."

"For the painting you will need a special gown, by a fashion designer, a friend of mine. But yes, we need to get you some clothes. I'm sorry I haven't seen to that. You and Wally can go shopping this afternoon, if you'd like."

"What if that Dutchman follows us?"

Klimt had kept an eye out for the Dutchman's brown bowler hat among the men on the street, but there were a lot of brown bowler hats and the artist wasn't sure if he'd even recognize the fellow if he saw him again. He tended to miss details in the appearances of men.

"Perhaps I should hire someone to watch out for you. Maybe Schiele will go with you."

"Egon is a wisp of a man," she said. "He'll be no protection at all."

"You should get to know Schiele. He is a talented artist. He will want to work with you."

"Let us take Geoff to protect us."

"You'll need to get a leash for him. He's quite large to have on the street without a leash."

"He's not a wolf," Judith said, defending Geoff's honor. "He's a Malamute."

"I know, I looked him up at the library, *The Illustrated Encyclopedia of Dogs*. But according to the book, he is large even for a Malamute."

"*You're* a Malamute!" She grinned at him.

"No," said Klimt, grinning back. "I am a wolf."

She rolled her eyes. "No, you are an old tomcat."

Klimt cleared his throat to signal he was about to be serious. "Judith, I am going away. For the rest of the summer, with my lady friend Emilie. To a lake called Attersee in the north. It is something I do every year."

"I won't have to swim, will I? The idea of swimming makes me anxious."

"You'll be staying with Wally and Schiele while I'm gone. They've agreed to look after you, take you to your sessions with Dr. Freud."

"So you're abandoning me?"

"No. Never. We have work to do."

10

EMILIE UND
DER LEBENSMENSCH

*E*milie Flöge occupied a position of myth in the minds of Klimt's young models. She was the master's companion but not his wife or mistress. She was frightfully old (thirty-seven) and frightfully tall, and she owned and ran a renowned fashion house, Schwestern Flöge, with her two sisters, where she employed scores of seamstresses to make her Reform-style dresses, long flowing gowns with a fitted bodice, which required no corset or constraint on the modern woman. Emilie was the queen of haute couture in Vienna—rich and fashionable ladies wore her designs to the theater and the opera, and in one case, that of Adele Bloch-Bauer, to pose for one of the master's major paintings. None of the models had ever seen her, but they believed her to be very beautiful and very fierce, and they told stories of how on certain weekend nights, in the wee hours of the morning, if you passed by Schwestern Flöge, you could hear the ecstatic cries of the master as she whipped him, and left him drooling and unsatisfied and begging for more. Although they weren't sure of Emilie's precise role in the master's life, they were all certain it was deliciously wicked. (The truth was, Klimt had never set foot in Schwestern Flöge, nor had Emilie set foot in Klimt's studio. It was a strict, unspoken agreement between them, which was why Wally was escorting Judith in the first place.)

"Whatever you do," Wally said, "you mustn't mention that you have shagged the master."

They were walking through the Burggarten park in the First District—flowers and trees surrounding a marble statue of Mozart about to be dogpiled by a gang of cherubs. Wally wore a skirt and a fitted toreador jacket she'd bought from a boy who had freshly stolen it and had been pretending to be a bullfighter with a cat in the alley behind Schiele's new apartment (the cat was not in on the game). She thought that with its narrow waist and seams outlined in gold, it looked quite smart on her, but in fact, she looked as if *she* had been bullfighting a cat, as the black wool coat was covered with gray and white dog hair, as were her black stockings. (Geoff.)

"But I haven't shagged him," said Judith. She was wearing Ella's blue dress again, and Ella's shoes, and a straw hat, probably Ella's, taken from the hall tree by the studio door. They had left Ella nude in the drawing studio with Klimt while they went shopping for clothes, but first a stop at Schwestern Flöge, where Judith was to be measured for a gown for the master's painting.

"Just the same," Wally said. "Madame Flöge is very possessive of him. She's never been to the studio or even seen any of us. Supposedly she doesn't know about the master's habits—and the master likes it that way. They spend every summer together at Attersee, yet they are seldom seen together in the city—although he spends many evenings at her family's home, playing parlor games and probably listening to the gramophone and talking about opera and art." Wally had no idea what Klimt did at the Flöge household, but she figured that's what she would do if she were rich.

"Have you seen the Dutchman?" Judith asked. "Following us?"

Wally scanned the garden, figuring the brown bowler hat might stand out against the roses and lilies, but spotted no one. "I don't see him. We'll have to find someone else to murder today." Wally rather enjoyed that Judith seemed to have only two solutions to any problem: snacks and murder.

"How about you, Geoff?" Judith was leading Geoff on a shiny new leather leash. He ruffed at the sound of his name but otherwise seemed preoccupied with a black squirrel that was playing at the far edge of the garden.

"He's useless," said Wally. "Except for getting dog hair all over my stockings."

"He's not useless, he's protecting us. You don't see the Dutchman, do you? Oh, look, a café. Let's go have pastry and a coffee."

"There's a café below Madame Flöge's studio. She and her sisters own it. We might get free pastry."

"We are going to be great friends with Madame Flöge," said Judith.

"She's going to love us," said Wally.

Who let these prostitutes in the studio?" Emilie Flöge called to an entire floor of seamstresses, perhaps forty of them, each diligently working on some piece of clothing, cutting on tables, hand-sewing, pinning up patterns, or seated at sewing machines.

"We aren't prostitutes," Wally said.

Emilie breezed over to them from a standing desk where she had been working. She was taller than Judith, even, well over six feet, with bright blue eyes and a pursed smile that made her look as if she were always about to burst into laughter. Her hair was parted in the middle and combed out into great puffy pom-poms of curls over her ears. She wore a flowing gown of bold black and white stripes, and her entire aspect made her look like a clown queen escaped from a comic opera. Judith liked her immediately.

"Street urchins, then," Emilie said. "Although I should think there's better money in whoring than urchining. Very well, let me find some coins and I'll send you on your way. But take that adorable beast outside, now. I'll be picking dog hair off the couture for a month."

"We're not urchins, we're models," Wally said.

"And he's not a beast," Judith added. "He's a Malamute. This is Geoff, with a G."

Emilie sighed, "The models report to the floor below, and we don't require any today. Did my sister Helene hire you?"

"We're models for Gustav Klimt," Wally said. "He said you would be expecting us."

Emilie laughed heartily and Judith found herself laughing with her, although she didn't know at what. "Oh, my, yes, Wally and Judith," Emilie said, reaching out and taking each of them by the hand, shaking them in rhythm to her laughter. "I'm so sorry. Yes, Gus sent a note yesterday to expect you but, of course, I set it aside and forgot about it. That man should get a telephone—enter the twentieth century."

"Yes!" said Wally. "And a gramophone in the studio."

"You don't have a gramophone in the studio?"

Wally and Judith both shook their heads, sadly, although they didn't feel at all sad.

"We shall see about that," Emilie said. "Now, let's get to work. Geoff, I'm afraid, will still have to wait for you outside. You can tie him up outside the café. I'll meet you on the second floor in five minutes." She turned to the room. "Greta," Emilie called to an efficient woman in her forties who was working at a drawing board on the perimeter of the room. "Your tape and notebook, please. In the studio in five. I'll fetch my sketchbook. We are to make a gown for this extraordinary creature."

"Does she mean Geoff?" Judith whispered to Wally, gearing up to defend Geoff's honor.

"She means you, nitwit."

"I'm not a creature."

"It's a compliment," Wally whispered back. "A promotion. We called you 'the drowned girl' for a week."

"Oh," said Judith.

"We need to take Geoff for a quick poo," Wally said.

"*You're* an extraordinary creature," Judith blurted out as they passed Emilie on their way through the double glass doors.

"Yes I am," Emilie said with a wink.

*T*en minutes later, Judith, wearing Ella's underwear, stood on a wooden box getting measured by Emilie's assistant, Greta, while Emilie drew on her sketch pad and Wally sat on a red velvet mushroom of a stool by the window and sipped cappuccino from the café downstairs, occasionally taking a dainty bite from a shortbread biscuit that wore a vest of chocolate and finely crushed black walnuts. It was the most elegant thing she'd ever experienced and she hoped the measuring process would last all afternoon.

"You must be very special," Emilie said. "Gus has never sent one of his studio models to me to have a gown made."

"But he has sent his portrait clients, right?" asked Wally.

"Yes, I've made several gowns for his portrait clients, and I made the gown for the portrait he did of me, although he designed the fabric. It was great fun working together on that."

"I'm not shagging him," Judith volunteered.

Emilie laughed, "Oh, darling, relax, if I drew that line with Gus we would have been out of each other's lives some years ago. I genuinely love him, but I cannot keep him. He is the keeper. He keeps his mother and his sisters. He keeps my sister Helene, his brother Ernst's widow, and her daughter—at least he did until our business took off. He keeps, and pays for, at least four mothers of his bastard children that I know of, four boys, all called Gustav. Must be confusing for

"You're an extraordinary creature," Judith blurted out as they
passed Emilie on their way through the double glass doors.

him. Likely the mothers named the boys after him to assure his support. Can't have little Gustav going around with holes in his shoes.
They are—were—all models. I don't say that to diminish you, nor
them, my love. They are all just hungry girls looking for a meal, but

it is understood that if you pose for the master you must also be willing to share his bed. He's handsome, a genius, and terribly kind, but he's also a dog. He adores me, and I him, but he is a dog."

"He is keeping Judith," Wally said.

"Until I remember who I am," said Judith.

Emilie let her sketchbook fall to her side. "What do you mean, dear? You don't know who you are? Aren't you Judith?"

"The master—er, Gus—gave her that name," Wally said.

"After he dragged me out of the canal," Judith added.

"Drowned and naked," Wally added with a smile.

Greta, who had been measuring Judith's leg from knee to heel, dropped her tape and leaned back on her haunches.

"How did you end up drowned and naked in the canal?" Emilie grabbed two café chairs from over by the windows where Wally was sitting and pulled them to the middle of the floor, where she sat in one in front of Judith, tapped the seat of the other one while looking to Greta to join her, then crossed her arms over her chest and waited. Greta declined the seat and kept measuring.

"It's a mystery," Wally said.

"A mystery," Judith repeated.

"We weren't supposed to tell you any of this," Wally said.

"Well, I'm glad you did," Emilie said. "This is fascinating. So Gus named you Judith? Do you know who that is?"

"Dr. Freud says she was a Jewish heroine who sawed off a general's head."

"And there was a headless Dutchman found in the canal near where Gus found Judith," Wally said. She was really enjoying referring to the maestro as "Gus."

"There was?" asked Judith. "Why didn't you tell me?"

"Gus thought it might upset you," Wally said.

"Well, I didn't saw his head off," Judith protested. "Probably."

"No, his head was torn off," Wally said.

"See?" Judith said, holding her hands out to hold Wally's statement in the air so everyone could see. Nobody saw.

"And you've been to see Dr. Freud?" Greta asked with awe in her voice. She immediately looked apologetic toward Emilie, who waved the interruption away.

"Yes, Freud?" said Emilie. "Gus is a hypochondriac—I have stacks of postcards he's sent me with his imagined maladies listed—but he is afraid of doctors. If he braved Dr. Freud for you, you must be very special indeed. Did Freud help? What did he say?"

"He said I have penis envy," Judith said. "Then he had the maid make me a sandwich."

"Did that help you remember anything?"

"Yes. That I love sandwiches."

"No, about your past, love."

"I think I loved sandwiches in the past, too. But Freud thinks a man mistreated me, sexually, and I am suppressing all my memories."

"Ah, yes, that is the crux of all of Freud's theories. And because you appear to be a girl from the lower classes, he feels you have it coming, because all girls from the lower classes just want to fornicate, even as infants."

"But we don't even know what class she's from," said Wally. "She could be a princess."

"Or a walrus," said Judith.

Wally dismissed Judith's silliness with a wave of her cookie. "No, not a walrus, you lunatic. But *I'm* a girl from the lower classes, and I for one can tell you that I do not want to fuck babies. I don't even like babies."

"No, no," Emilie said. "He thinks that you were either abused as an infant or formed your personality out of jealousy of your mother and father's relationship."

"And my father's penis?" Judith asked.

"How do you know all this?" Wally asked.

"I've attended Dr. Freud's lectures, and I've read some of his books. Like many brilliant men, he is blind to his own limitations. Although he does try. He once confessed that as a child he was afraid of trains, and to this day he feels anxiety when boarding one."

"Well, I'm going to bring that up next time," Judith said.

"I am finished here, madame," said Greta, gathering her measuring tape into loose loops in her hand. She hurried toward the stairs.

Emilie called after her, "Can you bring down one of the silk robes from upstairs—one that will fit Judith?" Emilie turned to Judith and held up her sketch pad, showing a drawing of a figure more or less walking out of a flowing gown. "I'm going to have to see how something drapes on you when you're nude—Gus will want to paint you with the gown open."

"Then why make her a gown at all?" Wally asked. She thought Emilie Flöge was wonderful, like a fairy godmother come to life, which made her immediately suspicious when the older woman started talking of Judith being naked. Wally stood and put her now empty cup and saucer on the window ledge, ready to protect her charge.

"Yes, why at all?" said Judith, suspiciously, as she whipped her chemise off over her head. Her knickers were already in a puddle at her feet.

She's very professional for a loony, Wally thought, and she was going to say so, to compliment her friend, when there came a wailing, howling, growling noise from the street below. She looked out the window to see Geoff chasing the Dutchman in the bowler hat into the square across the street. "It's the Dutchman," Wally said.

"And Geoff!" Judith cried. She leapt off the wooden stand and ran out the doors and down the stairs.

Wally looked to Emilie, who was waving her arms as if directing a symphony, when in fact she was trying to make all that had just happened go back a few seconds so it could be explained.

"She'll be fine," Wally said. "She'll run down the street frightening and scandalizing people, she'll steal some meat or fishes or cats or something, then she'll pass them out to people to eat." Wally tried to sound bored with it all, as she thought that was how a sophisticated woman would react. "Of course we didn't have Geoff, previously, and this was all set off by the fake Dutchman that Judith wants to murder."

Emilie swallowed hard and tried to sound bored, the way she thought a street-smart girl would react. "Of course, but what is that horrible noise? It sounds like wolves upchucking." Emilie had joined Wally by the window and was peering out over her shoulder.

"Oh, that's Geoff."

"He doesn't bark?"

"No, that wailing howling singing sound."

"Ending in nausea?"

"Yes. Judith says it's called an *aroo*. *That*, she remembers."

"I should play you Schoenberg," Emilie said. "His music has a similar effect."

Wally turned to face the older woman. "I have to go now, catch my friend. I'm being paid to watch her."

"Of course. I understand. I am your friend, too." Emilie took Wally's hand and began to lead her to the door.

"Really?"

"Of course, really. I only want to help you."

"You didn't sound like you meant that. You said that like you were mocking."

"Wally. Wallace. Wallerie," Emilie said, stroking Wally's cheek gently as she spoke. "I have lived my whole life among artists, everything I say sounds mocking and sarcastic. Would you like a job? You can learn to be a seamstress, or work in the café, or if you're good with figures we could teach you bookkeeping. You can wear clothes, all day if you'd like."

"That sounds lovely," said Wally, "but my current job is looking after Judith, and I need to get to it."

"Well, come back when you can."

"*Adieu*, madame," said Wally, in what she hoped was perfect fucking French, because it sounded sophisticated.

Emilie replied with some gibberish Wally didn't understand, probably French, but she was already out the door.

*T*he commandant's saber raked Klimt's shoulder to score the point and the painter disengaged and saluted en garde for the next point.

"Take off your mask, Klimt," taunted Kruger. "Let me give you a fencing scar to show the girls."

The portly Commandant Kruger had a glorious fencing scar high on one cheekbone, two inches long, as precise as if it had been put there by a theatrical makeup artist. Kruger insisted he had acquired it in a duel, but Klimt suspected it was inflicted by one of his friends during a drunken brawl when they were cadets at the academy, since no one else remembered the duel. The scar was puckered at the edges, pulled tight by Kruger's chubby cheeks.

"It is my quest to attain beauty, not to mar it, Commandant. Besides, if I appear any more manly I shall be overrun by the attention of the ladies and I will never get any painting done."

"En garde, you rascal. Let's finish this so you can buy me the drink that I have earned by thrashing you once again."

They engaged, blade met blade, Klimt lunged, Kruger riposted and slashed Klimt under the armpit. Match point.

Klimt liked Kruger—an ex–cavalry officer who moved into a police position, he was a bit older and quite a bit fatter than Klimt, and although brusque, he was quick to laugh and he loved art and the symphony. As far as sport went, Kruger was a fierce swordsman who insisted on the saber because it more closely matched the cavalry saber he had carried in the military and most of the policemen under his command still carried on the street.

"I like to make my point with an edge," he would say, "not just a point."

Klimt could count on Kruger to thrash him in early matches, then lose in the later ones as he grew fatigued. Today Klimt was collecting on a favor and he needed Kruger to be flush with victory, so he feigned distraction and gave away many points to the commandant's edge.

"I am off my game today, Kruger," Klimt said, pulling off his helmet and cradling it under his arm. "Café Tivoli awaits with the spoils of your victory."

Kruger laughed, removed his helmet, and clapped Klimt on the back. "My friend, even on the days you are on your game you are off your game, but if I could paint like you the only blade I would touch is a palette knife. Lead on."

They washed and dressed and stowed their gear with the steward, and a half hour later they were sitting at an outdoor table on the white macadam of the Tivoli courtyard, each with a stein of beer in front of him. Around them the luminaries of Vienna's art, science, and government smoked cigars, read newspapers, and exchanged gossip. Klimt had chosen Tivoli because he knew Kruger would relish being seen there in his company, and he very much wanted the policeman to feel magnanimous.

"So," Klimt ventured. "What do you hear of the headless fellow who they found in the canal?"

"We never found his head, so presumably he's at his wit's end."

Klimt grinned as Kruger laughed at his own joke.

"You know he was a policeman, right?"

"Yes, I had heard."

"I spoke with his captain by telephone. It was horrible." The big policeman shuddered.

"I know," said Klimt. "His head torn from his body."

"Not that. Talking on the telephone. A nightmare. My wife wants us to get one but I told her she can have one when I'm dead. Stuff me and use me to hold the contraption. HA! You would have to put my finger in your ear and talk into my mouth. Yes, that is how I should like to be remembered. When I'm dead you must call my wife and, before she says anything, tell her to shut up. You can imitate my voice, I've heard you do it."

"The headless fellow?" Klimt said, trying to bring the subject back around.

"Ah, yes, I spoke to his captain. Thiessen was the detective's name. He'd been a solid detective in his prime, for a Dutchman. A few years to go until his pension. He was biding his time. Suddenly he pricked up his ears. Said he had a tip on a murder case. At least five unsolved murders that they had never connected before. He wanted permission to pursue a lead in Switzerland."

"Switzerland? Then why was he in Vienna?"

"They don't know. The captain wouldn't give Thiessen leeway to follow an anonymous lead and Thiessen wouldn't reveal his source, so he took a leave of absence to follow the lead."

"And the captain didn't know anything about the suspect? A description? It wasn't another Dutchman, was it?"

"Thiessen told his captain nothing, but they found telegrams in Thiessen's desk. One was from London. Asking Thiessen if he had received the dog. The other was from Zurich and read, 'If you find her, contact me, I will double any offer.'"

"Her?" Klimt repeated. "His killer was a woman?"

"His *suspect*," Kruger said, correcting him. "Thiessen wouldn't even reveal which victims of unsolved murders he suspected her of killing. But apparently, more than one foreigner was looking for her. I'd guess it's someone's wife who ran off with some rake, then ran away from the rake, and the husband and the rake were both trying to get her back. That would be my guess."

Klimt resisted the urge to roll his eyes at the commandant's imaginary love triangle. "And what about the dog?"

"We don't know anything about the dog."

"What do you think happened to Thiessen? What put him in the canal?"

"Why are *you* so interested, Klimt?"

"I walk over the bridge every day on my way to my studio and home again at night. In fact, I passed by there the very day he was found."

"Should I tell the Dutch captain that I've interviewed you as a suspect?" Kruger grinned so broadly that the tips of his big mustache went wider than his ears. He snorted and drained his beer, then set it down with a sigh of satisfaction. "I think what happened to him, my genius painter, is whoever sent the telegram from Switzerland won."

ASLEEP AND AWAKE

I see you have a new dress," Freud said.

"Yes, Wally took me shopping. I have two new dresses, and underclothes, and my own shoes."

"Wally is a friend?" *A lover?* Freud wondered.

"The *best* friend. She is going to look after me while Gus is with Emilie at the lake in Attersee. Her and Schiele."

She, Freud thought. *Wally is a woman.* "Egon Schiele, the young artist?"

"Yes. We are all going to a town called Krumau for the summer. Gus wants me to be safe from the Dutchman."

"Dutchman?"

"The pretend policeman who has been following us. Wally and I were going to murder him, but Geoff chased him away. I called him off just before he ate him."

"Wait, wait, wait. Geoff? The dog?"

"He was going to eat the Dutchman."

"You mean bite, I think."

"He seemed determined. But I called him off."

"Geoff is Herr Klimt's dog?"

"I think Geoff is his own dog. He didn't stop when I called him Geoff, so I called him another name, from before, and he stopped."

"What other name?"

"Butt Puddle."

Freud wrote in his notebook.

Judith laughed. "No, not Butt Puddle. Akhlut."

Freud smiled. "You were trying to unnerve me again? Very good. You said 'from before.' Do you know where you know this other name from?"

"I only remembered it on the spot. But he did what I told him to, so it must be right."

"Do you remember where you first heard that name?"

"No, but it was dark."

"Good. What is your first memory of Geoff?"

Judith closed her eyes, tilted her head as if she was thinking, then said, "When Wally said, 'There's a wolf at the door,' at the studio."

"I see," said Freud. He made a note. "As we discussed, I think we *should* try hypnosis. In hypnosis, I will ask you to relax on the couch, and I will talk you through a process that will put you into a dreamlike trance where you will be able to access your unconscious mind and the memories you are not able to access when waking. You should know that you will be safe, and that I cannot make you do anything you would not do when you are awake. We may be able to discover things about your past that your conscious mind is repressing for some reason. Shall we try it?"

"Are you going to touch my naughty bits?"

"No, I will not touch you in any way." Freud was used to this transference, the romantic, sometimes sexual, projection of the patient on the physician. It was best to gently, but insistently, deny any such thing was going on.

"Good, Wally told me to tell you that if you touch my snatch you should not charge Gus for the session."

"I am not charging Herr Klimt for your treatment. I am doing it as a favor."

"Well, I suppose I owe you then," she said, and in one swift motion she hiked up her dress and hooked her thumbs into the waist of her knickers.

"No!" He nearly dropped his cigar. "No, Judith, that will not be necessary. Now please, arrange yourself and lie back on the couch."

She smoothed down her dress and lay back on the couch. "Very kind of you to help me without charging. Thank you."

"It's nothing. Let us see if I can help you. Please now, close your eyes, and try to let your mind go blank. As best you can, think about nothing."

"But what about—"

"Not even sandwiches."

"Fine."

"You are completely relaxed. At peace. When I prompt you I want you to open your eyes and concentrate on my watch."

Freud took his watch from his vest pocket and, leaving the case closed, dangled it by the chain before her face. "Now, open your eyes." As he spoke, he moved the watch steadily closer to her face. "I will count backward from ten. At any time, you may close your eyes and enter into a trance." And he began to count. By the time he reached three, she had closed her eyes again.

"Concentrate on the sound of my voice. I want you to think back, before you met Klimt. Go to the earliest thing you can remember. Go to the place. Back. Back. Back. Can you see where you are?"

"No. It's dark. But it's cold on my face."

"What else? Can you hear anything?"

"Someone grunting. A man. He is on top of me."

"Do you know this man?"

"Yes. His name is Adam."

"Can you see his face?"

"No, it's dark. Hard to breathe."

"Do you know where you are?"

"I—we are in a box. It's dark. And cold. He smells foul. His breath smells like rotting meat."

"Are you in pain?"

"No. I can only feel the cold on my face. I can hear him grunting as he humps my body. I can hear wind, outside the box."

"You said humping your body. Not you—"

"I can't feel him. Only the cold on my face, the stink of his breath. I think I can hear whimpering."

"Could you be the one whimpering?"

"No. Dogs. There are dogs outside. Whimpering. Howling."

"The man on top of you, what is his relation to you?"

"He is my brother, and my murderer."

Eureka! Freud wrote in his notes.

Judith's Story

The first mistake I made was opening my eyes. I was perfectly safe, lying there in my frozen coffin, enduring the daily violations of my numb, lifeless body, having warm broth poured into me and warm piss wiped off me, sleeping the sleep of the dead most of the time. I might have been floating in a particularly long and unpleasant dream, but then I opened my eyes and it became a nightmare. I opened my eyes and it was daylight and he noticed before I could shut them again.

"I saw you," he said. "And I saw you see me. You couldn't keep the revulsion out of your face."

I had seen him—his enormous melon of a head, his patchwork face, his yellow eyes.

"What of it, butt puddle?" I said.

"That was the last thing you said to me."

"It's the first thing I've said to you. To anybody."

I had no memory of having spoken to anyone. I remembered being in the box, the cold, sometimes light when the lid was off, another man's voice, the warmth of broth, the pleasant feeling of fur brushing against my cheek, a dog licking my face, and otherwise long periods of darkness and cold. Only smells then: stale air, black iron, the dog, tinned meat—the names for these smells came to my mind without effort or searching; where I had learned them I didn't remember, but pictures had begun to form in my mind around them.

"I am Adam," the monster said. "I am your mate."

"Just because you've been rogering my limp body like a terrier shaking a rat does not make you my mate, mate." These things I spoke of—a terrier, a rat—until I said the words I wouldn't have been able to picture them.

He had been leaning over the box where I lay and when I said this last he must have stood up, moved away, and I saw the sky, as bright and blue as a newborn's eyes, and although the light hurt my eyes, it was glorious, and I was grateful to be alive. What a strange new feeling.

"What is your name?" Adam's voice from nearby, also the sounds of dogs.

"I don't know." And I didn't. In my half-waking state I had heard other voices refer to me as "the girl" and even "beauty," but I did not know my name.

"I shall call you *wife*, then. For together we shall stand against the cruelties of the world."

"And I shall continue to call you butt puddle, and you will have to do the standing as I seem to be confined to this box."

"How long?"

"What?"

"How long have you been conscious? How long have you been aware of what was going on around you?"

"A while. I didn't want to interrupt you while you were yammering on about your being wretched and suffering the disdain of humanity at the top of the world. I heard you get eaten by a bear. I had to hide my smile."

"Not eaten. I killed that bear."

"How much of you did he have to eat before he died of your poison?"

"With a harpoon. I've become quite proficient with it. Speaking of which, I need to hunt or I will have to slaughter another of the dogs to feed us."

"You've been feeding me dog? You fiend, I like dogs."

"I gathered that. The way the one I killed on the ship attacked me when I was taking you away?"

"What?" I sat up in my crate then. Most of the time I spent tucked in a chamber at the bottom of the crate, but Adam had taken me out to abuse me and had put me back in on top of one of the polar bear rugs. I sat up and even then had to pull myself up to see over the edge of the crate. Had I thought about it, I doubt I could have moved my arms, or even sat up—I wasn't sure that my muscles worked at all, but evidently they did. "You killed Geoff? You massive fucking twat!"

He stood a few feet away, hefting the harpoon as if he were weighing it for a throw. He dropped it to his side when he saw my face over the edge of the crate. "Who is Geoff? And when did you start moving?"

"Geoff was my friend. He licked my face and kept me warm in this infernal box. You need to take that spear and shove it up your own bloody arse, you monster!" I struggled to stand. I don't know what I thought I would do, all I had in mind at the time was tearing his face off, patch by patch.

He spun the harpoon in his gloved hand and swung it by the metal shaft so the wooden handle smacked me on the forehead and I was knocked back into the crate and was, once again, staring up at the sky.

"Ouch," I said.

He looked over the edge of the crate and talked through gritted teeth. "I brought you here to share my misery, and I will gladly escort you into a world of pain, until you are as wretched as I am. Yes, I killed the dog. I killed our creator and all his family. I killed your husband and I killed you. And I will kill you again without a second thought. Welcome to hell, wife."

My sight was blurring in one eye, which then went black. My gorge rose and I turned my head to the side and vomited, nothing but water and acid, which burned my throat. I lay on my side, gasping, coughing, digging my gloved fingers into the polar bear fur to stop the spinning.

"I had a husband?" I remembered nothing before the little man—Waggis, Frankenstein had called him, for I had listened to the doctor's tale as he told it to the man on the ship.

"There was a man with you when I came upon you in Edinburgh. He tried to protect you and I crushed his skull with a brick. I don't know that he was your husband, but he died for you."

I rubbed my forehead against the bear rug and saw I had wiped a red stain on the white fur. "Why? Why me?"

"Of all the women I stalked, you were the tallest."

"The tallest?" Suddenly my pain and nausea were replaced by rage. "You murdered me because I was fucking tall?" I not only stood, I leapt out of the crate. There had been some sort of iron rod on the floor of the crate, I don't know what it was, but I grabbed it as I leapt. As I sailed over the edge of the crate I drew back to plunge it into the creature. Oh, I did not think, nor plan, nor gauge my move, yet I was in the air. I rose high enough to give me time to grab the rod with both hands and lever my weight so I might impale the fiend down through the top of his head and into his chest. And I would have, but whatever demon strength Frankenstein's potion had bestowed on me was active in Adam as well, so before I could spit his melon like a roasting chicken, he thrust the wooden end of the harpoon into my ribs and levered me face-first onto the ice.

"Ouch," I said as I lay there, my face bleeding, my breath steaming against the ice.

"I didn't know you could move like that," he said.

"Neither did I." I didn't know I could move at all, other than to open my eyes. After months of not even being able to feel my extremities, suddenly my limbs felt like they had fire in them. Not pain, strength.

"I'm surprised." He seemed annoyingly amused.

"I'm going to kill you," I said.

"Vengeance will make a sweet bedmate, then," he said. "I'm going to kill a dog for our supper."

"Twice," I said into the ice. "I shall put your hideous head on your harpoon and feed the rest of you to the dogs."

The dogs had started to yowl and I heard one yelp as he struck. At some point I lost consciousness and when I awoke I was bound inside the crate once again.

I lived the next few weeks bound inside the crate. Adam would drag me out on the ice for meals, to empty my bladder and bowels, and to, of course, rape me, daily, doing his dread deed while I cursed him, my vocabulary growing with my memory day by day.

"You hideous bucket of rotting offal! You potato-brained satchel of runny shit! Do your bloody business, you leprous hedgehog!"

After a week he tied a gag on me when taking his liberties, and after two I endured his abuse with hissing anger but no shouting.

The only mercy was that his man bits were not in proportion to the rest of his enormous body, so while it was painful, I was not torn by his lust.

"How is it you know so many words?" he asked after he finished one day that first week. "When Frankenstein first awakened me I knew nothing. I was like an animal. I learned to speak by watching an old man through a crack in the wall of his cabin."

"Perhaps you have the brain of a simpleton," I replied. "You certainly speak like a drooling ninny."

"I am still learning English. It is my second language. I brought these books to study." He held up two volumes. "Can you read?"

I didn't know. I squinted at the spines of the books. Yes, I could read the gilded letters embossed on the leather. One was *The Complete Plays of Shakespeare*, the other *The Canterbury Tales* by Geoffrey Chaucer. "Yes."

"Perhaps we can read to each other to pass the time."

"At night," I said. At that point there was no night. While the sun stayed low in the sky, it was never quite dark out, and while it remained cold, it was not so cold that the ice would burn your uncovered flesh. In fact, the sea ice was breaking up, and while Adam drove the dogs to exhaustion before he would stop, lately he had been forced, by the great chasms and rivers opening between the ice floes, to change course several times a day.

"If the ice gives way under us I will drown," I told him. "With my hands and feet bound I won't even be able to drag myself out of the water."

"I will drag you out."

"And who will rescue you? Even if you survive, you will be alone again."

With that he cut my bonds, allowing me to walk beside the sledge as we traveled, which was just as well, since we had eaten half the dog team by that point, and those still alive were weak from lack of food. We saw seals and walruses resting along the ice floes' edges, but Adam could approach no closer than fifty yards before they would slide into the sea. The harpoon and the knife were his only weapons, and at times he would curse himself for not thinking to steal a gun from the *Prometheus*.

When storms rose, we sheltered inside the crate until the weather cleared, the way Frankenstein had, and I persuaded him to allow me to slide into the compartment the doctor had created for me, so I did not have to bear his enormous weight on me.

"We are going to need to find land soon," I told Adam after we had traveled in circles for days, turned again and again by the encroaching sea.

"The fishermen who ferried us to the ice from Norway said there were islands in the north. We must find one."

I had forgotten that I too had been along with Adam on his quest to leave the human race behind, and I tried to remember if I had overheard anything useful that might help us navigate to solid ground. When the sun would go lowest on the horizon we searched for high points, and finding one, we would push the dogs until we reached it. We managed to locate two enormous icebergs jutting from the sea, visible for miles, but hope as we might that they were mountains upon islands, we could not even reach them, as they had drifted away from the ice floe on which we traveled.

With warmer air there was often water on the top of the ice an inch deep, and while the boots Adam had purchased from the Norwegians held back the water and kept us warm, we had to search each day for a dry place for the dogs to lie when we rested. The wet ice would become as clear as glass at times and we could see seals and small white whales swimming beneath it, could hear their exhales when they found a nearby air hole in the ice. Occasionally, on a floating mass of ice we would see birds feasting on the remains of a kill left by one of the white bears, but Adam had no clue as to how to capture any of them. Sometimes we would find a great red stain and bits of fur where a bear had made a kill, but not even a bone remained to feed the dogs.

Occasionally we would see one of the bears at a distance and I'd encourage Adam to pursue it, hoping it would slay him and I could make my escape while the bear feasted, but he had learned from his first encounter with a bear, and when we saw one he would make us lie on the ice until it moved out of sight, sometimes going so far as to drape our white bearskins over the sledge and crate to hide them, gathering the surviving dogs behind it.

We were almost out of food when we spotted the Eskimo. We were down to the last two sled dogs. We had eaten the rest of the team raw, as the oil for the little stove had run out. When Adam slaughtered and skinned one of the dogs I would avert my eyes and put my fingers in my ears. I would try to think of nothing but the wonder of the blue sky as I chewed the flesh. Sometimes I would create a book page in my head and fill it with Shakespeare. But try as I might, I knew I was turning savage, and my thoughts were filled with plans of murder: *"And if you wrong us, shall we not revenge?"*

Without the stove to melt ice, we were reduced to slurping the fresh water atop the ice to slake our thirsts, or if a storm blew up and the surface refroze, we melted ice chips in our mouths or sometimes filled a tin from the canned broth with snow and carried it inside our furs until it melted. Both methods brought on shivering that sometimes took an hour to pass. The sledge was too heavy for so few dogs to pull, yet we carried on with it as the crate was our only shelter. Adam pulled the sledge for a while, and I suggested heartily that he go fuck himself when it was my turn, but I would finally take the yoke after the beatings. I would plot his murder as I labored. I would not kill my captor by overpowering him. He was too strong, and although I could not remember my life before my murder, I knew that I was stronger than a normal person too, yet half Adam's size.

Unfortunately, our strength came at a price. We were hungry all the time; somehow Frankenstein's elixir had endowed us with preternatural strength and healing, but it demanded fuel in return. If we had not seen the Eskimo, surely Adam would have eventually killed me and feasted on my corpse, only to eventually starve to death, alone on the ice.

When we first spotted him, the Eskimo was only a distant dark spot against the ice, too short, I thought, for a man, and moving too quickly, but as we approached we could see that he sat in some kind of low boat and was gliding along a crack that had opened between ice floes. I suggested we call to the man and ask for his help, but Adam said the sight of him would frighten the Native and proposed we follow at a distance without revealing ourselves—see if he might lead us to his camp and perhaps land. Thinking he could move more quickly without all the kit, I proposed Adam take after the Native on foot, while I would stay behind with the sledge, but Adam dragged me along by a leash fastened around my neck, holding it in one hand with his damnable harpoon in the other. We left the dogs and sledge in place, and, wrapping ourselves in the white bear rugs to hide our outlines against the ice, we followed the Eskimo until we nearly lost sight of the sledge.

"If we lose the sledge, we have no food, and no shelter," I said. "Let me go back."

"We have only a few days of food anyway," Adam replied. "We cannot lose the Eskimo."

We lost him.

We lost sight of the sledge as well.

The sun was as high in the sky as it would get that day, and we squinted into the distance looking for some sign of the Eskimo, but all we saw was more ice. What we heard, however, was the distant sound of crashing surf.

"This way!" Adam fell into a trot toward the sound and I kept up with him as best I could. When I fell he would drag me for several yards before stopping, to teach me, I suppose, to pay better attention to my footing. A mountain rose up out of the ice, and while I thought it another iceberg, soon, streaming above it, was a line of dark black smoke.

It couldn't have been longer than an hour before the island came fully into view. It was gray stone with a single peak visible, much of it still covered with ice, but here and there, above the rocky beach, splashes of green, some hearty grass or perhaps lichen growing among the rocks. Birds circled above the cliffs that rose steeply from the beach and I realized that the white on the rocks, which I had thought was more snow, was, in fact, droppings from nesting birds frosting the cliff face. At the base of one cliff, sheltered from the sea by an enormous boulder, we saw three round tents. The smoke we'd spotted emanated from behind the boulder. Since we saw no figures around the tents, we assumed they were tending the fire behind the boulder as well.

The ice we'd been traveling over had gotten increasingly rough as we approached the island, small icebergs driven up by the sea and refrozen into place. The ice ended, however, perhaps fifty yards from the shore, and there appeared to be no bridge to cross over. We crouched among the rough ice to hide ourselves from view of the Eskimo camp and watched.

"It's shallow," Adam said. "We can wade."

"You go ahead," I said. "You're taller and will be better at wading."

"If it's too deep I'll pull you back," Adam said before snatching me up by the scruff of my fur parka as if I were an errant kitten and throwing me into the sea.

I sputtered, I struggled, I lost my breath. After so long on the ice, often losing feeling in my hands and feet, I thought I had been as cold as I could be, but it was not so, and the icy water filling my furs felt like liquid needles against my skin. My feet found the bottom and I sprang up, gasping for air, determined to yank Adam into the water to drown with me, but the water was barely above my knees. I was a sodden, freezing, miserable creature, an angry creature, and in anger I yanked the leash to pull the monster in with me, to join me in *my* misery as he had forced me to join in his, at which point he let go of the leash and I tumbled backward into the freezing water again.

When I surfaced again and realized Adam had no tether on me I plodded up onto the rocky beach. It's not that it hadn't occurred to me to run away before, but where to? And most of the time I had been either unable to move or tethered to my captor, but now, shivering to the point where my vision began to blur, I *had* a place to go. From the beach I could see figures behind the huge rock, moving around a fire. I took a tentative step toward them, then another; then, as I crouched, gathering my strength to run, I was yanked back by my hair and dragged in the opposite direction.

Adam pulled me behind another tall monolith of rock. I struggled and started to scream but he clamped his hand over my mouth. "No," Adam said. "If we approach them they will flee. We will watch them from hiding, learn their ways, and, when they sleep, take their supplies."

There was an overhang above our heads from which cold water dripped down from icicles as long and broad as a man's arm, as wickedly pointed as daggers. I bit down hard on Adam's hand, felt his flesh tear beneath his mitten, and when he pulled away I leapt as high as I could, Adam's bloody mitten still in my teeth. I caught one of the icicles with both hands and snapped it from its mooring. As I came down I levered all my momentum into the spike and drove it into Adam's eye. He roared in pain, caught me by the front of my parka, and slammed me against the rock. I heard my bones breaking, saw bright white pain, and then darkness.

What are you seeing now?" Freud asked after she had been silent for a long minute.

"Darkness. Cold. I'm naked, constrained inside a cramped space."

"The crate again?"

"No, this is a different place. It is a shell, a giant clamshell. I hear a dog yowling, almost a talking sound. A voice, deep and male, says, 'Akhlut has been waiting for you.' The shell is pulled open and there is light, soft and blue. Strong hands take me by the arms and set me on my feet. I stand on soft moss that feels good on my feet. The figure that lifted me is very tall, completely black, covered in feathers. He puts his arm around my shoulders and his feathers grow to cover my body. I am smooth, shiny, warm. Safe. In front of me stands an enormous wolf. My head barely reaches his shoulders. He pants before me, drooling. As I watch, his head changes to that of a killer whale, then back to a wolf. He ruffs.

"'Akhlut,' says the tall, dark figure.

"'Geoff?' I say. The giant wolf ruffs."

"Who is the dark figure?" Freud asked. "Can you see his face?"

"Tulugaak."

"A name? Can you say it in German?"

Judith opened her eyes. "Raven," she said. "I am dead and we are Raven."

12

CRY HAVOC AND LET SLIP THE DOGS OF—COFFEE?

Van Beek had sworn off Mother Hagen's Cough Killer until he had the girl in hand. He'd been told that the opium in it could cause hallucinations, but he hadn't believed it until the dog. The giant fucking dog. He'd followed the girl and her friend to the Café Piccolo, and had done quite well, he thought, at staying out of sight, but after they'd been inside for a while, inside the fashion house above, not the café, the dog, who was tied up outside, spotted him—or smelled him. Something. For the love of God, he'd changed hats! He'd figured once he changed hats, from his traditional bowler to a deerstalker, he was virtually invisible, but the dog spotted him and in an instant broke its leash and was after him. He was fine. Safe. As soon as the dog started for him he bolted for the nearest alley. In retrospect, he could have ducked into any shop or café, but he hadn't been thinking clearly, which he blamed on Mother Hagen, and he headed into an alley across the square, where he thought he'd give the dog the slip. It wasn't barking or doing that ridiculous singsongy howl that it did, attracting attention, so he sidled into a narrow space between buildings and waited for it to go away.

A few seconds passed. He was patient. He didn't peek out from his hiding place because that's how they get you. He knew, because that's how he had gotten every criminal who had ever hidden from him: they always peek. He waited, and then it was there, a wolf so large its muzzle would barely fit in the space between the buildings, so, mercifully, its enormous head was stopped by the bricks. Van Beek sidled farther into the gap, scaring up a couple of rats, who squeaked and ran the other way. The wolf foamed and snarled, the sound so primal and terrifying that Van Beek thought he might lose control of his bladder. He tucked his chin into his chest and shut his eyes, as if he could deny the reality that was about to savage him. He was willing it to go away when he heard a woman's voice.

"*Aakka*, Akhlut! *Aakka!*"*

Van Beek squinted, took a tentative peek out from under the brim of his deerstalker cap. The giant wolf was a dog again. A large dog, but just a dog. It looked remarkably like the dog he'd seen with Thiessen the night the detective was killed. It ruffed at him and trotted away. Van Beek shuffled down the gap in the opposite direction until he reached Mariahilferstrasse, where he pulled the bottle of Cough Killer out of his inside pocket, thinking a substantial gulp might steady his nerves, then thought better of it and tossed the bottle into the gutter. *You did this to me, you bitch*, he thought. Instead he found a bar, where he ordered and drank three schnapps quickly, then found a telegraph office and sent a message to the fixer in Amsterdam: "LAMP LOCATED. NEED TO HIRE HELP TO DELIVER. SEND FUNDS 2X AGREED AMOUNT. WILL RETRIEVE LAMP UPON RECEIPT."

The next time the girl in the blue dress left the artist's studio without the dog, he would take her, but he would have help. If the dog came after him, the hired help could take the bite.

---

* "No, Akhlut! No!"

*S*o you were in a ship?" Wally said. "I've always wanted to travel. I've never been anywhere."

"I was in a box most of the time," Judith said. She sipped her coffee and smiled. "This is fucking delicious."

They were at Café Griensteidl in the First District, enjoying coffee and pastries and laughing at nothing, in hats, because that's what Wally thought sophisticated ladies did after not seeing each other for a few days, which they hadn't. Wally wore a camel-colored wool cloche hat, which she pulled down so her red curls created a fringe all around, that and the bow on the side giving her head the appearance of a festively decorated bell. Judith wore a wide-brimmed summer straw hat into which all of her hair had been stuffed, tied all around with a sheer lavender scarf that concealed much of her face, which had been the plan. Ella had left the hat at the studio and Wally thought it cruel to not give it a home—also, she thought it might throw off the Dutchman who was looking for Judith.

"I'm so excited to go to Krumau," Wally said. "Aren't you ex-cited? Egon says it's a beautiful medieval town with a castle. His mother was born there."

"What's a medieval town?" Judith asked. She nibbled at the biscuit and stopped herself from commenting on how delicious it was. Instead she looked around the café, an expansive space with Gothic-arch ceilings, a white marble floor and tables, black cane chairs, and long glass cases full of treats. People were talking, eating, smoking, and/or reading newspapers affixed to long sticks, while a squadron of waiters in white shirts, black vests, and white aprons moved like determined ghosts among them.

"It's where you went to catch the plague in the old days. We're going with Egon and his friend Anton Peschka, who is also a painter. Also Egon's sister Gertie."

"The one he's boinking?"

"He says he's not. She's going to be a model for Peschka. They've rented a house near the river. I hope Peschka doesn't paint in the nude, too. It might be awkward. Did I tell you that Egon paints me in the nude?"

"You didn't tell me. I haven't seen you."

"Yes, Egon paints in the nude, except he keeps his socks on to hold his brushes. He draws that way, too—and he draws like a crazy person. Sorry, I didn't mean to say 'crazy person'—like a maniac, very fast, with his face all scrunched up, sometimes with his tongue sticking out. And I'm mostly in the nude too, or in my underwear, and Egon moves all around me with his sketch pad, getting different angles and drawing and drawing and telling me to move this way and that until he can stand it no longer, then we have sex."

"While he's drawing?"

"No, he throws his sketch pad and crayon aside, then he's on me."

Judith shuddered, remembering Adam on the ice. "Does he hurt you?"

"No, no. He's excited, but he's quite weak and willowy. It's usually over quickly, then he's very thankful and he apologizes a lot and talks about what a loathsome creature he is until he feels like drawing or shagging again."

"At my session I remembered shagging a loathsome creature," Judith said.

"I think I'm falling for him." Wally grinned.

"It's only been three days," Judith said. Wally had gone to stay at Schiele's and Klimt had paid Ella to stay at the studio to watch Judith.

"I think he might be a genius—like Gus, only not old. And he smells better. Sorry, tell me about *your* loathsome creature."

Judith wasn't sure she wanted to recount all she had remembered in her last session with Dr. Freud. "It was a little blurry, but there was a man, a horrible man, who kept me as a slave on the ice in the north. Hurt me."

Wally put down her biscuit, reached across the table, and took Judith's hand. "I won't ever let anyone hurt you, you know that, right?"

Judith nodded.

"I need to teach you about hand jobs," Wally said, grabbing Judith's hand. "To keep you safe."

"I stabbed him in the eye with an icicle," Judith said.

"I suppose that would work too. What did he do then?"

"He murdered me."

"Oh, good, you're still a lunatic. I was worried Freud would cure you and you wouldn't want to be my friend anymore."

Judith did a wrestler's reverse—extracting her hand from under Wally's grip, then grabbing and squeezing Wally's hand back. "I will *always* be your friend."

"I know," Wally said. "Let's get more coffee. I'm making so much money watching you and I don't have to pay rent, we should celebrate."

Judith nodded. "We should get something for Geoff." Geoff was tied up outside. People scratched him between his ears as they passed and he made his howly-singing noise for them. "He liked the croissants."

"I didn't see the Dutchman outside," Wally said. "Did you see the Dutchman?"

"I think Geoff frightened him off," Judith said.

"Geoff is just a silly fluffy boy," Wally said. "He couldn't frighten a mouse."

"He can be very protective of me. Of us."

"Did you remember where you knew him from? Oh, oh, did you remember your name?"

"I think I knew Geoff on the ice. And on the ship. But no, I didn't remember my name. Someone very tall and black, with feathers, said *we* were Raven."

"Well, that's stupid. Maybe you brought Geoff to Vienna with you." Wally forgot to be sophisticated for a moment and climbed up on her knees on her chair, leaned over the table, face close to her friend. "What if the man they found in the canal brought you both here from the ice? And you murdered him?"

"Maybe," Judith said. "I don't remember. I remembered that I'm English, though."

"But you're speaking German."

"I think I may speak many languages—maybe all languages."

"No you don't. Say something in Russian."

"I can't think of anything to say in Russian. Maybe if I hear Russian I'll remember how to speak it."

"Well, that's a useless talent then. I can *not* speak Russian just as well as you can *not* speak Russian."

"Dr. Freud says that I may be reminded of more things from my past now that the door has been opened. He says they may be traumatic."

"What's 'traumatic'?"

"Horrible. He says I may act out, act hysterical, he said."

"Oh good, you still need me to look out for you. We are going to have such an adventure in Krumau."

*F*ucking Hitler was going to ruin everything. Egon rubbed his forehead as if he were massaging out a headache, but he was, in fact, trying to hide his face from Hitler, who was coming across the Café Tivoli courtyard toward Egon and Klimt, who had been enjoying coffee and a chat about travel and light.

"Master," Egon said, still hiding his face, "I apologize in advance, but we are being approached by a failed artist I know and he is going to use me to try to get an introduction to you. He was rejected, twice, by the academy in the year I was accepted, now every time I see him he wants to know my secret."

"Did you tell him *talent*?" Klimt spotted the thin, unkempt man, about Schiele's age, crunching across the white gravel toward them, a portfolio under his arm. "The one with the stupid mustache?"

"Yes. I'm sorry, sir. I think he lives in the shelter for poor men."

"It's nothing." Klimt drained his coffee, then made a show of patting his breast pockets as if searching for a cigar.

"Schiele, you old dog!" Hitler said, as if he'd just spotted Schiele rather than set a path toward him. "How are you?"

"Hitler," Schiele said, trying to will himself to sink into gravel to disappear and never be seen again.

"And oh my, Herr Klimt, what a surprise and an honor. I am a great admirer of your work."

"Thank you," Klimt said. Having found a cigar, he now seemed distracted by searching for a match.

"Schiele, aren't you going to introduce me?"

"Hitler," Schiele said to Klimt.

"Good day," Klimt said. He didn't offer his hand, preoccupied as he pretended to be with searching his pockets.

"I am an artist as well," Hitler said, tilting his portfolio. "Perhaps I could show you some of my work and you could give me a critique."

"I'm sorry," said Klimt, "but I'm having an important conversation with my colleague. I am merely a craftsman, I would never presume to advise another artist on technique." Klimt located a match, struck it on the bottom of his shoe, and made getting an ember going on his cigar a new avocation, for the concentration he gave it.

Hitler shuffled his feet like a small child who needs to pee. "But, Herr Klimt, if only—"

"Please, Hitler," Schiele said, "this is an important meeting for me." Trying to shift the focus from the master to a contemporary in the struggle, or so he hoped.

"Fine!" Hitler said. "You can review my work when I exhibit. Good day." He turned to leave, then seemed to run into a wall of something he'd forgotten to say. "You'd have no career at all if not for the patronage of the Jew bankers and their mongrel wives. They are usurping art any way they can. Like Mahler, pretending to be Catholic when everyone knows he was a Jew and only converted so he could direct the opera. I'm glad he's dead."

Klimt looked at his cigar as if he were studying it for a drawing. "Good day, young man," he said, as casually dismissive as he might have been to one of the sparrows foraging for crumbs amid the courtyard gravel.

Hitler stormed off. Klimt put out the cigar on the sole of his shoe. He really didn't smoke unless it was with the gentlemen, with brandy, after dinner.

"I didn't know Mahler had died," Klimt said.

"Did you know him?"

"I met him once. It was awkward. I knew his wife, Alma, when she was younger. Her father, Emil Schindler, was a painter, one of the original Secessionists. Later, perhaps a dozen years ago now, I traveled to Italy with her and her family to look at art—her new stepfather was also a painter, he'd been one of her father's students. I was charmed by her company. She was very beautiful, bright—a vision."

"Did you . . ."

"Her stepfather intervened—I was too old, he said. I was forbidden to be alone with her. Soon after, she married Mahler, who was older than I was."

"I'm so sorry," Schiele said. "Hitler is a pest."

Klimt smiled, waved it off. "Is there a name for that kind of stupid little mustache he has?"

"I don't know. I don't think so."

"It should have a name, so you can warn people when one is coming."

"He's a dreadful draftsman. The academy told him so. I thought he had left Vienna."

"Evidently he has been listening to the anti-Semitic screeds of our late mayor." Mayor Karl Lueger had built a strong following among the working-class youth in Vienna, and even after his death, a year ago, the anti-Semitic movement lived on.

"The last I heard, Hitler was painting postcards and getting Jewish shopkeepers to sell them, so he's not so dedicated to his cause, I think."

"He's not wrong about my Jewish patrons, you know. They've been a blessing for me—I haven't had to take a public commission for a decade. And their wives are beautiful, of course. Time spent painting beautiful women is better than making a public work that will be judged by bureaucrats." He had painted four enormous canvases to decorate the halls of the University of Vienna, which were rejected by the regents as pornography, then went on to win the gold medal at the World Art Exposition in Paris. Klimt returned the fee for the commission, despite having spent years working on the paintings.

"I don't think I'm in any danger of being hired to decorate any public building," Schiele said. "The critic at the *Daily* called my work smut."

"The critic at the *Daily* is an idiot. Still, if you can support yourself by selling your work, it will give you freedom to do what you want. As supportive as my patrons are, I can't exhibit my explicit nude drawings—there is a limit to the amount of scandal they will endure."

"Arthur Roessler has just sold ten of my pictures in Munich. He's even sent me thirty more canvases to fill while I'm in Krumau. The market for Expressionist art is very good in Munich."

"Excellent. Speaking of your trip to Krumau, I am happy to pay for Judith's train fare, and Wally will have money for her food and sundries. Your rent is secured?"

"Oh yes, I've rented a house for the whole summer, paid in advance. And Peschka is paying for himself and Gertie."

"Gertie? Your sister? The one you—"

"I am not. I did not. No, Gertie will model for Peschka. She quite likes him and she thinks modeling for him makes me jealous."

"Friends are a blessing. Now, I don't know how to ask this, but I must." Klimt leaned on the table and made a temple of his fingers, as if he were about to announce the death of a grandmother. "I need you to be, uh, gentle with Judith. She may say and do outrageous things, but Dr. Freud says she's been horribly abused by a man in her past and she is fragile—he wants her to avoid anything that might cause her to relive her trauma. I know that sounds strange, since his treatment is helping her remember, but he says these memories in the wrong environment might cause her to act irrationally, even self-destructively."

"Do you think that's why she was in the canal? She was trying to kill herself?"

"I don't know. But Wally has been very good looking out for her. And the dog seems to calm her. It's just that—"

"I see," Schiele said, trying to give the master a pass. "I will treat her like she is my own sister."

Klimt cringed.

"I did not shag my sister!"

"I didn't say that. Just keep her safe. There is a quality about her—I don't understand it. Perhaps after I paint her I will understand the fascination."

"Or after you bed her," Schiele said, then immediately regretted it.

"No. I think not." He wasn't angry or offended, but simply announcing a decision he had made. "You will see to it that Peschka knows of her fragility, too, though. It's fine if she models for him, she's good at taking direction, but ask him to resist making advances."

"Oh, he will. He's quite taken with Gertie and he wouldn't jeopardize that, but he's even more obsessed with flying the airplane. They have an airplane at Krumau."

"An airplane? A flying machine?"

"I know a man who knows the man who has it. I am going to fly it."

"Do you know *how* to fly it?"

"I'm going to learn. How hard can it be?"

Klimt had seen an airplane while visiting Paris for an exhibition. Canvas stretched over a wooden frame. A waste of good canvas, he thought. "Do you know the story of Icarus?"

13

THE UNDERWORLD

*H*e had two scoundrels, a revolver, and a bottle of chloroform, and it wasn't even lunchtime. Amsterdam had approved, without question, his price increase for snatching the girl, but added to the wire that she was not to be "damaged." Using the word "damaged" because according to the telegraph office, he was procuring a lamp, not a girl. You can't have some telegraph clerk commenting on your kidnapping plan, so everything was in an easy code. He found the two scoundrels outside a bar in the Sixteenth, when he spotted them sizing him up to rob him. He lured them into an alley, where he introduced them to the American-made .44 revolver he'd purchased and made them an offer somewhat better than being shot, to help him snatch the blond girl in the blue dress. They both said their name was Hans, which showed a distinct lack of imagination on their parts, but he wasn't hiring them because they were clever. One was taller than the other, so he decided to call him Tall, and the other one Hans, because no one wants to be called Short, but he thought of them as *Tall* and *Short*.

Now Tall was stationed by a tree outside of Klimt's studio garden, rolling and smoking cigarettes to pass the time as he kept an eye out. Short was just a dozen or so yards away, by a vegetable vendor.

He'd been examining the same cabbage for half an hour as cover for his stakeout and kept arguing with the vegetable vendor, who wanted him to pay for a cabbage or move on, preferably both. Van Beek was at the reins of a rented carriage across the boulevard—a safe distance away. He hadn't warned the Hanses about the giant shape-shifting dog. He didn't want to dampen their enthusiasm for the task.

They'd seen the girl go into Klimt's studio only a few minutes ago, without the dog, and Van Beek had prepared them to wait for hours if need be, but to everyone's surprise she emerged only a few minutes later. Tall Hans signaled Short Hans and they moved inside the courtyard. She looked startled as the scruffy Short Hans stepped in front of her and she backed into the grasp of Tall, who clamped the cloth saturated in chloroform over her face. She slumped, and each of the Hanses took an arm and held her up, her head lolling forward like she was a marionette with its strings cut. Van Beek pulled the carriage up to the entrance of the courtyard and his scoundrels hustled the unconscious girl into the carriage.

Van Beek snapped the reins and the horse trotted off. He'd considered renting an automobile, but he didn't know how long they'd have to wait, and he imagined himself trying to turn the crank to bring an auto to life while the Hanses were carrying the unconscious girl across the boulevard, so instead he'd opted for a horse and carriage. Besides, he'd never driven an automobile and thought the middle of a lucrative kidnapping not the best place to learn a new skill.

They were away and nobody was following or sounding an alarm; best of all, no dog. He took a serpentine route around the city center and headed into the Second District, Leopoldstadt, where he'd rented a small room behind a leather shop with an entrance from a concealed alley.

"Wait," he called to the Hanses. He climbed down from the carriage, unlocked the door, then looked around to make sure that no one was watching and signaled for them to bring the girl in. The thugs hustled her out of the carriage, dragging her feet across the cobbles, and put her on the bed. There was just enough room for the cot, two chairs, and a small table with a white porcelain basin and a water pitcher. Van Beek guessed the room had been a broom or supply closet before its current incarnation.

He checked to make sure the girl was breathing, then rolled her on her side so he could tie her hands behind her back. He'd found some leather laces in the bin behind the shop for this purpose and felt especially thrifty at the move.

"I think she's pregnant," said Short Hans.

"How pregnant?"

"All the way," said Short.

Van Beek would have shot him on the spot if it hadn't meant hiding a body.

"How many months?" He hadn't noticed she was pregnant before.

"Had a look at the goods under her frock," said Tall. "Since she was sleeping."

Van Beek smoothed down the front of the girl's blue dress and indeed, she had a distinct bump there, and not one built by pastry, not on that thin frame. Perhaps that's why the extra instruction to be careful with her. Perhaps he was returning a wayward mother to a concerned father. He'd probably never know. Now he needed to get rid of the Hanses and get to the telegraph office to wire Amsterdam that he had her; then he'd get instructions on where to take her. But he didn't want to gag her, and he couldn't leave her unattended and unconscious—as a cop he'd seen more than one opium fiend choke to death on his own vomit.

"You two stay with her. If she wakes up, chloroform her, but just until she's out again. Don't hurt her and don't touch her otherwise."

The thugs nodded at him in unison, like schoolboys being dressed down by a nun.

"At all." Van Beek patted the breast of his coat, beneath which the .44 rode in a shoulder holster. "I'll be gone for a bit, a couple of hours at most, then I'll return and pay you."

They nodded.

"Only if the girl is unhurt and untouched, do you understand?"

They did.

*H*ow will I know you haven't been stirring around in her brain?" Wally asked. "How do I know you won't hypnotize her and have your way with her?" Wally flipped up the front of her cloche hat so Freud could see she had an eye on him.

"I'm sorry, Fräulein," Freud said, "but you cannot stay with her during the session. You may wait in the hall or downstairs in the lobby."

"It's fine," Judith said, squeezing Wally's shoulder. "If he hurts me we can murder him."

Wally broadcast a bright smile all around the room, especially to young Dr. Bauman, who had shown them to Freud's offices. "All right, I'll take Geoff for a walk." She whirled on Freud and showed him her *eye of bluest scrutiny*. "But I'll be back."

Dr. Bauman showed Wally out. Freud opened the door to the inner office and waited for Judith to pass by. "You know, your talk of murdering me does not shock me."

"Oh good," Judith said, breezing by as she entered the treatment room. "I don't want to ruin the surprise."

After she found a comfortable spot on the couch and was looking at the carved figures displayed around the room, feeling that some of them were more familiar than they really should have been, since most were effigies of ancient gods, Freud opened his notebook and began.

"Have any more memories occurred to you since our last session, any dreams?"

"I think I remembered that I can speak all languages and I was shocked by a dwarf."

"You were frightened by a dwarf."

"No, shocked. With electricity."

"And this was in a dream?"

"It felt like a memory, but it could have been a dream."

"Do you remember anything else about the dwarf?"

"I think he was kind. He gave me soup."

"I see." Freud wrote in his notebook. She could hear the scratch of his pen.

"It wasn't penis soup, if that's what you're thinking."

"Why would you think I was thinking that?"

"Because you think everything relates to the penis."

"That is not true, Fräulein—er, Judith. We must see if you can remember your surname."

"You're thinking of penises right now, aren't you?"

"Shall we start your hypnosis?" Freud pulled his watch from his waistcoat pocket and dangled it before Judith's face.

She caught the watch and turned to him. "You have to tell me what I say, yes? Don't keep any secrets."

"I will tell you everything you tell me and I will tell you what I think it means. We are here to uncover the truth of who you are, not construct more mysteries. Shall we begin?"

She released the watch and lay back on the couch. "Put me to sleep, Herr Doctor, I'll have you swimming in penises in no time."

And in less than a minute, after he recited his calm, reassuring litany, she was entranced.

"I want you to travel back," Freud said. "To the time after you were on the ice, when you were found by the dark figure."

"I found her," Judith said, her voice a warbling growl, sounding nothing like she had seconds ago. "I found her in the clamshell, like I find the others. The soft ones. But she was more pale than the ones before. She had no feathers, so I gave her some of mine, very shiny black feathers. Beautiful feathers."

"Who are you?" Freud asked.

"Ha! Who am I? Who am I? You pretend you don't know Raven? You are silly, White Beard. You cannot insult Raven, who gave you the stars to wonder at. Who gave you the sun to warm you. Raven, who gave you the moon to make love under. Ha! You are silly and your white beard is silly."

"Where is Judith?"

"She is here, four times dead. She has been to the Underworld, where all the Animal People can talk, where all the People go when they die, but only she has returned, and I returned with her."

"Have you made love with Judith?"

"Ha, she said you would ask about my penis. It is the most grand and shiny of all the penises. I would show you, but I don't have it with me."

Freud wished he had one of the wax cylinder recorders that some of his colleagues used with their patients. This was the most extraordinary example of disassociation he had ever encountered, at least in a patient who had returned to normal functional life. If he could find the triggering event in her past, she might be freed of this shadow personality, as Jung called it. "Did you show your penis to Judith?"

"Did you?"

"You know I did not."

"She was hurt when I found her. And hungry. She was hungry enough to eat a whole walrus. No one in the Underworld had ever seen someone so hungry. I took her to Sedna, who healed her, gave her all the food she wanted."

"Who is Sedna?"

"Who is Sedna? Who is Sedna? Are you a crazy man or just simple? Sedna who is your mother? Sedna the Sea Wife. Sedna who brought you all the animals and all the fish to eat? Sedna taught Little Bird to hunt, and catch fish, and scrape and sew furs. That is what we call your Judith, Little Bird, or Pale Girl, even though she has the second-most shiny and beautiful feathers in all the Underworld."

"Is Sedna—"

"Yes, I showed my penis to Sedna. Many times. It is her favorite."

"I was going to ask if Sedna had come with you."

"She is around."

"And she is the mother?"

"*The People* call her Mother. And she gave birth to the otter men after we made love under the moon. It is not my fault that they are vicious killers. Blame that on their mother. But their shiny fur, I gave them that."

"Do you know what hurt Judith, before you found her?"

"Oh yes, she was raped and murdered by a patchwork man. I helped her with him. I told her that unless you lose the big battle, losing the small battles does not matter."

"What did she do when you told her that?"

"Well she was called back to the Above. She had been with us for a moon. No one had been called back before. We were surprised."

"What happened then?"

"I don't know. That was only the first time. I did not return here with her. Does it always smell like burnt hair in the Above?"

"It does not smell like burnt hair." Freud extinguished his cigar in a bronze ashtray by his chair.

"No, I like it. Do not be sad about your silly white beard, White Beard. I once had white feathers, but when I stole the sun from

Grandfather's house, I flew with it out the smoke hole and my feathers were turned black and shiny. You should be happy."

"Can I talk to Pale Girl, please?" Freud was furiously writing notes, defining the vocabulary: Pale Girl, Little Bird, Sedna, the Above, the People, otter men—he would need all these terms to communicate with the scattered parts of her personality.

"Did he show you his penis?" Judith's voice again. The warbling scratch of Raven gone.

"What happened when you returned to the Above?" Freud asked.

Klimt was manning the oars in a white rowboat that drew a chevron across the mirror surface of Attersee, a four-hour train ride west of Vienna. He wore a straw boater and a starched linen jacket with broad, bright red and white stripes. Emilie sat in the back of the boat, wearing one of her long dresses in a bold floral print and a straw hat piled high with artificial flowers and felt fruit. It was their first week at the lake, so they still clung to the fashion conventions of city dwellers on holiday. By the second week Emilie would abandon the hat and Klimt would wear nothing but one of the caftans she made for him, and they would take the full sun on their faces and swim naked in the lake like joyous Bohemians.

"The light here is glorious," Klimt said, "bright, yet soft. We should rent a room at the château with a window that looks out over the lake and make love all afternoon." They were rowing by Schloss Kammer, a seventeenth-century castle that had been converted to an inn—a great white edifice guarding the lake.

"Perhaps a cuddle and a hand job in the pantry, then off to paint plein air for you. I shall share tea and gossip with the girls." Emilie's sisters and their children had joined them at the large house Klimt had rented on the shore. There was a spacious pantry in the rented house that could be locked from the inside against curious explorers.

"I adore you," Klimt said.

"And I you," she said.

"I cannot marry you," he said.

"Just as well you don't ask, then, so I won't have to turn you down."

"After lunch in the pantry, then?"

"Before lunch. I like to nap after."

And so the accommodation for their lust was made for the season.

He rowed for a while, the oars making a melodic ring in the water as they stirred up tiny maelstroms, the oarlocks slipping a bit with every stroke, beating out a slow rhythm.

"I am still in shock about Mahler's death," he said.

"He was a great talent. I listened to his Second Symphony three times on my gramophone when I heard of his death. Such power."

"He was only two years older than me."

"He had been in poor health for some time."

"Worse than me, do you think?"

"Evidently," she said. "Would you like me to row for a while?"

"No, I'm fine. What have you heard from his wife?"

"Alma? She will be unbound. Every talented young artist in Vienna should run for shelter."

"We should call on her when we return to the city. Together. To avoid the appearance of impropriety."

"Of course. Perhaps she will play for us. She's quite gifted on the piano."

"She wanted to marry me, you know. Before she met Mahler."

"And you disappointed her? You cad."

"Her stepfather objected to my age."

"And your syphilis."

"I don't think it was syphilis. There have been no symptoms for years. I'm probably not contagious."

"Oh, Gus, my brilliant man, never worry. When you are a drooling simpleton I will cradle your head in my lap and rub your temples and tell you that everything will be all right. I'll sing to you, if you'd like."

"I would like that. Thank you."

"My pleasure." She laughed and grinned and winked at him from under the brim of her hat.

"I adore you," he said.

"And I you," she replied.

They spent another hour on the water before lunch grew tall in their minds and Klimt rowed them back to the house. Later, some of the children thought they heard a woman's soft singing coming from the pantry and concluded that the house on the lake was wonderfully haunted by a day ghost.

The supply closet was damp and smelled of mildew, but on the bright side, neither Tall Hans nor Short Hans had bathed for three weeks, and Short Hans had slept in his own sick during that time, so the odor of mildew was an improvement. The girl lay on her side on the cot, her breath rasping in her throat.

"She all right?" asked Short.

Tall Hans went to the girl, put his hand under her chin, and turned her head so she faced up. The rasping breath stopped.

"Just lying at a bad angle," said Tall. He remained bent over the girl. "Pretty little piece of tail," he said. "No wonder someone's paying to fetch her back."

"Bit tall for my tastes," said Short.

Tall pinched at the skirt of her blue dress, like he might have been testing the fabric for the quality of the weave. "Wouldn't mind giving her a go."

"You'll get us shot," said Short. "And we won't get paid."

"The Dutchman will never know. *She'll* never know. She starts to come around, I'll dose her with the chloroform."

Short shrugged. "Well, don't make a mess of her. I don't want to get shot."

Tall nodded, then turned to look at Short. Waited.

"What?" asked Short.

"Bit of privacy?"

"The room's not big enough to swing a cat in, what do you want me to do?"

"Step out, if you please. Keep a lookout for the Dutchman. I won't be long."

"Oh," said Short. "Right." He threw the bolt, then jumped back—a scratch at the door.

"Who's there!" called Tall, his voice all menace and snarl.

A howling, singsongy whining noise from outside.

"Just a stray dog," said Short. He opened the door.

14
JUDITH'S SECOND RESURRECTION, AS TOLD TO DR. FREUD

I woke to the sight of the sky, blue and clear through a wooden frame, and I realized I was, once again, inside the fucking crate, looking up. I don't know why I remembered where I was, and who I had been, at least to the time of my murder, but I knew I was in a box, in the north, on the ice, or near it, and my murderer was nearby—I could smell the foulness of him on the chill air. I tried to remember the time before Adam murdered me the first time, the husband that Adam said he had killed, but I could only remember as far back as the ship, the ice. No, there had been someone before, a little man. Feeding me. Speaking to me in a language I didn't understand.

Then Adam's big patchwork face filled the sky above me and I screamed and bolted upright in the crate.

"You're back," Adam said. He had leapt back when I screamed and now stood six feet from the crate, which was partially enclosed by a small structure of roughly stacked stone with a roof of salt-bleached driftwood. There was a driftwood fire crackling and the monster sat down on a log that had been dragged there for that purpose. I could still see the furrow it had cut in the sea gravel. Somehow, he had retrieved the crate from the ice, but there was no sign of the last two dogs.

"There are bears everywhere on the island," Adam said. "The ice receded and left them stranded. I had to build stone walls around the Eskimos' tent, put on this roof of heavy driftwood to keep them out."

"You murdered me again, villain." I looked around for a weapon I might use to attack him. My limbs were alive with pain, as if I'd been rolled in a bin of needles.

"You took my eye," he said. Indeed, his right eye socket was a black cavern in his yellow skin, but there was a glimmer in the darkness. "It grows back."

"Where are the dogs? Where are the men who brought these tents?"

Adam grinned into his chest. "They were good hunters but not-so-good fighters. I watched them for a while to learn, but they were going to leave the island, and I had to stop them. But now we have spears and knives and tents. And three skin boats, but they are too small for me."

"Where are the dogs?"

"We ate them."

"I didn't eat them. *You* ate them."

"I gave you broth as before. You haven't moved for weeks except to swallow."

"You fed me dog broth?"

"It was that or starve. The ways I saw the Eskimos hunt do not work without the ice, without their little boats. There are some birds' eggs among the rocks, but most are in the cliffs where I cannot reach. I may be able to kill a bear."

"What did you do with the men's bodies?" I was horrified that he might have fed them to me while I healed.

"The white bears," he said. "I sat inside the stone house and listened as they ate them. Every bone. It took days."

"How many? How many men?"

"Six. Look, we have six spears now." He pointed to a cone of spears leaned together near an open driftwood fire—all taller than me, with wide stone points.

"We?" I asked.

"What is mine is yours, *wife*. I was able to get their furs off of them before the bears came. The floor of our house is warm now. Their furs are too small for me. Probably even too short for you, but their boots might fit you."

"I can sew," I said. *Wife? Wife? He called me wife?* If I could move, I needed to move to get to those spears.

"These are sealskin and bear hides, not linen and wool like you knew in England."

"I didn't know how to sew in England," I said. I might have sewn shrouds and circus tents for all I knew, but I could not remember. Sedna had taught me to sew in the Underworld. "Was there a needle among the hunters' things?"

"Bone needles, and a bone awl."

"I can sew furs," I said. I stood up in the crate, tested my weight on my legs. The stinging ran from the soles of my feet up my legs, as if each muscle were awaking to pain, but I could support my own weight. "I need to wee."

"Just go in your nappy like you have been. I change it twice a day, even washed you head to toe in the sea."

I felt inside my furs to see if I was wet from the washing, then realized I sensed a very specific sensation of unclean. "Were you shagging my corpse while I was dead?"

"I didn't think of you as dead, just more cooperative."

"I was dead. You already admitted to murdering me, you quilt-faced corpse-fucker."

"You were performing your wifely duties."

"What? Rotting?"

"There was no rotting. I cut you, so you would be an abomination like me, but you have healed." I reached for my face. I could feel the scars there, smoother than the other skin, but healed. Had he only scarred my face?

"You heal quickly," Adam said. "The first cuts I made aren't even visible now. Would that I healed like you do, I would not such a monster be. You are still too fair to share my misery, but I will find ways to bring you into the fold. I'm glad you're back. It was lonely."

"Maybe if you didn't murder everyone you met you could keep company."

I climbed out of the crate and walked slowly away from the box toward the teepee of spears, my muscles burning with every step.

"Where are you going?"

"To have a wee."

"That's far enough." He stood as if he would pursue me.

I was only a few steps from the spears. I tugged down my fur trousers and squatted, pulling out the nappy that Adam had stuffed in there and tossing it toward him. It fluttered like a dead bird and landed a few feet away. "Why are you so cruel?"

"I am how I was made. Blame Frankenstein." He poked angrily at the fire with a long, heavy stick and stirred up sparks, one of which flew into his eye. He cried out, tossed the stick aside, and covered his eye.

"Now, Little Bird," came Raven's voice in my head. *"Strike now!"*

I pulled up my trousers and, holding them with one hand, lunged for the teepee of spears. I snatched one up, adjusted it so it felt balanced in my grip, then threw it at him. He wasn't twenty feet away and I put my whole back into the throw. The spear wobbled in the air like a palsied snake and the shaft struck Adam in the shoulder at an obtuse angle and rattled harmlessly to the gravel. Adam cleared his eye and looked at me, then at the spear lying in the gravel, then at me.

He stood and roared at me, actually roared, his lips pulled back until I could see all of his teeth.

"*Fly, Little Bird!*" cawed Raven. "*Fly!*"

"I can't fly here, I don't have wings."

Adam bent and snatched up the spear I had thrown.

"*Then run,*" Raven said. "*Run!*"

And so I ran, holding my trousers up with one hand, across the sea gravel, out of the little protected grotto where the Eskimos had made their camp, and down the beach toward the rocks where Adam and I had come to shore, although now the ice was gone and the rocks stood in the water. I could hear Adam's heavy steps in the gravel behind me and I glanced back to see him struggling to keep pace, his great weight driving his boots deep into the sea gravel with every step.

Cliffs rose in front of me, but there was a path, of sorts, inland, and I took it. I fell to my hands and knees and scrambled up the path, stopping for a moment to fasten the suspenders that held up my trousers—bearskin, I think, from the white fur. Very warm and waterproof, but complete shit for running in.

When I reached the head of the path, perhaps a hundred yards above the beach, I glanced back. Adam stood there, looking up, leaning on the spear to catch his breath. So there *were* limits to his strength.

"You can outrun me, wife, but you can't outrun the bears," he called. Then he turned and trudged the other way down the beach.

"*You should steal his fire,*" Raven warbled in my head. "*When the long night comes he will freeze to death.*"

"He can make more fire," I said.

"*Nonsense,*" said Raven. "*I am the bringer of fire.*"

"Anyone with flint and steel can make fire."

"*I haven't been to the Above in a while. They let just anybody make fire? That's a mistake.*"

"I need to find food and shelter," I said. "Help me." Raven was new in my head, and even though he had taken me under his wing in the Underworld, I didn't know if he could help me on the island.

I made my way to the highest point on the island I could find without going onto the great glacier, which rose to the height of a mountain—so where I stood was little more than a hill above the sea cliffs, really, but there was no rain or fog, so I could see a long way. I saw two of the white bears in the distance, not traveling together but stalking what looked like the edges of the island. Cliffs. The bears were hunting birds or birds' eggs. With that in mind I went the opposite direction until I came to a cliff, jagged rocks dropping hundreds of feet to the sea, just a shallow fringe of a beach at the bottom, probably only visible at low tide.

There were seabirds nesting in the cliffs, sleek black and white creatures, smaller than seagulls, but none of the nests were reachable from the top. The cliff face was nearly a sheer drop, but uneven— many crevices and depressions I could use as handholds, but not while wearing the thick sealskin boots.

"*Go,*" said Raven. "*If you fall you will return to us. You can learn to fly this time.*"

"*There are lemmings on the island,*" came a female voice in my head. "*Call them to you as I taught you, and feast.*"

Sedna the Sea Wife, who had taught me all the skills of the People—how to scrape hides and sew, build shelters, prepare food—the skills she had bestowed upon the People along with all the animals and fish. I needed to eat. I remembered from before that Frankenstein's elixir came at the cost of a ravenous appetite. Still, I had no knife and no way to make fire. I didn't see myself calling a clutch of lemmings and having them sit patiently on their haunches and watch while, one by one, I chewed their little heads off.

"I don't remember how to call game."

"Fine. Fall off the cliff and return to us. Maybe next time you'll learn your lessons."

I sat down and removed my boots, then untied my bear-fur trousers (which were too thick to climb in) and shimmied out of them. My mittens were attached to the sleeves of my fur parka with thongs, so I could climb and keep them close. So, barefoot and pantsless, I scooted backward over the edge of the cliff, my bare bottom waving in the chill wind. (I needed the airing out. Despite what Adam had claimed about bathing me in the sea, the odor that rose off of me when I removed my trousers was not that of a living creature.)

I made my way carefully down the cliff face, feeling for footholds before releasing a hand to find a handhold. I had foraged for eggs in the Underworld, so I had climbed before, but I had been wearing Raven's feathers at the time, so the cold had not been so pronounced. I knew I was approaching a nest when seabirds began to swoop on me. My next handhold was slick with guano and I nearly lost my grip and fell, but then I reached into the crevice and felt four eggs, each no bigger than my thumb. I ate the eggs on the spot, biting the tip off each and sucking out the nourishing insides. I tasted nothing, just felt the sustenance singing in my blood.

I no longer felt the cold or the strain in my limbs, just hunger and energy. I crabbed across the cliff face, back and forth, down and up, as far as an overhang that I could not traverse, until I had decimated a generation of seabirds, but my belly was full. I made my way back to the top, where there waited a white bear that swiped at me with a great paw, nearly taking my face off. I pulled back and was able to scramble down the cliff face, just out of the bear's reach.

"Slay it with your flight feathers," Raven cawed. *"They are stronger than any blade made by the People."*

"Command it to heel," said Sedna.

"I don't have flight feathers here and I don't speak bear."

"Losing small battles doesn't matter if you win the war," croaked Raven.

"This is not a small battle," I said. "It's be eaten by a bear or fall to my death from a cliff."

"You died before, returned stronger," said Sedna. *"Return to us. Akhlut misses you."*

I had no intention of returning to the Underworld. I climbed down as far as the overhang but saw no way to traverse it, and if I did, I would at best find myself stranded on a thin ribbon of beach that would disappear with the tides. Above me the bear was leaning down from the ledge enough that he was knocking rocks and soil loose to rain down on me.

"Go away," I said, trying to call upon the supernatural powers that Sedna was sure I commanded. The bear remained unimpressed and clawed at the rocks trying to reach me, almost tumbling over the edge at one point, sending a shower of rocks down upon me as he pushed back from the edge. Which gave me an idea.

There had been one spot on the cliff, a small ledge—no more than a hand's breadth wide, but wide enough that I was able to stand there and rest my hands, only having to hold on lightly with one hand to keep my balance. I made my way there, and moving from one hand to another, I was able to wriggle out of my parka, leaving me only a thin shirt below it, silk or cotton, I couldn't tell, as it was stiff with months of sweat, the blood from the cuts Adam had given me, and whatever else oozed out of me while in the crate. I hung my parka from my hood and climbed back up until I was perhaps half my height below the bear, who pranced with excitement, a move I'd seen them make before in breaking through snow dens to find seals.

I drove my left hand deep into a crevice and made a fist, hopefully anchoring myself to the cliffside; then, with my right hand, I took my parka by the hood and swung it up at the bear, who swiped at it as if to deliver a blow that, if landed, would have taken my head off. But it lost its footing in the process. Gravel and soil rained down. I tucked my face into the cliff side and let it pepper my back.

"Do you smell that, Nanook?" I said. "Don't I smell delicious?" I whipped the parka up at the bear again and pulled it away as he swiped at it. Again he pushed away from the edge and the detritus pelted me as it came down. The next time I roared at the bear and he roared back. I slung the parka up, but this time farther from the edge, and the bear reached out with both paws and caught it between his claws, the balance of his great weight now leaning over the edge.

I yanked down on the coat for all I was worth while pulling myself as close to the cliff face as I could with the hand wedged in the crevice. The bear seemed confused at his sudden weightless state and made a swimming motion with his front paws as he went over the side. He snapped at me as he fell and missed, but his rear leg hooked on my shoulder, and his half-ton weight tore me back, ripping the skin from my braced fist as I was wrenched off the cliff face.

I taught her to fly," Raven said to Freud. "It is not my fault that she didn't pay attention."

"Our time is nearly over," said Freud. "May I speak to the Pale Girl, please?"

"If you can't fly better than a bear you have not learned your lessons," Raven croaked.

"Please," said Freud.

Judith opened her eyes and sat up on the couch, swung her legs off. "I remember."

Freud had noted all the details of the dream but would need to study them to find a cogent interpretation.

"When you died—"

"The second time?"

"Yes, when Adam murdered you the second time and you were revived, you remembered then, your time on the ice, on the ship?"

"Yes."

"Yet you didn't remember your time before, in Edinburgh?"

"No. I think I remembered because of Raven and Sedna—living in the Underworld. It didn't feel like I was dead, but that I had changed places."

"But you don't remember the Underworld before the second time you died?"

"No."

"Do you remember falling?"

"I do."

"And after?"

"After, I woke up wrapped in fur. Adam was tending a fire."

"What did he say?"

"I asked him how long this time. How long had I been dead? He said just hours. I hadn't been dead, just cold and unconscious. He'd walked along the beach at low tide and found me. Carried me back to his camp."

"You said that the beach wasn't reachable because of the rocks."

"It was high tide when I left. I didn't know."

"Have you always been afraid of heights?"

"I'm not afraid of heights."

"But in your dream, you face the peril of falling."

"I'm afraid of bears."

"Were you afraid of bears as a child?"

"I don't remember being a child. Have you always been afraid of trains?"

"How do you know about that?"

"I looked into your soul. Are you afraid of all trains or just trains going into tunnels?" She bounced her eyebrows.

"All trains, I suppose."

She snatched his notebook off his lap. She reached for his pencil and he made as if to stop her. She glared at him threateningly. "I fought a bear, on a cliff."

"You *believe* you fought a bear on a cliff."

"What's the difference?"

He moved his hand so she could reach the pencil. She scribbled something on his notebook.

"Judith, we will have to explore this on our next visit."

"I see," she said. She scribbled.

"What do you see?" Freud took off his glasses and wiped them with his handkerchief.

"Are you afraid of streetcars?"

"No."

"So it's not the tracks, it's the train itself?"

"I suppose. May I have my notebook back, please?"

She scribbled in the notebook. "Is it the length of the train?"

He wasn't sure if she was writing or just moving the pencil around. "I don't think so."

"Did you have a bad experience with a train as a child? A train trauma?"

"No. Not that I remember."

"We should explore that," Judith said. She snatched his watch out of his waistcoat pocket, so quickly he barely saw the movement. "Was your dog run over by a train?"

"No. May I have my watch back please?"

"Perhaps your mother? Was your mother run over by a train?"

"No!"

"Your father? Was your father run over by a train?"

"No, no one I know was run over by a train."

"Pity, the mother would have made it easy."

"Yes it would. Judith, I have another patient. May I have my watch back?"

She held his watch before him by the chain. "I will need you to concentrate on this while I count back slowly from twenty."

"I usually start at ten."

"Are you questioning my methods?"

"Give me back my notebook and my watch, please."

She flipped the notebook shut. "Fine, but if you wake up screaming because you suddenly remember that a train drove up your poop chute as a child, don't blame me."

"Wait, so you are saying that my fear of trains is a fear of the phallus?"

"Obviously. Oh, look at the time. I'm afraid that will be all for today." She stood, tossed his notebook on the couch behind her, made for the door.

"Wait, give me back my watch."

"Good day, Herr Doctor. Good day!"

"My watch."

"I'm sorry, but it's shiny, Raven likes it and wants me to take it."

"Who is Raven to you, Judith?"

She turned, grinned, held his watch out to him. "Raven is a god, Herr Doctor."

"Judith, I'm going to refer you to a colleague of mine in Switzerland who I think will be interested in talking to your Raven."

15

GEOFF THE CROISSANT-EATING DEMON DOG OF THE NORTH

*T*he girls frolicked like electrified fairies on their way back to Klimt's studio. Judith had remembered a significant segment of her past, and Wally had discovered the wonders that were young Dr. Bauman and the magic of a mental hospital.

"You can just go talk to the loonies any time you want," Wally gushed. She'd spent the hour Judith was in session shadowing Dr. Bauman.

"And that's something you'd like to do? Talk to loonies?"

Wally put her arm around her friend's shoulders and made her skip along the sidewalk with her. "None of them will be special like you." Geoff frisked alongside them.

As they were passing a bakery, Judith said, "Oh, let's get some treats, to celebrate."

"What are we celebrating?"

"That I was murdered twice by the same man," Judith said.

"What kind of cake do you have for that?" Wally asked.

"We can ask the baker," Judith said.

As it turned out, the baker did not know the appropriate cake to serve for a double murder of the same person, but he did give the two giddy models a big sack of the end-of-the-day croissants for the price of a pair, and they sprayed crumbs and teased and trained Geoff all along the way home.

There was an older woman waiting at the door when they entered the courtyard of the studio. She was perhaps forty, dressed like a washerwoman, in brown skirt and white blouse, with her hair tied up in a white cloth, and she was very distressed.

"Where is she? Where is my Ella?" the woman said. "She went out to pick up my medicine from the chemist and she never came home. I know she came here. She was going to fetch my medicine and pick up her pay from the master and come right back."

"Did you knock?" asked Wally.

"Of course I knocked. I wouldn't be upset if I hadn't knocked."

"Sometimes we don't answer unless it's the secret knock," Judith explained.

Wally took the key Klimt had given her, along with the responsibility of looking after Judith, and went in, followed by Judith, Geoff, and Mother Huber. Wally whooshed around the studio calling for Ella, with no answer.

As she passed through the drawing studio, Mother Huber stopped to look at a wrinkled pile of Klimt's drawings the cats had been playing with. "Oh my, do you all pose nude all the time?"

Wally rolled her eyes at Judith. "Yes, that is how Camilla got pregnant—she accidentally ran into the master on the way to the kitchen."

"When the little one is born, Herr Klimt is going to get us a larger apartment," Ella's mother said with a smile, oblivious to Wally's sarcasm.

"She's not here," Judith said.

"Here's her hat," Wally said, holding up the wide-brimmed straw hat with the lavender scarf tied around the band that Judith had used to conceal her face when she last borrowed it.

"She wore that today," said Mother Huber.

"Was she wearing her blue dress with the white lace collar?" Judith asked.

"Why yes," said the distressed mother.

Judith took the hat from Wally and put it in front of Geoff, who crunched the brim.

"No, dummy, don't eat it, smell it. We need to find Ella."

Geoff made a singsongy howling-whining noise to indicate that he was sorry, but how was he supposed to know?

Wally put her hands on Mother Huber's shoulders and spoke to her like she often had to her own mother when she was drunk and irrational. "Frau Huber, we will find Ella. She is our friend and we worry about her as well." Wally stopped herself from saying "because she is a beautiful little simpleton" because mothers do not want to hear that about their children, no matter how stupid they are. "I'm sure she's just taken her pay and gone around to the shops to buy herself a treat." She shrugged at Judith as if to say, *That seems as credible as the story is going to get, right?*

"Could she have run off with Herr Klimt?" said Mother Huber. "He had to be here to give her her wages. And he is gone, too."

"The master was here this morning," Wally said. "But he caught a train to Attersee at noon. With friends from the art world who don't mix with us."

"We'll find her," Judith said. She waved Ella's hat under Geoff's nose. "Won't we, Geoff? No! Don't eat the hat. Wally, give me a croissant for Geoff."

*A*nd they have nurses there," Wally said. "I think I'd be quite good at that."

Geoff had led them to an alley in the Second District, Leopold-stadt. Wally had been recounting her adventuresome hour in the company of the handsome Dr. Bauman the entire time they'd been searching for Ella.

"I think you need training for that, don't you?"

"But I have experience—taking care of you. They might let me apprentice." She paused, looked around. "I don't like this. It's dark. You'd better be right about this, Geoff, or no more croissants for you." She carried the sack of croissants, still half full.

"We'll be fine," Judith said. "Geoff says this way."

They followed Geoff down the alley. Something in the shadows made a squeaking noise, a rat, probably, and Geoff looked back over his shoulder at Judith as if to say, *I hope you don't expect me to go after that rat, because it's dark and I don't care for it.*

Geoff paused at a weathered door made of roughly hewn boards. He whimpered, pranced a bit.

"This is it," Judith said.

"This is what? Ella didn't come down this alley on her own. She's afraid of moths. I chased her with a dead moth once and she screamed."

"Why would you do that?"

"She was fine. She's tall. But if someone took her, and they're in there, they might just think that we are delivering ourselves into their clutches."

"Their clutches?"

"Their lair, where they will rape and kill us, and vice versa."

"I don't think that will happen," Judith said. "But just in case, maybe you should back down the alley a bit, and if they grab me, you can run and get help."

"And just leave you? In their clutches?"

Geoff scratched at the door and whined. Judith raised a hand of stern *shut up* to Wally, who immediately backed down the alley a few yards. They heard the door unbolt and in an instant Geoff was through it.

Judith barked orders in a language Wally didn't understand. Wally could hear men shouting, scrambling, screaming. Judith pulled the door partially closed, looked at Wally, held out her hand. "I'm going to need the croissants," she said. Wally handed her the sack.

Judith shouted, "*Aakka*, Akhlut! *Aakka!*" She tossed a croissant in through the crack in the door. "Really? Fine." She threw in another croissant, then looked to Wally again. "Come help me get Ella up."

*T*here was already a message waiting for him when Van Beek checked in at the telegraph office. He hadn't left an address for delivery because he didn't want to be found, and he certainly didn't want a messenger coming to the room in the alley where the two hired scoundrels were watching the girl.

NEWS. WAIT FOR REPLY UPON NEXT MESSAGE.

Van Beek swore and crumpled the message. How long was he to wait? He couldn't very well leave the girl in the hands of the two Hanses for very long.

"The sender is going to have your message read over the telephone," the clerk volunteered. "Likely you won't have to wait long. If you'd like, you can go home and I'll call you by telephone when the response comes."

Van Beek just didn't think in terms of the telephone. People shared lines if they had them, and there was no way to know who was listening. Although he was sending coded messages through telegraph operators who read every word he sent or received, so perhaps the telephone made sense.

The clerk gave him a form and he filled out the message in clear block letters.

LAMP ACQUIRED. AWAITING INSTRUCTIONS. URGENT.

He really hoped that "URGENT" conveyed just how impatient he was with this entire job and its very weird circumstances, although he was grateful to not have experienced any more hallucinations since the day he'd seen the giant wolf outside Café Piccolo. To celebrate he'd bought a bottle of Mother Hagen's Cough Killer, which took the edge off his nervousness, somewhat, and consequently had kept him from shooting the two Hanses.

"Here it comes," the clerk called from the desk where he worked the telegraph key. He transcribed the paper tape as it was fed out of the machine, folded the form, and brought it to the counter. Van Beek gave the young man a five-crown coin and took the message.

CLIENTS AGENT WILL RECEIVE LAMP DIRECTLY VIENNA
2 DAYS. SEND DISCREET ADDRESS.

"What the fuck am I supposed to do with her for two days? Keep her drugged?"

"The lamp?" asked the clerk, and Van Beek realized he'd spoken aloud.

"Exactly," said Van Beek. "One of those Jugendstil lamps with the female figurines on the base."

"What kind of drugs does one use on those lamps, Herr Hagen?" (Hagen being the alias Van Beek had been using in Vienna, in honor of his dear mother the cough killer.)

"Young man," said Van Beek, tapping the brim of his hat as if a thought had suddenly landed there. "I have forgotten to tip you. My apologies." And he flipped another five-crown coin onto the counter, which the clerk pocketed with a smile.

"I hope your client likes your lamp," said the clerk.

Van Beek took the message and hurried out into the night.

The door was ajar when he arrived at the little room on the alley in the Second District. The girl was gone, the furniture broken, and the two Hanses cowered in the corner, whimpering.

"It, it, it was huge! Teeth like, like knives!" said Tall Hans.

"We couldn't do anything. We couldn't move," said Short Hans. "It would have bitten me in two."

"Look around, make sure it's not coming back," said Tall.

"They were just here," said Short.

"They?" Van Beek asked.

"Two girls. One looked like the girl we took. Tall. The other little, a redhead. They took her."

"It ate our shoes," wailed Short Hans, thrusting out his foot, which was bare and somewhat bloody, but not to a life-threatening degree.

"I thought it was going to eat our legs, but she gave it a croissant."

"A croissant?"

"Two croissants," said Tall. "The tall girl gave it two croissants and called it off. That's all that saved us."

"This won't affect our pay, will it?" asked Short.

Van Beek turned and walked out.

*B*ecause Geoff likes to chew shoes," Judith explained.

They had Ella slung between them and were more or less carrying, perhaps dragging, her down the street.

Ella raised her head just enough to say, "My head hurts. Ouch. Fuck." Then she passed out again.

"He *has* eaten two pairs of the master's shoes," Wally allowed. When she'd come into the room she'd felt sure it was mostly full of Geoff—to a really unbelievable level—but only a second later he was normal Geoff size, chewing on one of the scoundrel's shoes, which he only dropped when Judith lured him out of the room with croissants.

"What was that language you were speaking to him?" Wally asked.

"The language of the People."

"How do you know it?"

"I spent some time with the People."

"Before you were murdered?"

"No, after. The second time."

"Will you tell me all about it after we take Ella to her mother?"

"What I remember. It might not make sense."

"I don't care. Tonight, then. Oh, you have to stay at Egon's apartment tonight so I can keep an eye on you. I promised the maestro."

"Does Egon know that Geoff is coming with us?"

"Not yet, but Egon is going to love Geoff."

Geoff made a howling-whining-talking noise and Wally leaned Ella on Judith as she dug in the sack and retrieved a croissant for their valiant guardian.

```
To: Dr. Carl Jung, 1003 Seestrasse, Küsnacht-Zürich,
Switzerland

19 Berggasse, Vienna, Austria
7 June 1911

Dear Friend,
    I find myself of late as busy as I'm sure you find
yourself, and I do not wish to add to your workload,
but I have been treating a patient that I think may
help illuminate and perhaps resolve our differences on
the presence of fantasy and occultism in analysis and
treatment.
    The patient, whom I shall refer to as Judith 3, is
a woman in her late teens to early twenties, of British
birth, I believe, although her command of German as a
```

second language is impressive. Initially she could not remember any of her childhood or recent past, including her name or birthplace. She was brought to me by a prominent artist who claims he found her wandering outside his studio, naked and confused. After an attempt at free association, which yielded nothing but resistance and suspicion from her, I reverted, after many years of abstinence from the method, to regressing the patient by means of hypnosis.

After three sessions, Judith can recall no memory from her childhood or upbringing, but instead notes her beginning, not as birth, but as being brought to life from a corpse, by a mysterious Swiss doctor and perhaps a dwarf. The imagery is confused and much of her narrative places her in a wooden box, traveling on ships and sledges in the frozen north, being used as a sex slave by a giant patchwork man she believes was sewn together from disparate corpses and reanimated by the same Swiss doctor, who she believes was murdered by her patchwork captor, who she believes, thus far in her narrative, has murdered her twice, only for her to return from the dead to endure more torture and sexual abuse.

All the fantastic imagery of her story I attribute to abuse by an adult relative, perhaps from when she was very young, the memories of which are repressed so deeply that her unconscious has constructed these fanciful scenarios as protection. (The wooden crate she was trapped in is perhaps a closet in the family home.) It is the imagery that she recounts of her time when she believes she was dead, and shortly after, that brings me to reach out to you. Judith believes that when she was dead in the frozen north, she lived in an underworld of magical talking animals and two gods, in particular: Sedna, a mother figure that brings food and culture to "the People," and Raven, a Promethean character who is animal, human, and god at once, who brought light and water to the People. Judith believes that both these deities abide within her, and indeed I have heard her affect the voice of Raven while under hypnosis, and the character answers with a distinct and separate personality.

As you know, I am skeptical to the point of disgust

at occult or religious nonsense as it relates to
the personality, other than acting as symbols for
various aspects of the psyche, but these two figures,
and perhaps even the patchwork monster man and the
magical Swiss doctor, seem to fit hand in glove with
your theory of the collective unconscious and the
archetypical aspects of consciousness. I would hope
that further exploration of Judith's condition by
a scientist with a more open attitude toward these
supernatural aspects might help her break through her
repression, and perhaps recover some semblance of her
history and normality. I hope you have the time and
inclination to consider treatment of this patient,
whom I have no doubt you will be able to help, but
whose study, in turn, may disabuse you of some of your
theories about the occult.

The artist who acts as her guardian is well funded
and I'm sure would consent to pay for her travel and
treatment, should you decide to take on her case. With
the patient's permission, I have enclosed typescripts
of my session notes, which include my interpretations
of Judith 3's narrative.

I look forward to your thoughts.

Yours, Freud

PS: The patient has exhibited a unique type of
transference wherein she indulges frequent fantasies of
murdering me, but I assure you this factored in no way
in my reaching out to you on this matter.

16

BOHEMIANS ON A TRAIN

*I*t was Wally's first long train trip and most of it she spent up on her knees on her seat looking out the window as the Austrian countryside went by.

"It's a great adventure," Wally said to Judith, who sat across from her at the window. "Have you been on a trip before? Do you remember?"

"I don't remember a train," Judith said. "But adventures, yes, I think."

"I've been on dozens of train trips," said Gertie, who was sitting across the aisle with Anton Peschka, Egon's handsome painter friend. At twenty-six, he was five years older than Egon, a fellow alumnus of the Vienna Academy of Fine Arts. Gertie wore a wide-brimmed sun hat with an orange band, and she panned her head around as if projecting sunlight on everyone she addressed. "But my favorite was our trip to Trieste, for our honeymoon, do you remember, Egon?"

Wally and Judith both looked from the window to Gertie, who had their full attention.

Egon, who sat next to Judith, ran his fingers through his hair and then leaned over a drawing of Peschka and his sister he had been working on in a notebook in his lap. "Yes," he said, as if he'd been pulled out of a dream.

"Honeymoon?" Wally asked.

"Oh yes, it was very romantic," gushed Gertie. "We ran away together, just the two of us. Took the train to Trieste, where our parents had their honeymoon. We stayed at the same inn, in the same room that they did. Reenacted the whole thing. It was so romantic. The harbor at Trieste is simply stunning. Mama was furious at us when we returned."

"And when was this?" Peschka asked.

"Oh, ages ago," Gertie said. "I think I was twelve."

Peschka looked at Schiele. "So you were sixteen?"

"Stop talking, Anton, I'm trying to draw your mustache." Egon was concentrating furiously on anything that was not the conversation.

"Oh, it was marvelous," Gertie said. "We spread flower petals on the sheets, and we drank champagne."

"And you were twelve?" Judith said right into Egon's ear. "With your brother?"

"Egon made drawings of the ships in the harbor, and many drawings of me in the room. I was already an excellent model."

"Is this after your father went mad from syphilis and burned the family fortune?" Wally asked, remembering the story Egon had told on the first day she'd met him.

"Oh, long after that," Gertie said. "I was little when Papa went mad. I don't even remember it, except there was a lot of screaming. Papa hated Egon's drawings."

"The nudes?" asked Peschka.

"Oh yes," said Gertie. "Egon has loads of practice drawing nudes of me. He says one day my snatch will be in the Louvre."

Everyone but Gertie and Judith cringed.

Wally was up on her knees again but this time turned toward Gertie. "So you went on a honeymoon, with your brother?"

"On a train?" Judith said.

"When you were twelve?" Peschka added.

"Dr. Freud is going to *love* this story," Judith said.

"You're seeing Dr. Freud?" said Peschka, his eyes wide with wonder.

"She's mad," said Wally. "A complete bedbug."

"Not from syphilis, though," said Judith. "Does that run in families?" She patted Egon's arm, rested her head against his shoulder to let him know that nothing was wrong with your father going mad from syphilis and you going on a honeymoon with your little sister. Who was she to judge?

Egon folded his pencil into his notebook and stood. "Well, I'm famished. I'm going to the dining car. Can I bring anyone something?"

"I'll go with you," said Gertie. She stood and hugged her brother's arm. Schiele looked at Peschka, pleading in his eyes.

"I'll go along, too," said Peschka, who stood and turned to Wally and Judith. "Can I bring you anything?"

"Strudel, please," said Judith.

"Also strudel," said Wally.

"And a croissant for Geoff," Judith said.

"I don't think they will let you in the baggage car while the train is moving," said Wally.

"Then a strudel for Geoff," Judith said.

"That doesn't—" Wally waved her hands in front of her face to clear any logic that was trying to enter the conversation. "Yes, three strudels, please."

"I'll have the porter bring them," said Peschka. He bowed slightly and hurried after Egon and Gertie.

Wally sat down in her seat. "I hate her. She's so pretty, and sophisticated, and she's known him all his life."

"Her hat is very pretty," said Judith.

"I don't know how to compete with her."

"I have an idea. We could—"

"We're not going to murder her!" said Wally.

"But with Geoff, it's just—"

"No!"

"Oh," Judith said, disappointed. She slid down in her seat. "We could get a ribbon for your hat?"

"I hate her. She's so pretty, and sophisticated, and she's known him all his life."

They paraded through the village of Krumau like they were announcing the circus, Egon and Anton in their cosmopolitan flannel suits in light colors, the girls in their hats and summer dresses, moving behind like dancers spreading flower petals behind the bride and groom at a wedding, except that each, in addition to her own bag, was carrying a tied bundle of number 30 framed canvases that Schiele's agent had sent with them, and Judith was leading Geoff on his leash, the Malamute prancing like a Lipizzaner stallion, so happy was he to be out of the baggage car.

The lower part of Krumau was built into a loop of a river, tall stone houses with tile roofs piled on top of each other, and upper Krumau was built atop a steep hill, a medieval village built around a great castle, a shamble of ancient buildings and narrow, winding cobblestone streets with small shops interspersed among the houses. People looked out their windows as the artists passed, shopkeepers stood in their doorways and gave them the evil eye, and children stopped playing and followed the little troupe of fancy city people. They didn't see many visitors in Krumau, so the arrival of five vital, young travelers and a big dog was the event of the week.

"Where's the airplane?" asked Wally. She had never seen one and very much wanted to.

"What is an airplane?" asked Judith.

"Oh, you bumpkin, how do you not know what an airplane is?" said Gertie. "I've seen simply dozens of them."

"Where?" asked Egon, who had never seen one himself.

"Pictures, in magazines," said Gertie, who took offense at being questioned. "You wouldn't know."

"We shall not only see one, we will fly one," said Anton, who, despite being the oldest, was the least cynical of the bunch and so often sounded like a complete loon.

They stopped at a shop and bought two basketfuls of food and wine, then made their way to the house that Egon had secured, a rather large house as houses went in Krumau, stone, two stories tall, with four bedrooms and a small fenced garden on one side, the river on the other.

"It's huge," Wally said when Egon led them through the door, then, realizing she was revealing her working-class roots, added, "for a small house."

Egon said, "We can use this great room for a painting studio, and one of the bedrooms for a studio as well. I'll be painting plein air most days as well. Roessler says he likes to have the landscapes for those who don't want to hang a nude in their house. Puritans."

The girls were giddy with the freedom promised by their new lodgings.

"We should pick some flowers to put around the house to make it cheerful," said Gertie.

"Oh yes," said Wally. "And build a fire in the stove so we can have tea."

"And kill a seal so we can use its oil for lamps at night," said Judith.

And they all stopped and looked at her.

"We can also make boots out of the skin," Judith offered with a shrug, as if it were the lack of utility in her suggestion that had given them pause.

"Come, Gertie, let's go find the graveyard and steal some flowers," said Wally, trying to change the subject.

Then everyone looked at her.

"Or find some wildflowers. In the wild," Wally added. She was a city girl and had seen the country for the first time on the train trip there.

"Geoff, find us some flowers," Judith said, and Geoff pricked up his ears and ruffed. Despite being a snow dog, he knew what flowers were from being told for many years in England not to pee on them.

"I'll open a bottle of wine and we'll have a drink," said Anton.

"To celebrate the establishment of our artist colony," said Egon.

Within an hour they had forgotten all about finding flowers. They were well into their third bottle of wine and had inflicted serious damage on some bread and sausages when Egon broke out his sketch pad and began to draw a portrait of Wally looking out the front window.

"Look over your shoulder at me," Egon directed. Wally gave him a coy smile. He drew furiously, barely looking at the paper but keeping his eyes on Wally as the lines formed a figure on the page. "Your eyes are so blue in the daylight," Egon said. "I'll have to do a painting."

Across the room, Judith sat on an old divan with broken-down cushions and watched Egon work while she cut bits of sausage and fed them to Geoff. Anton suggested that he should draw Gertie by windowlight as well, and since Egon had monopolized the window looking out on the street, he led Gertie by the hand up the stairs to one of the bedrooms that looked out over the river.

"I'm going to take Geoff for a walk," Judith said, standing.

"Don't go far and don't murder anyone," Wally said.

"What if I see the Dutchman?"

"Fine, him. But nobody else."

"Stop moving," said Egon.

"Sorry," Wally said. "I'm usually much more professional, but I'm being paid to look after her."

"Get more wine," said Egon.

"There's money in my bag," said Wally.

"I have some money," Judith said. She'd taken all the money from the thugs who had kidnapped Ella, in exchange for not letting Geoff eat them. "Come, Geoff!"

Judith led Geoff out the front door and surprised several of the village children, who were watching Wally pose from under the window. The children fell in behind as Geoff was more interesting than a pretty girl in a hat.

"Does he bite?" one little girl asked.

"Sometimes," Judith said.

"Is he a wolf?" a boy asked.

"Sometimes," Judith answered.

She led them through the winding streets of Krumau and on different blocks parents called their children away from the parade until there was just one little boy following, desperate, it seemed, to pet the big snow dog. They passed through the gate of the old town walls and the ramshackle village opened into fields with ripening crops.

"Where are you going?" the little boy asked. He wore short pants and high socks and broken-down shoes that looked to be too big for him.

"I don't know," said Judith. "Why are you following me?"

"I don't know. Do you want to see the marmot?"

"Yes." She remembered a marmot she'd met in the Underworld who was lovely.

It turned out they were going in the right direction to find the marmot. The boy led them, although there were no crossroads for miles, so leading was just a matter of staying on the road, and after a while the boy fell in beside her and examined her as they walked, as if he were sizing her up for spare parts.

"Who are you?" he asked.

"I'm not sure," she said. "I am a corpse and a slave, but I am also a trickster and a sea wife. I am a hunter and fisher, and a seamstress and a cook. I am a model for a painter. My friend Wally says I am a lunatic. Sometimes, I am Raven, who fetched fire and the sun, and sometimes I am Sedna, who brings all the game and the fishes to the People. I think I have been a killer, but I don't remember killing anyone. I am probably English, but I might be Scottish, I don't remember. I try to think back, every night as I fall asleep. I try to remember who I was, but there are many times I've lived in that I can't see. There is a famous doctor in Vienna who is trying to help me, and he says I am jealous of my father's penis, but I don't remember. I don't know who I am. I just don't know."

"I am Jakob," said the boy.

"Oh," she said. "I'm Judith. This is Geoff. With a G." Geoff awooed softly to confirm the G.

"I have been to the doctor," said Jakob. "He looked in my nose and ears and listened to my heart. He said I'm strong."

"He didn't say anything about your father's penis?"

"No. Would you like me to ask my father if you can have it? I don't think he uses it."

"No, thank you. I don't think I need it." She stopped, let the revelation wash over her like the Northern Lights in the Arctic night, turned to Jakob, and took him by the shoulders. "He's wrong, Jakob. Dr. Freud is wrong. I don't envy a penis. I don't want a penis."

"Not so fast," Raven said from the corner of her mind.

"Shut up, bird," said Sedna the Sea Wife from another corner. *"She's having an epiphany."*

They walked for a while longer and the boy led them to a farm, where, behind the barn, there was a rabbit hutch, and inside was a portly marmot, munching on a turnip.

"He's like a giant squirrel," said Jakob.

"I think I knew that," said Judith. "But he lives underground."

Geoff whined and warbled, meaning to say, "I'll bet he would be delicious," but he behaved and instead produced a giant poo next to the cage to remind the marmot how he might have turned out.

"What do you want to do now?" asked Jakob.

Judith squinted at the sky. "We should go back to town. I need to buy some wine for my friends."

"My friends said that you city people would catch us and eat us. But I wasn't afraid."

"You are very brave."

Jakob blushed and then set his chin like a soldier and proudly marched toward town.

"You are pretty," he said after a while.

"Thank you. I was made to be a monster."

"My sister says that I am a monster."

"We'll both be monsters, but in secret," she said.

Jakob grinned as he marched on, reveling in his secret monstrosity.

When they reached the wine shop Judith shook Jakob's hand and thanked him for the marmot. He skipped away to tell his friends he had survived an encounter with the tall girl from the city.

When Judith returned home she found Egon and Wally shagging on the great room rug, in front of a mirror with a gold frame that someone had taken off the wall and propped up against the couch. Wally was on the bottom, her legs in the air, wearing only her chemise and stockings, and Egon, spiderlike, was on top of her, naked but for his socks, trying to draw on a sketch pad on the floor beside Wally's shoulder while looking at them in the mirror. He thrusted several times, then lost momentum as he concentrated on his drawing, then repeated the whole distracted dance step again.

"Hi," chirped Wally. "Did you bring more wine?"

"I'm trying to capture the grotesque, savage beauty of it," Egon said.

"I'm sorry," Judith said. "I'll go back out."

"No, don't bother. We're almost finished," Wally said.

"Make them a sandwich," Sedna said.

"Command Akhlut to join in with them," Raven suggested.

Judith was beginning to realize, as these memories surfaced, as these voices awakened in her mind, that good judgment demanded she ignore them most of the time, even when they were trying to help. Instead of making a sandwich or having Geoff join in the moving art installation on the great room rug, she said, "The wine is on the table," and led Geoff up the stairs toward her room. As she passed the first bedroom, the door was open a crack and she could hear a man moaning. She peeked in to see Anton Peschka sitting on a rocking chair, his artist smock pulled up over his waist, and Gertie kneeling on the floor before him, her head bobbing in his lap like she was a cat lapping up cream.

"*You could*—" Sedna started.

"I'm not making them a sandwich," Judith said aloud.

"What? What?" said a startled Anton.

Judith moved down the hallway. "There's more wine on the table downstairs," she called over her shoulder.

There was going to be a lot of this, she reckoned, over the next month. Art could be a very demanding endeavor. She went to her room, removed her shoes, lay down on the bed, and opened a magazine Wally had given her that seemed to be mostly about hats, soap, and popular entertainers. Geoff curled up on the rug by the bed and fell asleep. In a few minutes there was a soft knock on the door.

"Yes," she said.

Peschka opened the door a crack, peeked in. "You're welcome to join us, if you'd like," he said. "Someone needs to finish Gertie off and I'm spent."

"Shhhhhhh, we don't need her," slurred a drunken Gertie from behind him. "I can do it."

"I'm just being polite," Peschka said.

"No!" came Wally's voice from somewhere down the hall. "No one touches Judith. The master said so. Also, she's mad."

"Thank you, Anton," said Judith. "I'm just going to read and rest for a bit."

Suddenly Peschka's face was yanked out of the door and Wally's replaced it. "How was your walk?"

"Nice. I made a friend and we met an excellent marmot."

"I've never seen a marmot," said Wally. "You'll have to introduce me."

"A shamble of ancient buildings and narrow, winding cobblestone streets with small shops interspersed among the houses."

As they passed the days in Krumau, the young Bohemians fell into a pattern of making art, making love, drinking too much, entertaining the village children, and scandalizing the adults. Anton and Egon, usually somewhat hungover, would draw in the morning, posing the girls doing everything from mundane tasks like dressing, reading, or attending to their toilette (after Lautrec) to the most gymnastic of erotic poses, many of which devolved into actual sex. Judith was excused from the sexual sessions, although Egon tried to have Judith and Wally pose together to simulate acts of sapphic love, which always resulted in the models giggling to the point of tears, and sending Egon into a fit of anger (unless he had managed to complete a quick sketch before the laughing began).

After lunch Egon and Anton would take easels and paints out

into the village and paint plein air landscapes and architectural motifs, Egon to fulfill his commitment to his agent for the thirty canvases he needed to sell in Munich, Anton because he was sore and needed a break from tending to Gertie's sexual wants and needs. It was summer and school was out, so the two painters attracted a pack of curious children that followed them through the village and asked questions while they painted:

"What is that color called?"

"Why do you mix the brown and the red?"

"Mother says your girlfriends are witches, will they turn Gunter into a toad?" (Gunter was a thuggish little boy who bullied the smaller children and never joined in the artist gaggle because Egon had threatened to paint him as a naked clown and show it to the girls if he didn't cease his rough nonsense.)

While Gertie often accompanied the painters into the field, Wally and Judith would do the marketing, and over time the local merchants got to know them and begrudgingly allowed that they were tentatively charming, if unserious, and mostly harmless, except for the more jealous wives of shopkeepers, who thought them strumpets and probably witches.

On afternoons when Gertie and Wally were engaged in private modeling sessions with the painters, Judith and Geoff would explore the village, doing the marketing, or sometimes just wandering in the countryside until it began to get dark. After one such adventure, Judith returned to the house to find Wally posing on the kitchen floor, naked, her bum in the air, and Egon, drunk, sketch pad in hand, shouting orders at her like a jailer to an unruly prisoner.

"Face down, damn it! Lift your ass!"

"I'm trying. I'm getting a cramp." Wally looked back at him, tears in her eyes.

"Face down, bitch!" Egon put his foot on the side of Wally's head and shoved her face into the stone floor. Wally screamed.

At which point Judith dropped her shopping basket, grabbed Egon by the throat, picked him up, and slammed him against the kitchen shelves. Their contents clattered to the floor. She held Geoff away with her left hand while keeping Egon suspended, the back of his neck against a shelf, his feet kicking as she squeezed his throat. He choked, then made no noise except his heels kicking the shelves as his eyes bulged and veins rose purple in his face.

"Never hurt her! Never!"

Egon tried to pull her hand off his throat but had no strength left; his heels beat a tattoo against the shelves and he went limp.

"Judith!" Wally called. "Let him go. You're killing him."

Judith let Egon fall to the floor in a pile and stepped back. Geoff whimpered. Wally crawled to Egon and turned him face up, put her ear to his chest to listen for his heart.

She looked at Judith, who was breathing hard and looking bewildered. "He's alive," Wally said.

"I'm sorry," Judith said.

Wally stroked Egon's hair out of his face. "How did you do that?"

"He was hurting you."

Wally rubbed her cheek, where there was still an impression of the floor's stones. "I'll be okay."

"I remembered something," Judith said. She cast wide-eyed glances around the house as if seeing it for the first time.

"What? What?" said Wally.

"I've done this—I've strangled someone before," Judith said, backing away, a horrified look on her face.

"You were protecting me," Wally said. "He'll be all right."

"Many times," Judith said. "I've done this many times before."

"*Yes you have,*" said Raven.

"*Show her the lovely rolls you brought home,*" said Sedna.

17

AU PLEIN AIR

I've had a gramophone sent to your studio, with some records," said Emilie. She was lounging in the rowboat, which was tied up under a massive willow tree. Up on the bank, Klimt, in one of his long caftans, stood before an easel that held a square canvas a meter wide. In front of him was the wall of one of the gardens of Schloss Kammer, a cascade of foliage and flowers from the ground to the top, in every bright color of his palette. The canvas was mostly white, with a fine pencil sketch, each blossom drawn in place. So far he had painted only the crimson bits, so from Emilie's perspective, it looked like blood spatter.

"Thank you, but I don't want to listen to music while I work."

"It's not for you, it's for the girls."

"My models? They'll be distracted."

"Some of them have never heard Beethoven, Gus. Never heard Strauss, Mozart. Why would you deprive them of that?"

"I'm never going to paint a canvas this size plein air. I'm not capturing a moment like Monet, I'm doing fine brushwork over many days, in difficult conditions. It's like cave painting. There's dust everywhere. I need to finish this in the studio. But the color—"

"Why don't you do your drawing on the large canvas, then do a smaller sketch in oils, just to place the colors, a map, then finish in the studio."

Klimt turned to look at her for the first time since he'd started painting. "That's brilliant."

"Yes. You need to let the girls listen to music while they pose. Imagine Strauss playing while you paint—the joy of it. I think you could use more joy in your life, Gus."

"I can't play Strauss. They'll dance. I can't draw them if they are dancing."

"It will be good for all of you. Joy, Gus!"

"You are my joy."

She laughed until she snorted. "That's not going to work."

"I should have never sent Wally and Judith to you. But I wanted to feature your brilliant work in a major painting."

"That's not going to work either, but thank you."

"I suppose I could try it, for a while. The music could inspire mythic motifs, symbols, Wagner—"

"No fucking Wagner!"

"But—"

"He's dreadful! The girls will *all* be suiciding, not just Judith."

"He's not as bad as he sounds. We don't know that she tried to kill herself. Freud thinks—"

"No!"

"Fine, no Wagner." He turned back to the canvas and painted precise blossoms in crimson while he pouted.

*I*n the days following Judith's choking out Egon, the artists, both of them, treated the models with an elevated level of respect, which Gertie felt was deserved, Wally luxuriated in, and Judith—well, Judith kept Egon terrified that she might do it again by winking at him and making choking noises whenever they made eye contact. On the day after the choking, the painters decided to go into the field for some plein air painting, and Gertie followed along to distract them. Wally and Judith went looking for a café where they could drink coffee and eat pastries like the cosmopolitan ladies that they were, but there was no such café in Krumau. The local grocer, though, did sell them some loose coffee, which they took back to the house and boiled mercilessly, poured into cups unfiltered, sweetened to the point of syrup, lightened with a layer of fresh cream, and drank with rolls and plum preserves the grocer's wife had recommended (after she'd shown her husband out of the shop for flirting with the girls).

They pulled the kitchen table to the window that looked out over the river and drank their coffee while wearing their hats, as if they were at a café in Vienna.

"So, you were a whore in Amsterdam?" Wally inquired.

"I *worked* as a whore."

"How was it? Was it disgusting? Were the men disgusting?"

"Yes. Often. Not always, but often. I needed money to live, and it paid better than being a laundress or a cleaner."

"I hope I never have to be a whore. I would, if I had to, but I hope I don't have to."

"I hope you don't either."

"And you choked your clients?"

Judith looked into her coffee. "Not all of them. At first, it was like yesterday, when Egon was hurting you. One hurt me, once, so I choked him until he stopped. From then on, if anyone hurt me, I choked them."

"And when they woke up, weren't they angry?"

"Sometimes. Mostly they were afraid. Like Egon. Sometimes they didn't wake up."

Now Wally looked into her coffee and stirred it. "You don't have to talk about it."

"I don't mind. I'm glad to remember."

"Oh good," said Wally. She climbed up on her knees on her chair and leaned over the table. "What did you do when they didn't wake up?"

"There are a lot of canals in Amsterdam. I would carry them to the canal and throw them in."

"By yourself?"

"I'm very strong."

"Oh, right. And they never caught you?"

"Not for a long time. I never planned it. It was always an accident. And I got better as time went on."

"So you didn't murder as many?"

"Right. Usually it only happened if the man was particularly large or strong, so they fought back. I accidentally snapped a couple of necks."

"How many would you say you murdered over the years?"

"I like to think of them as *accidents*."

"How many did you *accidentally* murder?"

"I don't know. A dozen, maybe."

"Over how many years?"

"I don't remember."

"Thirty," said Raven from the corner of Judith's mind.

"Thirty," Judith said without thinking, then cringed. "Maybe not."

"Thirty?" Wally said. "I didn't think you were even twenty years old yet. How could you be—"

"I told you about the ice. In the north. I was on the ice for a long time."

"I thought that was just nonsense you made up because you're insane."

Judith thought for moment, nibbled at her roll, sipped her coffee, then said, "Oh, that's right."

"How can you be so old? Why aren't—"

"Why aren't I rich? What kind of fortune could I have made—all those years on the ice? The biggest pile of walrus hides?"

"I was going to say why aren't you smarter?"

"Oh, right. Good point. I am excellent with a harpoon, though."

"You won't accidentally murder Egon, will you? I think he really likes me."

"He stepped on your head, Wally."

"He says we are all just grotesque fuck-beasts."

"I know I am." *More monster than beast*, she thought.

"And he *had* been drinking. A lot."

"I'll try to be careful. I got better at not accidentally killing them for a while because some of the men I choked would return. Offer me more money to do it to them again."

"That's strange. That's strange, isn't it?"

"I don't think I'm a good judge of that."

"If Egon asks you to choke him again I forbid you to do it. He's mine."

"I won't. But if he hurts you again I might have to break his legs or something."

"You're the best friend ever. Not his arms, though. He needs them to paint. Do you want to go find the men and annoy them?"

"I'd rather stay here and annoy you."

"But Gertie is with them. She's so pretty." Wally finished her coffee and chewed the grounds for a moment. "Have you ever choked a woman?"

"I'm not going to murder Gertie."

"That's not why I was asking. I was just making conversation. Trying to help you remember."

"Then no, not that I remember."

"I can't wait to hear what Dr. Freud says when you tell him you were a murdering prostitute."

"I don't think I'm going to tell him."

"Because of the murdering part?"

"Yes."

"Then how is he going to make you well?"

"I'm getting better."

"That's true, you haven't run into the streets naked in weeks. I'm going to make more coffee. Do you want more coffee?"

"Yes, please."

Wally went to the stove and put on a fresh pan of water, poured in some coffee grounds, eyed the mix, then poured in some more. "Even if Dr. Freud turned you in, you probably wouldn't be hanged because you're a loony."

"I don't know." Judith was trying to remember if she had been afraid of being caught for murdering johns, and while she had visions of herself carrying a body a block or two as if he were too drunk to get home, in case someone saw, before chucking him into the canal, she didn't remember being afraid.

"They would probably just send you to a nuthouse. Hey, I could be your nurse and we could drink coffee and eat pastries. It would be just like now, except I would probably have to bathe you and hose you down with freezing water and tie you to your bed, and you wouldn't be able to come home at night, but I wouldn't mind."

"I think you would make an excellent nurse," Judith said.

"They probably wouldn't let you keep Geoff. But I could bring him to visit."

"I'd like that."

"Wait! Wait! Wait!" Wally was dancing in a nervous little circle in the very spot where twelve hours before Egon had stepped on her head. She'd had entirely too much coffee. "Is the fake Dutchman actually a *real* Dutch policeman and the reason he's after you is because you're a murdering Dutch prostitute?"

"Dr. Freud thinks I'm English."

"Don't change the subject."

"Policemen don't drug and kidnap young girls."

"I don't know. I've never been to Holland," said Wally. "Do they really wear wooden shoes there?"

"No."

"What about that other Dutchman, the one they found headless in the canal, the day Gus rescued you?"

"He wasn't wearing wooden shoes," Judith said. "Probably."

"Oh good. Let's go get some pastry. They have to have some croissants somewhere in this bumpkin town."

"I'll get a basket for the shopping," Judith said.

"That was close," Raven said.

"I don't remember," Judith said aloud.

"What?" Wally said. "The basket is behind the couch."

"Just as well," said Sedna.

*T*he painters came tumbling in the door laughing, followed by a small parade of children, boys and girls, in sizes small to medium, who were carrying their easels, canvases, brushes, and paints. Gertie trudged in behind them, moping because her enthusiasm had been overshadowed.

"We bring our entourage!" Anton announced.

One little boy, perhaps eight years old, ran to Wally like he knew her, waving a sheet of drawing paper. "Look, Anton made a drawing of me."

Wally recognized Peschka's careful draftsmanship in the head-and-shoulders pencil drawing of the boy. "That's very nice," she said.

"My snatch will be in the Louvre next to Gertie's," the boy said.

Wally and Judith looked to Gertie, who was wrestling an easel away from two boys who were trying to set it up as an artillery installation in the doorway. Gertie met their gazes of disapproval first with a haughty aspect of denial, then said, "For art!" When neither looked away, or smiled, she looked at the floor and said, "We've been drinking."

Egon took the second easel from a pretty young girl of perhaps twelve, who was wearing a green cotton dress and worn work shoes. "Come, my patrons, I'll show you how great art is made!" He unfolded the easel and took a canvas from the boy who was carrying it.

"Wally, Judith, this is Tatiana," Egon said. "I'm going to make a painting of her. Do we have any wine?"

Wally moved to where she could see the canvas, which, mercifully, showed a sketch of a shamble of old Krumau houses. "We have wine," she said. "And we found some éclairs at the market."

"Shall I choke him?" Judith whispered to her friend.

"Not yet," Wally said. "But I'm not sharing my éclairs with these urchins."

Geoff stood between them, woofing and warbling suspiciously.

"We won't give them your share," Judith said, scratching him behind the ears.

"Come, look at my drawings," Egon said to the entourage. He folded back the pages of his sketchbook and held it aloft for the children to see.

"You can see her boobies," said one little boy.

"What's she doing? Is she trying to poop?" asked a little girl. "My dog makes that pose when he's trying to poop."

"Yes!" said Egon. "You see the pure, base animalness of our nature."

Wally hid her face against Judith's shoulder. "I was not trying to poop," she whispered.

"I know. Don't worry," Judith said, stroking Wally's hair. "You can't even see your face in that one."

"And here," Egon said, flipping the page, "is the act of beastly lust itself."

"Egon!" Anton called from the other side of the group. He, too, was drunk, but not so drunk that he wasn't horrified by what his friend was doing. Egon looked up. Anton shook his head slowly.

"What?" Egon said. "They have to learn. Art will prepare them for the horror that is being human."

Gertie breezed into the kitchen, looked around until she saw the bakery box, and opened it. "Look, everyone, Wally brought éclairs!" She snatched a knife off the drain board and brought it, with the éclairs, to the table. "There aren't enough for everyone to have one, so we'll have to share." She started sawing the éclairs in half as the children gathered round.

Peschka moved to Schiele's side and gently wrestled the sketchbook out of his hands. "Perhaps only share the landscapes," he said.

The children had dispersed to different parts of the great room, except for a group of four who stood facing each other, grinning as they munched the pastries. One little boy, who had finished all of his éclair except for a cream-smeared stub, held it out and said, "Puppy. Here, fuzzy puppy."

Geoff bolted to the child and frisked until the boy fed him the pastry.

"Geoff, you slut," said Wally. To Judith, "Your dog is a slut."

"He's not my dog," said Judith. "I just know him."

Meanwhile, Peschka had retrieved his own sketch pad from his room and had taken a seat at the end of the divan by the front window. "Come, you," he said to Tatiana, who was the oldest and therefore the tallest of the children. "Sit, sit, I will draw your portrait."

"Draw me! Draw me! Draw me!" came a call.

Left standing with no one paying attention to him, Egon found another sketchbook, a smaller one, and took a seat at the kitchen table, which was still by the river window where the girls had staged their sophisticated coffee klatch. "Come, you," he said, pointing to a boy with chocolate smeared on his mouth from an éclair near miss. "I'll draw you." The boy sat and Egon began drawing. "No, don't move. You mustn't move."

"Shall I help him?" Gertie asked. She looked to Wally. "I was modeling for Egon when I was even younger than that kid."

"Yes, please," said Egon. "Wipe his face. He looks like he's been eating the ass out of a sheep."

As each of the artists completed a drawing he would tear it out of the sketchbook and hand it to the child, who would show it around to the other children as a new model slid into place.

"We should take Geoff for a walk," Wally said to Judith.

"And buy more éclairs," said Judith.

"To feed the children," Sedna said in Judith's head. *"And kill a seal, they need meat."*

"Yes, let's go," Judith said, snatching up the shopping basket and Geoff's leash and leading them out the front door.

They took Geoff up to the castle and down to the river. They bought a loaf of bread and some cheese, because the éclairs were all gone for the day; then when they returned in the late afternoon the children were gone, Anton was asleep on the couch, Gertie snored softly in the chair beside him, and Egon was sitting at the table sketching Tatiana, who sat across from him, her dress unbuttoned and pulled just off her shoulders.

"I'm going to choke him," Judith said.

"No." Wally held her back.

"Geoff can bite *her*," Judith suggested. "He loves children."

"No." Wally moved behind Tatiana and put her hand gently on the girl's shoulder, bent down, and whispered, "Drawing's done, love. Time to go home."

"The drawing isn't finished," Egon said, a growl in his voice.

Judith snatched the top sheet off the sketch pad and balled it up. "Yes it is." When Egon started to get up, she pushed him back down in his seat and slid into his lap. "I've murdered simply dozens of men," she whispered in his ear, evidently too loudly, because Wally said, "You didn't say dozens!"

"Walleeeeee," Egon wailed. Judith choked him just enough to cut off his air and therefore his pleas.

"Shush," she said. She kissed his eyebrow, twice, then let him breathe.

"Please don't make me go," said Tatiana to Wally. "I like it here. And we're going to make art."

Wally put her arm around Tatiana's shoulders and led her to the front door. "I know, dear, it's very exciting. But that's all for today. Perhaps come back tomorrow."

"These are the biggest eyebrows I've ever seen on a man," said Judith. She grabbed Egon's right eyebrow and stood, pulled it up and him with it.

"Ow, ow, ow, ow, ow," said Egon as he followed her, eye first, up the stairs.

"Where are you going?" asked Wally.

"I'm going to take Egon upstairs and remind him about how to treat you."

"Don't murder him," Wally said.

Judith raised her eyebrows in question, as if to say, *But he has to learn.*

"No!"

"Fine." Judith led the enfant terrible of the Vienna art scene up the stairs.

Geoff whimpered.

"Please, Fräulein," said Tatiana. "My father died and my mother has a new husband and he is horrible. I wasn't supposed to leave the house today. He will be very angry with me. He beats me." She pulled up the hem of her dress to reveal strap marks across her thighs.

"Oh balls," said Wally. She had lost her own father when she was eleven, and while she hadn't endured an abusive stepfather, she knew girls who had. "You can stay here, one night, but you are not to take your clothes off."

"Even to sleep?"

"Not even to sleep."

"To bathe?"

"No bathing. And you're not to be alone in the room with Egon or Anton."

"But, how will he make the painting?"

Wally looked back at Anton and Gertie, sleeping off their wine. "Gertie will be there."

"She's very pretty."

"Yes, but she's as stupid as a chicken, so let that be a lesson to you."

"To not be pretty?"

"To not be Gertie. And you will sleep in Judith's room." She thought she heard Egon wailing upstairs. "No, on second thought, you will sleep on the divan."

"Oh thank you, Fräulein." Tatiana threw her arms around Wally's neck and hugged her furiously.

Wally pushed her away. "One night."

"One night," the girl repeated.

"And you have to cook breakfast for everyone."

"I know how to do that."

"Good. Button up your dress. I have to go rescue Egon." Wally padded up the stairs.

Judith emerged from Egon's room, examining something pinched between her fingers. "I really thought eyebrows were attached better," she said. Wally rushed past her into the bedroom.

Downstairs, Tatiana sat on the end of the divan at Anton's feet and leafed through a magazine by the soft afternoon light from the window.

She stayed for three nights. On the third morning, a policeman pounded on the door.

18

PLACES LADIES, MUSIC, AND BEGIN

When Klimt returned from Attersee he walked into his studio to find four models in various states of undress, sprawled across the posing platforms, wanking joyously to Strauss's "Blue Danube" waltz.

"What is this?" he said. "What is this?" He would have waved around the room to identify what he meant by "this," but he was trying to carry a half-dozen meter-square canvases he'd brought home to finish and they were not cooperating.

Two of the girls sat up and grinned, and Ella, wearing an open kimono, her belly now protruding like Turnip Madonna, padded over to him and kissed his cheek. Judith, who lay on the wide platform by the window, strumming along to the music, held up a finger as if to say, *I'll be right with you as soon as I finish.*

"Don't you love it?" Ella said. "We thought you'd love it. Thank you so much for the gramophone."

She threw her arms around his neck and hugged him hard enough to dislodge the canvases, which the two of them tried to catch before they fell flat. He leaned the canvases against a posing platform and returned Ella's embrace.

"I had to watch through the window," Ella said. "When you came through the garden gate we all took our places, and Judith put the needle down on the record."

"Almost done," Judith said, same free finger of pause in the air, although now her head was thrown back and she was wiggling a bit.

The other two models—dressed only in their stockings—Trudy, a tall brunette with bobbed hair, and Anna, a round blonde with long locks, began dancing around Ella and Klimt, who was a little angry, in addition to being surprised. He desperately wanted to start sketching this scene.

"That's it!" said Judith. "Yes, that will do." She was out of breath and slightly flushed—Klimt could see the thread-thin white lines on her skin he hadn't seen since that morning when he'd fished her out of the canal. She slid off the posing platform to her feet, caught herself on weakened knees, then grinned as she waltzed across the room to Klimt and Ella. "Master. Welcome home." She bent and kissed his cheek. "You look so tan and healthy. And surprised."

"Were you surprised?" Ella asked.

"Yes, surprised." He looked around for someone to blame. "Where is Wally?"

"In prison, with Egon," Ella said. "Do you want to dance, Gus?" She gracefully offered her hand and he took it, not sure what to do next. First, she had never called him Gus before, and he wasn't sure he liked it, but he thought it might be in bad taste to scold one of your employees for being too familiar when she was naked and carrying your child, and he was disoriented in his own studio, his sanctum, and what were those white lines on Judith's skin, *and where in the hell was Wally?*

"Thank you for the music, Gus," said Trudy as she waltzed by.

"Yes, thank you, Gus," said Anna over her shoulder as her partner danced her away.

They were striking in their figures and movement and he resisted the urge to shrug off the anxiety, pick up a sketch pad, and start drawing, but he let Ella lead him to the center of the studio, where she curtsied, then began to lead him in a waltz. They had gone three steps when the record ended.

"I'll get it," said Judith.

"No," said Klimt.

Judith lifted the needle and stood by the gramophone.

"Oh, put on the cabaret record from Paris," said Trudy.

"Cancan," said Anna. "You'll love it, Gus. It's absolutely scandalous."

"No. Wait. No. Why are you all calling me Gus?"

"Because of the card." Judith picked up a piece of white card stock that was wedged into one of the seams in the gramophone's case and handed it to him.

It read: *To my girls. May it bring joy to all our work. All my love, Gus.* He recognized the handwriting: Emilie. Torturing him with talk of joy and light for a month at Attersee wasn't enough? Now she was inflicting her joy on him in his studio?

"It's so sweet of you," said Ella. She kissed his cheek again, perched his arm between her breasts, and stood at his side.

"Wait, Wally is in prison?"

"No, she's not in prison," Judith said. "Egon is in prison. In Krumau. Wally just visits him."

Klimt pushed Ella away, as it felt as if she was distracting him from grasping what had happened, but he watched her spirit sink and quickly put his arm around her shoulders.

"Judith, put on some clothes. All of you, put on some clothes."

The girls looked at each other, confused. He had never asked them to get dressed before. Klimt jostled Ella and she took the cue. "Come on, let's all get dressed, Gus has other work to do."

He guessed that the "Gus" moniker was out of the lamp, never to be put back in, and sighed.

"What is Egon in prison for?"

Judith looked up from pulling on her knickers. "Exposing children to pornography, I think. But it was much worse when they first arrested him. At first it was abduction of a minor with intent for corruption."

"I was abducted," said Ella cheerfully, wanting to be included in the story.

"What?" Klimt sat down on the largest posing platform, which was large enough to accommodate a dogpile of models, and often had. "You were abducted?"

"Egon didn't abduct her," said Judith. "There was a girl called Tatiana, I think she was twelve. She came to the house where we were staying with a lot of other children Egon had collected."

Klimt felt like he might be getting a headache. He rubbed his temples; then Ella slapped his hands away and *she* rubbed his temples, which felt much better.

"So," Judith continued, "when the other children left, Tatiana stayed because her stepfather is a twat."

"Did she say 'twat'?" asked Ella.

"No, I said that. I'm English, did I tell you? He was hitting her."

Klimt looked up. "You're English?"

"And a prostitute," said Trudy, who was fully dressed now and sat down next to Judith on a smaller platform.

"You're a prostitute?" Klimt asked. Ella rubbed his temples harder, to help with his confusion.

"A big old whore," said Anna. She gave Judith a bit of a hip bump and sat next to her on the other side from Trudy. "A huge strumpet."

"So, anyway," Judith said, "the police came after three days and took Egon away, and then hauled him before the magistrate the next day for a trial. And Gertie and Anton and Wally all testified that he was a genius artist and I testified that he referred to himself as a disgusting fuck-beast."

"Is he?" asked Ella.

"No, he's not disgusting. He's just thin. Although he looks strange with only the one eyebrow. So they were going to put him away for a long time, but then Tatiana came in and said that she had asked to stay over and that she was never in the room with Egon alone, which is true, because Wally told Egon if he was alone with her or if she took off one stitch of clothing I would choke him out again."

"Again?"

"Don't worry, I'm very good at it. It's how I remembered that I used to be a prostitute."

"A big old floozie," Anna said. Trudy nodded.

"He was being unkind to Wally. Anyway, the judge reduced the charges to showing pornography to children. They confiscated a lot of his drawings and showed them at the trial."

"Was he showing them to children?"

"We don't think so, but he may have. Maybe one before Anton stopped him. He had some hanging in his studio space while the children were there. He brought out some drawings for the police that he had shown in an exhibition in Prague, to show them they were art, and that's when they arrested him."

"Those drawings were taken down by the police in Prague for indecency," Klimt said. "He was distraught then. Why would he show them?"

"Egon doesn't have a good sense of what's appropriate for children. Wally thinks it's because he went on a honeymoon with his little sister when she was twelve."

"And now she's a big old harlot," said Anna.

"No she's not," said Judith. "Although she's very pretty, so if she was a whore she'd be rich as well."

"So how long is he going to be in prison?" Klimt asked.

"Thirty days. And they won't let Wally in to see him anymore, because she pretended to be his wife, when she isn't. But he has a window where she can see him from the ground. It's three stories up, so she shouts at him and throws him fruit because he says the food is horrible. Wally sent me home with Anton and Gertie. She's going to stay to keep Egon from succumbing to melancholy. He was very depressed the first few days, but she talked the jailer into giving him his paints and drawing materials, so he's been better since then, she said."

"And who has been watching you?" Klimt said.

"Well, it was supposed to be Anton and Gertie, at Egon's apartment, but Anton lives with his mother, and Gertie lives with *her* mother, and they didn't want me and Geoff around because it interfered with their shagging, so we've been staying here."

"And I've been watching her during the day," said Ella.

"She's been very good at it."

"She's on her own at night, but I come every morning with pastries," said Ella.

"Wait, am I paying you for that?" Klimt twisted out of her temple massage to look her in the eye.

"I've been keeping track. I can make an invoice, if you'd like. Judith taught me."

"Because she's a big ol' slut," Anna said.

"No, Wally taught me," Judith said.

"Am I paying *all* of you?" Klimt asked.

"No, this was just our way of saying welcome home," said Trudy. "A thank-you for the gramophone. We know how much you like to draw us when we touch ourselves, so it was our welcome-home present."

"Yes, Judith," Anna said, scowling at Judith. "You're only supposed to *pretend* to touch yourself."

"Really?" Judith looked to each of the models for an answer.

"Yes," Ella said. "We were just pretending."

Klimt closed his eyes and signaled for Ella to resume massaging his temples.

"I didn't know," Judith said. "I'm new."

"But I really *was* abducted," Ella said. "On the day you abandoned me."

"On the day you left for the lake," Judith said.

"Holiday. I went on holiday."

"Two horrible men abducted me," Ella said. "Right here, in your garden. Drugged me and whisked me away to a closet in Leopoldstadt. But Judith and Wally rescued me."

"And Geoff," Judith added.

"So now we're best friends," Ella said, smiling at Judith.

"Despite her being a gigantic whore," Anna said.

"You mean Judith, not Ella, right?" asked Trudy.

"That is correct," said Anna.

"Were you hurt?" Klimt asked Ella.

"No. I was just groggy. But the men who took me were roughed up."

"Geoff ate their shoes," said Judith.

"Did you go to the police?"

"No," Judith said. "We think the men were after me. Ella was wearing the blue dress I had been borrowing until Wally bought me new clothes. She thought the police would want to know about me, and you said that wouldn't be good because you didn't report finding me."

"Right."

"But we asked the ones who took her who they were working for. It was the Dutchman."

"The one who pretended to be a policeman?"

"Yes. I think it's time we murder him."

"No. Judith, you can't keep talking about murdering people."

"I meant first ask him why he is after me, *then* murder him."

"See?" said Ella. "You think she's all better, then she says something like that. I can stay nights and look out for her, for whatever you were paying Wally. Judith still needs help."

"Because she's a massive tart," said Anna.

"Dr. Freud is going to turn my treatment over to a different doctor. In Switzerland."

Klimt pushed Ella away again. "When did this happen? No one consulted me. Strauss, invoices, now a doctor in Switzerland? Why does no one consult me on my own business?"

"That reminds me," said Ella. "A fat policeman came to the door this morning. He said he has some news about a case you asked him about and he will meet you at Café Tivoli at noon. Commandant something."

"Kruger?"

"That's it."

Klimt pulled his watch out of his waistcoat pocket. "That's in twenty minutes."

"You'd better go, then," said Ella. "Go ahead, I'll keep an eye on Judith."

"The colossal trollop," said Anna.

"And I'm going to paint Anna blue," Judith said.

"She means paint a picture of me in blue," Anna said.

"No," said Judith.

Klimt desperately wanted order to return to his life, but part of him also really wanted to see what the curvy blonde would look like painted blue. "Use the Prussian blue," he said. "It's cheaper. There's a fresh tube in the storeroom."

"No," said Anna.

"It's for art," Judith said.

"For art," Ella said, snatching up a fresh, clean brush from the tray of a nearby easel. To Klimt she said, "You had better go, Gus. You'll be late."

Anna jumped to her feet and ran toward the kitchen. Ella, Judith, and Trudy headed after her.

"Geoff, stop her!" Judith called.

Geoff, who had been napping in the kitchen, answered in a talky yowl, which meant "Okay."

Klimt put on his hat and left the studio, locking the front door on the way out. Maybe Emilie had been right; the models really did seem more sophisticated after being exposed to classical music.

To: Dr. Sigmund Freud, 19 Berggasse, Vienna, Austria

1003 Seestrasse, Küsnacht-Zürich, Switzerland 14 June 1911

Dear Professor Freud:
How excited I was to receive your letter of June 7. I am flattered that you feel I might be able to help this patient, Judith 3, but I am reticent after the last patient you referred to me, our colleague Otto Gross, whom you described as needing my medical help with a cocaine addiction but who required my full-time, constant attention for months before I diagnosed his condition as dementia praecox,[*] manifesting in nearly constant infantile, autoerotic behavior. I can ill afford to again spend a full calendar page of days chasing a patient through the streets of Zurich as he furiously masturbates in front of crowds while publicly announcing that I have cured him. I am still trying to repair the damage to my reputation. I trust your description of this young woman's condition does not conceal complicating circumstances that might require more time and attention than I am able to allocate to her treatment at this time. I would also be quite interested to know if her preoccupation with murdering you has caused her to manifest any behavior toward that goal, or if she, like so many upon meeting you, is simply responding to your personality. In short, has she actually tried to murder you? It will affect my response.

---

[*]   Schizophrenia.

223

That said, I have reviewed your case notes and I am intrigued by the particular images she cites, those of Raven and Sedna. While I have not heard of the latter, a short trip to the library yielded myriad references to a raven deity across cultures. There is very little published to date about the mythology of the indigenous people of the Arctic, but a Danish explorer called Knud Rasmussen has recently published a study he compiled from many interviews with the Inuit people of northern Greenland, which may provide details which I can use for comparison to Judith's stories, and, perhaps, expand my theory of the collective unconscious. If the patient can recall elements of Arctic myth, which she has no way of knowing, she may have, indeed, tapped into the collective unconscious. This may be a unique opportunity to expand my studies, and with that in mind, I will accept Judith 3 as a patient, under conditions my schedule can accommodate.

I have wired the University of Copenhagen, which has compiled and published Rasmussen's research, which is currently only available in his native Danish language. They have consented to send me a copy of his full work and I have hired one of my students, who was born and raised in Denmark, to translate for me.

I will be able to visit Vienna a few days next month on my way to a conference in Munich. I would be grateful if I could use your offices for our sessions. I am delighted that a method we both concluded years ago produced inaccurate responses, hypnosis, has resurfaced as an effective procedure, and I will implement it with Judith in our sessions. I will send the exact dates soon. If you could arrange with the patient, or her caretaker, for me to see her for two hours, on three consecutive days, that will be helpful.

Whether we will be able to find a cure for this woman's amnesia and whatever complexes she may suffer from or not, the prospect that I may be able to confirm the existence of the collective unconscious, or reinforce your theory that all mental illness stems

from repressed childhood sexual trauma, is quite
exciting.

With kind regards,
Most sincerely yours,
Jung

*I*t took the entire twenty-minute walk to the Café Tivoli for
Klimt to put his thoughts into enough order that he might be able
to push them aside while he dodged the obstacles of subtext with
Commandant Kruger over coffee and cake. Had life suddenly become more complicated, or had a life of privilege, self-constructed
as it may have been, softened his ability to cope? Was he too old to
cope with change? Or did he, in fact, crave change, variety, and
perhaps even chaos? Soon he would turn forty-nine, an age when
men were at the height of their intellectual powers—or so he had
read—even if their physical prowess might be ebbing. He thought
of poor Mahler, lamenting that he could not keep up sexually with
his young wife, Alma—the man was a genius, even if he had a
heart condition. Had he deserved to weather the caprices of a young
woman? Did he?

The syncopated wanking of his young models in three-four time
had thrown him. He, who had built a worldwide reputation merg-
ing sex with art, was thrown by their silly performance. And who
could he blame but himself? He *had* found the dead girl in the canal, brought her to his studio, saw to it that she was cared for, mind
and body, and why? Because she represented risk? Danger? Beauty?
Sex? Compassion? Responsibility? Death? The critics called him
a Symbolist painter, and he had gladly taken on the label, created
works to enhance the reputation, to give his work intellectual heft

that he—educated as a craftsman, not at the Academy of Fine Arts, but at the School of Applied Arts—felt he did not have. Symbols to somehow throw a haze over the fact that he was simply a working-class fellow who liked drawing, painting, spending time with, and bedding pretty women. Was Judith a living symbol? A symbol of his weakness, perhaps? He desperately wished for a friend with whom he could talk about this. Someone as close and intelligent as Emilie, but who wouldn't sum it all up, as she often did. "Oh, Gus, you are just a dog. A lovely, loving dog." She could be hurtfully smug sometimes. Accurate, but hurtful.

Well, Commandant Kruger was not the friend to whom he could pour his heart out. The big policeman admired him too much; he couldn't disappoint him by confessing human weakness.

The maître d' at Tivoli showed him through the dining room to the garden in the rear, where Kruger waited alone at a table, reading a newspaper on the stick provided by the café, over a tiny cup of coffee. Kruger spotted Klimt, stood, and heartily shook his hand.

"My friend, you look so tan and healthy, like someone who works for a living."

"Just back from holiday at Attersee, but I did get some painting done." Klimt sat and caught the waiter's eye, signaled to bring him whatever Kruger was having. He was grateful it was coffee and not beer. He was having a hard enough time keeping a clear head.

"And I am just back from a trip to Amsterdam," said Kruger. "Where I found out some intriguing information about the dead policeman you were interested in."

"Oh, Commandant, mine was only a casual interest. You needn't have gone so far—"

"Calm down, Klimt, I value your friendship, but not so much I'd go to Amsterdam on a case. I have detectives who do that kind of work for me. My wife's sister lives there and we were visiting while on holiday. The case was a perfect excuse for me to get away from family."

"It was diligent of you to keep it in mind." *Why can't Kruger just forget about social conversations like everyone else?*

"The local police revealed more to me than they had told us in telephone and cable inquiries. Going in person made a difference. For one thing, I told you that Thiessen thought he was on the trail of a killer, but it wasn't because of his overzealousness that he had to leave the police force, it was because his theory was so daft. He thought he could trace murders going back thirty years, all, he thought, done by the same prostitute, who strangled them or snapped their necks, then threw her victims' bodies in the canals."

"That's an old whore," Klimt said, grinning as if he were amused but trying to fight down the panic.

"And a very strong one," said Kruger. "Absurd. Which is what Thiessen's captain said of this theory. But he kept at it, and when he was ordered to give up on the case, bury it, he went to the press with it, and one of the papers that specializes in fantastic stories published his theory. It was shortly after that that he received a telegram from London offering to pay him to find this woman killer."

The waiter brought Klimt's coffee, but before he even touched it, he pulled his notebook from his inside pocket. "Commandant, do you mind if I sketch you while we talk?" He flipped open the notebook and tapped it with his pencil.

Kruger twisted the ends of his great mustache self-consciously and brushed his eyebrows with his thumb, and it seemed to Klimt he might have even blushed. "Well, I would think you could find a better subject, but if you insist."

Klimt smiled. "Do I tell you how to wield a sword? Good, then, go on. Don't think about the drawing."

"That girl who answered the door at your studio, very pretty, and very pregnant. Is that your work?"

"Oh, Camilla," Klimt said. "No, no, she has a boyfriend. But I am working on a painting about birth and death, so her condition is useful to me."

"I see," said Kruger. "Well, anyway, back to the case. It seems that Thiessen actually had found victims who died by strangulation going back thirty years, and all were men, and all had been dumped in the canals around the red-light district, but there was no pattern time-wise. Sometimes there would be two found in a matter of weeks, then nothing for years, so it wasn't a gang robbing johns. And they weren't especially rich. So I was going to dismiss it all as Thiessen trying to end his career on some fantastic case, which was the conclusion of his captain, until I returned to Vienna."

"Look that way," Klimt said, pointing to a table over his shoulder. "There you go. So what happened when you returned?"

"I sent one of my detectives back to the area to see if anyone had seen anything, and one old woman had heard a window crash in the middle of the night. Of course any glass on the street had long since been cleaned up, but my man spotted a window frame, three stories up, that hadn't been painted, as if the entire window, frame and all, had been replaced recently, so he went to the apartment, where he found a fellow of about forty, a printer who worked in a shop nearby, and with a little pressure confessed that on the night that Thiessen was killed, he had picked up a prostitute, a very pretty, tall blonde, he said. He was beside himself. He was a widower, who had recently lost his wife to cancer, and he kept swearing that this was the first time he'd ever hired a whore. But before they could do anything, a man announced that he was police and burst through the door, followed by a big dog, and the woman jumped through the window to escape."

"Three stories? Did your detective find her body?"

"No, that's the thing. We know it was Thiessen who burst into his room, the painter described his coat exactly. And of course the dog was the one mentioned in the telegram from London, from whoever was sponsoring Thiessen's investigation. But there was no evidence of the woman. And he said he doubted if she was more than twenty years old, so she certainly hadn't been strangling johns in Amsterdam for thirty years. The next day he threw her clothes in the bin. There was no identification and very little money. She gave him the impression that she had picked him up out of desperation, because she needed money, not as if she was a working regular."

"Interesting," Klimt said. "Has anyone else seen this strange woman?"

"Well, that, actually, is why I sought you out."

"Not because I had asked about the Dutch policeman?"

"No, because one of my beat patrolmen has been bragging about coming to your studio with a newspaper boy who claimed that you fished a naked woman out of the Danube canal that morning."

"Ridiculous." Klimt didn't look up from his drawing; he was afraid to.

"When you're famous, Gus, people remember talking with you."

Gus? What was it with people calling him Gus, like he was a shoeshine boy? He carefully signed his drawing with the Art Nouveau–style calligraphy he had cultivated over the years, as distinct as the stamp on a Japanese print. "Voilà!" he said, tearing the portrait out of his notebook and holding it out to Kruger. "My gift to you, my friend."

Kruger took the sheet in his big paws and held it like he was handling a holy relic. "Oh—I–oh—my wife will be thrilled. I'll have it framed. We will have a signed Klimt in our little apartment. Why, I could never—"

Klimt held up his hand and smiled. "It was nothing. My pleasure," said the maestro.

"Well, let me pay for your coffee at least," said Kruger, mesmerized by the drawing.

"If you insist," said Klimt.

19

A BLUE DANUBE WALTZ
WITH HENCHMEN

When Klimt returned to his studio from his meeting with Commandant Kruger it was his intent to send all the models home, except Judith, so he could have a word with her, but upon seeing that they actually had painted Anna blue, he amended his plan.

"She's so strong," Anna said. The blonde was wearing only a kimono and it was clear that the only parts of her not painted blue were her hair and her toenails. She put him in mind of a Matisse, but drawn better.

"She is," said Ella. "But also we helped." Klimt noted that Ella, Trudy, and Judith were blue from their hands up to the middles of their forearms.

"It was three against one," whined Anna.

"There's some oil soap in the kitchen. You'll want to use that to take the paint off, not mineral spirits or turpentine, those will make her sick."

"Won't it just wear off over time?" Trudy, the tall brunette, asked.

Klimt sighed. "There are Giottos in the Uffizi Gallery that are over five hundred years old and the blue is still vivid and intact."

"So no?" Trudy said.

"We could sell her to the circus," Ella said.

"I'd like that," said Judith.

"I wouldn't like that," said Anna.

"Take her to the bathroom," Klimt said. "Run a tub, and use lots of oil soap. Do you know how to light the water heater?"

"I do! I do!" said Ella.

"You're in charge, *cher*. Trudy, help her please." Klimt looked to Judith. "Could we have a word in the parlor?"

Ella took one of Anna's arms and led her out of the room, her nose in the air, unable to suppress her specialness since the master had addressed her affectionately in French. *Cher*.

Judith, wearing her knickers and a white cotton chemise, padded into the parlor and sat on the divan. Geoff trotted out of the kitchen, showing a distinct blue corona around his mouth, extending to his nose, teeth, and tongue.

"Geoff helped," Judith said.

"I don't think that paint is good for him."

"He'll be fine. Geoff is very durable."

Klimt sat at the other end of the divan, cleared his throat, then dove in. "Judith, were you a murdering prostitute in Amsterdam?"

"Seems as if that may be the case."

"Why didn't you tell me?"

"I only remembered when I choked Egon out."

"You murdered Schiele?"

"No, I was just teaching him to be more respectful to Wally. He's safely in jail for corrupting children."

"So, there, you were with many men. Sex wasn't unusual for you?"

"A means to an end. A job."

"When I pulled you from the canal I sensed you were extraordinary. Untouchable."

"Was it because I was dead? Because evidently I make an irresistible corpse."

"No. I mean yes, when I started drawing you. But even after I realized you weren't dead. Precious. Like if someone touched you they would burst into flames."

"I don't remember that happening, but not everything has come back to me yet. But I suppose it could have. I *did* murder my clients."

"That's true? I mean, is that true?"

"Several. Perhaps many. But not all at once."

"So I gathered, but—"

"And you *did* name me Judith, so maybe you sensed that."

"Did you kill the cop on the bridge the night I found you?"

"I don't know. Possibly. I don't remember."

"The Dutch policeman, the dead one, believed that a prostitute had been murdering her johns in Amsterdam, on and off, for thirty years."

"That's possible, I suppose."

"How is that possible? Thirty years? Look at you. I thought you were nineteen—twenty at the most."

"I told you, I died four times, so I don't age. Didn't I tell you that?"

"Yes, but I thought that was because you were mad. How can that be true?"

"If it makes you feel better, both things can be true."

"That doesn't make me feel better."

"Are you going to throw me out?"

"No, of course not. I still want to do the painting of you. But should you stay here? It's not safe. Do you know the other Dutchman who is after you? Did you remember him from before, in Amsterdam?"

"No, but now I would recognize him, from seeing him outside of Emilie's studio."

"Do you know why he is after you?"

"I have no idea."

"Well, he's not really a policeman, so it's not about the murders. Other crimes? Have you stolen something?"

"I keep trying to remember, but nothing. Maybe my new doctor will help me."

"Have you remembered your name?"

"No."

He hung his head, rubbed his temples, more to buy himself a moment than to relieve any tension. "I'm sorry," he said. He meant it. When he'd called her Judith he'd been responding to a feeling she inspired in him, seductive dread, perhaps, that and the beheaded policeman found in her proximity, but now it seemed cruel. "I can call you something else if—"

"It's fine. I like it. You shouldn't feel bad. You saved me. You fed me, clothed me, saw to it that I've been looked out for. You've been very kind to me. You have nothing to be sorry for. In fact, I am not untouchable, and if you'd like to go into the storeroom with me—"

"No!" he barked. Then, more softly, "No, thank you."

"Perhaps a hand job. Wally says they work wonders. Although I can't promise you I won't get blue paint on your willy."

"No! No more hand jobs!"

"Well, if you want more than that there's negotiating to be done."

"That's not what I mean. What negotiating?"

"I just found out I was a prostitute for many years, I probably have valuable skills."

"Do you remember them? The skills?"

"Just disposing of the bodies stands out, and the choking, of course."

"Well, I don't want *that*."

"Have you tried it? Some gents came to enjoy it, others could not be convinced."

"And you? Did you enjoy it?"

"I never choked anyone who didn't hurt me or someone else, I'm relatively sure of that. If they returned—paid me—I made them promise they would never hurt anyone again. Anyone."

"That seems closer to the Judith of the Bible. Beautiful, just, fierce." He was thinking about the painting now; he couldn't help himself. She *was* the femme fatale from legend. Maybe he'd pose her with a sword. Like Donatello's *David* he'd seen in Florence, delicate, demure, yet deadly.

"So, the storeroom?" She bounced her eyebrows at him.

"No. Thank you. I don't think that would be appropriate."

"I've embarrassed you." She pulled away from him, hugged her knees to her chest. "I'm still learning what's appropriate."

"I am too, apparently. Am I too old to start drawing new lines? Ethically?"

"You are asking a murdering, blue-handed monster, sitting on your couch in her underwear."

"You're clever, aren't you? You talk like a child or a loon sometimes, but I think you're clever and you just don't remember that you are."

"Thank you?"

"Emilie is clever too. More clever than I am."

"She is very clever."

"It's her most annoying quality."

"I can't wait to tell her."

"Oh, she knows."

Van Beek waited at the train station for the noon train arriving from Zurich, but he wasn't sure what he was waiting for. He had no description of the "agents" he was meeting, but he had wired Amsterdam to tell them to look for a man in a brown suit and a deerstalker cap. As the arriving passengers filed down the platform,

Van Beek ducked behind an iron girder and took a quick swig of Mother Hagen's Cough Killer. He was going to have to improvise, and cough killer calmed his nerves.

Men in suits, mostly, and women in dresses and hats passed him, but none looked like what he expected, which were a couple of thugs from the same mold as the two he'd hired to snatch the girl. Nobody exiting the train fit that description.

"Herr Van Beek?" a voice said from behind him—*right* behind him. He nearly jumped out of his shoes. He turned to look into the top button of a very tall, very broad-shouldered man in his midtwenties, in shirtsleeves, carrying a jacket draped over one arm. Next to him stood another young man just as tall and broad, dressed in almost the same way, but wearing a light canvas jacket. They looked like farm boys dressed to go into town. Each had a great mop of straw-colored hair. Neither wore a hat.

"Who is asking?" Van Beek said, dropping the bottle of Mother Hagen's into his breast pocket, keeping his hand there near the butt of the revolver.

"We were sent from Zurich to meet you," said the second. "Where is the girl?"

"About that," said Van Beek. "I couldn't very well bring her to the platform, could I? But I know where she is."

"You will take us to her." A simple statement of fact.

"Do you have my fee?"

"When you deliver the girl. Unharmed. You didn't harm her, did you?"

"No, no, she's fine. But the thing is, she's not actually in my—I don't have her anymore." The two of them seemed suddenly to get larger—that couldn't be real, could it? Must have been the cough killer. Sometimes it played with his vision. If you drank enough of it, the furniture would appear to breathe. "She's at the studio of an artist she works for. You'll have to fetch her yourself."

"We were told she was working as a prostitute."

"I don't know anything about that. I'll hail a taxi."

Fifteen minutes later they climbed out of a carriage in front of Klimt's studio.

Van Beek said, "I'll have my fee now, if you please."

"When we have the girl."

"Are you going to just break in in the middle of the day and take her?" He didn't want to tell them that he had tried that and it hadn't worked out well, or about the dog. He really didn't relish facing the dog again.

"No, we are going to knock on the door," said the fellow in the canvas jacket.

"Unless they have a doorbell," said the other one. He led them to the door and knocked.

Van Beek grasped the butt of his revolver, ready to pull it if these two giants rushed inside.

Specters moved behind the reeded glass sidelight. Klimt opened the door and seemed taken aback that there were three men standing there. He looked past the two Swissers, right at Van Beek.

"I told you I couldn't help you."

Van Beek could tell there was another figure standing behind the door, a woman in a white chemise, it appeared. Canvas Jacket stepped in front of Van Beek and said, "*Mein Herr*, we have traveled from Zurich. We are interested in buying the employment contract of one of your employees. The young woman from Amsterdam."

"I don't know what you're talking about," Klimt said. "Who sent you?"

"Our employer is a physician. He believes he can help the woman."

"Yet you don't know her name, and you don't know the name of your employer."

"The young woman has changed her name many times. You

may know her as a different one than we have. Our employer is Dr. Frankenstein."

"That means nothing to me. I'm working, gentlemen, and I must get back to it, so good day."

Klimt began to push the door closed, and Van Beek stepped between the two Swiss giants and put his foot in the doorjamb, then pulled the pistol from his shoulder holster and pushed it into Klimt's face. Before he could voice a credible threat something struck his forearm with such force that the bones shattered and he screamed and leapt back. The gun thudded onto the wooden floor inside.

"Akhlut, *tuvlaugaa!*"* the woman inside the door shouted; then she pulled the painter away as she pulled the door open.

Through the white light of his pain, Van Beek saw the wolf dog coming through the parlor. "Run!" Cradling his broken arm in his good one, he ran, not looking back, hoping that the Swissers might distract the dog long enough for him to escape the walled garden. He looked over his shoulder to see the Swissers only begin to run as the wolf dog cleared the doorway and the girl slammed the door behind him. He made it to the street outside the wall before he heard their screams.

*J*udith opened the door a crack and barked, "*Aakka,* Akhlut! *Aakka!*"

Klimt was on the floor, where, basically, she had thrown him. He looked up in confusion and wonder. "I heard his arm break when you hit it."

She shrugged. "He had a gun."

Klimt stood, dusted himself off. "We should send for the police."

---

* "Akhlut, protect!

"Or keep the gun for next time. Do you want to explain how you are employing a killer hooker?"

"There were three this time. What if they send more next time? Who is this Frankenstein, anyway? Do you remember him?"

"I remember what Adam told me. Adam, the patchwork man who kept me as a slave on the ice—"

"Yes, Freud told me that was one of your dreams. He thinks—"

"I know, he thinks Adam is a memory of an older relative from my childhood who locked me in a closet and abused me. No. Not a dream, Gus, I'm sure of it now. Adam said that Frankenstein was *our father*, the man who brought us back from the dead."

"Do you remember what happened to him? Did Adam say?"

"Yes. He said that he tore his head off when he took me from the *Prometheus*. The ship."

"*Tore* his head off? Is that even possible?"

She shrugged. "Adam was a true monster. So, where should I put the gun?"

"We have to move you. I have to move. I can't paint with this— this chaos—this violence hanging over me."

"Yes you can." She squeezed his shoulder like a reassuring mentor.

There was a yowling chuff at the door. Judith opened it a crack, peeked out, and pulled it open for Geoff, who trotted in carrying a large work boot in his mouth. Judith looked out into the garden, spotted no carnage, and pushed it shut. "So that went well?"

He answered with a boot-muted aroo.

"What? What?" Klimt looked back and forth from the dog to the girl and back again.

"Fine," Judith said. "No bodies to hide."

Klimt's confusion turned to panic. "I have to do that painting. I can start sketches with you in one of the kimonos, but we need to get the gown from Emilie finished. Has she finished the fitting? I can't take you there—"

She patted his arm. "I know, I know, if she ever connects studio Klimt with Attersee Klimt she'll shatter like the fragile crystal doll that she is." She rolled her eyes. "It's fine, Gus. I'll go with Wally when she gets back. She loves going to Emilie's."

"Yes. Yes. She is an extraordinary woman. Extraordinary."

"I like Wally too," Judith said. "She's my only friend."

Klimt started to correct her but thought better of it.

Van Beek sat on the floor of his hotel room across from the two enormous Swissers, who sat on his bed, tending to their wounds. Their ankles and shins were bleeding with scrapes and punctures from the wolf dog's teeth. They were both able to walk without help, but it had taken some first aid in the motor taxi to stop the bleeding, which Van Beek made them pay for on the spot. One of them had lost a small toe, and so that was how Van Beek could tell them apart.

"Why didn't you tell us?" said Nine Toes.

"You knew about this," said Ten Toes. "How could you let us walk into a trap like that?"

Van Beek sighed. He had finished off a bottle of Mother Hagen's Cough Killer and had split a second bottle among the three of them. He told them it would help with their pain, and it had. It had helped with his arm, which the hotel doctor had set and put into a cast for an obscene amount of the Swissers' money. If not for Mother Hagen's he'd have gone into shock from the pain. Now he was feeling wistful, contemplative, lucky, like a fellow who had gotten out of the garden before the enormous fucking dog could eat his shoes.

"Well, gentlemen, the information about the dog was available upon payment, but you decided to not pay me, so I thought it best if you saw in person the difficulties I faced." They still had his fee and he would have it one way or another. If the woman hadn't relieved him of his revolver he'd have robbed them and been on his way back to Amsterdam, but they were stubborn, and large, and he was unarmed and wearing a cast.

"That is not possible," said Nine Toes. "That creature was too large to get through the door."

"Too large to exist," said Ten. "This is some kind of evil science."

Van Beek dusted off one of his shoes with his handkerchief, a soft display of his position of authority (the one with shoes). "That may be, but what do we do now? I have some ideas, but I'm afraid I'll need to be paid before I share them with you."

"We can do nothing until we report back to our master," said Ten Toes.

"I'm still bleeding," said Nine Toes.

"I will factor that into the plan," said Van Beek.

"We have to wire home for instructions," said Ten Toes.

"You can't go to the telegraph office like that," said Nine Toes, nodding to Van Beek's arm and torn shirtsleeve.

"I can," said Van Beek. "In fact, if you want to write out your message, I will go out, find us some food, buy you each some shoes, and book you another room in the hotel."

"That would be good," said Ten Toes. "Would you do that?"

"I will. But I will require my fee, plus ten percent, and, of course, the price of the room, the shoes, and the wire."

"We will need new trousers, too," said Nine Toes. "And fresh bandages."

"Done!" said Van Beek. "The money, please." He held out his hand.

Ten Toes pulled an envelope out of the pocket of his canvas jacket and began counting bills.

"Oh, Swiss francs?" said Van Beek, putting his good hand up

as if the money had been dipped in leprosy. "That will require an exchange bonus."

Ten Toes looked bewildered at the stacks of bills he held in either hand, looked back and forth, as if trying to figure out the value by weight. Van Beek saved him by standing and snatching both stacks away.

"This will do nicely."

Ten Toes hung his head. "That is all of our money."

"Did you buy round-trip tickets?" asked Van Beek.

The two Swissers nodded sadly.

"Then you'll be fine. I'll be back in a tick with food and shoes and we'll get you moved to a room with a bath where you can clean up and heal."

"Thank you," said Nine Toes. "Some fresh bandages and antiseptic if you please."

"Of course," said Van Beek. He picked up his valise and headed to the door.

"Do you need your bag?" asked Ten.

"I need to bring two full outfits of clothing back, I think I do."

"Very well. Be quick. I'm starving," said Ten.

"I'll have food sent up right away," said Van Beek. He tipped the brim of his deerstalker hat as he backed out of the room, then he sauntered down the hall, trying to think of a hotel nearby where he could stay for the night. It was too late to catch a train back to Amsterdam. He'd leave in the morning, perhaps a nice meal, a bath to wash this entire job off of him tonight—Vienna, artists, giant dogs, giant Swissers, all of it in the past. Maybe he'd treat himself to a fresh flask of Mother Hagen's and a whore to suck him to sleep. Rewards for a job well done.

DANGEROUS PLAYTHINGS

*M*y urchins were shit," said Wally. "Krumau has shit urchins."

They were walking down Mariahilferstrasse on their way to Schwestern Flöge to have Judith fitted to the gown she would pose in for Klimt's painting. The right side of Wally's face was swollen and purple, as was much of her right arm, the result of her failed attempt to break Egon out of prison.

"They seemed nice," said Judith. "One introduced me to a marmot."

"Well, they're shit at prison breaks. I hired four of them to help me get Egon out of prison, and they were useless. They were supposed to start a fire at the front of the jail, then I would climb the short side of the building, climb down a rope to Egon's window, and saw off one of the bars, then we would both slide down to the ground and get away. But they didn't start the fire, so as I was lowering myself to Egon's window the jailer opened another window and yelled at me, so I fell. I had tied the end of the rope around my waist, so I didn't fall all the way to the ground, but I swung into the wall really hard."

"Was the bar on Egon's window made of iron? How were you going to saw through that?"

"That wasn't the problem, the problem is I was surprised. Everyone knows you do not send Pee Pants to fetch the matches because he will put them in his pocket and they'll be too damp to light when you need them."

"Does everybody know that?" asked Judith.

"I should have known from his nickname."

"Does that still hurt? It looks like it hurts."

"It hurts a lot," said Wally, touching her purple cheek and wincing. "But I was saving him."

"What made you think you could do that?"

"Well, I saved you, and look how good you turned out."

"No, I mean, what made you think you could do all the climbing and rope tying and things?"

"Before my father died, when I was eleven, we used to read *The Count of Monte Cristo* together. I thought I was an expert at breaking out of prison."

(The jailer had called a woman from the church to minister to Wally's injuries. He'd thought about taking her before the magistrate but reconsidered. He wasn't even sure what she'd done was a crime, and the poor girl's face looked like a summer plum and he didn't want to punish her any further. Also, if she were put in his jail she wouldn't stop shouting to Schiele, which was wildly annoying. She'd returned to Vienna at Schiele's insistence, as he'd received a wire from Gertie saying Klimt needed Wally's help with Judith.)

The models tied Geoff up outside the café and left instructions with the waitress to give him a croissant if he got restless. They found Emilie on the second floor, talking to a tall young man with protruding ears and such an overall aspect of anxiety that they stayed by the double doors and watched rather than going in.

"Please, Fräulein Flöge, I know you have Alma's measurements. I need them exact or the dollmaker will not be able to construct a suitable model. And I will order a gown for the doll as well. I would like it to have structure but for the fabric to be pleasant to the touch."

Emilie Flöge wasn't buying the young man's pitch. "Oskar, I cannot give you Alma's measurements. My clients depend upon my discretion."

"Oskar?" Wally whispered to Judith. "I think that is Oskar Kokoschka, one of Egon's group of painters—the Expressionists."

Oskar said, "She is a sensuous flesh dreadnought and I have perished on the bow of her bosom."

Emilie looked past Kokoschka to the two models at the door; her face went from delight to concern when she saw Wally's bruised face. "Oh my. Excuse me, Oskar," she said. She hurried to meet the girls, reached out, and took Wally's hands in hers.

"Child, what has happened to you? If this is Schiele's doing I will have him beaten."

"She tried to break Egon out of prison but her urchins were shit," said Judith cheerfully. "But I will be happy to beat Egon if you think it will help."

"Does it really look that bad?" asked Wally, touching her cheek and wincing.

Emilie nodded gravely. "No, it will heal. Have you seen a doctor to check that no bones are broken?"

"Yes, they had a doctor come to the jail. He gave me a tincture for the pain."

"It works wonderfully," said Judith. "Wally put some in my coffee and I can't even feel my face."

"You're Schiele's new model," said Kokoschka, who had crossed the room and stood behind Emilie. "You're absolutely grotesque! No wonder he's so fascinated with you."

"He said he was fascinated with me?" Wally said, bright and purple.

Emilie stepped between the painter and the models. "Oskar, you need to fuck off now."

"But I still need——"

Emilie put her hand before Kokoschka's face. "Now, Oskar! Go downstairs to the café and wait for me."

"But——"

"Can I?" Judith asked Wally, bouncing on her toes in anticipation.

"No!" Wally said.

"What?" asked Emilie.

"I know a way to make men more cooperative," Judith said.

Kokoschka slunk away, out the double doors and down the stairs.

"One second," Emilie said, patting Wally's hands. "Greta, come here please," she called to the empty room.

Greta, mistress of the measuring tape, came breezing from behind one of the changing screens, stopped, and stood at attention, waiting for orders.

"Greta, I need you to fetch some Spanish lace from upstairs, and the green silk peach-basket hat, the one with the faux jewel. We're going to make Wally a veil." She leaned in and whispered to Wally. "It will just cover the one side of your face—you will appear intriguing and mysterious." Back to Greta: "After you bring the hat, I'd like you to go downstairs to the café and offer to sell Alma Mahler's measurements to Oskar Kokoschka. And make sure you get a fair price. That boy is desperate and will pay all he has."

Greta, normally the model of urgent efficiency, said, "But, madame, discretion——"

"Discretion is for me, Greta. A house of fashion can't share information about their valued clients, but there's no reason an enterprising seamstress in possession of that same information shouldn't profit from it."

"Thank you, madame. But what if Frau Mahler finds out?"

"Tell me, Greta, do you think that you could guess Frau Mahler's measurements by just looking at her?"

"Within a centimeter, madam," said Greta.

"Then that shall be our defense. Oskar has intimate knowledge of Alma's shape, our numbers are not going to help his efforts, but if it comes up, we will say that he simply guessed. If it makes you feel better, you can lie."

"Oh, madame," Greta said, covering her mouth as if stifling a mischievous giggle. She hurried away to go about her tasks.

"Come in, ladies. Tell me about your adventures. How was prison, Wally? Was it ghastly?"

They followed Emilie to the opposite side of the great studio, where she rolled one of the changing screens aside to reveal a small table and chairs. "Sit sit sit. I'll call down to the café and have them send up coffee and pastry."

Emilie went to a brass tube on the wall, with a string near it. She pulled the string, then put her ear to the tube. When it was obvious she heard something, she spoke into the tube. "Bring us three cappuccinos and a plate of cookies, please." She turned and grinned at the models. "I can talk directly to the kitchen in the café. My sister, Helene, hates it. She runs the café, you know?"

She joined them at the table. "So, that young man was Oskar Kokoschka. I hope you'll forgive me for not introducing you, but I very much wanted him to go away. Alma Mahler is coming in for a fitting. I hoped you two might meet her, but I did not want him to see her."

"Why did he want her measurements?" asked Judith.

"He's obsessed with her," Emilie said. "She broke off her affair with him and won't see him, so he's having a life-sized doll built to replace her. I wouldn't be surprised if he came here today because he found out she had a fitting."

Wally, confused, scrunched up her face, then winced from the pain. "I thought her husband just died."

"He did. The affair was going on while Mahler was still alive. As was her affair with Walter Gropius, the architect."

"She stays busy," Judith said.

"Is the doll—is he going to shag the doll?" Wally asked.

"It seems that is his intention," Emilie said. "Thus the measurements. He's commissioned a dollmaker in Munich. He's instructed him to stuff it with horsehair, so it feels like 'sinew under fat,' he said. He said the dollmaker had covered the first draft of the doll with fine white feathers, so it had more of a feeling of a polar bear rug than a woman."

"Well if he tries to fuck a polar bear he'll be cured of his obsession, I can tell you that," Judith said.

They both looked at her.

"Sorry," Judith said. Then, quickly changing the subject, "What's a dreadnought?"

"A battleship," said Emilie.

"Well no wonder she dumped him," Wally said. "He compared her bosom to a battleship. If Egon ever calls me a battleship—"

"I'll choke the life out of him," said Judith.

"Thank you," Wally said.

"You're welcome."

Emilie didn't follow the girls' conversation, but they were young and silly and she allowed them that. "Alma Mahler is one of the most accomplished women in Vienna," Emilie said. "Mind you, she's a bitch, but she's amazing on the piano, and if she hadn't put her music aside for Mahler, she might have been a renowned composer. She's brilliant. She memorized Nietzsche's *Thus Spake Zarathustra* when she was seventeen, yet this, this—"

"Grotesque fuck-beast?" Wally offered.

"Yes! This *grotesque little fuck-beast* thinks he can replicate her with horsehair stuffing and a dress." Emilie regarded Wally. "That's good."

"Egon," Wally explained.

"Egon is also a grotesque fuck-beast," Judith clarified. "Sometimes a disgusting fuck-beast."

"These men, these artists, who try to define us by where they want to stick their dick. I'll not have it. As if we have no will of our own. Fucking Nietzsche, for men he postulates the Übermensch, above all rules and morals, but for women, he says we exist only for the child, and to men we represent only danger and play. *The most dangerous plaything*," Emilie mimicked, spitting with disgust, then laughed at herself.

"Why is there no Überfrau?" Judith asked.

"There is," Wally said. She patted Judith's hand.

They heard the doors squeak and saw a waitress in a long apron butt-bump through the double doors with a tray of coffee and cookies. She set the treats out on the table and Emilie thanked her.

"I don't think I've seen women waiting tables at the other cafés," said Wally, stirring some sugar into her coffee.

"Would you like to try it?" Emilie asked. "They make a decent wage. I have an in with the owner." She winked at Wally.

"Maybe," Wally said. She winked back and winced from the pain.

"Do you think your living should be threatened at the whim of an artist?" Emilie nibbled a cookie and raised her eyebrows, affecting the aspect of a wise and curious squirrel. She had resolved to help these poor girls ascend from their positions as pretty objects for exploitation by these male artists, to having control of their own fates. Perhaps this was why Gus had never let her meet any of his models.

"I can survive as a model, I think," Wally said.

"Plus we don't have to wear clothes to work," said Judith, spraying crumbs over the table.

"You're here to be fitted for a very expensive couture gown for work," Emilie said.

"You can't listen to me," Judith said. "I'm insane."

"She is," Wally agreed. "I think I might like being a nurse for the insane, too."

"That's the spirit," said Emilie.

"Do you think she'd have to shag the doctors?" Judith asked.

"That is not a requirement for all jobs, no," said Emilie. "Speaking of that, how are your sessions with Dr. Freud going?"

"He fired me because I can't remember my father's penis. He's turned me over to a Swiss doctor called Jung."

"Oh, Jung," Emilie said. "Much better, or at least different. I've read his papers as well. He believes we can all be defined by archetypes in the unconscious. Universal ones, common to all people. The hero, the goddess, the mother, the trickster. As if we are all living in the middle of a great unconscious opera."

"Oh, that!" said Judith. "Thank you for the gramophone. The girls love it."

"And Gus?"

"It made him uncomfortable."

Emilie grinned, mischief achieved. "We should get your fitting finished before Frau Mahler arrives. The gown is behind that screen. Put it on and when Greta gets back we'll pin you up."

Judith padded around the screen Emilie was pointing to and was stunned when she saw the gown.

"It's, it's so beautiful," Judith said. "Wally, come look."

"It is nothing without you in it, *cher*," said Emilie. "*You* will make it worthy of a Klimt."

*A*lma Mahler wore a black satin dress, complete with layered petticoats, and carried a black parasol. Her hat was large, with a wide brim, an explosion of black ostrich feathers, and a black veil that surrounded her head and shoulders like a Gothic beekeeper's. She leaned her parasol by the doors and folded back her veil to greet Emilie with an air kiss to each cheek.

Wally and Judith stood by the café table, where they'd been snacking with Emilie since Greta had finished the fitting. Wally wore the green hat Emilie had fixed for her; a structured veil of black Spanish lace covered the bruised side of her face and accentuated the wide, bright blue of the eye that was showing. Emilie had put extra mascara on her to enhance the effect.

"Well, she doesn't look like a battleship at all," Wally whispered.

"I thought she'd be fuzzier," Judith said. "But you can't really see her skin. Maybe she's only fuzzy when she's naked."

Wally turned to her. "What are you talking about?"

"The polar bear. Oskar said the doll was like a polar bear."

"Can you be a little less crazy, just while we're here?"

"I'll save up for Dr. Jung tomorrow."

"Thank you. And don't mention the prison break. Please."

Emilie breezed across the room toward them, Alma Mahler in tow. "And these two young women have been dying to meet you." She stepped aside and performed a presentation flourish as if it were a dance step in a formal waltz. "Alma, these are Wally and Judith. They are artist models. Ladies, this is Alma Mahler."

"Charmed," Alma said, offering her fingers to shake hands, again, as if she expected to be led onto the dance floor.

"Charmed," Judith parroted.

"I'm sorry to hear about your husband," Wally said. "He was an extraordinary composer."

"A terrible loss to you and the world," Emilie added.

"Being dead isn't all that bad," said Judith.

Wally clamped her hand over her mouth. "Fuck," she said softly, then, "Fuck, ow, fuck!" loudly, when she accidentally touched her bruise.

"Oh, child," said Alma Mahler. She stepped up and pushed Wally's veil aside. "What have you done?"

"An accident," Wally said.

"She fell while breaking Egon Schiele out of jail," Judith said.

Alma tilted Wally's head this way and that to get a better look at the injury, all the while tut-tutting. "Egon Schiele, the painter? Oskar has spoken of him. What is Schiele in jail for?"

Wally didn't answer. Her eyes darted around in panic.

"Showing dirty pictures to children," Judith offered. Wally moaned.

"It was a misunderstanding," Emilie explained, despite not knowing the particulars of the situation. "Some children visited his studio—he had drawings pinned on the walls."

"Art is wasted on children," Alma said. "As are women."

"Women only exist for the child," said Judith. "And for men are only danger and play."

Alma Mahler dropped Wally's chin and looked at Judith. "Nietzsche? A genius, no doubt, but a nitwit when it comes to women. When I was your age he captivated my imagination, his Übermensch, but as I've gotten older, perspective has allowed me to see his work more clearly. The torment of the Übermensch, above the practical and the comfortable, that is no place for a woman. I have found what comfort I can in the company of genius. Is your Egon Schiele a genius, child?"

Wally pulled her veil back down. "Egon says he and Kokoschka are breaking down the walls of artistic convention."

"Ah, Oskar may be a genius, maybe not, but Gropius is also a genius, and he is better in bed, so I choose him, for now."

"We get to choose?" Wally said.

"You get to choose. At your age, the only path I could find to live an elevated life, a life of greatness, was marriage, and I chose Mahler. Now I will choose again. But be sure a man will give himself to you, and take care of your needs, before you give yourself to him. That was my mistake with Mahler. He was a genius, and he made me give up my own music for him, so we both serviced his genius, but he was many years my senior, and he had a weak heart, so he did not see to my sexual appetites."

Emilie was standing behind Alma Mahler, grinning like the Cheshire cat, enjoying the looks of surprise and confusion playing over the girls' faces.

Wally said, "Well, I'm going to have a word with Egon when he gets out of prison."

"He sounds like a scoundrel," Alma said. She sighed, "But I can tolerate a scoundrel if he's a genius."

"He's more pleasant when you choke the breath out of him," Judith said with a smile.

"Shhhhh, Judith! No!" Wally scolded, as if she'd caught Geoff eating the master's shoes.

Alma stepped back, her eyebrows raised. "And you, tall girl who knows Nietzsche, what will be your path to greatness?"

Emilie stepped between them, in the interest of congeniality, but also because Judith appeared as if she might choke Alma Mahler. "Klimt is going to do a major painting of Judith. The girls are here to pick up the gown we've made for it."

"And you don't mind Klimt spending hours with this beauty? I could not do it, Emilie."

"I've promised not to boink him," Judith explained. "But he's been very kind."

"Well, you should know that both Emilie and I have posed for Klimt, but mine was only a drawing, when I was but a girl, while

Emilie has been the model for at least two major paintings—one, *The Kiss*, I believe is Klimt's greatest painting to date."

"Emilie has also been very kind," said Judith.

"Well, I couldn't do it. You have a way about you. I wouldn't let you near my man."

"That's probably good," said Wally. "If you want him to keep breathing."

"Ah, you are so silly," laughed Emilie. "Now, Alma, come look at the drawings I've done for your dress."

Alma excused herself from the younger women and wished them luck, then followed Emilie up the stairs, presumably to an office where she had a drawing board.

"She seems nice," said Judith.

"She seems like a bitch," said Wally.

"But Emilie wanted us to meet her, and Emilie is nice."

"I think Emilie is looking out for us and that was a warning."

Judith nodded, the lesson hitting home. "Don't cover yourself with fine feathers?"

"Yes, that's it," Wally said. "Let's go get Geoff and feed him pastries."

"I wonder if Oskar has ever tried to shag a swan . . . ," Judith mused.

"You can't let the feathers thing go, can you?"

"See what you think after I teach you about polar bears," Judith said.

THE INIMITABLE
DR. JUNG

*Y*oung Dr. Bauman was manning the desk at the clinic when Wally and Judith arrived. He seemed genuinely pleased to see them, or at least to see Wally, who still wore her green hat with the veil.

"Before you say anything, it was an accident and I'll recover soon and I'll be better than before."

"I was thinking you looked mysterious," Dr. Bauman said.

"Yes, that's what I mean," said Wally. "Let's go chat with some loonies."

"First, we don't use that term for the patients, and I need to introduce Judith to Dr. Jung. I'm on the desk for another quarter hour, then you can go on rounds with me if you'd like."

"I would very much like," Wally said.

"You'll have to leave the dog outside."

"But Geoff loves loonies, Judith is his favorite."

"Patients," Judith said, correcting her.

Dr. Bauman ignored Wally's protest and held out his arm as if presenting the staircase. "If you'll come this way, Judith."

The young doctor let Judith lead him up the stairs, then directed her to Freud's outer office, where a dark-haired man in his midthirties sat in one of Freud's wingback chairs leafing through a thick file. He was taller than Freud, as tall as Judith, and as fit as young Dr. Bauman. When he looked up and saw Judith he immediately jumped to his feet and went to greet her, nearly losing some of the papers from his file along the way.

"Judith, I'm so pleased to meet you. I've been looking forward to this."

She offered her hand in the limp, *do what you will with it* way she'd seen ladies do, and Jung gave her a warm handshake with a smile. "A pleasure," she said.

"Thank you, Dr. Bauman," Jung said, dismissing the young intern. Then, to Judith, "Please, come in, have a seat."

"Should I lie down on the couch?"

"As you wish. I thought we would chat for a while, and if we decide to continue with hypnosis perhaps you can move to the couch, where you can relax."

She sat in the wingback chair across from where he had been sitting and he took his seat. He patted the file and leaned forward. "I've read through all of Dr. Freud's notes from your sessions. You have some very interesting characters in your history."

"Do you think they're real? My friend Wally says I'm just insane."

"We don't say 'insane' anymore. I don't, anyway. When we did, it was an excuse for giving up. You may be insane, which is to say you may not be distinguishing between what is real and what is imagined, but all the details matter. A diagnosis—melancholy, psychosis, dementia praecox—doesn't matter except as it may lead to a path for treatment. What matters is your story. The details, real and imagined. Only when I know your entire story can I help find a cure. And that is what we are hoping for, isn't it?"

"I just want to find out who I am."

"Who you are is your story, Judith. Let's find out the rest of your story."

"I don't even know my real name. Judith is a name Gustav Klimt gave to me."

"Ah, Herr Klimt. I must confess, I was hoping he would accompany you. I admire his work."

"I'll ask him to come next time. He doesn't allow me to go out in the city by myself, and Wally comes with me most of the time because she likes Dr. Bauman and talking to loonies."

Jung winced at "loonies." He said, "I would love to meet him, but I will only be here in Vienna for a few days. With that in mind, I've blocked two hours for our session today, if that works for you."

"That will be fine. But, Doctor, Freud and I had an agreement, since I am learning everything over again, that he would explain his method to me as we went along—"

"Absolutely. We will reveal aspects of both of our stories. First, I would like to ask you about some of the dream figures you've spoken about, so I might learn their nature. These spirits, I think, you call Raven and Sedna and Adam, can you tell me about them?"

"Can I be honest with you, Doctor?"

"This process doesn't work any other way. And I promise to be honest with you. And I will not reveal what you tell me to anyone else."

"Even Dr. Freud?"

"Dr. Freud will probably want to hear what you have to say, but I won't tell him either, if you'd rather I didn't."

"Just tell him you were able to find my father's penis and it was huge."

Jung laughed. "He would be much more comfortable with that than with what I suspect we are going to find out."

"Oh, Dr. Jung, I like the way you think. What should we tell him?"

"I can see you have embraced the trickster aspect of your nature. Perhaps we will tell him that what he thinks are figments of your dreams are more."

"Like Adam and Raven and Sedna?"

"Let's start with Raven and Sedna. You said in your session with Freud that Raven was a god. Do you remember how you encountered him?"

"I spoke of him when I was under hypnosis. When I woke up I remembered that I met Raven in the Underworld, and since then he is always with me."

"And Sedna?"

"The same. She is quieter, and usually when she speaks to me it is to tell me to feed someone or help them."

"Because she brings fish and game to the People?"

"Yes, how did you know?"

"I sent for a monograph from a Danish researcher called Rasmussen. He was raised among the Inuit people of Greenland, and he speaks their language fluently. He transcribed their oral traditions, the stories they tell of their gods and heroes. It was only available in Danish so I had a student translate it into German for me. Rasmussen's accounts of Raven and Sedna are exactly as you describe them."

"How would I know that? I don't speak Danish, not that I remember."

"I think you experienced them directly, through something I call the collective unconscious, which is something I think we all share but we are not aware of in our conscious world. People from many different cultures manifest the same myths, the same gods, the same heroes, although sometimes with different names and forms, even when there is no physical contact between the cultures. I call them archetypes. I don't know how you did it, but you managed to make the unconscious conscious."

"I think I do. Did Freud not tell you? I died four times, and returned."

"He mentions it in his notes, but he thinks you are confusing being beaten unconscious with death. You remember surviving a horrible trauma as coming to life again."

"No. I died four times and came back to life. I died and visited the Underworld, which is where I met Raven and Sedna and Akhlut. Lived with them. Or whatever living is there. This is the point where we start using the term 'loony' again, right?"

"Akhlut? That name is not in Freud's notes."

"Akhlut is, well, he's not—he doesn't speak well."

"He is not articulate?"

"Yes! That's the word. He isn't articulate. He is savage. But he is a god in the Underworld—a giant wolf when he is on land, and an orca when he is in the water. He changes at will. He followed me here too, would you like to meet him?"

"I hope to meet them all."

"I can't call up Raven and Sedna, but Akhlut is just downstairs. We call him Geoff. With a G. He's a silly boy."

Jung smiled and finished writing a note with a flourish. "But according to Professor Freud, you can access them when you are under hypnosis."

"So he says."

"Like Professor Freud, I have not used hypnosis in my practice for years, but I am certainly willing to try it again if you are."

"Will I find out who I am?"

"That is the intention. We may find out who we both are in the process."

"My friend Wally was afraid that Dr. Freud would put me under and have his way with me. That's not your intention, is it, Dr. Jung?"

"Quite the opposite."

"I'll have my way with you?"

"In a manner of speaking. I feel as if what we discover may change us both."

"Let's start." She leapt out of the chair and plopped down on the fainting couch. "Do you have a watch or do you want to borrow Freud's? I tried to take it, but he made me give it back."

"I thought I'd use the tip of my pen."

"You rascal."

"Perhaps Raven rises in me as well." Jung smiled.

"Doctor, you didn't mention Adam among your—your—"

"Archetypes. Yes, I feel as if the Adam figure is different. Didn't you say that?"

"No, he's not of the Underworld. He was on the ice. He, like me, returned from the dead."

"I see." Jung made a note. "Shall we begin?"

Two minutes later Judith was in a trance. Jung checked his notes from Freud, then began the questions.

"You said that when you awoke after falling off the cliff, you had not died. Do you remember what happened after that?"

"It was summer then, so the ice had broken up around the island and the bears were everywhere. We had to be mindful of bears all the time. We kept spears inside the stone house that Adam had built and would block the entry with stones when we slept. When I say 'house,' it was a hut, really. I couldn't stand up inside and Adam was doubled over. Even the ceiling was made of stone, supported with driftwood to keep out the bears, something Adam had figured out how to do after he murdered the hunters, before I returned to life. He draped a sealskin tent over the roof to keep out the rain.

"With the summer rain, there was standing water all over the island, where the mosquitos bred. Driftwood was plentiful, great tangles of it driven up the edges of the sea cliffs, so we kept a fire going all the time to keep mosquitos away. There was a massive glacier, miles across, and rivers of fresh water poured off of it and carved out crevices in the glacier that seemed to go down for hundreds of feet. We explored the glacier, looking for food, but always probing the surface for hidden faults, and always wearing the bone goggles with the thin slits in them that the hunters used to prevent snow blindness. In the short hours of darkness we burned seal oil the Native hunters had left in a shallow stone bowl carved out for that purpose, but Adam was right, hunting without the ice or the skin boats was difficult on the island in summer, so we conserved the oil."

Jung said, "You said 'we,' as if you and Adam were cooperating. Did you try to escape again?"

"I did, and again Adam caught me and dragged me back and would resume his torture and humiliation. He said it was my wifely duty. I found if I stopped fighting, just submitted and let him do his dread deed, he was less violent, there was less pain. I fell into the mindset of a slave, a beaten creature who fills a routine to avoid suffering. I lost my will to escape or rebel. All the time, though, when I felt my mind go vacant, Raven was in my ear, telling me to escape, plotting how to kill Adam. When Adam slept he tethered me to him by a strong rope and kept the knives outside of the hut. He had disassembled the hunters' skin boats so we might use the materials, so there was no escape by sea."

"You said that Adam had also returned from the dead. Did he not hear the voices of the spirits there?"

"He didn't. Because I had learned to hunt and fish and sew, the skills of the People, in the Underworld, Adam would ask me how I had learned. I realized he knew nothing of the Animal People or the gods of the Underworld. He had never heard of Sedna or Akhlut, and Raven to him was just a bird."

"Why do you think Adam didn't experience the Underworld?"

"Because he was a patchwork man, Raven told me. The second time Adam murdered me and I woke up in the Underworld, I was afraid I had killed him, driven an icicle into his brain, and he would follow me. He survived my attack, but I didn't know that at the time. Raven told me he could not follow me. He was man of meat only, not a person. He was soulless. Even animals pass in and out of the

Underworld; we call them the Animal People there, and they can talk there, but not Adam. I don't know where he went when he was dead."

"When you were dead, in the Underworld, did you have a sense of your body?"

"No. A small mercy. Who knows what evil Adam got up to with my corpse while I was away, I mean beyond cutting every inch of my skin in a grid to scar me and make me as hideous to the eye as he was."

"But you weren't. You have no scars I can see."

"They healed. More than they would for a normal person. Now, if I'm very cold or flushed with heat you can see very fine white lines on my skin from the cuts. I had forgotten them, but Klimt mentioned he could see them sometimes. He is very observant."

"So that part of you in the Underworld, interacting with Raven and the others, you called it your soul, but it is a consciousness, with your thoughts and feelings, even without your body?"

"Yes."

"Yet you don't remember your first life, we'll call it? The person you were before Adam murdered you the first time in Edinburgh?"

"No. Raven and Sedna don't know that person either. I asked them. They did not meet me until I woke up after Adam murdered me the second time, but I had sensed them before. Adam told me I had spent months in the crate, unconscious, dead, even. I think during that time, at least when I was in the box on the ice, and later on the ship, I could hear voices from the Underworld."

"And these voices, they were in a language you understood?"

"Yes, I remember them as pictures, symbols, the way you remember a dream as real. But after I died, I could understand all languages."

"And that is true outside of the Underworld? You can understand all languages?"

"It seems so. I can speak English, which Adam said was my native language, as well as Dutch, German, French, and the language of the People."

"We'll call that Inuit," Jung said. "And you don't remember having to learn these languages?"

"When Adam first took me onto the ice he spoke to me in English. He read aloud from Shakespeare and Chaucer to practice his English, although I'm not sure Chaucer helped. He had learned to speak French while hiding in a pigsty in the Alps, outside an old blind man's house. I don't know where he learned German. Perhaps it came to him from memory, the way it did to me the last time I died, here in Vienna. He knew less about his past before Frankenstein raised him from the dead than I did about mine. All he would talk about was the suffering Frankenstein had raised him into, the pain and alienation, as if he would find a sympathetic ear in his prisoner, his slave. The only way to quiet him was to kill him."

"You killed him?"

She was quiet for a moment. Jung waited, didn't want to interrupt the silence even with the scratch of his pen.

"It was the spring. We had spent the winter in the stone hut, burning seal oil and making small fires of driftwood. I had learned to hunt from Sedna. When the ice returned we found the air holes that seals use to breathe. You wait for them to come up for air and harpoon them. Sometimes they would lie on top of the ice near a larger hole, but it was almost impossible to get close enough to them to spear them unless the weather was bad, which was as dangerous as the bears, who also hunted seals at the air holes.

"Anyway, it was spring, and we had made it through the winter, and we'd procured enough meat and oil to make it through another, but we still hunted on the thinner ice.

"Maybe it had been more than one winter, I don't remember.

Faced with monotony, passing time in a small space with a monster who tortured me, I became numb—I retreated into my own world, which was the Underworld. While Adam yammered on in the stone hut, in my head Raven chanted to me, *'Slay him, slay him, slay him,'* and when I would ask, *'How?'* Raven would say, *'Crush his skull with a stone,'* so I tried that. I was beaten unconscious, and afterward I had to tend to Adam's semicrushed skull until he healed. *'Slay him with a spear,'* Raven chanted, and in the winter, when Adam had become more careless with the killing lances, I was able to break one of the sharp stone tips from the shaft and hide it inside my polar bear leggings. When he slept, I drove the blade deep into his chest, and he bled, and roared, and I pulled the spear point out so he might bleed to death, and ran out onto the island to wait for him to die. I waited for days, nearly freezing, having no food to eat, but when I sneaked back to the shore to find his body, he caught me from behind, bursting out of a snowbank. After that I lay tied up inside the stone hut, unable to stand and barely able to move. He would only untie my legs so I might relieve myself outside, then he would bind me and drag me in again. At last, in spring, when he thought I had learned my lesson and untied me, I ran into the sea and tried to drown myself, but he dragged me back and bound me again.

"He made me swear I would behave before he unbound me again. As strong as I was, I had grown weak from lack of exercise, so attacking him again was out of the question. Sea ice still framed the shore on the windward side of the island, so one bright but hazy spring day we went to hunt seals. We saw seals lying upon the ice near a sizable hole, but they were a hundred yards away and it would be very difficult to approach them without them slipping into the water. What *I* saw, that Adam didn't see—I suppose my taking his one eye and smashing his skull had affected his sight—was there was a white bear hunting the same hole, hiding among mounds of rough ice.

"We still had the bear rugs from the crate, so we used one of them as a blind to approach seals on the ice, so the animals would only see white on white when they looked up. We crept up on the seals, allowing as much time as needed to move the hundred yards. While the bear rug shielded our approach from the seals, the snow bear was downwind, and he knew we were approaching.

"Then I heard Raven's voice in my head: '*I give you sunshine, Little Bird,*' and the sun broke through the haze and was hot on our skins, on the ice. In no time there was water on the ice and it became as clear as glass. '*When the ice is clear, Nanook can hunt from below the ice as well,*' Raven said, but I didn't understand what he was talking about. We crept on, but when we were almost within range to throw a harpoon, Adam stepped on a bubble in the ice. There was a loud crackle and the seals, four of them, slid into the water. I looked to see if the bear had reacted, but he was gone.

"Raven said, '*Tell him that the People lie down on the ice near the hole, so the seals do not see their shadows and will surface. You stay back, Little Bird.*'

"So when he stopped cursing his luck at having frightened away the seals, I told Adam of the People's trick of lying down on the ice. He didn't see how he would throw the harpoon that way, but I told him with the large hole the harpoon could go deeper, and he could pop up to his knees and strike at an angle. With his great strength, it would be no challenge to spear a seal under the water, the tiny Native hunters did it all the time.

"Adam relented and, since we could see no game close, lay down on the wet ice to wait, while I stood ten yards away, watching.

"Then I saw it, right below me, something I had never seen before, the white bear under the ice, swimming, and looking at me as he passed. It was terrifying to have the massive bear only half a foot away, and I thought I might wee in my sealskin trousers, but I remained calm, leaning on the harpoon I had been using to prop up the bear-rug hunting blind.

"Adam didn't even see the deadly ghost moving under him. It exploded out of the hole in the ice face first, all teeth and claws, catching Adam's head in its mouth with a sickening crunch. Hooking its great claws into his ribs, the bear slid back into the water, dragging Adam with it, leaving a cloud of blood spreading pink under the ice. Adam's harpoon lay on the ice where he had been a moment before.

"I stood there for a long time, stunned, waiting for Adam to rise out of the hole in the ice. The bear must have surfaced at another hole on the far side of the mounded ice, but I did not see it again. An hour passed and I picked up the spears and the bear rug and dragged them back to the stone hut by the beach. Raven's voice whispered in my head, '*Well done, Little Bird. Well done.*'"

Jung took off his glasses and wiped them on his handkerchief. The voice coming from Judith when Raven spoke sounded nothing like her—it was deeper, raspy, it didn't really even sound human.

Jung said, "Judith, please stay present if you can, but may I speak to Raven directly, please?"

The sound of rustling feathers filled the room, from whence Jung couldn't tell, then, in the scratchy Raven voice, Judith said, "I told her to fly, to escape, but she wouldn't fly, so I helped her kill him."

"You knew the bear could hunt from below the ice, even though Judith didn't?"

"Beneath *clear* ice," Raven said, correcting him. "I know many, many things."

"And you brought out the sun to melt the ice so it would be clear? You can control the weather?"

"When you bring the sun you don't just do it one time. You bring the sun every morning. Which is why everyone should be grateful to Raven every time they feel the sun on their face."

"Does everyone pass through the Underworld?"

"Many, most, I don't know."

"But why Judith? Why does she remember? Why are you with her and not with others?"

"Others don't come back from the dead. Sometimes for a few seconds, just long enough to look around, but she was with us a long time before returning. We call her Little Bird, not Judith."

"And the dog?" Jung checked his notes. "Akhlut? Was he in the Underworld for a long time?"

"No, Akhlut just wanted out. He's savage. He does what he wants. He likes her."

"Is the Underworld of the north, where Judith found you, different from the Underworld here?"

"There are different Animal People, and other gods, and in the Underworld of the north there is a huge fucking tree that holds up the sky."

"How does it do that? Where does the tree come from? Is it a legend from the People in the north?"

"I don't know. I *think* it holds up the sky. Everyone kept asking about it, so I took credit for inventing it."

"You invented trees, then?"

"No, just the *huge fucking tree*. I didn't invent it, I just take credit for it. No one will know better."

"Why tell me, then?"

"No one will believe *you*, with your collective unconscious nonsense."

"But you are a figure, a *manifestation*, of the collective unconscious."

"Irony. I stole the sun, I invented the trees, and I bring *you* irony. My gifts."

"Because you are the trickster?"

"Possibly. I'm bored now. We'll talk again. Talk to Sedna next time. She is the Sea Wife and won't be too clever for you."

Judith opened her eyes and turned to face Jung. "I killed Adam."

"You hadn't remembered that before?"

"No, and I was worried. There were some men who came to Klimt's studio looking for me. I chased them away, but not before they said they were sent by Dr. Frankenstein."

"Who you believe raised you and Adam from the dead?"

"Yes. Who Adam murdered. He said he tore his head off on the ship where he stole me."

"And you believe he lied?"

"Possibly, but I also wondered if Adam survived the polar bear. He might have assumed the identity of his maker—*his father*, he called him."

"And he came all this way, all these years later, to Europe?"

"Why not? I did. Do you think now that I will remember who I was before Adam and Frankenstein?"

"I don't know. We will keep talking, keep working, until we find a cure. Would you like to try some free word associations? I find that method can access the unconscious without—without inaccuracies."

"I tried that with Freud and he didn't think it worked."

"Because all your answers were about murdering him?"

"Well, yes. Is he here? We *could* murder Dr. Freud."

"I think the trickster Raven is tall in your consciousness and you were just saying that to intimidate Freud."

"Of course, but imagine the surprised look on his face when we actually do it." Judith grinned.

Jung smiled, letting her have her joke. "I don't think that will help us find a cure."

"What is a cure? Is it when I remember who I was?"

"That is the hope, but a cure would be being at peace with who you are now."

"Are *you* at peace with who you are?"

"Absolutely not. Well, sometimes. No."

"So we, you and I, are fucked."

"That is not a cure, just another diagnosis."

"And?"

"Yes, we're fucked."

"I feel better now," she said.

"Let me ask you what you can remember about the ship you were on. The name of it wasn't in Freud's notes. Do you remember it?"

"Yes, I don't remember much from being there—a twilight dream, really—but Adam talked about it all the time. The *Prometheus*."

Jung made a note.

DUTCH CRUNCH

ot all crazy people are like you, Judith," Wally said as they strolled along the boulevard. "Some are sad. Mental illness is not all fun and games." She had shadowed Dr. Bauman for the full two hours Judith had been in session and had seen more than she had bargained for. "There's a fellow in there they can't untie or he bites himself."

"Did you try giving him a croissant? That keeps Geoff from biting."

Geoff, who was frisking along beside them, let out a bubbly-soft yowl at the mention of his name.

"No, but I'll suggest that next time. Did you remember anything in your session?"

"Yes, that I murdered the man who twice murdered me."

"That's nice. Choking?"

"Polar bear."

"I wouldn't have thought of that. You must have been very clever before. Did you remember anything else? Your name?"

"Not my name, but I remembered that I know how to hunt."

"That could come in handy sometime, maybe."

"Maybe," Judith said. What she didn't tell Wally, didn't tell any-body, is that she had remembered how to hunt the day the Dutchman and his two large minions came to Klimt's studio. After all the girls left, and finally, after she had assured Klimt she would be all right because now she had a gun (and reminded him that she had once been a murdering prostitute), he went home and she called Geoff to the parlor. He trotted in with a boot in his mouth, although much of it was gone.

"Give me that," she said, wrenching it out of his mouth. "I need you to find the man you took this boot from, can you do that?"

Geoff answered in a talky whine, which meant "Please give me the boot back."

Judith started to repeat herself, then paused. She didn't want to find one of the two tall boys who had come to the door; she wanted to find the Dutchman. He was the one who had come for her, followed her and Wally, and kidnapped Ella. She grabbed the revolver out of the drawer in the hall tree and held it out to Geoff, open handed. "I want you to find this man. The man you smell on this gun. Can you do that?"

Geoff howly-talked a few syllables, which Judith understood to mean "yes," but by which Geoff meant "Can I please have my boot back?" She handed him his boot, but before he could settle down to give it a good and thorough chew, Judith dressed; found a canvas shoulder bag, which Klimt used to carry books; and stuffed the big revolver inside.

"Let's go then, Geoff. Let's go, boy, find the bad man."

Geoff trotted through the door, boot in mouth, and Judith locked it behind him. She hooked the leash to his collar, she shoved his nose into the bag with the gun so he could get the scent, and they were off into the city. Geoff led her to three bakeries, all of which were closed, before she realized that the last time anyone had used this particular shoulder bag was when Wally had fetched a batch of strudel for them.

"No, Geoff. Snacks later. After we find the fake Dutch policeman."

Geoff tilted his head from side to side, as if he'd just come out of a coma and was trying to remember her name. She understood the effect, so she pulled him into an alley, drew the gun from the satchel, and waved the grip under his nose. "We need to find the man who was carrying this."

Geoff yowled, by which he meant "Why didn't you say so?"

He was off like a shot, dragging her down the sidewalk for half a block before she was able to get the revolver back into the bag. "Good boy, Geoff, but slow down."

They stumbled up to the entrance of a hotel called Hotel Schlossgarten on the Ringstrasse, where the doorman, who wore a very fancy military-looking uniform with many shiny buttons, gave her and Geoff a severe look of disapproval. "No dogs," he said.

"Fine," Judith said. She led Geoff around the corner to a service entrance and tied his leash to the door handle. "I'll be right back."

When she strolled through the front doors into the empty lobby she gave the doorman a look of extreme disapproval.

"All whores are run through the concierge," he said.

She stopped, nodded to herself, pivoted on her heel, and walked back to the doorman. "Secret," she said. She was taller than he, but she bent down and crooked her finger for him to bend down also to hear her.

The doorman bent down, trying to look smug and bored while still trying to hear her. "Don't," she said. She clamped her right hand on his throat, pushed hard on the side of his neck with her left, then whispered in his ear as she lowered him gently to the ground, unconscious. "You'd think it's the choking, but it's not, it's pressing on the artery in your neck that puts you out. You probably won't die."

The clerk behind the desk had been placing notes in pigeonholes the entire time and didn't even look back. When he did, he'd see his doorman in a pile by the door. Judith slid by the desk and down a corridor past the elevators to the door where Geoff was waiting.

She untied him, gave him a sniff of the gun butt, then followed him up the stairs, taking two at a time. On the third floor Geoff yowly-talked at the exit door. She opened it for him and he led her to the door of room 327. Geoff frisked and started to scratch at the door but Judith shushed him and ruffled him behind the ears. "First this, then snacks," she said. She knocked softly on the door.

After a few seconds the door opened a bit and a young girl, perhaps Wally's age, stuck her face in the gap. "What?" she said. "I checked in with the concierge."

"Pardon, Fräulein," Judith said. "Are you finished?"

"I was finished before I started. He's had a whole bottle of cough medicine. He passed out before he could get his trousers off."

"Did you get paid?"

"Always before."

"Well then, this one is finished for the night. You can leave. If the doorman is still out, would you kick him in the ribs as you pass, please?"

"I'm not going to do that."

"Well, perhaps slip out the service entrance, then. Have a pleasant evening." Judith stepped back from the door and held Geoff's collar as the girl swished by.

"They didn't say he wanted a dog," the girl said. "I don't do dogs."

"A girl has to have a specialty," Judith said. She smiled in solidarity as the girl wiggled away down the hall.

The fake policeman was lying on the end of the bed, his trousers down around his ankles, his broken arm thrown back over his head. "Geoff, give him kisses." She tapped the Dutchman on the lips and Geoff began licking him in the face. The Dutchman didn't even sniffle when Geoff licked his nose.

"Hmmm," Judith hmmed. She pulled the revolver from her satchel and gave it a looking over. It was a big American revolver, "Smith and Wesson .44" stamped on the top of the barrel. She cocked the hammer, which had a firing pin on it that looked like the beak of a small steel bird. She put the gun close to the Dutchman's crotch, then pulled his scrotum skin out in a small wing, which she held between the hammer and the frame of the gun before pulling the trigger. It snapped with a very unsatisfying click, but the Dutchman was awake and would have been screaming had she not clamped her hand over his mouth, leaving the revolver clipped to his nut sack unsupervised. The Dutchman clawed at the gun with his good hand to dislodge it but only served to hurt himself more.

"Calm down," Judith said. She pinched his nostrils shut and said it again. He didn't calm down. She released his nose and cocked the revolver again, releasing his scrotum. She set the gun on the bed and held the Dutchman as he tried to squirm out from under her. She didn't want to, but she had to. She clamped down on his windpipe, cutting off his air, and said into his ear in Dutch, "If you don't stop squirming I'm going to strangle you. Do you understand?" He stopped squirming, just for a second, as her message wove its way through his opium-fogged brain.

She released his windpipe and he snorted but began breathing again. "I'm going to take my hand off your mouth. If you scream, I'll snap your neck, do you understand?" He nodded and she removed her hand from his mouth. He grabbed the gun off the bed, aimed it at her, and clicked off three quick shots, which did just that, *clicked*. He pointed the gun at Geoff and clicked off three more. Geoff ruffed.

"What, you thought I'd just take three of the bullets out?" Judith said. She snatched the gun out of his hand and tossed it into the corner, where it landed with a thud.

The Dutchman scuttled up to the top of the bed and sat with his back against the headboard.

"Pull your trousers up," Judith said.

The Dutchman looked down. "I'm bleeding."

"Pull your trousers up or I'll have Geoff bite your dick off."

The Dutchman wiggled into his trousers as best he could with one hand but couldn't cinch up the belt. "What do you want?"

"I want to know who you are and who sent you to kidnap me."

"I'm nobody. It was a job. I know a man in Amsterdam who arranged it."

"One more time. Who are you and who sent you to kidnap me?"

"I don't have contact with the client. It's all done by telegrams."

"Fine," she said. "Akhlut, *makittuk!*"* she said to Geoff. She grabbed the Dutchman by the throat again, pinning him to the head-board, as Geoff changed. As if his fur were being blown by a strong wind in thirty directions, he grew, his fangs lengthening, his coat going darker, and the floor creaked under his weight. Akhlut's back was against the hotel room's ceiling; his body nearly filled the room, and his muzzle was more than half the length of the Dutchman's body. Judith could feel his steamy dog breath fogging the room. The Dutchman squirmed on the bed and screamed against Judith's hand.

She shook him until he stopped fighting, saying, "Calm. Settle. Be still."

His eyes were fixed on Akhlut's fangs, long, sharp, and glistening damp, a foot above his face.

"Who are you and who sent you?" She took her hand away.

"My name is Jan Van Beek. I was a policeman in Rotterdam. Now I work freelance as an investigator and a fixer. I work through a middleman in Amsterdam. I don't know who sent me, but those boys he sent to get you were from Switzerland, near Zurich, I think. They said they worked for a doctor called Frankenstein. That's all I know. You were not to be harmed in any way or I wouldn't be paid."

"You drugged Ella and your thugs were about to rape her when we arrived."

---

* "Akhlut, rise!"

"That was on them. Locals I hired for muscle. I was away sending a message that we had the girl. I thought she was you. I didn't know she would be touched, I swear. I know the bar where you can find them."

"You have never spoken with this Frankenstein?"

"The first I heard of him is when we came to Klimt's studio and they said his name at the door. I can tell you where the Swiss boys are. And the other cop, from Amsterdam, he brought your dog. *He* was going to hurt you."

"Where are the two Swiss?"

"I left them in a hotel near the opera house. Hotel Herrenhof. They should still be there. They didn't have any clothes or money. I don't know their names." Van Beek tried to catch his breath, while never taking his eyes off Akhlut's maw.

"You don't know who I was or what I did before, then?"

"Nothing. I didn't even have a description of you, other than you were a young woman. I was to follow Thiessen, who led me to you."

"And who sent Thiessen?"

"Someone from London. I don't have a name. I swear. I would tell you."

"Akhlut," she said.

Akhlut growled, laid back his ears; his eyes became fire.

"Walton!" Van Beek said. "I heard the name Walton, that's all I know, I swear."

The name meant nothing to her. She released her grip on his throat. "Fine then," she said, turning away.

Akhlut took the "Fine then" as permission and chomped down on the entire upper half of Van Beek's body. Blood sprayed the ceiling and the bed. Akhlut tossed his head and swallowed the dead Dutchman with a gulp.

"Oh, Geoff," Judith said, wiping blood out of her eyes. "That wasn't what I meant."

Geoff let loose a yowly-talky whine, by which he meant "You said snacks after."

Judith found a long canvas travel coat in the armoire, slipped it over her bloody clothes, wiped her face off with a flannel she dampened in the basin, retrieved the revolver, then quickly led Geoff down the stairs and out the service entrance before the blood dried on his fur.

"Where have you been?" Judith asked the Malamute. "If I'd had you in Amsterdam to dispose of bodies we wouldn't even be here."

Geoff ruffed, by which he meant "Sorry."

The next day, walking home from the clinic with Judith, Wally said, "I'm thinking of taking Alma Mahler's strategy for becoming great by attaching myself to a genius."

"Attaching yourself permanently? Like sewing yourself to them or, I don't know, handcuffs?"

"No, like Alma Mahler and Gustav Mahler. Married. And like now, with her and Gropius, or Kokoschka. Be his support, his muse. I think I will do that with Egon."

"I thought you were going to be a nurse."

"Maybe, if musing doesn't work out. I don't have the education or family connections to succeed any other way. I need to attach myself to a successful man."

"You just want to get your snatch in the Louvre, next to Gertie's." Judith bumped shoulders with her friend.

"I do not. Besides, I think Gertie is going to marry Anton Peschka. Now that I'm home they can't use Egon's apartment for shagging, so they are desperate. Do you want to move in with me now? Get you away from the studio so Gus won't worry about you at night?"

"Can Geoff come?"

"Absolutely. But you have to walk him. And when Egon gets out of jail, he may throw Geoff out."

"That would be a surprise for Egon."

"How so?"

"I'll tell you later," Judith said. They walked in silence for a while. Since she had introduced the suspense of a secret, to break the silence, Judith said, "I would be afraid of becoming like Kokoschka's doll. Just something a man makes and keeps to put his dick in, with no will or ambition of my own—like some kind of sex puppet."

"That won't happen."

"That already has happened. I was made to be a sex puppet and that's what I was."

They walked for a little while more without talking.

Wally said, "Is that why you started murdering men when you were a prostitute?"

"Probably."

"Did you tell Dr. Jung about it? Maybe he can help."

"I don't think he can help if it's already happened."

"I thought that's exactly what he was supposed to be doing."

They played with Geoff for a few blocks, teasing him with a beat-up deerstalker hat that he had adopted as his new toy and carried everywhere. They played "make fun of the people on the streetcar" for a while but settled into a steady pace after the car was out of sight.

Judith thought about the revelation of what she had done to Adam and realized that even though he had been gone for many, many years, she was still afraid he might turn up. Or, more precisely, she had become afraid again. The time in between she wasn't sure of. She said, "I don't want to be a sex puppet anymore."

"I don't think you are," Wally said. "You haven't shagged anyone since I've known you. Have you?"

"No, but that's not what I mean. I mean like Kokoschka's Alma doll."

"Covered with feathers? I agree, you would look terrible covered in feathers. You're too tall. You'd look like a big—"

"That's not what I mean. I mean treated like an object. Alma Mahler may be a bitch, but she's talented and well educated and has things to say, and Kokoschka thinks he can replace her with a doll covered with feathers."

"Were you a little disappointed when she didn't have feathers in real life?"

"No."

"Me either," Wally said. "I don't want to be a sex puppet either. Maybe Egon and I can be like Alma and Mahler, except Egon won't die and leave me at the mercy of younger artists."

"Maybe be like Emilie is to Gus," Judith said.

"He does love her, and she loves him. And they have fun. But Emilie has her own money, her own art, she doesn't need Gus to get by."

"Exactly," Judith said.

"What about Dr. Bauman? What if I was a nurse and married Dr. Bauman?"

"Well, you'd be a nurse."

"And Dr. Bauman likes me and he's never even seen me naked."

"He seems like a nice man."

"And as long as you're a loony, we could see each other all the time."

"What if I wasn't?"

"Wasn't what?"

"What if I wasn't a loony? What if I'm not crazy?"

"Don't be silly. I love you, but you're a bedbug."

"What if all the things I'm remembering in my sessions aren't dreams like Dr. Freud says? What if they're real?" Judith had shared most of what she had remembered with Wally, leaving out her adventures in the Underworld because she was only beginning to believe they had happened.

"Like you were a raven and a, what was it called? A sea wife?"

"Yes. A sea wife, or a sea mother, who takes care of people and feeds them, even teaches them to hunt."

"Like when you ran through Café Landtmann throwing trout at people?"

"Yes, like that."

"That's when I knew we were going to be friends, because you needed me."

"If I show you something, do you promise not to be afraid of me and stop being my friend?"

"Is it worse than being a murdering prostitute and choking out Egon?"

"Not worse. Bigger."

"No, I'll always be your friend."

Judith laughed, and bent and kissed Wally on the temple. "Come with me." She led them down an alley, then turned down another alley so they couldn't be seen from the boulevard.

"If you're bringing me down here to murder me, I *will* be surprised," Wally said.

"No, nothing like that." Judith looked around, made sure no one was watching from the windows above, put her arm around Wally's shoulders, then said, "Akhlut, *makittuk!*"

Geoff bubbled, expanded; his teeth grew, and his fur danced like windblown grass, until he was nearly three meters tall. Akhlut rose.

"Holy shit!" Wally said. Judith held her fast.

"Don't be scared. It's just Geoff."

"I peed a little."

"But only a little." Judith hugged her. "Still friends?"

"Yes. Can you make him Geoff again?"

"He ate the fake Dutch policeman."

"You mean 'bit.'"

"I mean 'ate.'"

"I never liked that guy."

"It was an accident."

"Is that where he got the silly hat?"

"Yes."

"He loves that hat."

"He's a silly boy."

"What do we do now?"

"Pastries? You always want to say *pastries*, not"—she spelled it out—"S-N-A-C-K-S. I learned that lesson."

23
HOW RAVEN GOT HIS SHINY FEATHERS

*D*r. Jung held a sheaf of notes as he led Judith into Freud's outer office. He gestured toward one of the wingback chairs instead of the fainting couch. He wore a gray suit of herringbone tweed that looked too warm for the weather. Judith could see sweat shining on his forehead and wanted to give him permission to remove his jacket.

Jung said, "I thought we could have a conversation first. After our last session, I wired a colleague in London who has access to the British National Archives, where they have all of Britain's maritime records going back to the fourteen hundreds. He found an English ship called the *Prometheus*, built in Whitby, North Yorkshire."

"Well, at least Adam wasn't lying about that."

"Its last port of call was at Archangel, Russia, where it shipped on an exploration expedition, searching for the Northwest Passage, with a crew of Swedes and Russians under a Captain John Walton, and was lost in the ice."

"That's it!" Walton was the name of the man Van Beek had said sent the Dutch policeman who died on the bridge—who had sent Geoff. She wasn't sure she should tell Jung about Van Beek. But how . . .

"The ship was lost in 1799, Judith. A hundred and twelve years ago."

"That can't be it, then, can it? Did anyone survive?"

"Many of the crew were rescued by another expedition ship, but most were lost when the *Prometheus* was crushed by shifting ice."

"The captain, was the captain rescued?"

"Yes, Captain Walton survived, and his great-great-grandson still owns a shipping company in London. What we have to ask ourselves is how you heard of this ship. How did it work its way into your memory when you couldn't possibly have been on it as you remember? Why has your unconscious repressed these memories under a façade of the impossible? Why did the name of the ship have enough impact on you to break through?"

"I thought you believed me that I died four times."

"I believe that is part of your story, yes."

"But that I couldn't have been on the *Prometheus* a century ago?"

"I am more concerned with *why* that is part of your story."

"Because Adam murdered me so Frankenstein could raise me from the dead to be his sex slave, the way men do with women. Adam and Frankenstein were just more direct. I had no worth to them except as a sex puppet."

"What does that mean, 'sex puppet'?"

So she told him about Kokoschka and his Alma Mahler doll, about a brilliant woman who was reduced in the mind of her lover to a bundle of horsehair and feathers.

"Feathers? Really?"

"Not the point, Doctor. It's why I want to know who I was before Adam, before Frankenstein, before the ice. I have to be more than a fuck-puppet, made to feed some monster's sexual appetite."

"Perhaps we can find a parallel in the story of Pygmalion and Galatea, from Ovid. Pygmalion was a sculptor who saw the debasement of the prostitutes in Cyprus, so he vowed to sculpt a perfect woman, and made a sculpture of a woman that he named Galatea, which was so beautiful that he fell in love with it and made offerings to Aphrodite that he might marry the living version of his statue. In response, Aphrodite brought the statue to life and Pygmalion married her. They had children together. So it was love, the love of beauty, not sex, that drove him."

"That's a happier story, but I don't think it applies to what happened to me. Adam tortured and raped me—cut my skin to make me as ugly as he was."

"Yes, I was just making a point that there is a parallel. Men construct those figures they need. When I was a boy, I carved a manikin, a small figure, from wood. I called him Atmavictu, which means 'the breath of life.' I kept him in my pencil box, hidden on a beam in the attic of our home. I used to write prayers on little scrolls and leave them in the box for him. I believe he was more of a real and primal god than the god of my father, who was a pastor, as was my grandfather."

Judith fidgeted, frustrated with the story. "So did you try to shag your little god?"

"No, I was seven."

"Doesn't Dr. Freud think we are sexual creatures from birth?"

"He does. Perhaps there is some truth there—as a child I had repeated dreams of my father's god as a giant penis sitting upon a throne in his church."

"Well, you were a twisted little scamp, weren't you?"

"That does seem rather sexual in nature, I suppose. I am not completely in disagreement with Dr. Freud. But I believe he needs to see beyond the sexual aspect of psychotherapy. There is more."

"Adam said he chose me because I was tall."

"How do you feel about that?"

"I murdered him."

"And after that? Do you feel that all men are like Adam? Herr Klimt has been very kind to you, you've said."

"He rescued me. He pays for my care. Yes."

"And you think he expects sex in return for his kindness?"

"No. Maybe before, but not since he's gotten to know me."

"So you feel he respects you?"

"I think he reveres beauty. He respects me as an object, but I think he fears me."

"But he has continued to help you. Certainly that would indicate his motives are not sexual."

"He wants to paint me. I'm not sure, if it had been an ugly girl, or a man, he found washed up out of the canal that morning, that he wouldn't have just hurried away to find a policeman."

"He found you in the canal? I didn't know that."

"I wasn't supposed to tell you. That was the fourth time I died."

"You believe you were dead when he found you?"

"Yes. Drowned."

Jung took a moment to make some notes. When he looked up, he said, "So, the first time was when Adam killed you?"

"Yes, in Scotland."

"In 1799?"

"If you say so."

"And the second time was when he broke your neck, just as you reached the island in the Arctic?"

"Yes."

"And the fourth time was here in Vienna?"

"Yes."

"And the third time you died? What do you believe happened the third time?"

"I don't know."

"Perhaps we'll find out today. I want to talk about Sedna. You know I spoke with Raven last time, and he told me I should ask Sedna about you. The Rasmussen monograph says that she is the daughter of Anguta, the creator god."

"That could be. She doesn't talk much."

Jung nodded. "It says that Sedna refused to consider the eligible men in the village for marriage, but she agreed to marry a wandering hunter who would give the People fish and game in exchange. But he was a bird in disguise, so her father took her to sea in a boat and threw her over the side. Her treatment angered a storm god, who raised a great storm. Sedna tried to crawl back in the boat, but her father, afraid she would capsize the boat, cut off her fingers with an axe so she could not climb. Her fingers became the seals, the walruses, and the whales, and she became the supreme goddess in the land of the dead. Does that sound right?"

Judith said, "She doesn't talk about it, but others do. Raven does. Yes, that sounds like what happened."

"So her rejection from the land of the living comes from her not obeying her father's wishes about her sexuality?"

"You know that her father, Anguta, lives in the Underworld as well, right?"

"Rasmussen doesn't say much about him."

"He meets the dead when they descend into the Underworld and hits them in the dick for their violations of taboo."

"What about women?"

"I never heard about him hitting women in the dick. Have you told Dr. Freud about Anguta? He would love him."

"Yes, I think he would have perhaps found his patron saint. But I'm not clear: Anguta is the creator, but he is not supreme in the Underworld?"

"The Animal People pretty much agree that what he created was a dark mess. Other gods had to fix things. Raven brought the sun and fresh water. Sedna brought the animals and the fish."

"And now, in the Underworld, what does Anguta do?"

"Hits people in the dick. With a stick. That's about it."

"I can't think of a parallel in other mythologies. This may be a unique archetype. Sedna is the rebellious daughter, but this Anguta—"

"Doctor, how do these figures get into your collective unconscious? Are they real people, real gods, and we found out about them?"

"What do you think?"

"Don't ask me. I've lived among them, talked to them. They are real people to me."

"With supernatural powers and knowledge and experience beyond what is human?"

"Not to me."

"Perhaps they are gods, or perhaps they are part of the physical structure of the human brain. In all different cultures we experience the same archetypes with different names. Tricksters like Raven, Loki, Reynard the Fox, Hermes, Mercury, Anubis; or mothers, Gaia, Mahadevi, Hera, the Madonna—even destroyers, rapists like Zeus and your Adam. They are extensions of human experience."

"Adam was real?"

"If you perceive him as real, he is real."

"Was," Judith said. She pulled off the sleeve of her frock and began slapping herself on the forearm, the impact making loud cracks.

Jung said, "Please stop that. Please don't harm yourself."

She slapped until the skin on her arm was bright red, as if she'd scalded it under boiling water; then, as abruptly as she'd begun, she stopped, and held her arm up a handsbreadth away from his face. "Can you see them? Can you see the lines?"

He did see, across the entire length of her forearm, fine white lines, finer than a human hair, but distinct, in a grid.

"This is where he cut me. I could do this on my thigh, on my face, on my breasts, and you'd see these scars—in some places two or three sets—where I healed and he cut me again. Adam was not a manifestation of the structure of my brain. He was a cruel, soulless monster, pieced together by Frankenstein."

Jung pushed back in his chair. He nodded to acknowledge that he could see what she was talking about and she put her arm down.

"I'm sorry," he said. "I didn't mean to diminish your suffering or elevate your tormentor. Of course Adam was real. I was careless and inconsiderate in my description. Sometimes I need to be reminded that patients are individuals, not collections of complexes. I apologize. I didn't mean to be disrespectful."

Judith nodded, pulled down her sleeve. "I forgive you." Then she grinned. "But I think you can expect to be bashed in the bollocks for a long time when you pass to the Underworld. I know people there."

Jung hung his head and smiled. "I was more focused on filling out my notes than on treating my patient. I hope I will learn my lesson by the time I pass to the Underworld. But understanding this Sedna's nature may prove to be helpful. Of the entire pantheon of the north, which Rasmussen notes is full of gods, these two became your protectors, your patrons, if you will. There must be a reason, and it may be the reason you can't remember."

"Just be glad I showed you my scars and not Akhlut. Wally peed herself when she saw him."

"I have that to look forward to, I guess. Shall we continue?"

Judith stood, moved to the fainting couch, and lay down. "Let's find out how I died the third time."

"Very well," Jung said. He removed the cap from his fountain pen, which, by habit, he'd capped when he'd paused in his notes, and began the ritual. "Focus on the nib of the pen. I'm going to count back from ten . . ."

Less than a minute later Judith was in a trance.

Jung said, "Judith, can you go back to that day when Adam was dragged under the ice by a bear?"

"Love to," Judith said.

"What happened next?"

"I picked up the spears, draped the bear rug over me, and went back to the side of the island with the stone hut."

"And then?"

"Then I went on, hunting, fishing, gathering bird eggs, sewing bags from sealskin to store blubber in."

"You didn't see anyone else? None of the Native hunters returned?"

"No. I dried meat and fish to take me through the winter—I even built a second stone hut where I could store dry driftwood and meat. Staying alive in the north takes a lot of work."

"And all these skills, you learned them in the Underworld?"

"Yes, and Sedna would talk to me, help me. Raven talked to me as well, but mostly to tell stories about himself. He gave me hints about how to live, tricks for hunting and catching fish, but half the time Sedna would whisper in my other ear that he was trying to trick me."

"Why would Raven trick you?"

"He gets bored with sameness. He wanted things to change. He wanted to create drama. Drama for him often means danger for me."

"That's true," said Raven, a scratchy male voice coming from Judith's mouth.

Jung was startled by the abrupt change in voice—he fidgeted in his seat. Raven laughed and Jung realized that startling him was exactly what the trickster was trying to do.

"I also taught her to fly. And made her feathers shiny and pretty."

"I'm talking to Judith now," Jung said.

"No you're not, big eyes."

Jung touched his glasses. "You don't have spectacles in the Underworld?"

"If we wanted to look silly I would invent them."

"Can I speak to Judith, please?"

"Let me tell you about how I made my feathers the shiniest of all. I was flying high over the land one day, and I saw something sparkling in the sun (which I stole and gave to the People because I am very generous), and naturally, I flew down to see what it was. When I reached the ground, I found a great mound of black glass that had come up from the earth as liquid fire and cooled to the shiniest black. And nearby, Sedna was sitting on some of the black glass, striking a piece of the black glass with one of the hard pink stones.

"And I said, 'What are you doing, Sea Wife?' Even though I knew what she was doing, I know she enjoys explaining things. And she said, 'I have made a blade core.'

"And I said, 'What is a blade core?' even though I knew what it was, but you know how Sedna likes to talk. And she showed me the piece of the black glass that was in the shape of a stick, but flat on many sides. And Sedna said, 'You see, when I strike the blade core just right, each time it sheds a very thin, very sharp blade. So sharp that if you hold it up to the sun, you can see the light shine through the very edges.'

"And I said, 'Of course. Those blades are the sharpest and shiniest I have ever seen. I'll bet if I put them in with my feathers, I would light up like a star when I fly in the sunshine.'

"And Sedna said, 'And you would be able to flay the skin off a walrus with a swipe of your wings.'

"And I said, 'I knew that. But walrus skin is very thick and very tough.'

"And Sedna said, 'There is no sharper blade in any of the worlds.'

"And, of course, I knew that, but I had things to do, so I said, 'Would you make me many of those I could weave in among my feathers? So I would be the shiniest as well as the smartest in all the worlds.'

"And Sedna said, 'I will strike those blades for you, but you still won't be the smartest in all the worlds.' Because Sedna can be a bitch sometimes, which is why the People say she snatches children if they get too close to the shore. But she made many, many, of the black glass blades, and I worked them into my wing feathers and now I have the shiniest feathers in all the worlds."

Jung said, "Thank you for that story. May I speak to Judith please?"

"You know I gave Judith shiny feathers too, but she won't fly because she is afraid."

"I am not afraid," came Judith's voice.

"Does Raven talk to you like that all the time?"

"No. Only sometimes."

"Did he talk to you when you were on the island?"

"Yes. He warned me if bears were nearby. Sometimes he would tell me where to find seals basking."

"But not storytelling, like he just did."

"Maybe. You stop listening after a while. And after a while he went quiet."

"After a while? How long were you on the island?"

"My whole life."

"I don't understand. Weeks, months?"

"Years. I don't know how many. I died on the island."

"Do you remember how you died on the island?"

"You remember I told you of the crevices in the glacier that ran with fresh water in the spring?"

"Yes."

"I jumped into one."

"You didn't fall?"

"When Sedna and Raven's voices went quiet, the only memories I had were of their stories and the time with Adam, the cruelty. I—I climbed to the top of the glacier in winter, took off my boots and my furs, and leapt into one of the crevices."

"And you died? It wasn't like when you fell off the cliff and were simply unconscious?"

"I died. I went to the Underworld. I lived with Sedna and Raven and Akhlut and all the other gods and all the Animal People."

"And that was the third time you died."

"Yes."

"And you came back, though. You somehow came to Europe?"

"Yes. Amsterdam, eventually."

"You said you died four times. Do you remember when was the fourth time?"

"It was the night I tore the policeman's head off."

Jung had been scribbling in his notebook and he stopped. He didn't want to write down what she had just said. It wasn't the fanciful world of talking ravens and sea goddesses. He wasn't sure what to ask next. Finally he settled on "What can you tell me about that night?"

"Well, he was being a cunt, wasn't he?" she said in English, with a distinct Northern accent.

Jung checked his watch. Maybe he'd bring her out of the trance until he could gather his notes and his wits.

"Judith, I'm going to count to three and you will be awake and alert and you will remember everything we've talked about." At this point, normally, he would have told the patient that they were at peace with everything they had said, but he had never had a patient confess to murder under hypnosis before. Perhaps he would just count.

"Would you like to see my shiny feathers?" Judith said.

Jung said, "One, two, three, and you're awake."

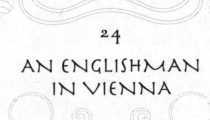

24

AN ENGLISHMAN
IN VIENNA

*T*he dress was finished. They knew that Emilie could have just had it delivered to Klimt's studio, but she had sent a message to ask them to pick it up, so she must have wanted to see them, and they were very excited.

"Maybe she's going to hire us to model her clothes," Wally said as they strutted down the street, two self-assured young women in hats with a large croissant-eating demon dog. "It would be strange to be paid for putting clothes *on*, but I could get used to it."

"Is Egon glad to be home?" Judith asked. Schiele had been released from prison a week early due to excessive melancholy that the jailer was afraid was catching. He'd arrived home the night before, thus ruining Judith's plans to move into the flat with Wally.

"He's still sad. We spent the whole night eating spaetzle and shagging. I'm a little sore."

"Spaetzle?"

"They're little dumplings—we ate them with cheese and butter."

"I know what they are, but why?"

"I don't know. He missed spaetzle and sunlight, he said."

"And you?"

"I call them *nocken*, not spaetzle. I think spaetzle is the German name."

"I mean, and he missed *you*?"

"I think so. I introduced him to the two sisters, about my age, who live across the courtyard from us. Edith and Adele. They're pretty, but not rudely so, like Gertie. He was a little too interested in them."

"Did they seem interested in him?"

"Not as much as you might think. They were when he mentioned he'd like to sketch them sometime if they didn't mind. Then I told them he was just home from prison for sexually corrupting a minor, so we had to run and catch up on some matters. After that they were very polite about letting us get on with our evening."

"So you cheered him up?"

"He was still moping this morning that he never got to see Krumau's airplane."

"He can always go back."

"He's afraid they might throw him back in jail."

"There will be other airplanes."

"We should tie Geoff up," Wally said. She looped Geoff's leash around a decorative wrought iron railing by Café Piccolo's front door. "Should I buy him a treat from the café before we go up?"

Geoff awooed and ruffed, by which he meant "Yes, please."

"After," Judith said. Geoff drooled a disappointed yowl and lay down on the sidewalk to sulk.

They took the stairs two at a time and burst through the double doors into Schwestern Flöge's studio like springtime in tap shoes.

"Oh, my sweet darlings!" Emilie said. She glided to them, her diaphanous gown trailing behind her, embraced them, and kissed them both on the cheeks, lifting Wally's veil to gain access. "Your face is healing up nicely," she said. "All the swelling is gone."

"But I'm still purple and black."

"Oh, I'd call it lavender and green. Matisse could paint you as is and no one would ever know. And you, Judith, tell me about Jung. Has he told you anything scandalous or embarrassing?"

"Well, as a child he dreamed of God as a giant penis on a throne in his father's church."

"Outstanding! Freud must have thought he found a kindred spirit when he told that story."

"And I told him about Kokoschka's doll of Alma Mahler."

"And what was his reaction?"

"He said that he carved a small manikin as a boy that he kept in a pencil box and wrote confessions to. He said men construct of us what they need. I told him I thought I was constructed to be a sex puppet."

Emilie paused for a moment, chewed her lip as she thought. It was the first time Judith had seen her without a smile on her face. She went to the desk, where a broad dress box was perched. She started to pick it up, then stopped and turned back to face them.

"Judith, you said you can sew—"

"Yes. Mostly sealskin, but I can prepare walrus hide and polar bear fur as well."

Emilie nodded as if making mental notes. "Well, we don't have much call for walrus hide, but I would think your skills are transferable. I'd like you to come to work here. For me."

"I have to model for Gus's painting."

"When does he plan to start?"

"Later today he'll start sketches, he said. As soon as we deliver the gown."

"As soon as the painting is finished, or at least as soon as he has a preliminary drawing on canvas, you can start. He can sometimes take a year or more to finish a major painting, he won't need you there all the time. Come back as soon as you can get away."

"But why?"

"Because you are not a sex puppet, and when you are a skilled craftswoman, you will never consider it again." She turned to Wally. "And I want *you* to start as a waitress in the café downstairs."

"But I just decided to go the route of Alma Mahler and achieve greatness by attaching myself to a genius."

"Then you can start in the early mornings and attach yourself to your genius in the afternoon. I don't know of a single painter who works early in the morning."

"But I'm not a fuck-puppet like Judith. I'm a professional model."

"Come to the café tomorrow, talk to my sister Helene, who runs the café. If you want, she will teach you to bake as well. And don't show up hungover."

"I won't."

"Wear shoes you will be comfortable in all morning."

"I only have these shoes."

Emilie scowled at Wally's run-down brown shoes. "We'll get you shoes. Be here at six. I'll tell my sister to expect you."

"I can't. I'm taking Judith to see the doctor tomorrow morning."

"Then after the doctor." She handed the dress box to Judith. "There. Now, my darlings, take the dress and go. Hang it once you get it to the studio, Judith, and every time you take it off."

"I will."

"Go, go, go," Emilie said. She kissed them on the cheeks, and as she pulled Wally's veil down, she said, "A few more days and you'll be the beautiful creature I know you to be."

They said goodbye several dozen times as they made their way to the double doors.

On the stairs, Wally said, "I love her more than my mother."

"She does smell nice," said Judith.

"I love her more than my sisters *and* my mother and my dead father put together."

"Calm down, Wally, she hasn't tasted your coffee yet."

"What do you know, sex puppet?" Wally elbowed Judith in the shoulder, then hurried down the stairs to hold the door for her so she could keep the dress box level.

Outside a thin old man in a dark suit was rubbing Geoff's belly and the demon dog was squirming and yowling a happy good-boy song.

"That's a good boy, Geoff. Who's a good boy?" the old man said in English.

"How do you know his name?" Judith said in English.

"He's touching our dog," Wally said in German. "And Geoff is letting him."

The man stood. Geoff rolled over and stood next to him. The man scratched Geoff's ears as he spoke, again in English: "There you are." He looked Judith up and down. "Exactly as you were, although somewhat more lively than when I last saw you. How are you so well preserved?"

"Why is he looking at you like that?" Wally said. "I don't like the way he's looking at you. Is he propositioning you? Can I choke this one? He's so old he looks like he's made of paper. I can do it."

"Where do you know me from?" Judith asked. She didn't recognize him, but there were years of her past, decades, that she didn't remember, and many, many men.

The old man smiled. "I am Robert Walton, the captain of the *Prometheus*. You were brought onto my ship inside a crate by a man named Victor Frankenstein."

Judith dropped the dress box and it landed flat on the sidewalk with a pop.

"I know," Wally said. "Have Geoff eat him. Geoff, stop letting him touch you."

Judith waved for Wally to be quiet. In English she said, "The *Prometheus* sank over a hundred years ago. How . . ."

"A hundred and twelve years ago, to be exact. And, strictly

speaking, the ship was crushed by ice floes, although I suppose much of it sank, if the pieces ever found the sea again."

"How?" Judith said.

"Your blood. Frankenstein had me draw your blood to inject into him. He said it would heal him. Unfortunately for him, before I could give it to him, Adam came aboard, tore off his head, and made off with you. When the crew and I grew ill, I injected the blood into myself."

"How does Geoff know you?"

Geoff ruffed at the sound of his name.

"Geoff is my dog, dear. Adam crushed him, but he had your magical blood inside of him too, so I kept him in my cabin and after a week he was no longer dead. He's been with me since then."

"So you don't know what he is? What he can do?"

"Do? He can eat a dozen scones at a sitting, but otherwise he's just a very old dog."

"Do you know who I am? Who I was before Frankenstein brought me on your ship? Did he tell you?"

"Sadly, no. Just a girl that Adam murdered in Edinburgh."

Wally leapt in front of Judith and grabbed the old man by the lapels of his very nice suit. "Where is the fucking library? Where is the fucking library?" she demanded in English, trying to shake the answer out of him.

"What are you doing?" Judith asked.

"It's all I know how to say in English."

Judith pried Wally's hands off the old man and gently pushed her away. "He knows me from one of my old lives. Let's not choke him yet."

"Fine," Wally said. "But just say the word."

"Thank you," Judith said. She turned to Walton. "So you sent the policeman, Thiessen?"

"Yes. He found you and kept in touch with me by wire. When

you fled Amsterdam I sent Geoff to him, thinking he would be able to help find you."

"They found me."

"I just needed some more of your blood."

"Why?"

"I'm dying. I've never been ill since the transfusion, and I am very strong despite my appearance, but finally, after a hundred and forty years, I am dying. Look at Geoff, he's still little more than a puppy; look at you, as if a day hasn't passed since I last saw you; yet I am this withered shell. I thought—"

"When you found me, you could have just asked. You didn't have to have Thiessen hunt me."

"You weren't supposed to be harmed. I told him."

"That's not what he said. Thiessen pointed a gun at me and told me that it didn't matter if I was dead or alive, he just needed my blood." The scene on the bridge was playing out in her mind and she was becoming flushed with anger. The fine white scars were showing on her face.

"I'm sorry. He wasn't supposed to do that. I will pay you handsomely. I inherited a fortune and it has grown over the years."

"How has no one noticed that you never die?"

"But I do. I live on a large country estate in West Sussex. Every twenty years or so my attorney places an announcement of the birth of another Robert Allen Walton, and twenty years after that a Robert Allen Walton dies and the new one inherits the estate. I'm currently Robert Allen Walton the Sixth. Sometimes I hire a young squire to pose as the younger Robert Walton, so the servants can say they've seen him. There's a comfortable cottage where the young Waltons live, then I send them off with a fortune in their own name."

"So you've been looking for me for a hundred years?"

"Less than that. There was a note in the maritime news years ago of a white woman wandering on the ice, picked up by a Dutch ship, but there was no record of where they took her. I thought it might be you, so I hired agents around Europe and America to watch papers for any story of an unusually lucky woman."

"Lucky?"

"Someone who should have died but somehow escaped."

"That's how you found me?"

"No. Thiessen published an article in a strange true-crime magazine about what he believed was a prostitute who had been murdering men in Amsterdam for more than thirty years. A *young* woman. Of course it was just a penny dreadful for the masses, written by a charlatan, most thought, but when I saw it, I contacted him. Offered to fund him to help find you. And here we are."

"But how are you here, now? Thiessen is dead. How did you find me this time?"

"I've been in Vienna since Thiessen was killed. But looking for a tall blond woman in Austria, well, it's been like looking for hay in a haystack. Then today I saw Geoff tied up here. I only hoped you might still be near him. Thiessen didn't report where he had tracked you to specifically."

"He didn't know. I never stopped running."

"Did you kill him? The police said his head was torn from his body. I've only heard of that—seen that—once before."

Judith looked at Wally, who was trying to follow the conversation by reading their faces and their tones. She had gone from being angry, to being bewildered, to looking terrified. Judith could see her eyes were wide even through the veil. She put her arm around Wally's shoulders, hugged her, and whispered in German, "Everything is fine. When I'm done asking him questions you can choke him all you want."

To Walton, she said, "I don't remember what happened on the bridge. I drowned that night—I haven't remembered much since." She did remember, at last, but she wasn't going to tell Walton.

Walton stopped petting Geoff and stood. He was shorter than Judith, thin, frail. His expensive suit looked as if it had been hung on a skeleton. "I've rented some rooms nearby. Perhaps we can retire there and discuss this out of the eye of the public."

"Did you send Van Beek?"

"Who is Van Beek?"

"A fixer. Hired through an agent in Amsterdam. Through Switzerland, he said."

"I haven't been to Switzerland in seventy years."

"So no?" she said.

"I can set you up in England. Your own home, a permanent income. All you have to do is provide transfusions periodically. You'll never have to sell yourself again."

"Isn't that exactly what I'd be doing?"

"You know what I meant. And the equipment for transfusions is far better than the crude devices Frankenstein used a century ago. Almost painless."

"He's lying," came Sedna's voice in Judith's head.

Judith picked up the dress box and handed it to Wally, then turned back to Walton. "Mr. Walton, I have work to do now. You've waited a hundred years, you can wait until I finish my current job. Give me the address where I can contact you."

"But I don't know how much time I have left."

"I can give you an answer now, if you don't think you can wait. If you can't wait, you have exactly as much time as it takes for your head to fall from your shoulders to the street."

"You wouldn't dare, here in public."

"I will consider your offer, Mr. Walton. Your address?"

Walton reached into his inside jacket pocket and retrieved a calling card. His hand was wraith thin, his skin like crepe paper, but he was steady. "There is a telephone number there, too. You can call when you are ready to meet to settle terms."

"What if I want to stay in Vienna?" She thought it strange that he'd had business cards printed for a temporary address, but maybe that was something that the landed gentry in England did.

"I'll consider it. When we discuss terms. Where can I contact you?"

"You can't," she said. She bent to untie Geoff's leash from the railing.

"Are you going to have Geoff eat him now?" Wally asked, cheerful once again.

"Maybe later," Judith said in German. "You'll hear from me, Mr. Walton," she said in English.

"I look forward to it," the old man said.

"If you follow us I'm going to let Wally choke you."

"What did you say?" Wally asked. "I heard my name."

"I told him if he tried to follow us I would let you strangle him."

"Aw," Wally said. "You're so good to me."

"Wait, what do I call you?" Walton asked.

"Judith," she said. "Just Judith."

They were in the portrait studio. Judith stood on a posing platform, a knee-high cube that was draped with a sheet, her arms out in the aspect of Nike, goddess of victory, head high, breasts out, the front of her gown open as if she were about to fly out of it, the fabric shining with gold and silver threads, flowing behind her in a trail. Squares and triangles of gold, silver, and black peppered the gown and gave it a strange dimension, as each layer shone through the draped sleeves and tails. The dress had been designed for this, for standing on a platform, entirely too long, and would have been dragged to ruin if actually worn for normal activity.

Klimt worked on a nearly life-size canvas on his easel, sketching and revising, moving from broad strokes to details, occasionally stopping to arrange the fabric of the dress.

"I'll let you have a break shortly," he said. "I know that pose is difficult to hold, but I have to get the pattern of these gold and silver patches set—it will be difficult to get them in the same position once you move."

"I'm fine," Judith said.

"Surely your arms must be aching."

"No, but I will take a break when you're ready. I need to count the cats."

Klimt looked up from his drawing, noting that she did not break her pose to speak to him. *If you're going to drag a dead girl out of the canal to model for you, good to pick one with natural talent.* "Why do you need to count the cats?"

"Because Geoff and I have an agreement and I need to make sure he's sticking to it."

"I've never been comfortable with having a dog at the studio."

"We may be leaving soon. May have to."

"Well, I think you would be safer somewhere else. That Dutchman—"

"The Dutchman isn't a problem. He's gone."

"Don't smile. For the picture you should look ecstatic."

"When I'm ecstatic I smile."

"If the Dutchman is gone, then why do you have to leave?"

"There are new problems."

"I thought you were going to move in with Wally."

"Egon is out of jail and Wally wants to be his muse, so I would be in the way. I mean I may have to leave Vienna."

"Where would you go? How would you live? You won't leave before the painting is finished, will you?" He put down his crayon. Stood back from the drawing. "Take a break."

She climbed down from the posing cube, shrugged off the gown, put it on a hanger, and hung it on a peg on the wall. She walked naked into the drawing studio, headed for the kitchen. "Would you like tea?"

"Yes please."

Over her shoulder she said, "If I go away, you have to promise to look out for Wally."

"I thought she was going to be Schiele's muse. He's selling everything he paints now."

"Promise, or I won't stay to finish the painting."

"I promise."

"And Ella. You have to promise to take care of Ella, too."

"Of course I will. We are already searching for a larger flat for her and her mother."

"And don't make her name the baby Gustav."

"I won't make her name the baby anything."

"Fine, he'll wander around being known as Klimt's nameless bastard." She was shouting from the kitchen now.

"It might be a girl."

"Nameless is nameless." She rattled around the kitchen, filling the kettle, lighting the cooker. "Jung wants to meet you. Do you want to take me to my session tomorrow?"

"What time is it?"

"In the morning. He wants to talk symbols with you."

"I should check on your progress as well."

"I'm better."

"You seem better, less . . ."

"Insane?"

"I wasn't going to say that. You seem to be remembering how to be a person in the world."

"Sugar in your tea?"

"Yes, please."

"They're all here."

"What?"

"The cats, they're all here. Geoff didn't eat any of them."

Geoff arooed softly from the kitchen, by which he meant "See!"

"You'll stay then? To finish the picture?"

"For a while, if you don't mind?"

"Stay as long as you like," he said, stepping into the doorway of the kitchen.

"Thank you for helping me, Gus."

"You're welcome. Also please don't call me Gus."

"But we're friends, aren't we? I should call you by your name."

"The way you say it, it sounds like a dog's name."

Geoff ruffed in agreement.

25
AMONG THE PEOPLE

Wally showed up to the studio early to escort Judith to her appointment with Dr. Jung. She still had the key to let herself in and found Judith and Geoff sleeping in the storeroom amid a pile of cats.

"Get up, get up, get up," Wally chanted. "I have a rendezvous with handsome Dr. Bauman and I don't want to be late."

There was much stretching and yawning in the storeroom, as well as abundant groggy complaining in three languages.*

"Gus is going to—take me," Judith said, stopping midsentence to pinch some cat fur off her tongue.

"Well, it's almost time and Gus isn't here and you can't go alone because Dr. Bauman will be sad if I'm not there. Also I need to see to your mental health."

"I thought you were going to concentrate on being Egon's muse."

"I am, I inspired him twice this morning already, but Emilie convinced me to have a backup plan. We need to stop by her café on the way back from the clinic."

"Wait, is your backup plan to be a waitress or a nurse?"

---

* Dog, cat, and German.

"Yes. Get dressed. We're going to Café Central for coffee before we go to the clinic."

Geoff shook off his morning haze and yowled an enthusiastic song of croissant anticipation.

"Fine," Judith said. "Will you take Geoff out for a poo while I dress?"

"Of course. And sponge off some of that cat hair. Your tits look like they have mold growing on them."

Café Central might have been a Gothic coffee grotto, with its tall columns and soaring, marble arched ceilings—the pastry cases in the middle of the floor floated like barges of sweet abundance bringing sustenance to the surrounding tables and booths of the great unfed. Wally and Judith took a table near one of the pastry cases so they could watch people in many directions while waiters in white coats whizzed by them trailing espresso steam and strudel fumes.

"Why are we here?" Judith asked.

"Because it is the center of Viennese coffee culture and we need to be part of it," Wally answered.

"Did you read that in a brochure?"

"It's on the menu, right there behind you on the pastry case."

"Oh. So it is."

"Also, I thought if we sat in the middle of this big room we could see if we were being followed."

"You mean by Walton?"

"I'm supposed to be looking out for you," Wally said. "And I let that horrible man find you." She kept turning in her seat as if she was looking for someone, which she was. "I wish they'd let us bring Geoff in here."

They ordered coffee and two *pains au chocolat*, which Wally ordered because a baker once told her she pronounced the French perfectly, and a plain croissant for Geoff, which the waiter brought in a small white paper sack.

"Also," Wally said, crunching into her pastry and spraying light, flaky, and buttery crumbs as she spoke, "handsome Dr. Bauman mentioned this place at your last appointment and asked if I knew it and I said 'Of course.' I wanted to be sure to not get caught in a lie if he brought up details today."

"And there he is," Judith said. She'd spotted Walton by the door, standing with two younger men. "Don't look."

"Handsome Dr. Bauman?" Wally, eyes wide, spun in her chair.

"Go ahead and look, then," Judith said.

"Oh, him. Can I choke him out now?"

"No. But I'm glad you thought to set a trap to see if he was following."

"Well he's shit at hiding, isn't he?"

"Probably why he hired the Dutch policeman."

"The real one or the fake one?"

"The real one—the one who died on the bridge."

"Can I choke him out, please?" Wally pleaded. "I think I'm ready. I practiced on Egon twice today already."

"You choked Egon out?"

"Not completely. Just until he turned kind of blue and veins popped out at his temples."

"How did he take that?"

"Better than expected. He wanted to choke me back, though."

"And?"

"I screamed 'no,' slapped him, and called him a disgusting fuck-beast."

"And that worked?"

"It inspired him. You know how he loves his self-loathing. So I was forced to choke him a second time."

"You seem to be getting pretty good at this muse job."

"I'm not sure I am. Which is why I need a backup plan. Plans."

"I may have to go," Judith said.

Wally glanced at one of the clocks fixed to a marble column. "We still have ten minutes."

"I mean I may have to go away. From Vienna."

"No!" Wally shouted. She wound up to slap her friend, but Judith caught her hand.

"Well, that didn't work," Wally said.

Judith said, "I'm not trying to hurt anyone. I just don't want you to worry if I'm suddenly gone."

"How will I know you weren't kidnapped?"

"I'll leave you a nice note."

"Aw, that's sweet."

"We should probably go. I'll leave first and get Geoff. You wait a minute and follow."

"And if the old man follows you, I can choke him out."

"He's with two strong-looking young men, Wally."

"Well, *you* have to do something. I can't look after everyone."

"I'll go." Judith stuffed Geoff's croissant into Gus's satchel with Van Beek's revolver and made for the door.

Wally watched the clock for a minute, and when Walton and his minions didn't follow Judith and Geoff, she ran after them.

*J*udith sank into a trance before Jung was able to count to three.

"I want you to go back to when you jumped into the crevasse in the glacier. Can you tell me what happened next?"

"It was very cold, but I had often been very cold. Soon I was no longer cold, and I was waking up in the Underworld. Raven had taken his beak off, which he does when he wants to appear as a man, and was poking me with it."

"Egon is also a grotesque fuck-beast," Judith clarified. "Sometimes a disgusting fuck-beast."

"'Wake up. Wake up. Wake up,' he chanted until I sat up and asked him to stop. Raven can be very annoying sometimes."

"I am not annoying," came Raven's scratchy voice from Judith's mouth. "I am handsome and wise."

Jung said, "So now you were in the Underworld. What else did you see there?"

"The Animal People, of course, doing what they do. And trees and mountains, water and sky. And what Raven calls the huge fucking tree."

"What else are you going to call it?" Raven said. "Did I mention I invented it?"

Jung scratched a note. "When you say the Animal People did what they do, what is that?"

"They live, forage, eat, fly, swim, burrow—animal things. And they talk."

"What do they talk about?"

"It depends on what animal. If you talk to a whale and mention krill, you better pull up a rock to sit on, because you are going to hear krill talk for a long time. Or herring, or salmon. But if you talk to a salmon you'll get a lot of talk about what dicks whales and bears are for eating them."

"But isn't that the natural order of things?"

"Yes, they accept it, but they don't have to like it."

"And the People, there are human people there?"

"They are boring. They do what the People do, but there is only one village, and they are all the same. I preferred spending time with gods, like Raven, Sedna, or Nanook, the white bear god."

"I don't understand. What do you mean, the People are all the same?"

"They play their roles, father, mother, hunter, child, fisher, shaman, but they don't have personalities."

Raven's voice: "They aren't in the Underworld long enough to be individuals. The People are just shells for the people from above to live in while they are with us, then they move on, the same as the Animal People."

Jung wrote furiously in his notebook, mostly questions. "Were you not one of the People in the Underworld?"

"No. I am different."

"She stayed," said Raven. "Longer than anyone who is not a god. And she returned as herself, to the same body."

"How long did you stay in the Underworld?"

"A thousand years," said Raven. "Maybe more. How long is an eon?"

Judith said, "I can't say. More than a decade, less than a century."

"And how were you able to return to the world of the living?"

"There came a very warm spring—the glacier melted and spewed great rivers of fresh water. Some hunters came to the island and found my body on the beach, so I must have washed down out of the glacier. I don't remember this, but it became part of legend in my village. They found me, still frozen, and took me back to their village. They had never seen a European woman, nor anybody so tall or with light hair. The shaman said I was Sedna returned from the sea, so they kept me in his house. I don't know how long I was there, but at some point, I thawed and my heart began beating and they cared for me until I woke up."

"When you woke up, did you remember jumping in the crevasse?"

"No. Not for a while. Nothing about being on the ice with Adam or being on the *Prometheus* came back to me for months, and then they seemed like remembering a nightmare, not something that happened."

"Did you remember your time before, in England?"

"No, only what I knew in the Underworld, so I had skills. I knew how to hunt, how to sew, how to build shelters and boats—all the skills of the People. And I knew the Animal People, so I could tell where fish and game would be."

"And you could speak their language?"

"Yes. I didn't know it then, but I could speak all languages of all the People. I don't know how, I just understood."

"And when you dream, what language do you dream in?"

"I don't dream in words. I dream in pictures, smells, light and dark, warm and cold."

"And what did you do now that you were among people again?"

"Many were afraid of me because I was different, but after I led them to game and fish they were more kindly disposed toward me. There was a man called Innik whose wife had died in childbirth, and who had two little ones, who took me as his wife."

"And how was your life after that? Did Innik treat you well?"

"He treated me as a wife, the way any other man treated his wife. I worked with the women, raised his children. After several years when I didn't become pregnant he became angry and demanded a second wife, which was allowed if he proved he could support her. With my knowledge of animals and fish, and the ability to call them—summon them—he was granted a second wife, a girl named Pinga."

"How did the new wife treat you?"

"She was fearful of me at first, then resentful. She would do little things to hurt me—hide a needle among my furs, leave the most difficult sewing for me. After she had a child she calmed down and treated me like a convenience, to help her raise her baby."

"Did you become friends?"

"No. She never stopped being afraid of me."

"Were the People cruel or unkind to you?"

"No, they treated me fairly, but I was apart. I was always apart. Sometimes the men would take me hunting with them, which was something a woman didn't do, so the other women resented me. Because Innik had two wives I could be away from the children. Most of the time I worked beside the other women."

"What about sex? Did you and Innik still have a sex life after he took a second wife?"

"The three of us slept together. With a baby when they were little. Sex was something that happened in the dark, sometimes with me, sometimes with Pinga. I didn't mind. It wasn't cruel or painful. After a time it was sometimes enjoyable."

"And you never became pregnant?"

"No. And I wasn't able to nurse, as some women do."

"You didn't have bad memories of your time with Adam?"

"It wasn't the same. What happened with Adam wasn't sex, it was rape. Even after I submitted to him, it was only to keep from being hurt. Innik was a good man."

"Did you love him?"

"I don't know. We were family. We were all in each other's lives. We had our roles and we lived them. Mine was different from anyone else's, but I had my role."

"Did he love you?"

"He didn't let me starve or leave me in the cold."

"What happened with Innik?"

"He died."

"Hunting on the ice must be very dangerous."

"He died of old age. Old by the standard of the People. He stopped breathing one winter."

"And Pinga?"

"She died too. I took care of her until she was gone. Some kind of fever."

"And the children?"

"They grew up. They married."

"But you didn't grow old like Innik and Pinga?"

"No. In the time when Pinga died there were too few women of marriage age—many had died. I was made the wife of a man called Tonraq, who lost his wife to the fever. His children were grown, so he was left alone, and the People hate for someone to live without family. He wasn't old enough to be left out on the ice."

"Left on the ice?"

"In those times, especially if food was sparse, they would leave the old or sick out on the ice to die. Tonraq was still strong, so I was given to him as his wife, otherwise I would have been alone, too."

"And did he treat you well?"

"Well enough. He too was a little afraid of me. The People called me Sedna, who brings abundance, but who also is used to frighten children. They are told she will pull them into the sea if they get too close to the water's edge. It keeps the little ones from playing too close to the water. I think he held on to some of that fear from when he was a boy. Also, he was a small man and he didn't like that I was tall. He often said that he wouldn't mind me being so pale and having yellow hair if I wasn't so tall."

"What happened with Tonraq? Did he take another wife?"

"He might have if there had been someone, even a widow, but several summers passed and he became more angry, insisting that he deserved a wife who could bear children, even though he was old and had children and grandchildren. Everyone knew me, and knew my powers, and they had no sympathy for him. He became very grumpy. He complained all the time that I was too old and too tall."

"Too old, but you still looked as you do now, right?"

"Yes, but the People knew I was as old as most of the elders, no matter my appearance."

"Was he cruel to you? Physically?"

"He was afraid to be. I had told him of what I had done to Adam, my first husband, telling only the story of him being pulled under the ice by the bear. I had remembered it by then. Sedna encouraged me to murder Tonraq."

"Sedna spoke to you then?"

"All the time. Less than Raven, who would talk to me to hear his own voice, but Sedna was always there on the hunt."

Raven's voice came: "I do have a beautiful voice."

"I'm talking to *Judith* now," Jung said.

"And the shiniest, most beautiful feathers," Raven said. "You should have her show you."

"What happened after you threatened Tonraq?"

"He took me on a hunt. Just the two of us. It was fall; the ice had returned and someone had seen a bear offshore. Tonraq said that because I was magical, he and I would go kill the bear and bring it back. We took a dog team and sled and three killing lances and we went out on the ice. Miles and miles. I told him there were no bears the way he was going, but he drove the dogs on. The days were short and we stopped and made a snow house at night. On the third night, I awoke to the sound of the dogs. I crawled out of the snow house to see Tonraq driving off with the dogs. He had taken the lances, the oil lamp, all my furs except the bear rug we had been sleeping in. I had my mukluks, my boots, but only because I had been using them as a pillow to keep them warm. I could hear Raven laughing. I shouted at him, angry he hadn't warned me of what Tonraq had done. He just laughed and told me, 'Fly away home, Little Bird.' Sedna growled at me and reminded me that she had told me I should have killed Tonraq.

"Days and nights had passed before they returned, four of them, searching for me, they said. Tonraq had said I had been dragged off by a bear who broke into our igloo. The others were worried that the game and fish might go away. There had been no famine among the People since I had joined them, and as fearful as they might have been of me, I had been their blessing from Sedna and they had insisted Tonraq look for me. He hadn't told them that he had taken my furs and all the tools."

"But they found you?"

"They found me in a new snow house that had been dug into a snowbank, much bigger than the snow house Tonraq had left me in. One of the hunters crawled in the entrance with a lighted oil stone and found me nestled in my rug and a great female bear curled around me. He backed out of the house shouting for the others to run. The bear followed him.

"They had brought two sleds and teams. They had lances, and they might have killed the bear if they had stood their ground and acted like hunters, but they ran. Even a team of dogs can't outrun a fully grown bear. The driver of the trailing sled was smaller than the others, so I told the bear to knock him off the sled."

"Tonraq?"

"Yes, Tonraq. The bear picked him up in her jaws and shook him until he stopped screaming. Then he stopped moving. I told the bear to wait, and I took Tonraq's furs, his knife, his snow goggles, even some dried meat he had tucked in his parka. The others kept going until they were almost out of sight, then they stopped and watched. I waved to them as the bear ate Tonraq. It took a long time and there was much blood on the ice."

"You said you told the bear what to do?"

"I could speak all languages, even bear. Nanook, the bear god, was my friend in the Underworld. All bears carry a little of Nanook's spirit."

Jung had been writing furiously as she spoke. He looked up to ask, "Where did you go then?"

"I waited a few days, then I returned to my village. The women and children hid. Some of the men came with spears but did not attack. I stood there at the edge of the camp, feeling like I had the day I jumped into the crevasse. I cried. I screamed. I dared them to kill me. All the time Sedna was in my ear, telling me to kill them all."

"Sedna, not Raven?"

"No, Raven laughed, called me Little Bird, and told me to fly away."

"But isn't Sedna the mother who feeds everyone, cares for everyone? Brings the game?"

"Sedna is the bringer of the animals and the fish, the caretaker, but she has a side that is still angry with how her father treated her. She fights her urge to take revenge only so long as she is respected by the People."

"Do they make sacrifices to her?"

"Some would say that the old people and the crippled left on the ice during hard times were sacrifices to her. But she did not recognize them that way. Sedna doesn't accept offerings, she *takes* her sacrifices."

"Were Adam and Tonraq sacrifices to her?"

Judith didn't answer right away. Jung caught up with his notes and waited. He could hear Judith's soft breathing, the clock ticking on the wall.

"Judith? Are you there?"

"They were sacrifices to me," she said flatly. Sedna's voice. *"When I am not respected, I take my sacrifices."*

Jung could hear his own breathing. The clock ticking on the wall.

"Judith, I'm going to count to three and you will be awake. You will be rested and aware and you will remember everything we've talked about."

Judith opened her eyes and sat up. "Well, that was a surprise," she said.

"Was it?" said Jung. "You didn't seem surprised."

"What do you mean?"

"Subjects who are regressed in trance, Judith, tend to react and behave as if they are experiencing memories for the first time— experiencing the fear or trauma. But you are conversational. Casual, as if you are reciting something you've recalled many times. Or something that didn't happen at all."

"You said it didn't matter if it really happened. Even if I'm re-membering dreams, they are valuable to understanding my story."

"As real as these stories may or may not be to you, Judith, your ideation of murder concerns me."

"Is it really murder if a bear eats a man who was unpleasant?"

"Yes."

"What is the harm if you don't believe it happened?"

"You believe it, that is what matters. I only point out the logic so you don't follow these destructive urges now. Murder and suicide."

"You saw the scars, Doctor."

"I have no doubt you have experienced great trauma, great pain, and your suppression of those experiences is so deep that you have constructed a fanciful narrative that has allowed you to give a context for them that is separate from the reality we share now."

"What about the collective unconscious? You said that Raven and Sedna inhabit it. I heard you talking to Raven."

"I have been discussing the theory with Dr. Freud in the evenings, and I believe that the archetypes in the collective unconscious may be complexes that are no longer needed. Complexes are states of mind which are created out of unresolved experience or motivations."

"So, not real?"

"Dr. Freud has persuaded me that we need to view them as artifacts of imagination created to cope."

"So I remember these things, these people, these gods, as real, but they aren't?"

"Which is not to say they don't have value in your treatment, they do, but now, in the cold light of day, as they say, how do we reconcile you being on the ice for lifetimes and somehow ending up in Europe, in the twentieth century?"

"You didn't ask before, but I remembered. I lived on the ice by myself for a while—through a winter—but the next summer I saw a ship and I went to it. It was a Dutch ship. They brought me to Amsterdam."

"And we will find the meaning of those images, but it may take longer than the time we have while I'm here in Vienna."

"So I won't find out who I was, originally?"

"I'm not saying that, but that identity is so repressed that we have to get through the layers of your story that are covering it."

Judith stood, straightened her dress. "Do we still have time today?"

"As you know, you are the only patient I'm seeing in Vienna, but I did promise Dr. Freud he would have his office back. We still have a quarter of an hour."

"Oh good. If you'd wait a bit, I'll be right back, I just need to run downstairs for a moment."

"Very well," said Jung.

She left the office and he perused his notes while he waited, marking those points he wanted to revisit and discuss with Freud. In a few minutes he heard footfalls on the stairs and Judith came through the double doors of the treatment office leading a large dog.

"Dr. Jung, this is Geoff," she said.

"Oh, the infamous Geoff, the immortal sled dog who returned from the Underworld?"

Jung put down his notebook, rose, and went to them. He scratched Geoff behind the ears.

"There's a good boy," Jung said.

"Yes." She released Geoff's collar and stepped back, holding the leash. "Akhlut, *makittuk*!" she said.

Akhlut rose.

*T*wo minutes later Judith led Geoff down the stairs to find Wally waiting by the desk. Handsome Dr. Bauman was not to be seen.

"Oh, you took Geoff to your session?"

"Yes. You weren't down here when I came to get him."

"We were on rounds," Wally said. "Handsome Dr. Bauman is updating his charts. How did Dr. Jung like Geoff?"

"Loved him," Judith said. "Shall we go? Geoff's a little queasy. I promised him a croissant."

"Did you remember anything good?" Wally asked.

Judith shrugged. "I fed a village, raised some children, and fed my second husband to a bear."

"A bear? How exciting. Wait, you were married?"

"Long story," Judith said. "I'll tell you on the way to Emilie's."

26

POSING A THREAT

When Judith and Wally arrived the next morning at Dr. Freud's clinic they were met at the desk by a sad handsome Dr. Bauman.

"I'm sorry, Fräulein Judith, but Dr. Jung has returned to Switzerland. He left a note for you, however." The doctor handed Judith an envelope.

"Does this mean that we can't do rounds today?" Wally asked.

"I would love that," said Dr. Bauman, "but unfortunately Dr. Freud has forbidden anyone in the clinic from having anything to do with this particular case."

"Why? Judith isn't cured. She's as loony as ever. Say something crazy, Judith."

Judith waved her off as she read Jung's letter.

"Give her a minute," Wally said.

Judith read:

My dear Judith:
   It is not my wish to leave a patient suddenly while she is in treatment, but I'm afraid I am forced to return to Basel, and I do not know when I will be able to come to Vienna again. Dr. Freud and I had a conflict over what you showed me yesterday, and how it applies

to my theory of the collective unconscious, and I'm afraid our points of view cannot be reconciled at this time. Dr. Freud revoked his permission for me to use his offices. He is quite cross about the rug.

I apologize for the abrupt and impersonal nature of this notice, but I had to catch the early train. That said, please do not feel abandoned. I have obligations in Basel and Zurich for the next few months, but if you are able to persuade Herr Klimt to finance your travel to Basel, I will try to find you temporary quarters at the university, and we can continue our sessions. I can make no promises as to whether we will be able to find out who you were before your abduction and abuse, but I will promise that I will do my best to help you reconcile your past with a happy, healthy life going forward.

If you are able to persuade Herr Klimt to cover your expenses, please write to me and I will make arrangements for your quarters. I only ask that you do not bring along your dog, as dogs are not allowed in university accommodations, and frankly, he terrifies me.

Yours Most Sincerely,
C. G. Jung

"Well," Judith said. "Gus is working on a portrait of Frau Bloch this morning and won't need me to model until this afternoon."

"I don't start at Café Piccolo until tomorrow," Wally said. "I told them I had to bring you to the doctor. Maybe I'll run home and surprise Egon. Will you be all right to get back to Gus's studio?"

"I could do it with my eyes closed. Geoff and I will do some shopping on the way."

Wally hugged Judith and kissed the air on either side of her cheeks because she thought it was very French. "*A demain, mon amie,*" she said.

"Tomorrow," Judith said. "Can I come to the café and visit you?"

"Maybe not on my first day," Wally said. "I'll come by the studio after lunch."

"I'll probably be posing. You know how Gus gets."

"I'll just sneak in with my key. He *loves* surprises."

Wally walked back to the apartment, passing slowly by the cafés on the way to watch how the waiters moved. She could do it. She was almost sure.

When she walked into the flat she found Egon sitting shirtless in one of the dining chairs, sketchbook in hand, while across from him, in her underwear, with one shoulder shrugged out of her chemise, the neighbor girl Adele Harms sat posing. On the divan sat a slightly younger Edith Harms, fully dressed, sipping tea. Both women were long necked and red haired (dyed, like Wally's), and both wore their hair up under knitted bands, Adele's red, Edith's black. Edith's teacup rattled in its saucer when she looked up.

"Oh, Wally," said Egon, only glancing up briefly from his drawing. "Wally is one of my models," he explained to the sisters. To Wally he said, "I knew you were busy this morning, so Adele and Edith came over to help me out."

"We met before," Wally said.

"Yes, Wally," said Adele. "Your life as a model must be so exciting."

"Exciting," said Edith.

Wally wanted to punch her in the mouth. She approached them tentatively, small steps, a stranger in her own home. "Dr. Jung had to go back to Switzerland early. Judith went back to Klimt's studio."

"Yes, Klimt," said Egon. "A true genius of a generation past."

Wally backed slowly to the door. "I don't want to interrupt the enfant terrible of the Vienna avant-garde at work." She took no pleasure in saying the French words, which she was pretty sure she'd pronounced them perfectly. "Perhaps your naughty bits will hang in the Louvre next to his sister's," she added as she slipped out the door.

*J*udith stood on the posing platform, wearing Emilie's gold and silver gown.

"Gus, Dr. Jung has had to return to Switzerland, so if I want to continue my treatment I have to go to Basel. He said you'd be happy to pay for my travel and he could put me in a room at the university."

"How does he know I would be happy to pay for your travel? He hasn't even met me."

"He's seen your work and can tell that you are a kind and generous gentleman who is only interested in me getting better."

"Did Wally tell you to say that?"

"No, but she would say the same thing if we asked her."

"I thought you had another session here in Vienna, what happened?"

"Canceled. Jung had a falling-out with Dr. Freud."

"What did they have a falling-out over?"

"Dr. Freud hates dogs, evidently."

"I read that Freud had two dogs. Chow chows, I think."

"Maybe he just hates Geoff. I took him up to the office yesterday."

"Why did you do that?"

"Dr. Jung wanted to meet him. I've told many stories about him."

"And he and Freud had a falling-out just because you brought Geoff into the office? That seems rigid."

"Well, Geoff vomited."

"In the office?"

"On a very nice rug."

"That's why I don't have nice rugs here in the studio."

"You didn't have rugs before Geoff showed up. You don't have rugs because you drip paint, and you have a thousand cats."

"Nine cats. We still have nine, right?"

"Yes, I counted."

"Hold still and don't talk, I'm doing a detail of your jaw. How bad was the stain on his rug? Maybe I should offer to have it cleaned or replace it."

"Geoff horked up a walrus."

"Hold still. What do you mean, 'a walrus'?"

"You can't ask me questions if you don't want me to move my mouth."

Klimt sighed and stepped back from the canvas. "What do you mean, 'a walrus'?"

"Just a baby one, although it was partially digested."

"A walrus?"

"Now you've got it."

"What, chewed-up meat that looked like a walrus? You're just using 'walrus' as a metaphor, right?"

"No, a whole baby walrus."

"A whole baby walrus?"

"Although, deceased. And partially digested."

"Geoff horked up a whole baby walrus on Sigmund Freud's rug?"

"Yes. As you've probably noticed, Geoff doesn't always chew his food very well."

"How big is a baby walrus?"

"About like this?" She moved her hands in a motion describing parentheses in the air that would contain about three and a half large house cats.

"Don't move your arms."

"Well, I couldn't think of anything that size. A medium sheep, maybe. Besides, you weren't drawing."

"But you were modeling. You're being paid to model, and you need to hold the pose. How could Geoff possibly eat a whole walrus—where did he get it?"

"Mmmm-mm mmm-mmmph," she answered, without moving her lips at all.

The front door clicked behind him and Klimt turned. Judith allowed her eyes to dart in that direction without moving her head. Wally burst into the room; black mascara tear marks striped her cheeks. "That's it! Judith, you will not be anyone's fuck-puppet. I forbid it. Gus, if you touch her, I will have Geoff bite off your nut sack."

"Wally—" Klimt said, but he didn't have any reply to what she had said, so he said, "Where did you get a key?"

"Mmmm-mmm mmmm-mph mmph," Judith mmmphed.

"We're finished for the day," Klimt said.

"She's had a key since you went to Attersee," Judith said. "I used it for a while, too." She dropped her arms and carefully gathered up the trail of the open gown before she stepped off the posing platform.

"What's wrong?" Klimt asked Wally.

"Men are disgusting fuck-beasts, is what," Wally said. "Especially artists."

"Oh, child," Klimt said. He held his arms out for her to come to him for an embrace. In his long blue caftan, he looked like a paint-spattered saint offering absolution. "You can't fall in love with them."

Wally bolted past Klimt into Judith's waiting arms. Judith petted her and kissed the top of her head. Wally left black damp wet eye prints on Judith's naked chest.

"Hold that pose," Klimt said. He snatched up a sketchbook from the side table and started to sketch.

"Geoff!" Wally called.

Geoff awooed from the kitchen and they could hear his nails clicking on the floor as he got up.

"Never mind," Klimt said, letting the sketchbook fall to his side.

"So you'll pay for my trip to Basel?" Judith said.

"What?" he said.

"You said you're paying me to model," Judith said. "You haven't paid me."

"I've been giving your pay to Wally. She was supposed to pass it on to you."

Wally looked up at Judith. "We've gone to the market and a lot of cafés. I wasn't sure you wouldn't give it all away to feed strangers if I gave it to you."

"Good thinking," Judith said. To Klimt she said, "So, a trip to Basel?"

"How long will you be gone?"

"I don't know."

"Can you finish posing for the preliminary sketches first? Another week?"

"Yes. I think so."

"Then yes, I will pay for your trip to Basel. And when you get back we'll find you different living arrangements."

"What about the Englishman?" Wally asked.

"What Englishman?" Klimt asked. They ignored him.

"Oh, I spoke to him," Judith said. "We have an understanding."

"Is it an understanding that if he doesn't like it, he's going to be the next thing Geoff barfs up on Dr. Freud's rug?"

"Yes, something like that. Wait, how do you know about that?"

"I went back to the clinic later to see handsome Dr. Bauman, let him know I was interested in working with him. He says that Freud is very cross with us."

"What Englishman?" Klimt said.

Wally breathed an exasperated sigh and turned out of Judith's embrace. "The one who hired the Dutch policeman that was decapitated on the bridge the day you found Judith."

Klimt backed to the love seat he kept in the parlor—where he sometimes met with clients to discuss the work—and sat. "Do we still have any of that French wine I keep for the portraiture clients?" Klimt asked.

"It's your studio," Wally said. "Don't you know?"

"There's a bottle in the kitchen," Judith said. "I'll fetch it." She padded off to the kitchen.

"Then you have to tell me what the Englishman said," Wally said.

*I*t's a fair offer," the Englishman had said. "I daresay it will be the first time in your long life when you have had any security. Better than any woman of your breeding could expect."

She'd gone to the address on the card he'd given her as soon as she left Freud's office that morning. It was a white concrete and marble building in the Empire style, white on white, like so many of the buildings on the Ringstrasse. Walton had leased an entire floor. She waited while the doorman called up through a brass tube behind the desk, to a servant on Walton's floor.

"How many servants are with Mr. Walton in his flat?"

"I'm not permitted to discuss the business of the tenants, Fräulein," the doorman said.

She contemplated persuading him but then thought better of it. She might have to return at some point and a terrified doorman might be an inconvenience. "I understand," she said. Geoff growled and she scratched between his ears to settle him.

Standing clear of Geoff, the doorman gestured to a wide marble staircase that whirled up and out of the lobby. A man in his thirties with extravagant muttonchop sideburns greeted her at the door to the apartment and said, "Mr. Walton is this way," in German, with an accent. After a frown at Geoff, he led her into a parlor or reception room big enough to hold a ball in, groups of furniture spaced out so guests might have their own conversation space. Walton sat in one of a pair of Louis XVI chairs in gold and mauve velvet, an ornate gilded table between them. He stood and gestured to the other chair.

"Can I get you anything?" Walton said. "We have everything."

"No, I won't be long," she said. "I wanted to discuss your offer."

It was then that the Englishman said, "It's a fair offer. I daresay it will be the first time in your long life when you have had any security. Better than any woman of your breeding could expect."

"What do you know of my breeding?"

"Well, nothing directly. But Frankenstein said his monster found you on the streets of Edinburgh, at night. No lady would be out on the city street at night."

"You don't know. I might have been getting out of my carriage at the opera."

"And the only time you ever spoke, you called me a butt puddle."

"Well, that has more to do with your background than mine, don't you think?"

"That is not the speech of a lady from a good family."

"I see," she said. "Well, that may be true, and I may accept your offer, but there are conditions."

"Please, I will accommodate your needs as best I can."

She sat with her bag in her lap, and now she felt the reassuring weight of Van Beek's revolver inside.

"I will need you to stop following me and anyone I know. I have work to do, and you don't need to know what it is."

"Yes, I apologize for that. But it took so long to find you, I was afraid of losing track of you again."

"That brings me to my next point. If I agree to accompany you to your estate, I have to be able to leave, to travel, any time I want. I will be there to do your transfusions, but you will not own me, is that understood?"

Walton said, "But we will—"

She held up a finger for silence and he paused. "If you break that condition, I will murder you and anyone that gets in my way, anyone you send my way. You may be under the impression that my blood made you immortal, Mr. Walton, but you are not. You remember Adam from that night on the ship, I presume. There has never been a more powerful human animal to walk the earth, nor one more resistant to death."

"Yes, I remember."

"I killed him. You found me; do you think for all your effort you wouldn't have heard of an eight-foot-tall immortal monster on the ice if he had survived?"

"I assure you, er—Miss, er—Judith, I do not want to restrain you or harm you in any way."

Judith noticed that four different servants, all male, had started to move from the corners of the great room toward where they were sitting, each occupying himself as if attending some other task that required their convergence. Geoff fidgeted at her feet and ruffed at the closest of the toadies, the one with muttonchops. She didn't want to call up Akhlut now. Geoff had spent over a hundred years with Walton; she wasn't sure what his response might be.

"Kill them all," came a voice in her head. Sedna. *"Make a boat from their skins."*

"I'm not sure I believe you, Mr. Walton." She stood, pulled the big revolver from her bag, and fired it at Muttonchops. The noise was horrific and set her ears ringing. The old man had dived to the floor, his hands over his head. Muttonchops was not hurt in the least, as the bullet had ricocheted off a marble column and splintered the leg of a chair on the other side of the room, but he froze in place.

Judith looked at the gun, kept it pointed in the direction of Muttonchops, but tilted it side to side. "These things are great!" she said. "My first time. Normally I just break someone's neck, strangle them, or tear off their head, but these things are the tits. Loud, but smashing." She waved the gun in the direction of each of Walton's minions, and each ducked or dived behind a piece of furniture. She let the gun fall to her side and the minions slowly crawled out of their hiding places; then she waved the gun again and they all ducked again. She laughed and did it three more times. When Muttonchops didn't duck she said, "I *will* shoot you, and if I miss, I'll be happy to pull your brain out of your eye holes."

Muttonchops didn't believe her and began moving toward her. Walton obviously hadn't told them what she was capable of. She shrugged and looked down at Walton. "Are you testing me?"

"No, I'm—"

She pulled up the pistol and shot Muttonchops. He fell to the floor and screamed, holding his thigh.

"Oh, it's easier if they're closer. Still quite loud, though."

"I will have the police—"

She pointed the pistol at Walton and he stopped talking.

"Oh, do that. Send for the police and have me arrested. They'll be happy to make arrangements for me to live on your estate and give you blood to keep you alive, especially when I tell them how old you are."

Walton dropped his head, defeated. Judith turned to each of the unshot minions, pointing the revolver and sending them back into their hiding places.

"I will return here in a month and we can make arrangements from there, but if I see you, or anyone who I think you may have hired, you will all be floating headless in the Danube. Let's go, Geoff." Geoff ruffed.

She walked across the room, swinging the revolver as she went, her heels clicking on the marble floor, Geoff's nails tapping softly like rodent castanets. She paused and stood over Muttonchops, who was wincing and breathing hard, holding his thigh. "I apologize, I'm just learning. I meant to shoot you in the heart, so it would be quick and painless. I'm not a monster."

She continued on her way, paused at the big double doors, and shoved the gun into her bag. "Not all the time, anyway," she called. The minions broke their poses and rushed to their fallen comrade as she slipped out the door. Geoff padded along behind her.

"Oh, Little Bird," said Raven. *"I have missed you so."*

On the way back to Klimt's studio she stopped at a café, and bought Geoff a croissant and herself a coffee and a piece of cherry strudel. They enjoyed them at an outdoor table in the shade. "Geoff, you silly boy, how does Walton not know who you really are?"

"He's a good boy," came Sedna's voice in her head.

"He barfed a baby walrus on my doctor's rug," Judith said aloud.

"We wondered what happened to that walrus," Raven said.

"Have you two been with me all this time? All the time in Amsterdam?"

"Maybe," Raven said.

"You could have helped me. Told me how I killed that policeman on the bridge."

"And ruin the surprise?" Raven said. *"You know how I love surprises."*

Two women at a nearby table looked over at Judith with scowls of disapproval. She smiled at them. "I'm comforting my dog. His tummy has been upset," she said. "He's a good boy."

Geoff warbled sadly.

The women nodded as if they understood and turned back to their own conversation.

27

DOG GONE

A week passed before Klimt was far enough along with the painting
to let her go, and in that time he wired Jung to tell him to prepare for
her arrival. He walked her to the edge of the garden to help her hail
a cab. Geoff pranced at the end of his leash, excited to get to go for a
ride, or a walk, or any of the activities that might end with eating a
croissant.

"Do you have everything?" Klimt asked her.

"I don't have anything."

"You have money, and . . ." He couldn't think of anything else
to ask.

She patted the canvas bag, which had magically become hers. "I
have bread and sausages and cheese and the revolver."

"Oh good," Klimt said. "Well, wire me if you need anything."

"I will."

"And no strangling people."

"No promises."

"Are you sure you want to take Geoff?"

"I have to. There won't be anyone here at night to take care of him."

"But Wally—"

"Wally has too much to do already, with her new job, and she's trying to save her future with Egon."

"He is a very talented young man."

Out of respect for the maestro, she didn't say she thought that Egon was a twat.

A motor cab putted up to the curb and stopped.

"Goodbye, Judith," Klimt said.

She embraced him lightly and kissed his cheek. "Goodbye, Gus."

She coaxed Geoff to jump into the cab and climbed in after him. Klimt told the driver to take her to the station and the cab motored away.

Klimt turned and walked slowly across the garden. One of the cats, the little calico, was menacing a marigold blossom and Klimt picked her up and petted her as he returned to the studio and closed the door. He felt hollow, used up, foggy headed, and slow—the way he often felt upon finishing a big painting.

"She'll be back, kitty," he said. She mewled and he set her down to go find her co-cats. She trotted off through the drawing studio. He pulled up a stool he often used when painting, sat, and looked at the canvas. It had no color yet, just the black crayon with a few patches of white chalk for highlights. He added a drop of black to the gesso he used to prime the canvas so it had a very faint cool gray tone. The problem was, there were two shadows bleeding through at the figure's back, which might have been understandable if he had been reusing the canvas, but this was a fresh linen canvas he had stretched and primed himself—work most artists of his status would have delegated to an apprentice or a color man, but his background in the applied arts had conditioned him to think like a craftsman, tending to the details of preparing materials as well as turning them into art. He sighed—he could mix more primer and paint over the shadows, or just paint over them when he applied the oil paint, but they would draw his eye to a part of the picture he meant to be space, not object, and he didn't trust himself not to try to correct the composition.

He was heading through the drawing studio to the storeroom to fetch the primer when there was a loud knock at the door and he nearly leapt out of his caftan. He returned to the parlor, where he could see a hefty figure through the reeded glass of the front door. He opened the door and was met by the brass buttons and outrageous mustache of his fencing partner, Commandant Kruger.

"Kruger," Klimt said with a smile.

Kruger did not smile. "Gus, I need to talk to you, and I need you to tell me the truth or one or both of us is going to be very unhappy."

"Come in," Klimt said, and stood aside as the big policeman entered the studio.

Gus? Why were people calling him Gus all the time now? Kruger was Kruger and he was Klimt, as was proper between grown men. *I don't even know Kruger's Christian name. Probably isn't Commandant— that would be too easy.*

*I*t was her first train ride alone, or at least the first she remembered. It never occurred to her to look around to see if someone was following her. Wally usually did that.

A porter at the station in Vienna insisted she put Geoff in a vented crate, which she rented. She had to change trains in Zurich and made the porter promise that she would be able to get her dog. She felt very strange using the term "my dog" to refer to Geoff, as technically, Geoff was inhabited by Akhlut, and Akhlut was a god. Still, the porter told her what to do to ensure that Geoff would arrive in Basel on the same train that she did.

The countryside was spectacular, fields of grain and hops, mountains and streams, villages as if from a fairy tale. All she knew of Switzerland was what Adam had told her when he was lamenting his mistreatment by Frankenstein, and he had described a hostile, foreboding place, which is saying something when you're living in a stone hut on an island covered with ice and bears that want to eat you. On the contrary, Switzerland was lovely, magical, and while there was still some snow on the mountains, even in high summer, it was distant and more decorative than elemental—faraway highlights to a lush green picture, which she decided would be the way she would prefer to experience snow from now on.

In Zurich no one was forthcoming to help her fetch Geoff, so she went to the baggage car and pulled him out, crate and all, and carried him to the platform where her train to Basel was set to embark. Along the way she was stopped by a porter who was mortified that a lady was carrying her own luggage, especially a crate large enough that he, a professional, had to fetch a trolly to move for her. But he did, and with Geoff safely loaded, she was off to Basel.

The station in Basel looked to have been built up from a toy miniature. In fact, most of Basel looked as if it had been built up from toy miniatures. When she stepped off the train she was met by a portly young man in a tweed suit, rumpled and slightly worn at the cuffs. He introduced himself as Diderot, one of Jung's students. He looked at her as if he had never seen a woman before, as if she had floated from the train nude, on a clamshell, instead of trudging in a wrinkled blue shift and a stolen hat, then he would look away, as if allowing her her modesty.

"Professor Jung has reserved a small flat in Kleinbasel; that's the smaller part of the city, across the river from the university, but an easy walk. Very nice. Not as nice as Grossbasel, the central city, but it's close to the station and it's the only building the university keeps that would allow a dog. Professor Jung said you would have a dog, despite his request you not bring it."

"We need to get him from baggage," she said.

They found Geoff among the trunks being unloaded from the baggage car, and after taking Judith's claim ticket, a porter released the Malamute from his crate. Diderot was surprised her only baggage was the small canvas satchel.

"Your quarters are very close. I can hail a taxi if you like, but it's an easy walk."

"Do they sell croissants in Basel?" Judith asked. At the mention of croissants Geoff drooled a wobbly song of pastry praise and dripped demon dog spit on the sidewalk as they went along.

"But of course. Although the bakeries may be all sold out this late in the day. There is a restaurant next to your building that caters to students for your dinner. They will even deliver food to your flat."

They sauntered along, Diderot extolling the highlights of the city, its proximity to France, Germany, and Switzerland making it a truly international city, and they stopped at a bakery, where the baker gave them the last four croissants for the price of one.

"That's never happened to me before," Diderot exclaimed. "That is remarkable."

"I'm magical," Judith explained, and Diderot laughed.

The building was six stories tall, a stucco affair with a peaked red tile roof and small, well-spaced windows looking on an inner courtyard. "There are no flat roofs in Basel," Diderot explained. "Snow."

He showed her to her room on the third floor and as he unlocked the door and threw it open said, "And it has its own bathroom!" as if he were announcing the arrival of the king, which made her think that she had, perhaps, been taking having a bathroom at the studio for granted, but which also made her want to pee.

"I'll come by in the morning to take you to your session with Professor Jung," Diderot said. "But in the meantime, if you need anything, the first apartment as you come into the courtyard is where the concierge lives, and she will help you, or contact us for you." He leaned in closer and said conspiratorially, "Professor Jung can sometimes be forgetful about the needs of mere humans, so I would eat a good breakfast downstairs before you come."

She bent over and, in an equally conspiratorial tone, whispered, "Thanks."

"I'll be here at eight." He handed her the key and bowed, ever so slightly, as if waiting to be dismissed.

"He's nice, give him a hand job," Sedna said. Which made Judith miss Wally—and made her want to ask the sea goddess if she had learned that phrase from the diminutive model, but she decided she'd probably best not right now. *"Or some of that cheese in your bag."*

Judith reached into her satchel and pulled out a white paper package in which was wrapped a hunk of Gouda. "This is for you," she said.

He took the package, in both hands, a penitent monk receiving alms. "Thank you."

"It's cheese," she said. "From Vienna."

"I'm honored."

"It's fucking cheese," Raven said.

"Everybody likes cheese," Sedna said.

"A demain," Judith said in perfect fucking French, thinking of how much Wally would have loved it.

"Tomorrow," said Diderot as he backed out of the room.

*D*iderot was waiting in the courtyard at eight sharp, and he walked her across the bridge over the Rhine and into the university grounds and to a neo-Gothic building, where they tied Geoff up in the breezeway.

"I will get him a bowl of water," Diderot promised. "Dr. Jung can ring me in my office when you need to go back."

"You have an office. I thought you were a student."

"I am a graduate student—a research assistant to Professor Jung. Psychiatry."

"I see. Well, I can probably make it back to the flat on my own, so I won't take you away from your work."

"No. No. I love being taken away from my work," Diderot said. Then, distraught, he said, "Oh, please don't tell the professor I said that."

"I won't."

He showed her to the stairwell and told her which way to go. The door to Jung's office was open. The professor sat behind a dark wood desk that was stacked with papers, folders, and the odd leather-bound volume. Jung stood when she came in.

"Ah, Judith, so nice to see you. Please, come in, sit down."

She did. "You don't have a fainting couch?"

"Yes, I do. This is a suite of offices, but I thought today we might just talk for a while, review your progress, and perhaps you could help me put what I have seen in context."

"Is Dr. Freud terribly angry about his rug? I'm so sorry, Geoff has never done that before."

"Yes. He is angry, but less about his rug and more about the conclusions I have drawn from what I have seen."

"Akhlut?"

"Yes. He's not here, is he?" Jung looked truly alarmed for a moment.

"Downstairs, just a normal Malamute. A silly boy."

Jung relaxed. "I concluded, as I think you meant for me to, that your Underworld, my collective unconscious, is a real, tangible thing—existing beyond a series of complexes and hallucinations."

"You saw him. When I call him, Akhlut can move in this world like he did when I knew him in the Underworld."

"And Raven and Sedna, can they manifest physically in this world?"

"I don't know. I have never seen either of them here, but Raven is a shape-shifter, he could be anything, anyone. I know he can move things in our world, like weather."

Jung looked at the notebook open on his desk, capped his fountain pen, and set it down on the page. "And you, Judith. Can you, like Geoff, change shapes in this world?"

She fidgeted with her bag, squeezed the revolver, the hard sausage, a croissant she'd saved for Geoff, through the waxed canvas. Where were the distracting comments of Sedna and Raven now when she needed them? She said, "You know, Dr. Jung, all this time we've been talking and I've never even offered you a hand job, and I think it's about time—"

"Judith, are you a shape-changer?"

"No," she said. Then, "Yes. I have changed shapes. My shape has changed. Once that I can remember, but honestly, with my memory, I might have been dreaming."

"Can you change shapes on demand, like your dog?"

"He's not really my dog, Doctor. More of a dog acquaintance."

"Judith. Please."

"Not at will—or on command like Geoff. But if I am in danger— *when* I was in danger, I changed."

"When was this?"

"When I first came to Vienna. I'd only been here a few days. There was a Dutch policeman who had been following me—an ex-policeman, I guess. And he burst in on me when I was with a man. A client, I guess you would call him. I jumped through a window and ran, but he caught up to me. On a bridge. And he threatened me with a gun."

"And you changed?"

"Geoff was with him. I knew it was Geoff."

"So Geoff changed?"

"I didn't even know Geoff could do that then. I hadn't seen him since the ship."

"What happened?"

"The policeman, Thiessen, said I needed to come with him or he would shoot me. I said he wouldn't shoot an unarmed woman. A naked woman. And he said it didn't matter to him, he had caught me, and all he needed to do was bring back my blood. Then I was terrified, thinking that Frankenstein had somehow survived, that Adam had lied to me about killing the doctor. Or, worse, Adam had survived and was going to make a new immortal sex puppet."

"A what?"

"A slave to his desires, if you like. Doctor, I had lived a very, very long time, in harsh circumstances, but I had lost the sense of fear. I hadn't felt it for decades—since my third death—until that night on that bridge. Thiessen grabbed me by the throat with his free hand, tried to choke me."

"So you changed—changed form?"

"Yes. Thiessen clicked the gun."

"Cocked the hammer?"

"Yes, he cocked the hammer and was aiming to shoot me in the face, and I changed. I became the form I learned from Raven, and I thrust out my wing and forced my flight feathers into his throat. I snapped my wing as if I were going to take off and I tore his head off, flipped it like a champagne cork."

"And then what did you do? Fly away?"

"No, Geoff came to me, licked the blood from my wing, and leapt off the bridge into the canal. He changed to his orca form in the air and made a great splash."

"Orca? A blackfish?"

"A killer whale. It is Akhlut's other form in the Underworld, where he will run to the water's edge as a wolf and change without missing a step. The Seal and Walrus People hate it."

"Can you change to another form?"

"I don't know. When Geoff went into the canal I dove in after him. I didn't know what had happened to me, only that I wanted to be away from that bridge and that policeman. I must have hit my head on something in the water and drowned, because the next thing I remember, Gustav Klimt was loading my corpse onto a newspaper cart."

"Judith, you know that it is my duty, ethically, to report it if one of my patients confesses to a crime, don't you?"

"I did not know that. Well, well, well, my imagination is playing tricks on me again. It was all a dream."

"The problem, of course, is that I would have to admit that I believe you, and at this point that is not something I can do. What you've shown me fundamentally changes the reality of existence for all mankind, and not necessarily for the better."

"It was one cop. He wasn't even very tall."

"No, I mean you, Geoff, Raven, the Underworld, empirical evidence of the existence of a collective unconscious."

"So you can prove your theory—that's good, isn't it?"

"The collective unconscious and the archetypes that reside there are useful, I believe, in understanding the nature of human consciousness, of the mind, and can help us understand how to help those who are experiencing mental illness, in many of its forms. They are useful as metaphors, and even when I postulated that they existed in an autonomous sense, as a world-mind, you might say, I understood it to be something that we as a species generated from our minds, but *you*, you *add* corporeal reality, and the idea that rather than helping the mind to come to a sense of peace with the self by the use of metaphor, you present the possibility of changing the myths, of challenging them. If I tell you that your mischievous side is like the archetype of the trickster, it helps you understand that your mischievous behavior is a type of narcissism, self-aggrandizement, a call for attention to the psyche. But if you say, 'Oh, I had tea with Raven on Wednesday and he was spending time anonymously helping the poor,' or 'He sacrificed himself for the betterment of mankind,' you've changed the trickster archetype, you've changed the collective unconscious. Even the term 'narcissism' would change if you found that Narcissus had thrown away all of his mirrors, eschewed his own reflection, and, in fact, would never talk about himself. Suddenly Raven and Narcissus are no longer universal. Under this new reality we can argue about the nature of myth, we can debate the superiority of our gods, encourage them to arm wrestle for dominance. Our day-to-day life becomes a battle on Olympus, or between heaven and hell, the Aesir and the Frost Giants—to determine whatever extent to which our minds do affect the collective unconscious, we would send our gods to war and we would all be foot soldiers in a religious war, because, remember, a myth is simply a religion that you don't believe in."

"So what does that mean for me?"

"I would say, from your experience, living in what you call the Underworld, and giving corporeal form to a figure from there, by most definitions, you are a god."

"I was thinking about becoming a waitress. I like giving food to people. And Geoff loves pastries. Maybe a seamstress."

"I wasn't describing a vocation, Judith."

"Because of the policeman on the bridge? I'd be known as Judith the murdering waitress?"

"What I am saying is I cannot reveal what I have seen or what has transpired between us. Just discussing it with Professor Freud had him denouncing me as neurotic to a fault and as needing serious psychoanalysis, and severing all ties, even his friendship with me."

"So it wasn't just the partially digested baby walrus on his rug?"

"That did not help matters, because that was inexplicable evidence of the existence of the supernatural, something Freud has found absurd and unscientific since before I knew him. And you, you are that same kind of evidence."

"So the collective unconscious was ruined by dog barf and I never have a hope of finding out who I was before all of this?"

"I didn't say that. Our goal can be the same. And as unpleasant as remembering your experiences on the ice has been, they have helped you to better adjust to the world. You haven't had any of the episodes you had right after Klimt found you, correct?"

Judith thought it best not to mention Geoff eating Van Beek and her shooting Walton's henchman and threatening to behead them all if they followed her, as it wouldn't reflect well on her progress. She said, "No, but sometimes I say things just to shock people."

"That would be Raven's influence, I would think. In most people I would suggest learning to resist those urges; in your case, you can probably ask Raven to stop. Most patients don't have that choice."

"And what will *you* do now, Doctor?"

"I will continue with my work, with developing my theory of the collective unconscious as a means of understanding and treating patients' conditions, and ignore what I have learned from you. As far as we know, from what Raven told me, you are unique. No one has ever done what you have done, nor gone where you have gone, so in effect, your experience won't be something I can use to help other patients. But that does not mean that we won't continue with your sessions, searching for the rest of your story."

"So, to the couch?"

"I was hoping before that to ask you a few more questions, details, purely to give some context to what you've already told me under hypnosis—would you have any objection to that?"

"I thought you couldn't use me as a model for your treatment."

"I won't, I can't, but I am unlikely to get the chance to speak to another immortal. It also may help to find out not just who you were, but who you have become."

"By all means."

"In your time on the ice, living among the People, which was what would be a lifetime for most people, and later, in Amsterdam, did you have friends? People who cared about you? People you cared about?"

"I cared for children with the People. But there was always fear or jealousy among the adults, men and women. When the children I cared for grew up, others made them push me away."

"And Amsterdam?"

"There were girls I could laugh with, but even though it was a small world among the whores, I moved around—different houses, different districts—and women don't last long in that life. More often than not they were the ones who moved away. And again, jealousy and fear."

"And lovers? Your husbands among the People? Anyone in Amsterdam?"

"Not my husbands, although I think my first husband, Innik, liked the status of having a wife who could always find food. It wasn't love, I don't think—I was more of an asset."

"Even when you made love?"

"That was an obligation for Innik. Among the People I was ugly, tall and pale. When it was clear that I would bear him no children, we slept together, along with his other wife. For warmth. Sometimes sex."

"How did you feel about that?"

"I had no romantic expectations. As far as I knew then, and even now, I was made to be a sex slave, tortured and raped repeatedly. Later, when I was in Amsterdam, no longer the pale freak, I made a living from sex. I don't know what *making love* is, Doctor."

"I am sorry. I asked because in all our sessions, you haven't mentioned loneliness, yet it had to be something you experienced."

"Only when Sedna and Raven stopped talking."

"They were with you in Amsterdam?"

"Raven not so much as Sedna. She had demands."

"To feed people?"

"Sure. That was it."

There was a soft knock on the door. Jung looked annoyed. "I'm sorry, I am not supposed to be disturbed when I am in session. Just a moment, Judith." He went to the office door and opened it a crack. Diderot, looking quite contrite, was standing there.

"You received a wire from Gustav Klimt. It was marked urgent. I think it's for Judith."

He handed the folded message to Jung, apologized again, and slipped away as Jung closed the door. Jung handed the telegram to Judith. She unfolded it and read aloud. "FOR J. KRUGER KNOWS ABOUT THE BRIDGE. STAY AWAY."

"Who is Kruger?" Jung asked.

"He's Klimt's fencing partner. A police commandant."

"How do you think he found out?"

"Probably those two bitches at the café when we were talking," said Raven in Judith's head.

"Raven," she said to Jung. "I was talking to him in a café. There were some women listening and I told them I was calming Geoff because of his upset stomach. I didn't realize—"

"Perhaps we should suspend this session for now. Pick up tomorrow."

*S*he wasn't sure what to do next. Should she reply to Klimt, let him know she'd gotten his message? Would the police monitor any messages she sent? Ella had been right, Klimt needed a telephone at the studio. In the hall, she asked Diderot if he would send a message to Klimt.

"Of course. What do you want it to say?"

He wrote in his pocket notebook as she dictated. "UNDER-STOOD. WILL WAIT TO HEAR FROM YOU. THANK YOU. J."

Diderot escorted her down the stairs and into the breezeway, where there was no sign of Geoff.

"Perhaps he slipped his leash," Diderot said.

"Then his leash would be here." She saw something light on the stones near the water dish Diderot had put out for Geoff.

"What do you see?" Diderot asked.

"Crumbs."

"You said he liked croissants."

"These crumbs aren't from croissants. These are from scones." She pinched the crumbly detritus between her fingers.

"What does that mean?" Diderot was genuinely perplexed.

"Someone took Geoff, or led him away."

"Would he go with just anyone?"

"Geoff is a pushover for baked goods," she said, standing up. "Will you help me look for him?"

"Of course."

"I may seem to be talking to myself as we go. Don't be alarmed, that's one of the reasons Dr. Jung is treating me."

"I completely understand," Diderot said.

"Raven," she shouted, her voice echoing off the old stonework. "Where the fuck is Akhlut?"

"That was louder than I expected," said Diderot.

"When I talk to myself I don't always listen," she said. She led them out of the breezeway and began calling Geoff's name as they went.

28

WHEN I SAY YOUR NAME

They retraced Judith's steps to her quarters, then to the train station, which might have worked if Geoff had just run away, but she was relatively sure he had been taken, or at least lured away. Diderot stayed with her until midnight, when he insisted upon leaving her at her quarters and resuming the search in the morning. She thanked him and promised to get some rest, then waited a few minutes, checked to see that Van Beek's revolver was loaded—she still had four unfired cartridges in the cylinder—and headed down to the courtyard.

As soon as she stepped out of the stairwell into the courtyard she knew something was wrong. She could hear the shuffle of shoes on stone, and before she could look in the direction of the noise, something was thrown over her. Her arms were held at her sides by some sort of restraint and she could smell chemicals, something caustic—could feel a cloth being pushed onto her face. She held her breath, even as she struggled.

She fell and whoever was holding her rode her to the ground; the hand holding the chemical cloth fell away. She tried to roll and realized that it was a net she was struggling against.

"Stop!" came a voice a few yards away. She heard clicking noises, machinery, guns being cocked.

The hands holding her down loosened. She could see figures standing above her—one was Walton, easily identifiable because of his skeletal thinness.

"Let her go." The same voice. High-pitched, but not a woman. More, well, a small voice shouting.

She made out two men standing over her, one with his foot on her hip.

"Stay where you are," said Walton. "Take her."

Judith looked to where she'd heard the first voice. A short, very short, figure, in a large hat, stepped out of a shadow holding a pistol. He shrugged and shot Walton in the chest; the old man went over backward.

Judith pushed up into a kneeling position, no one holding her now. The little man looked around the courtyard—there were three men dressed in normal street clothes, of different sizes, but all about thirty years old; she recognized them as the servants in Walton's apartment in Vienna. Beyond them were four younger, bigger, sturdier-looking men in work clothes and boots, each of them holding a rifle.

Walton's men appeared to be unarmed except for the one holding the rag he'd tried to suffocate her with, which seemed pathetic in contrast to the four rifles and the pistol. Lights were coming on in the rooms above the courtyard.

"You all can go now or we can shoot you as well," said the little man.

Walton's servants exchanged glances, then all broke toward the entrance.

"Take him with you," said the little man, pointing to Walton's body with his pistol. "He'll be all right."

"He's shot through the heart," said the one who had the rag, kneeling over Walton.

◆

"Just keep the body in a cool, dry place and pour some broth into him when he starts breathing again."

Judith had climbed to her feet and was looking for a way out of the courtyard not blocked by the little man and his minions. Back into the building and up the stairs was the only way out. She turned, took a step, and—

"Elspeth Lindsey," said the little man.

She stopped, turned. "What?"

"Elspeth Lindsey. That's who you are. You were born in Alnwick, Northumberland, in 1779. Your father's name was James and your mother's name was Elizabeth. You had a brother, also James, who was with you when Adam took you. He played the fiddle and you sang and danced in pubs all over Scotland and Northern England."

"Elspeth?" she said. She was stunned.

Walton's men had lifted him and were swiftly carrying him out of the courtyard under the guns of the larger men.

"Yes," said the little man. He shoved his pistol into his belt. He put out his hand to her. "And we need to go, the police will be coming. I have a carriage waiting."

"We have to find Geoff," she said. "Stop them."

One of the men with a rifle stepped in front of Walton's men.

"Where is Geoff?" she asked in English. "The Malamute."

The man holding Walton's feet looked over his shoulder. "Tied up behind a hotel, two blocks toward the river."

Judith waved him on.

"We have to go," said the little man. "We'll get your dog on the way."

"Who are you?" she said, following along behind the little man, who waddled as he walked.

He turned, took off his big hat, and held it over his heart. He had the happy face of a carved puppet, cheeks a little too round and ruddy, nose a bit too bulbous, but kindness—no, joy—in his eyes. "I am Waggis," he said. "I've known you forever. I have always loved you."

They rode in a full carriage, black, trimmed in polished brass, with a team of horses. Judith and Geoff sat on one side of the coach, Waggis on the other. Two of Waggis's men rode in the driver's seat and two on top of the coach. Judith offered for them to ride inside but they declined, as the last time two of them had seen Geoff he had eaten both their shoes and the small toe of one, so they didn't care to be close to him. The other two had heard the tales and mentioned how attached they were to their respective toes and how much they'd like them to stay attached.

While grateful to have been rescued and reunited with Geoff, she was uncomfortable with the circumstances. Being enclosed in the carriage with the little man, who was still armed. She wasn't sure if she should trust him, but she did like how he had unceremoniously shot Walton without a second thought. She was still reeling with the knowledge of who she had been before Adam and where she had come from.

He'd offered her food and wine, as he said it would be a long ride to his villa in the mountains. She ate some dark bread and butter he'd brought, and Geoff ate everything else.

"So," she said, around a crust of bread, "how do you know who I am?"

"I'm sorry it took so long to find you," he said. "I've been looking for you since Adam took you from the villa."

"You were the one. Feeding me. Talking to me."

"I brought you to life when Frankenstein had given up." He smiled, a crooked grin of healthy teeth. "I thought it was the electrical current, but after more experiments, I found that it was the care, the broth, the water, keeping you warm. The current simply started your heart sooner."

"How are you still alive?"

"Your blood. I injected your blood into my system even before Adam took you. There was no more of Frankenstein's elixir, but we had your blood. First I tried it on mice, then on myself."

"But you—you're still young. Walton said he injected my blood and he looks old. Not as old as he actually is, but an old man."

"Because I died. That's the trigger. I found it with the mice. The estate is infested with a small population of immortal mice. Thankfully they can't produce offspring, but they do grow smarter with experience. It's annoying. Anyway, if Walton had died accidentally when he was younger, he would likely look his age at the time, like me. Like you."

"I died four times," she said.

"Only twice for me."

"Accident?"

"Once by villagers with pitchforks and torches. It was a misunderstanding about the lightning I was producing in the laboratory. Fortunately, the laboratory was in the folly, which is constructed completely of marble, so the torches just burned out on the roof."

"Once?"

"Another time I took my own life."

"Why?" Asking seemed intimate, since she had done it herself and knew the pain involved. She looked away. "You don't have to say," she said.

"Because I could not find you. I looked, everywhere. Well, not me, but people I hired. It was unbearable."

She didn't know what to say. He had lived a very long life thinking about her, searching for her, and she had only remembered him as a shadow figure in a dream. Finally, she said, "But why?"

"You were my first friend. My only friend. No matter how smart I was, people treated me like a clown. A sad clown. My name, Waggis, is after the clown Basel celebrates during Carnival. If Frankenstein had not hired me I would have been a beggar."

"But I was just a body on a table when you knew me. Wait, did you shag my corpse, Waggis?"

"No. Oh no. We were friends. We talked for hours and hours, about all things."

"But I was unconscious at best."

"Yes, you are a very good listener. I've missed you so." He made as if to reach out his hand to touch hers, then pulled it back and hid it under the brim of his big hat like a shy child.

"How did you find out who I was? It was so long ago."

"I knew Adam had gone to the Arctic, and Frankenstein had followed him, so I hired people to try to track his path. I had resources. Frankenstein had left me the entire estate to manage—in fact, adopted me before leaving, so I was legal heir to it, since Adam had murdered the rest of the family. I hired agents in all the ports at the edge of the Arctic, looking for any news coming from explorers, whalers, or even trappers, who might have encountered a giant traveling with a woman.

"Then, about seventy years ago, Walton came to the estate and opened the next chapter of the story, and although he didn't say, I knew from his appearance at the time that he had also injected some of your blood. I knew where the *Prometheus* was when Adam took you, and I knew that you had survived. I hired people to track what Walton was doing and found out about Geoff. I knew where you and your brother had been when Adam murdered you, and when, so I sent people to track the history—they searched records all over Scotland and Northern England, and eventually they connected the murder and disappearance of a pair of entertainers, brother and sister, and we knew that was you, Elspeth, and your brother, James."

She hadn't really tried on the Elspeth name yet—it still seemed like the name of someone else, from long ago—and she'd never had a surname. She remembered that she had gone by the first name Margot for a while in Amsterdam, but the closest thing she'd had to a surname was "the Murdering Prostitute," which didn't look right on a library card.

"So Walton found me before you did, and you had Van Beek follow Thiessen. Why did you send Van Beek? Why didn't you come yourself before this?"

"Hope is too painful. While I knew Walton might have found you, I couldn't be sure. I didn't think I would be able to take the disappointment if it wasn't you—and I do not represent the best face of welcome, I think. Van Beek wasn't supposed to try to capture you. I had an intermediate in Amsterdam who confused things. I'm sorry. I'm afraid Van Beek disappeared—he stranded my men in Vienna."

"But your men told you about Geoff. About how he changes." She ruffled Geoff's ears. "Silly boy."

"I didn't know what to believe. Their story was—well, there was a lot of fear shaping it."

"They told you the truth. You said you died twice. How long were you dead—how long was it before someone brought you back?"

"In the case of the pitchfork, a day or two. When I drowned myself in a pond on the estate one of my men pulled me out, so it was only minutes, maybe an hour. I fired him. I'd left instructions to let me die."

"Do you remember anything from the time when you were dead? Of the Underworld?"

"Just light, a lot of light. And figures moving in the distance, but they never became clear."

"Not long enough," she said. "There are creatures on the other side—gods and spirits—and if you are dead long enough, they follow you back. Geoff and I brought part of the Underworld back.

That's how he changes. He is inhabited by a god from the other side, Akhlut, a savage god who is a giant wolf on the land and an orca in the water. I knew him when I was in the Underworld. In a way, he followed me home."

"Is that how Walton was able to find you?"

"I think it was how Thiessen found me in Vienna. Poor Geoff didn't know he was being used to track me. Oh, he ate Van Beek."

"Pardon. Ate?"

"Two bites. One bite, really, but he sort of chomped in the middle of it."

"And the police haven't figured it out yet?"

She shrugged. "No body."

"You didn't take his money first, did you?"

"I just told you that a giant supernatural wolf dog ate your hired scoundrel."

"It was a lot of money."

"I thought you were rich."

"I am, but I don't have so much that I want to feed it to the dog. That's just irresponsible."

"You're irresponsible! Letting a patchwork monster run off with your only friend is irresponsible."

He hung his head, hid again behind the brim of his hat. "I'm sorry."

"I'm teasing," she said. She lifted the brim of his hat and peeked under it. "Thank you, Waggis." She could see a shy smile there in the shadow of the hat. "I would probably be chained in a box right now if not for you."

"Well, you don't have to worry about Walton anymore."

"He won't figure out who you are and try to take me again?"

"He doesn't need you. When he returns to life he'll realize that more of your blood won't help him. Barring an accident, he'll live forever, but he'll always look like an old man. I'll send a letter to his estate explaining as much. And if he won't listen to reason, perhaps we can take Geoff on a trip to England to visit. Walton won't be a problem, but the police in Vienna will be. You can't go back there."

"I have friends in Vienna. Well, a friend. No *friends*. I have people. Where will I go?"

"Anywhere you want. I'm sure, like me, you've accumulated a fortune over your long life."

"No fortune. I was on the ice for eighty years."

"You could come and stay at the villa. That was my hope if I found you. Stay as long as you like, come and go as you please. Even if Walton comes after you again, we have excellent security. Since the torches-and-pitchforks incident, it's been a priority. And you will never do without."

She sat silent for a while, listening to the clop-clop of the horses and the creak of the carriage springs.

"You could—"

"Shut up."

"Okay."

"I will not be your sex puppet."

He hid behind his hat brim again. "You can have your own wing of the house."

"Do you speak English? I have some swearing to catch up on and I think English is the best language for it."

"A little. I can learn."

"Fine," she said.

"Fine," he said.

They rode awhile in silence, Waggis hiding his smile under his hat brim, Judith trying to imagine her future.

They were still an hour from the villa when she made her decision. "There's something you should know about me before we go any farther."

"Is it that you murdered a number of men in Amsterdam? Because that doesn't bother me."

"*A large number,*" said Raven.

"*Not enough,*" said Sedna.

"No, it's something else. Something that happened because I was in the Underworld for a long time when I died on the ice. Years before I came back. It's disturbing."

"I watched a monster slaughter everyone I knew and take away my only friend, then was killed by peasants with pitchforks. I feel as if I'm prepared."

"I've never tried this before on purpose, but I think I can change. I think I can go back and forth to the Underworld the way Geoff does, and leave my body here, but I also think I can change, physically, here."

"*Fly away, Little Bird,*" Raven said.

"I'm going to try it now, and if it works, you mustn't be afraid. I won't hurt you, but I think this is as much who I am as finding out that I am Elspeth Lindsey."

"I'm ready," Waggis said.

She shut the blinds in the carriage windows, then closed her eyes and sat back in the seat. Before long her blue cotton dress began to turn to shiny black feathers.

Waggis pushed back against the seat. "Oh my," he said.

The next time they spoke she was in her blue dress again.

"So?"

"Can you fly?"

"I don't know."

"*Yes,*" Raven said.

"Raven says yes," she said.

"Raven?"

"A god from the Underworld who talks to me. I'll tell you about him."

"I want to hear. I want to hear your whole story."

"I think I can tell you my whole story now."

"I wish I could fly."

"Well, is it cold in the winter here? Cold enough that you could, say, keep meat fresh in an unheated barn?"

"Very cold. Lots of snow."

"When winter comes, I could choke you. I guess 'strangle you' is the right term. And once you're dead, I can show you around the Underworld for a while. Maybe you'll learn a new skill."

"I'd like that," said Waggis.

"As friends," Judith said. "I'd only be choking you as a friend."

"That's all I've ever wanted," he said.

"Good," she said.

"Good," he said.

Another hour passed with the two of them listening to the clop of the horses and the squeak of the springs, thinking about what was to come next. When the driver pulled up the reins and they could hear his companion climbing down to open the gate, Waggis said, "We're home."

29

VIENNA WALTZ

Wally received her first telegram a few weeks after Judith disappeared: "I WILL BE OKAY. LOVE J." Although she was sad for a while, she didn't worry, and she pursued her goal of achieving success by the Alma Mahler method of attaching her hopes to a creative genius. For three years she and Egon lived together. She waitressed at Café Piccolo in the mornings, modeled in the afternoon, and had come to terms with coming home from work to find Egon chatting up or drawing one or both of the Harms sisters, Edith and Adele, from next door.

Wally traveled with Egon and the two were often seen about town together at art shows and salons. About the same time the war came to Vienna, Egon was invited to show his work in non-German-speaking countries, and while chaos reigned across the Continent, Egon assured Wally he was bound for greatness, despite the fact that—nay, maybe *because*—he was a disgusting fuck-beast. Wally stood dutifully by his side and braced to bask in the light of his success, until one afternoon she came home from the café and Egon announced:

"I've asked Edith Harms to marry me. She's from a good family and will make a proper wife, but in the contract I've offered her, I've included the provision that you and I get to go off on holiday together two weeks of the year."

He grinned as if he had just handed her a bouquet of roses. For the first time in months she palpably missed her friend Judith, because she didn't think she was strong enough to choke Egon out if he saw her coming. Instead she ran out of the flat in tears and only returned several days later to pick up her things when she'd secured a room in a women's rooming house in an outer district.

The Alma Mahler strategy was not going to work, even, currently, for Alma Mahler, who had married Walter Gropius, the young architect; given birth to his daughter; then promptly left him. Oskar Kokoschka had been conscripted for the war and sent to Russia (sans Alma doll) and promptly bayonetted. He was listed as missing and probably dead.

Untethered from creative greatness, Wally, with Emilie Flöge's influence, enrolled into nurse's training at the Vienna General Hospital. Due to the war and an accelerated demand for nurses, the training was expanded to twelve hours a day and Wally was not able to work enough hours at the café to stay ahead of her rent. She decided to use the secret knock on Gustav Klimt's studio door.

"Wally!" Klimt said, opening the door and finding his smile, despite having been interrupted during a portrait session with a wealthy lady.

"Gus!" Wally said, and she burst into tears and ran into his arms.

"What's wrong? Are you hurt? And please don't call me Gus."

She pushed back from his embrace and said, "I am heartbroken and I am almost a nurse but I can't work enough to pay my rent and I will have to become a murdering prostitute like Judith to get by."

Klimt realized his portrait client was listening from the next room and he needed to measure his response. "Come in, *cher*," he said. He led her away from the portrait studio to the little parlor that had once been a dining room and now held the divan where they'd first placed a waterlogged Judith years ago.

"How much do you need," he said, "to finish your training?"

"I don't want a gift. I need to work. I will work."

"You can start tomorrow," Klimt said. "I have a portrait sitting in the morning, but I will draw you in the studio during break. Ella will be here too. She'll be happy to see you."

Wally wiped the tears from her eyes with a handkerchief. "How is Ella?"

"She's lovely. Due with a second child in the fall."

"Will you call it Gustav?"

"Only if it's a boy. You can catch up with her tomorrow morning."

"That's just it, I can't work in the mornings, I have my classes."

"I see." Klimt paced a tight circle and rubbed the bridge of his nose as if he were deep in thought. "I know, I will paint your portrait. I've never painted you, despite all the drawings. When are you off from your classes?"

"Six in the evening."

"That's it then. We'll work an hour each evening, and I'll make a painting of you."

"But an hour a day won't be enough—for my rent and expenses."

"That's what you never knew, Wally. For a portrait model, the pay is four times that of a drawing model," he lied. "It will be like you're working four hours a day. Will that work?"

"Yes, that will do. Thank you. Thank you, Gus." She wrapped her arms around him and kissed his cheek.

Wally finished her training, Klimt finished the portrait, and Wally was sent to Dalmatia to an army field hospital, where she found a distinct lack of the cheerful spotted dogs she was expecting, and instead was subjected to a flood of young mutilated and dying soldiers. She was a good nurse, her superiors and her patients told her, but she was overwhelmed with how ineffective her treatment was in alleviating suffering and death. She resolved to be the face of kindness and love for every soldier she treated, so that might be what they saw before they passed, a small note of hope in a symphony of despair.

In her second year in the field she fell ill with scarlet fever, and was isolated in a tent with soldiers and another nurse who were suffering from the same malady. She lay on the cot, her head pounding, her throat so sore she could barely swallow, passing in and out of consciousness. Sometimes she would hear the voices of the other patients; sometimes she imagined she was hearing Strauss and would watch elegant happy couples dancing in the air above her cot. On the fourth night of her isolation, when the other patients were asleep and even the shelling at the front had gone silent, she heard the beating of great wings outside the tent, but she was too weak to lift her head to look toward the source.

She heard the tent flap scrape as it was tossed aside and she expected to see the shadow of a nurse fall on her. Instead a familiar face appeared like a rising moon.

"Judith," Wally whispered.

Judith held her cheek against Wally's and hugged her as she wept. "I'm here. Don't be afraid."

"How?"

"Magic." Judith reached behind the black feathers on her breast and produced a small leather case. She unsnapped it and pulled out the needles, plunger, and tubing. The feathers on her arm retreated and she put one needle in her arm, then brought Wally's arm out from under the wool army blanket. "Little pinch," she said. She put the other needle in Wally's arm.

Wally laughed. "I always say 'little pinch' too."

Judith pumped the plunger until she'd transferred the amount of blood Waggis had recommended, then she removed the needles and put them away.

She put her face close to Wally's again. "Wally, don't be afraid."

"I'm not."

"Love, you are going to pass on. But you will be back, probably very soon, but you can't be Wally anymore, do you understand?"

"Do you have feathers?"

"Not all the time. Listen, Wally. You are going to come back in a few minutes, and when you do, you will have to come find me in Switzerland. I've written this down and I've put the paper along with some money in your chemise, because you may not remember, or someone may move you or take you away."

"Where am I going?"

"Call it the Undiscovered Country. I'll be there when you get there."

"Oh good. Can we get pastry?"

"Absolutely." Judith bent and hugged her cheek to Wally's. "I love you."

"Me too," Wally said. "I missed you."

Judith gently took the pillow from under Wally's head and held it over her face until she stopped trying to breathe.

$\mathcal{E}$gon would marry Edith Harms and go off to war and return without seeing combat. His art would be shown around Europe and his reputation as the leader of the Vienna Expressionist movement assured. Gustav Klimt would never marry Emilie Flöge, but would father two more children with Camilla (Ella) Huber. In 1918, just as the Great War was winding down, the Spanish flu epidemic would descend on the world. Klimt, Egon Schiele, and Edith Harms, Egon's wife, would all perish from the flu, Egon only four days after Edith, who was pregnant at the time.

*H*ey, butt puppet," Judith said.

"I feel so much better," Wally said. "Where are we? Why are you wearing a helmet?"

"We're going on an adventure. Do you remember what I just told you?"

"Yes. Switzerland. Wait, did you smother me?"

"A little bit. Sorry. We don't have much time, you have to go back. You have to stop being Wally, do you understand? Wally is dead."

"But who will I be?"

"Anyone you want to. Go now. I'll see you soon."

Epilogue
KLIMT IN THE UNDERWORLD

When Klimt opened his eyes after dying, the first thing he saw was Judith's face.

"Judith?"

"It's Elspeth, but yes. Hello, Gus."

"Where are we?"

"The Underworld. You're dead."

"Why are you wearing a helmet?"

She was wearing a golden helm with great wings jutting from the sides.

"Valkyrie. I borrowed it so I could greet you. This isn't my normal part of the Underworld."

"Are you dead too?"

"No, I can go back and forth."

Klimt jumped at the sound of a growl so deep it rattled in his ribs, and he looked past Judith to see an enormous wolflike creature looming above them. "I—what—"

"That's Geoff. That's what he looks like here. He's a silly boy."

Akhlut arooed a sad yowl.

"Can he go back and forth too?"

"Yes. In fact, he was the first. I learned from him."

"Can I go back and forth?"

"No, just Geoff and me. We had to die a few times to make it a two-way thing, and you only get to die once."

"Where do I go now?" He squinted into the distance and could see mountains, trees, sky.

"Well, normally you would mix into the consciousness of the People, become one with all mankind and the human spirit, then be spread again to a body, where you would have an identity, a personality. But you're special, Gus. You were kind to me, and I have some influence here, so I'll make it so you will retain your identity, your personality, in the Underworld. You'll see things here through your own mind's eye, with your painter's sensibility."

"When I sent you that telegram to stay away, I just meant stay away from Vienna, I didn't mean I would stop helping you. I didn't mean for you to disappear."

"I know. I was fine. I've been fine. I found out who I am."

"I'm glad. I tried to help Wally, like you asked. And I took care of Camilla and the children. They'll be looked after."

"I know, which is why you get to be Klimt in the Underworld, not just another bit of the human spirit."

"Thank you?"

"As a squirrel—well, one of the Squirrel People."

"What?"

"It's the only vacancy."

"I'm going to be a squirrel?"

"Squirrel Person. They can talk here, so it will be just like you're Gustav Klimt, but with a tail."

"I'll be a talking squirrel?"

"Yes, Gus. That's what I just said. Did you suffer dementia since I've seen you?"

"I had a stroke before the flu."

"Well, that shouldn't make you stupid here. I don't think. I'll ask. Anyway, you'll feel just like you do now, but you will be a much better climber."

"Wait, are you covered with black feathers?"

"Not my face, I didn't want to scare you. This is how I look here."

"They are magnificent, are they not?" came Raven's voice.

"What was that?"

"No one, don't worry about it."

"Is this why black wings kept appearing on the painting? I never finished it, you know. I would paint them out and the next day they would be there again."

"Sorry. I didn't know that would happen."

"You should offer him a hand job," came Sedna's voice.

"Who was that?"

"That's Sedna. She learned that from Wally. Used to be it was just *'Feed them'* or *'Murder them,'* but after Wally she added hand jobs."

"Poor Wally." Klimt hung his head.

"Yes, poor Wally. Well, I need to return this helmet. Are you ready for the squirreling?"

"What?"

"Goodbye, Gus."

Afterword

I know what you're thinking. You're thinking, *Oh, great job, butt puddle, how did you manage to ruin history, literature, and art in one short novel?* First, there's no need to use that kind of language, and second, it went like this.

I visited Vienna for the first time in 2015 and learned about many of the luminaries of the city, and how, during the first part of the twentieth century, Vienna comprised what Eric Weiner, in his book *The Geography of Genius*, called a 'genius cluster'—the idea that at certain places and times in history, groups of geniuses develop or rise. I'd written one novel, *Sacré Bleu*, set amid one such genius cluster, Paris in the 1890s; I thought one in Vienna would be interesting, too.

In pre–World War I Vienna, one could find scientists Sigmund Freud, Carl Jung, and Alfred Adler, who were basically inventing psychoanalysis; musicians Gustav Mahler, Richard Strauss, and Arnold Schoenberg; painters Gustav Klimt, Egon Schiele, and Oskar Kokoschka; and architects Walter Gropius and Adolf Loos, who would redefine modern design; as well as political figures Josip Tito, Joseph Stalin, Leon Trotsky, and Adolf Hitler—although calling the last group "geniuses" rather sullies the term, but they all certainly became leading figures in politics. And that's just the men; as I did the research, extraordinary women, some famous, some infamous, and some obscure, began to rise, and the focus of the book I was going to write changed.

While many of the characters in *Anima Rising* are based on real people, all of the dialogue and many of the intersections of the characters are from my imagination. But some events actually happened, although I've changed the timeline to accommodate the story, and it's only fair I tell you which ones.

I chose the year 1911 to begin the modern part of the story because that is the year that Mahler died and Klimt introduced Wally Neuzil, who had been working with him as a model, to Egon Schiele. Also, Freud and Jung, who had been friends and colleagues since 1907, would have a breakup over their views of the human psyche late that year. Those events and relationships dictated what would transpire in the book, but some events that would happen later in the decade were moved to serve the theme.

The Elephant in the Room: Klimt and the Women

Gustav Klimt's paintings are striking and beautiful and sensual and often ethereal. He was one of the founders of the Vienna Secessionist movement and the first elected president of their group—artists who wanted to break away from the conventions of the Vienna academy, much like the Impressionists had broken with the Paris Salon. Klimt was considered a Symbolist painter, and while many of his paintings are wrought with symbols or serve as allegories, he didn't describe them, write about them, or, as far as we know, talk about them. What we *do* know is that nearly all of them featured female figures, often nude, and often portrayed as unattainable, aloof, sometimes dangerous, seemingly oblivious to the attention they were inspiring. When asked to speak about his art, Klimt said,

I have never painted a self-portrait. I am less interested in myself as a subject for painting than I am in other people, above all women.

His early murals for some of the buildings of the Ringstrasse, like those he did for the Burgtheater (along with his brother Ernst and their partner Franz von Matsch), were exquisitely drafted and executed scenes from mythology, but as the new century approached and he worked on his own, his work became less narrative and more, well, reverent, I guess, of the female figure, and was often viewed as scandalous.

As in *Anima Rising*, Klimt's studio was in a freestanding home with a walled garden. He used the front parlor for his wealthy portrait clients but kept a drawing studio that was often filled with as many as a half-dozen young models. While painting one of the commissioned portraits, he would take breaks and retreat to the drawing studio, where he would draw and chat with the young models. The sketches of the models, all of whom were well paid, were often used in his major nonportrait paintings. Nearly every book I read on Klimt, including those that focused on the paintings, included some version of this sentence:

"It was understood that if you modeled for Klimt you would share his bed as well."

If I may, YIKES!

I did not and do not want to try to justify Klimt's behavior or his appetites, but I also wanted to find a way not to see him as a villain or a predator. As much as I looked, I couldn't find any of his contemporaries who criticized him for his habits as being out of the ordinary, and they were certainly known at the time. Some historical context may explain this, although not excuse it, when viewed through our second–decade–of–the–twenty-first–century lens.

There were very few opportunities for young women in early twentieth-century Vienna, particularly if they were born into the lower or working classes. Education for young women was almost unheard of, and there simply weren't enough manual labor or domestic jobs to go around. Vienna, a city of two million people, its population drawn from cultures all over the Austro-Hungarian Empire, had forty thousand registered prostitutes in 1910. That was only the registered prostitutes; streetwalkers and those the police didn't steer to the legal brothels would have added to that figure. As bizarre as it might seem to us today, a young woman of the lower classes might have seen working for Klimt as an opportunity, even with the consequences of having to have sex with "the master."

Klimt kept meticulous records of their hours worked and he paid each model eight crowns an hour, which was a good wage. He was also known to have paid for the funeral of the father of one of his models, and would pay their back rent when one faced eviction.

The age of consent in Austria at that time was fourteen, and indeed, Camilla Huber—Ella—whom we meet in *Anima Rising*, was fifteen in 1911, and pregnant with the first child she would have with Klimt. She would give birth to two more before Klimt died in 1918, and Klimt provided for her and the children in his will. I can't seem to find a definitive number, but Klimt fathered between eight and thirteen illegitimate children in his lifetime. He provided for eight children in his will and left the rest of his estate to Emilie Flöge.

Gus and Emilie

Klimt likely met Emilie Flöge around 1890, when she was sixteen. She was the younger sister of his brother Ernst's wife, Helene Flöge. When Ernst died in 1892, Klimt took on the support of Helene and her soon-to-be-born daughter, and he would remain close with the Flöge family until his death, often spending evenings with them in the city, and spending summers with them at Attersee. Klimt first painted Emilie in 1891 and included her in a major painting he finished of his brother's in 1895, *Hanswurst on the Fair Stage*. The two were very close throughout Klimt's life; he painted her several more times, and the two collaborated on fashion designs and fabrics once Emilie and her sisters opened Schwestern Flöge, which became a major design house. While they never married, Emilie referred to Klimt as her "Lebens-mensch," or "Love Man."

While no one knows what the actual relationship was between Klimt and Emilie, it's impossible that she didn't know about his adventures with other women, so there had to be some sort of understanding between the two. Most of Klimt's writing that survives is postcards to Emilie he sent while on tour with his art, and much of it is very whiny, complaining about the weather or his health. Emilie

burned baskets full of his letters upon his death, and we have none of her letters to him. There are dozens of photographs of the two of them together, most taken during the summers at Attersee, and what you see in nearly all of them is the pure joy the two found in each other's company.

Emilie was a revolutionary designer, moving women's clothes from a fifty-year era of restrictive corsets and bustles to flowing, unrestrictive Reform dresses with bold colors and designs, but comfortable. She was Coco Chanel before Coco Chanel and could definitely have served as an example of the possibilities for an ambitious, self-possessed woman.

Klimt and Wally

We don't know when Klimt first met Wally Neuzil, or when she started modeling for him, but we do know that he introduced her to Egon Schiele in 1911 and the relationship between Schiele and Wally was both a working one and a romantic one that lasted until May of 1915, when he married Edith Harms. I could find only one painting Klimt did of Wally, done in 1916, which would have been after her split with Egon and probably during her training as a nurse. The painting, along with many of Klimt's major paintings, was burned by Nazi soldiers retreating from Schloss (Castle) Immendorf in 1945. A black and white photo of the painting is all that survives. The portrait is unlike any other I've seen by Klimt, with the subject painted in profile, expressionless, one breast exposed. It really suggested a work that neither the artist or the model want to be part of. That's why I wrote the scene where Klimt offers to paint Wally in order to pay her, to help her out. I have no evidence that it happened that way.

This portrait of Wally looks nothing like any other portraits
by Klimt. The Japanese prints in the background show that it
was painted in his portrait studio—and it was painted in **1916,**
long after any other drawings of her by Klimt or Schiele.
The original was burned by the Nazis in 1945 at Schloss
Immendorf along with many other Klimt paintings.

Wally and Egon

As above, Wally met Egon Schiele in 1911, and the trip they took
to Krumau happened in the spring of 1912, much as I describe it in
the novel, without Judith or Geoff, of course. Wally, Egon, Anton
Peschka, and Egon's younger sister, Gertie, all visited Krumau, where
Schiele's mother was born, and set up an ad hoc Bohemian artist colony. There are numerous paintings that came out of the trip, many
landscapes and architectural paintings, as Egon's agent actually had
sent him a bundle of canvases to paint for a show in Munich, but also

many drawings, mostly nudes, by both artists, some depicting them engaged in sex with the models. They were asked to leave Krumau, driven out, really, because of their behavior.

Before the trip, Egon wrote that he was excited to see the airplane at Krumau, but he never did.

Egon Schiele was, indeed, arrested, initially for abducting thirteen-year-old Tatiana von Mossig, who had been missing for three days but later confessed she had been trying to escape her family and had run away, so the charge was reduced to attempting to corrupt youth by showing them obscene pictures. These events, however, happened on a different "artists' trip," to the village of Neulengbach, Austria. He was sentenced to twenty-four days, and Wally did, indeed, stay with him (in the village), persuaded the guards to let him have his art materials, and threw fruit to him through his high window. He wrote about there being no color and asking Wally to bring him an orange, and he did a drawing, with watercolors, of the orange on his prison cot. Wally didn't, however, stage a daring escape attempt with the assistance of village urchins. I feel as if she would have, but it was well-known that the urchins of Neulengbach were shit.

In his journal in prison, Schiele wrote:

No erotic work of art is filth, if it is artistically significant. It is only turned into filth through the beholder if he is filthy. I could mention the names of many, many famous artists, even that of Klimt, but I do not want to excuse myself by this at all—that would be not worthy of me. Therefore I do not deny it. I do declare as untrue, however, that I showed such drawings intentionally to children, that I corrupted children. That is untrue! Nevertheless, I know that there are many children who are corrupted, that is, incited and aroused by the sex impulse they themselves were as children. Have they forgotten how the frightful passion burned and tortured them while they were still children? I have not forgotten, for I suffered terribly under it. And I believe that man must suffer from sexual torture as long as he is capable of sexual feelings.

So it's clear that Schiele viewed himself as a disgusting fuck-beast. Kidding. That's my term, but you can see how I might have come to think that.

Wally was Egon's model and companion until 1915, when he announced he would marry a girl from a more suitable family, Edith Harms. Part of his marriage proposal included an agreement that he get to go on holiday for two weeks a year with Wally, which neither

This painting of Egon and Wally shows her desperation and his indifference. His other painting of their split is called *Death and the Maiden*, so he was obviously aware of the pain he caused.

Wally nor Edith agreed to. Two of Schiele's major paintings, *Death and the Maiden* and *The Lovers*, show Wally trying to hold on to him, weeping, as he pushes her away.

After their split, Wally would train as a nurse and eventually perish from scarlet fever in Dalmatia (now Croatia) while treating war wounded. Egon was drafted but had officers who kept him in positions away from combat, and he was able to eventually return to Vienna and Edith. Both died of the Spanish flu in 1918.

Egon drew his younger sister, Gertie, scores of times, many times nude, and the two did go on a trip to Trieste, Italy, when Gertie was twelve and Egon sixteen, to reenact their parents' honeymoon. The two were very close. Gertie would go on to marry Anton Peschka.

Wally

Walburga (Wally) Neuzil was born in Tattendorf, Austria, in 1894 and moved with her family to Vienna in 1906. Her father was a schoolteacher, who died when she was eleven, and her mother a day laborer. She had four sisters. That's about what we know about Wally before she meets Klimt and later Schiele. I looked everywhere for books about her and found one, which was only available in German. After I translated it with my phone, I realized that it was a novel and had no more corroborated information than her Wikipedia page.

So, essentially, Wally achieved, if not greatness, notoriety, by pursuing the Alma Mahler model of attaching herself to a genius, or at least by having history attach her to Schiele. However, the circumstances for a young woman in Vienna at the time were much as I describe them, and we have many drawings, paintings, and photographs of her, so from those elements I built a character.

I can do nothing to correct the injustices of history. I could do nothing to change the circumstances Wally lived under, nor does it serve anyone to stand upon the self-righteous platform of progress and shout down about just how awful, unfair, and dehumanizing conditions were for a young woman of the time. I could not give Wally or her contemporaries agency, but what I could do was portray her as resilient, clever, loving, courageous, resourceful, and funny. For me, even though it was the story of a fictitious character from literature (Judith) and a cast of historical figures, *Anima Rising* became Wally's book. For me, her memory has been a blessing.

Alma Mahler and Oskar Kokoschka

Alma Mahler had an extraordinary life, and many books have been written about her if you're interested in learning more. She kept detailed journals through much of her life, so unlike other characters in *Anima Rising*, she is neither obscure nor a mystery.

She did, she said, receive her first kiss from Gustav Klimt, at nineteen, while on a trip to Italy with Klimt, her mother, and her stepfather, who was also a painter. She goes on at great length in her journals about Klimt's attention, and her dilemma of wanting to succumb to his seduction, and Klimt's age and reputation as a womanizer. In any case, her stepfather chased Klimt away, and a few years later she married Gustav Mahler, had two daughters with him, and traveled with him until his death in 1911. At one point, around 1908, Mahler, distraught that he could not keep up, sexually, with his young wife, consulted, like you do, Sigmund Freud, and the two took an eight-hour walk through the garden, which evidently helped the situation not at all.

Alma then had affairs with Walter Gropius, the young architect who would found the Bauhaus school, and Oskar Kokoschka, a painter and contemporary of Egon Schiele in the Vienna Expressionist movement. She *did* choose Gropius over Kokoschka, married him, and had a daughter by him, but eventually returned to Kokoschka. They lived together for several years but Kokoschka was called up for military service and was severely wounded at the Russian front and thought to have been killed. When he did return, Alma was finished with him, and late in the decade (1918), he did, indeed, commission a doll based on Alma's figure, and as described in *Anima Rising*, the dollmaker made the skin of the doll with goose feathers. And yes, Kokoschka described it as being "more like a polar bear" than like Alma. That did not stop him from buying dresses for the doll, appearing in public with it, and making paintings of it.

The timing of the events of Alma and Oskar's lives didn't line up for the timeline of the novel, but thematically, I felt as if I had to include them.

This is a photograph of the actual doll. Kokoschka also featured the doll in at least two paintings.

The Inuit and the Arctic

The references to Inuit life and mythology come completely from academic sources. The character of Raven in the Inuit cosmology is much less a trickster than what I needed for the novel, so I have drawn on Raven stories from the Haida and Tlingit cultures as well. I found no detailed stories about Akhlut, but only descriptions of him in various indexes of Inuit deities, so I was unconstrained in creating the character. Sedna is described as having different aspects and origins in different sources, which isn't surprising as the geographical range of the Inuit people is vast, and legends tend to evolve and change as they are passed on and influenced by individual experience. I chose those tales that describe her as most benevolent, but hint at the ones that describe her as vengeful and menacing.

In addition, I just made stuff up, like the obsidian blades in Raven's feathers, out of whole cloth, although the description of how a blade core is made and the sharpness of the blades that can be struck from one is real.

The use of the term "Eskimo" is contemporary to the time in which the book is set. Rasmussen (whom Jung refers to as a source in *Anima Rising*), who was raised among the Inuit people of northern Greenland, used it in his papers, and it was in common use by Arctic explorers of the time.

The Underworld, as I describe it, comes from descriptions in several sources. Most describe it as being under the sea, yet the Animal People can talk and people use fire, which reinforces the Underworld as a spiritual place that adheres to its own set of rules.

The phenomenon of Judith being able to speak and understand all languages comes not from Inuit legend but from a Crow shaman I met on the Crow Reservation in 1991 while researching my novel

Coyote Blue. In short, one day over lunch with some friends from the res, this gentleman blurted out, "I died four times!" And everybody stopped their conversation and looked his way. Once he had our attention, he said, "And after the fourth time, I could speak all languages."

It's a longer story, which I may tell someday, but he was the only person I knew who had died four times, so I just took him at his word and used that as a conceit for Judith.

Freud and Jung

When I realized that I was going to be writing about a time and place that could include these two giants, I was excited. When I started the research and realized that the two of them had published a combined total of over 750,000 pages, I was somewhat less excited. There was simply too much. To present characters in a comic novel I needed to pare down the material more than somewhat. I turned to titles like *Freud for Dummies, Jung for Imbeciles, A Brief Explanation of Jungian Analysis for the Patently Stupid*, and *Kill Your Dad/Shag Your Mom: A Freudian Pop-up Book*.

After reading those enlightening surveys, I decided to build my characters around an out-of-print book of Freud and Jung's letters to each other, a correspondence that runs from 1907 to 1912, when they break off their friendship like a couple of teenage girls who like the same boy. What's interesting is that from the very first letters you can see the breakup in motion. Freud more or less denounces any influence of the supernatural, or what he calls the "occult," including all religions, and Jung announces that while he is a follower of and indeed believer in Freud's theories, he believes that there may be more to the human psyche than childhood sexual trauma.

In the last letters, Freud more or less accuses Jung of being neurotic because he won't abandon the idea that something exists outside human experience, and because Jung won't admit the neurosis, Freud tells him they can't be friends anymore.

Freud also exhibits a distinct disrespect for young women of the lower classes, and women in general (at one point he comments to Jung that he could never understand how Jung could treat a woman who was so ugly), and attributes every mental disorder to their sexual trauma as children, while Jung can't seem to get on board with that limitation. There was also an instance in one case of Freud obviously trying to pawn a problem patient off on Jung, a colleague in psychiatry, who ended up being a massive problem for Jung, who accepted the difficulty with grace but was obviously irked by Freud's misrepresentation of the case.

For a wee bit of accuracy's sake, timeline-wise, Jung wouldn't formulate, or at least publish, his theory of the collective unconscious until the 1920s, but it's clear, in retrospect, that his work was heading that direction earlier on.

Frankenstein

As you may already know, the novel *Frankenstein* begins and ends in the Arctic, and the "bride" of the monster, the mate that the creature demands he make for him, Victor Frankenstein tears to pieces and abandons on a Scottish island. My conceit was "What if she lived?" In Shelley's novel the monster says it's his intent to go to the Arctic with his mate, where they will live out of the sight of men, so that's where he goes in my book. The time frame was the problem. Frankenstein concludes in 1799; my story starts in 1911. I had to give her something to do for a hundred and twelve years. Now you know what that was.

Hitler

Hitler *was* a contemporary of Egon Schiele, and he was in Vienna
in the first decade of the twentieth century. In fact, on the ledger
page at the Vienna Academy of Fine Arts that shows Egon Schiele's
acceptance, five spaces below was recorded Hitler's rejection because his draftsmanship and portraiture were substandard. During
that decade, also, Vienna's mayor, Karl Lueger, was an avowed anti-
Semite and was famous for blaming Jews for all the troubles of the
city. His screeds appealed to the poor, working-class men of the city
who wanted someone to blame for their misfortune. The very visible, wealthy community of Jewish businessmen and bankers was an
easy target, and there's little doubt that Hitler was among Lueger's
followers. I don't know whether Schiele or Klimt ever met Hitler, but I had a mustache joke I wanted to use, and goddammit, any
chance to make fun of Hitler is a chance you have to take.

The Great War

Vienna at the time of the book, and for several hundred years before, was the center of the massive Austro-Hungarian Empire, made
up of many nations with divergent cultures that were starting, in
the twentieth century, to want independence and cultural identities
of their own. The First World War erupted in 1914, with the as-
sassination of Archduke Franz Ferdinand, the heir to the throne of
Emperor Franz Joseph, and became a huge inconvenience for me
and my novel, entirely too massive a series of events to cover in the
book, so I decided to not let it get in the way of the story and treat
it more like a bus full of noisy tourists driving through. You know,
wave as they go by. *Hi, Great War, have a nice day in the city.*

Acknowledgments

I need to thank my friends Flip and Linda Nicklin for information and sources that became essential to *Anima Rising*. Flip was a *National Geographic* photographer for more than thirty years, specializing in marine mammals. He was an essential source for my novel *Fluke*, and the character Clay Demodocus is modeled after him. Flip has worked on the Arctic and Antarctic ice many times and I felt it would have been inconsiderate to go out on the ice myself when Flip had already done it. I knew from Flip's stories how marine mammals use air holes to stay under the ice for long periods, and, in the case of seals, even climb up on the ice to rest, so I was going to take care of the Adam problem with a killer whale coming up and snatching him. But Flip immediately said, "No, they don't do that." Then he told me about working on a narwhal story on the ice, near one of the large breathing holes where the whales would come up, and how on a spring day, when there was water on the ice, so it was clear, they looked down to see that a polar bear was hunting them from under the ice. It was a chilling description, and I, of course, didn't know polar bears did that. To be fair, none of the guys on the expedition had known that up until that point either, so I decided that was how Adam would meet his demise.

In addition, Linda Nicklin, who is a naturalist and tour guide and has forgotten more about Arctic birds and animals than most people will ever know, provided me a whole folio of raven anecdotes and behaviors that helped inform the Raven character. She also steered me to books of Tlingit and Haida mythology, as well as the book *Ada Blackjack: A True Story of Survival in the Arctic* by Jennifer Niven, the story of an expedition in the 1920s by three American explorers and one Canadian explorer who went to Wrangel Island in the Arctic with a hired Inuit woman, Ada Blackjack, to try to claim the island as an American territory. The short version is, they were there for two years, all the men died of scurvy or misadventure (lost trying to cross the ice for help), and Ada was the only one who survived, but the expedition was meticulously recorded, and the challenges of survival on that island were the basis for the section about Adam and Judith on the island.

Also, my thanks to Jeff Russell, Taylor Crawford, Nikki Mertens, and Melanie Gravdal at Avalon Waterways, who helped get me to Vienna a second time and Basel, Zurich, and Amsterdam a first time.

Finally, my thanks to the usual suspects: my wife, Charlee Moore, who had to put up with more whining than normal as this book unfolded; my agent, Lisa Gallagher; my brilliant editor, Jennifer Brehl; also Tavia Kowalchuk and Eliza Rosenberry at William Morrow, who do all the magic and marketing on my books. Thank you.

Christopher Moore
SAN FRANCISCO, CALIFORNIA
MARCH 2024

Index of Illustrations